The Coming of Rain

The COMING of RAIN

Richard Marius

RUTLEDGE HILL PRESS
Nashville, Tennessee

FIRST PAPERBACK EDITION

Published in Nashville, Tennessee,
by Rutledge Hill Press,
513 Third Avenue South,
Nashville, Tennessee 37210

A hardcover edition of this work
was published by Alfred A. Knopf, Inc.

Library of Congress Cataloging-in-Publication Data

Marius, Richard.
The coming of rain / Richard Marius.—1st paperback ed.
p. cm.
ISBN 1-55853-142-4
I. Title.
PS3563.A66C66 1991
813′.54—dc20 91-23076
CIP

Manufactured in the United States of America

1 2 3 4 5 6 7 — 97 96 95 94 93 92 91

FOR RALPH NORMAN
AND FOR MY BROTHER JOHN

A friend loveth at all times
and a brother is born for adversity

—PROVERBS 17:17

The Coming of Rain

And the Lord spake unto Moses,
saying, He that killeth any man
shall surely be put to death.

—LEVITICUS 24:17

PROLOGUE

Bourbonville, Tennessee

June 24, 1885

IN THE BEST YEARS the summers in Eastern Tennessee are always hot. It is not the continuous broiling heat of the Mississippi Delta with its weary humidity, nor is it the steady narcotic torpor of the blazing sun in the piny woods of Alabama. In those places the heat slides down out of the sky like an avalanche in the middle of spring, and it chokes the earth until late September when it is gradually washed away by the autumn rains. Beneath its massive, unyielding bulk the people of those regions die, though their bodies keep up a feeble, biological pretense of life in season and out. Summer for the citizen of the Deep South is eternity drawn down like a shade into time. It is not that way in Eastern Tennessee, but it is still hot, and on some days the heat there is as terrible as it is anyplace on earth.

And in the early summer of 1885 there was drought. You can still read about it in the old newspapers preserved from that year. The onset of summer heat came unusually early, as if to assure perfect misery, and by the twenty-fourth of June it had not rained for fifty-three days. The heat waves rolled steadily upward from the baking fields. People's eyes ached both from the cutting sunlight and from the continuous involuntary effort to focus on something sharp and clear. Day after day the wavering heat put a blur on the world. It was better in the forest, but for lack of rain the fallen leaves cracked like thin glass breaking underfoot, and there was an ugliness among the trees that smelled of fire.

The land was all but dead. The countryside smoked with dust. The roads had disintegrated. Wagon wheels turned laboriously in them with a ghostly muffled grinding, and the hoofs of tired animals sank beyond the fetlock in the fine dust. The high, filmy veil of weightless ocher rising off the trampled roads reminded some men of the War and the dust raised by supply trains and moving troops, and they were startled at how close the War seemed on those still afternoons of merciless heat.

The whole world looked drained and sick. Cows were getting thin. You could see slats of bones under their scrawny hides, and they roamed hungrily over the dead fields and bawled so that your heart would almost break for hearing them. Chickens dragged around with their wings drooping from their bodies and their beaks open in thirst, and their stupid eyes were glazed and bewildered. The dust had risen so high in the atmosphere and hung so thickly there that it painted the sunsets an ugly red. At the end of day the sun fell behind the Cumberlands in a lurid pool of unnatural light, and to country people possessed of a rich Biblical imagination the devastated land seemed cursed by a plague of blood.

The oats were ripe, as was the wheat. Farmers were glumly preparing for the harvest, and they tried to lose themselves in the simple seasonal mechanics of getting ready. But they had little hope for this harvest. They would work their machines in a hell of dust, so they thought, and there would be pitiful reward. Worse was the prospect for the corn. It would be tasseling soon. If there were no rain by then, it would be too late. There would simply be no corn at all—nothing but the reedy stalks—and so there would be famine, and old people and children would die.

The creeks had sunk in their beds as had the river, and the mud along their banks congealed and stank in the heat. Everyone was waiting, deferring deeds and hopes from day beyond helpless day. Life was suspended in a slow rolling of time, and every morning waking men strode anxiously to a thousand windows and read the signs in the sky and found them wanting. The air was so dry that people continuously rubbed their tongues around to wet their mouths, picked at their clotted noses until they drew back blood-tipped fingers, and grew more grimly irritable with each seething day. In the smothering nights children cried out querulously in their sleep, and husbands and wives started up at the sound and settled back, withdrawing if their bodies touched, for they were too miserable, and life was too precarious for love. And on the afternoon of the twenty-fourth of June, when the drought had become so dolorous that people bore it as they bore life itself, hardly daring to dream and yet dully hopeful for some other state of existence, Mr. Simson was hanged, and weary people turned out for miles around to see justice done.

You could have seen them early that morning, filing toward Bourbonville under the copper sun. On horseback, by mule, in wagons, tramping like an army through the fiery dust. The land disgorged them.

His neighbors mostly. People who had seen him in church or else passed by him in the streets of the little town or on the roads beyond. People who had talked with him. People who knew him at a glance and some who only knew his name. They came to see him die.

But not *just* his neighbors. Like sluggish, constipated animals the trains down from Knoxville or up from the south expelled hard little gobs of Sunday-dressed humanity into the dust of Bourbonville, and there was a reporter sporting a vest in spite of the heat—red-faced, self-important, and young, from Chattanooga.

He wrote a good story that day, and you can still look it up and recapture something of how it was—the sweaty crowd jamming the shaded square, the clutter of wagons and horses and mules tied up along the brown streets and choking the fringes of the square itself, people lounging in the hot shade of the great trees, talking in nodding deliberation at one another, measuring the sky, waiting. Shapeless, sullen women in faded calico; men in washed denims; children in bulky homespun frolicking, unaware of death on the courthouse lawn. Adult faces bleak and austere with work and gaunt with the fatigue of the drought—all under the hard, hot sun which built the heat unmercifully with the swelling day.

Families staked out places on the side of the courthouse where the new scaffold stood. A lot of men drifted over to the other side of the square so they could watch the jail—which stood off to itself across a little street—and especially the barred windows on the second floor. Mr. Simson was in the second cell on the right as you looked at the jailhouse, and they tried to catch a glimpse of him. Failing that they speculated on the way he was spending the last morning of his life.

Mr. Simson had murdered his wife. It was one of those senseless, sudden explosions of violence which mark the annals of the poor. He beat her to death with a hammer one morning while she slept. It was early April. The dogwood tree outside her window had just burst into bloom, and people remembered that. Everyone knows that the dogwood has a spot of blood in the midst of its flower, and there is a sadness in dogwood trees which agrees with death.

The Simsons had a child who carried the news to town. Her name was Ardelphia, and she ran and walked six miles, naked except for a thin nightshirt, barefoot and hysterical. When Sheriff Hub Delaney and six hastily deputized and thoroughly terrified men arrived at the Simson place, they found Mr. Simson sitting on the side of the bed, gaping at them in a dreamlike trance, and holding the hammer. It was clotted with blood and hair. Mrs. Simson's head was crushed into the pillow, a shapeless pulp. Her yellow brain and red blood and gleaming shards of bone and mangled flesh were splashed across the bed and dripping on the floor.

The sheriff had been in the Union Army during the war, and he had fought at Shiloh and at Chickamauga, and he had seen the squalid gore of violent death. But the War had been over for twenty years. He took one look at Mr. Simson and the horror and ran out on the porch and vomited. Then he beat Mr. Simson up and hauled him off to jail.

Mr. Simson made no attempt to defend himself. No attempt, in fact, to do anything. Instead he continued in an aimless silence, unbroken for the rest of his life except for one sentence that anybody heard, and that was spoken on the scaffold a moment before he died and it had nothing to do with the murder.

At the trial Ardelphia testified that her father had sat at the supper table the night before the killing in a mood of bitter anger. He kept talking about the work he had done and the fact that in spite of all his labor they didn't have anything and never in all their lives would have anything and that people spurned them and that they all might as well be dead. When the girl tried to cheer him up, he looked at her with such sullen wrath that she became frightened and went to bed. In the morning she was wakened by the sound of muffled pounding and the labored breathing of a man at work, and when she went into the next room to see what it was all about, she did see. She screamed, she said. At that her father looked up and saw her and left off pounding his dead wife and made for her with the hammer. But she got away, and everybody knew the rest.

The spectators who packed the courtroom listened to all this with gasps of terror and loathing. Mr. Simson sat at the table reserved for the defense, shackled to a self-conscious deputy on each side of him. He was unshaven, and one thin leg was fastened to the table with a heavy iron chain. He was filthy, and he was unconcerned. Throughout the whole trial he gazed off into space at nothing. Nearly everybody agreed he looked like an animal, and from the very first people knew Mr. Simson had to die.

Still, John Wesley Campbell, attorney at law, volunteered himself for the defense. That was surprising. Mr. Campbell had been a major of cavalry in the Union Army, and Mr. Simson had been on the other side. People still noted these things in 1885—not that they fought over them. They simply chalked them up and made some of their judgments about people by referring to that bewildering war now receding into the past. Mr. Simson and Mr. Campbell were divided by that war, and since its end they had only talked briefly a couple of times. No friendship there. Furthermore, Mr. Campbell had a sharp eye for a dollar, and Mr. Simson didn't have a dime to his name.

But then Mr. Campbell was unpredictable. And even those who disliked him (and they were many) had to admit that he did a pretty good job under the circumstances—the chief circumstance being that his client wouldn't speak to him. All he could do was plead that Mr. Simson wasn't responsible.

The argument didn't get very far. Mr. Simson was the man they found holding the hammer, and if he wasn't responsible it was hard to tell who was, unless you blamed the whole thing on God. The jury deliberated only ten minutes and thirty-one seconds before bringing in its verdict. Guilty of murder in the first degree. It came so fast that some of the crowd who had gone out to the privies were still standing in line when others rushed out shouting the news.

Judge Simon K. Toliver was known to like Mr. Campbell and to admire immensely his knowledge of the law, but he had no choice but to sentence Mr. Simson to be hanged by the neck until dead and to implore God to have mercy on his soul. The judge was pretty good at sentencing people to death. He had a nice voice for it—deep and booming and austere—and everybody in the courtroom was impressed. Everybody except Mr. Simson, who flicked a crumb off his sleeve and didn't appear to notice anything else. A little muttered codicil to the sentence held that the costs of the trial and the hanging were to be paid for by Mr. Simson or by his heirs.

People almost guffawed at that part, and as it was a murmur of discontent passed through the courtroom. Everybody knew Mr. Simson's land wasn't worth killing an Indian to possess. That meant the county would have to bear all the costs itself. The whole question of money raised a lot of philosophical discussion in the valley. It did seem that the people who could afford to be hanged never did anything to get themselves hanged for, and that meant that the people who did get themselves hanged were mostly charity cases. It was a dangerous predicament for the county treasury.

The president of the Bourbonville State Bank and mayor of Bourbonville, Rufus Swope Mitchell, explained it all to Samuel Beckwith, Jr., just after the trial. In a way it was a strange sight. The older man, dressed in almost foppish elegance, leading the younger (Sam was not yet twenty years old) by the arm out under the trees, talking earnestly at him, explaining the mathematics of the case. Sam ran the old family farm five or six miles out of town to the south. His father was dead, and he lived out there with his mother. He was a quiet sort. He had few friends, and he read a lot—which was unusual for a young man in the valley—but he worked hard. Everybody said he was getting to be the best farmer around, and some said he was going to make himself rich. The girl Sam loved was with him on that day, and people saw them walking gravely together with the gesticulating banker, listening carefully, nodding their heads as he dramatically explained some stirring computation of figures. Afterward the boy and the girl were seen arm in arm happily laughing about something, and people remembered their outburst of fresh gaiety on that otherwise sober occasion. The girl was tall and blond—beautiful in an awkward, coltish way—and her name was Emilie.

Mr. Simson was arrested just in time for the regular meeting of circuit court. His trial came only ten days after his arrest. Much was made of the lucky timing of the two events. Some even speculated that he might have planned it that way—murder and a kind of quick, judicial suicide. However it was, the trial and the judgment rolled off like the turning of a key in a well-oiled lock. The hanging could take place before the month of June was out.

The people of Bourbon County were innately suspicious of the law. Those who disliked Mr. Campbell thought he just might pull something out of the bag at the last minute. But he did nothing but smoke his infernal cigars and shrug in irritation whenever anyone asked him what he planned to do. In the end he even stopped visiting his client. So the good citizens of Bourbon County did not have to wait long for their vengeance. They might well have been content had it not been for the drought.

But the drought filled them with misery. There had not even

been a trace of cloud for a couple of weeks now, and the customary deep haze of summer had been burned off the mountains. It was an unnatural vision, and the same unnatural deviancy was conferred on everything else in the world. The grass, for instance. It was burned and dead, and people who sat on the courthouse lawn felt the grass sting them through their clothing. It was only grass, but there was something quietly dreadful about it, and touching it unexpectedly was a little like touching a dead snake in the dark.

And people were thirsty, constantly and helplessly thirsty. The well under the courthouse pump had gone dry. You could push and pull at the handle and hear nothing but the dry sucking of shriveled rubber washers at the air in the pipes. There was one morose crowd packed into the Kingston Street Saloon and another at Dick's Place on the pike to Sweetwater, but whiskey doesn't really do much for thirst. It burned away the dust in people's throats, but not for long, and it couldn't take the place of water. But if you toiled up the hill and drank at the spring behind the Baptist Church, you were sure to be thirsty again by the time you got back down. So there was a continuous coming and going of people for water, defeated and disgusted with themselves and glowering with the heat.

Meanwhile the clock on the courthouse cupola above their heads summoned up the hours and tapped the quarters into place with the crashing of its bell, and the morning slipped along.

Just after eleven o'clock the Reverend Thomas Bazely rode into town. He came to preach the hanging sermon, to save Mr. Simson's soul. In his complete silence, Mr. Simson had not confessed his sins. The Bible said that if he didn't confess with his mouth, he was doomed to hell. Since Mr. Simson had been a Baptist, it was the affair of the Baptist preacher. So Mr. Bazely came riding in with the Keys of the Kingdom of Heaven dangling invisibly by his side.

Mr. Bazely did not look much like a preacher. He was small and undistinguished with a bush of flaxen hair and a little scruff of a beard that made his narrow face seem even smaller and tighter than it was. When he preached, his eyes flashed up dark and strangely wild, but you didn't notice his eyes out of the pulpit, for usually he tramped along the street with his head downcast and without speaking to a soul. His face was deeply lined, though he wasn't really old. You might have thought he hadn't slept well the night before, but he looked like that every day of his life. His lips were thin and pale, and there was a hardness about his mouth as if it had been carved out of a block of fine hickory. On Sundays year in and year out he flung the Gospel at the Baptists like a man throwing rocks. Many people were awed by him. Some were puzzled. John Wesley Campbell said simply and emphatically that the man was insane and evil, and some could remember those raw days after the War when Mr. Campbell had stood on the porch of his house and hooted as the preacher passed by. Once he called Mr. Bazely a lunatic to his face, but that was all a long time ago, and now the two men passed by one another with only a wordless hatred burning the air between them.

In one hand, swinging like an armed pistol, Mr. Bazely carried his Bible. It was a large book, bound in flopping black leather and showing faded red along the edges where the binding had worn thin. Mr. Bazely was educated. You could tell that, though he never cracked the slightest doorway on his past. It was the way he talked, the way he read the Bible. Even Mr. Campbell admitted the man had a way with words. He could spin off the great hard vocables of the Old Testament so that his tongue sounded like a lashing whip. "Ahithophel, Rab-shakeh, Amalekite, Leviathan, Sodom and Gomorrah." And he could rise to a vehement ecstasy on words like "Shear-jashub" or "Maher-shalal-hash-baz" or "Jeberechiah." Sometimes he simply lost his congregation to the violent coils of his own rhetoric, but his preaching was a memorable thing for people to see and hear whether they understood it or not.

His reputation endured for a long time in Bourbon County. You might say that in view of all that happened later you could expect people to remember him. But it was not just the shock of those events which kept his memory alive. People remembered him as a preacher of the Gospel, and in a very few the memory was so intense that they took up for him till they died. Little children were chilled down to the roots of their hair by his ruthless preaching. And long after his bewildering and violent death, grown men still had nightmares over things they had heard him say when they were young.

On this day he slipped off his horse on the street before the jailhouse and tied the animal to a post. People nodded hesitantly at him, and some mumbled greetings. Nobody ever knew how to approach Mr. Bazely. Today he ignored them all. Stalking out in front of the jail, he swept his dark eyes over the tier of blind windows on the second floor and began to preach. "The wages of sin is death!" His nasal voice cranked upward from the established text and hammered like shot against the wall.

The sheriff appeared briefly in the open door and peered at him blankly, then vanished in the cooler darkness of the jail's office and banged the door behind him. The crowd behind the preacher thickened. More and more people coagulated out of the square and lumped themselves in a shabby semicircle at his back, giving silent echo to his words in the gravely nodding heads of the women and the respectful attention of the men.

Mr. Bazely's origins were as mysterious as his person. To Bourbonville he was without father, without mother, and without descent. He turned up in the valley in the spring of 1865, like so many others washed out of the flooding of war. It became known that he was a preacher. The Baptists let him have their vacant pulpit one Sunday, and except for a brief time one summer years ago, he had preached in it every Sunday since.

In that summer, five years after the War, Mr. Bazely departed on a mysterious journey. He announced that he was going away for a while, and he bought a ticket for Knoxville and got on the train and vanished without a trace. One month passed and then two, and the Baptists had given him up and were on the point of looking for a new preacher when he returned. To the discreet inquiries as to where he had been, he made no real reply. "Business," he said in a grim tone which really dismissed the matter as nobody's business but his own. And after a while people let the matter drop, though occasionally they still wondered about it.

He lived alone in a clapboard and log house which squatted on a patch of land back in the hills. It wasn't much of a place, but he got his living out of it. He never asked for anything more. He received the twenty-dollar salary which the church paid him annually without comment, as if he had not given the subject a thought in a year. He probably hadn't. Except for the money he must have spent on that strange trip years ago, nobody ever saw him spend anything. Not on tobacco, for he neither smoked nor chewed nor dipped. Not on liquor, for he never drank. Not on seed, for he raised his own. Not even on coffee or sugar or flour, for his drink was milk and water, and he ate cornbread made of meal he milled himself.

He was not married. So far as anyone knew he never had been. And nobody ever heard the slightest acid droplet of gossip about himself and women. That was surprising for Bourbonville and even a little disappointing. Some still remembered the famous episode of the Reverend Elijah Armstrong Sutten, the last preacher at the Baptist Church before the War. After one of the most glorious revivals in memory, Brother Sutten was caught red-handed pumping a fifteen-year-old girl (large for her age) in the back of his wagon one half-mile from church. Even after the lantern was held up over them and outraged people were yelling for others to come and look, Brother Sutten did not desist. He kept on until he was done. In fact he speeded up so he could finish, and finish he did in spite of the girl's sweaty squirming to get away and the men who were struggling to pull him off. Then he took his beating and the jeering and the ritual tar and feathers with never a word of complaint. He and his wife and their three little children rode out in the same wagon two or three days later. They went West. Nobody ever heard from them again. He must have gone back to preaching since he was pretty handy at it. Nobody ever knew, but he was not forgotten. His exploit provided long nights of narration and theological and biological disputation until it was all sucked up by the War and nearly carried off to oblivion. (Oh yes, the girl—the one Brother Sutten worked on—she and her family went West too. Everybody who went anyplace went West.)

Nothing like that ever happened to Mr. Bazely. There was a half-remembered story that he had fallen desperately in love when he first came to the valley. But nothing came of it, and the woman was so respected that no one had the slightest suspicion that anything improper had taken place. If the story were true, Mr. Bazely's heart was constant, for certainly he never loved anybody else. At first some of the women, especially the widows, laid snares for him —polite little snares baited with cookies and tea and tales of spiritual woe and longing for the devout life and peace with God. But the cookies went uneaten, the tea undrunk, and the woeful tales fell into confusion under the hard scrutiny of the man who heard them in silence and responded at last that he would pray God to have mercy on the women's souls.

There was only one faint glimmer from Mr. Bazely's past. Really less even than that. Something more like the flashes of false light people think they see when their eyes are shut in a dark room. One doubtful story . . .

It was told by M. G. Galyon. Recounted again and again in a frightful tone of certainty and mystery. M. G. Galyon was the blacksmith in Bourbonville before the day a mule kicked him in the back of the head and converted him into the village idiot. He had been in the War, in the Union Army in Missouri and Kansas, and he claimed to have seen Mr. Bazely once, riding with Quantrill. That didn't make sense, a man like the preacher riding with the likes of Quantrill. But M. G. Galyon swore to it. He said he had seen Mr. Bazely in full gallop down the single street of a little Kansas town, houses roaring up in flame on each side of him, throwing a lurid glare onto his wild face. He claimed he lined the preacher up in the sights of his rifle, but that the preacher rode his horse over the top of him and gave him a stunning blow with a saber, only barely parried by the rifle itself. Then Mr. Bazely vanished in a lash of gunfire. M. G. Galyon said he *knew* he was going to die. The terror froze the instant in his mind like something carved out of ice. It was a face he could never forget, he said. Then the preacher came to Bourbonville and stepped behind the image, and it all moved again in the blacksmith's mind.

But everyone knew that M. G. Galyon was one of the most talented liars north of the Alabama line. He had been everywhere in the War, not only at Henry and Donelson but at Vicksburg and Gettysburg and at both battles of Bull Run and at Appomattox, and at the very last he had ridden part way home with Ulysses S. Grant. He had seen everybody of any importance. Not only Grant but Abraham Lincoln, Jefferson Davis, Alexander Stephens, Stonewall Jackson, Robert E. Lee, George Gordon Meade, William T. Sherman, James Longstreet, and the little nigger boy who held Booth's horse the night Lincoln was shot, Everybody said M. G. Galyon was a better man after the mule kicked him than he was before. A great many of the more pious sort saw in his idiot babbling the perfect punishment of God for a lying tongue.

Still, people wondered quietly among themselves and speculated in the slumberous nights about Mr. Bazely and about Quantrill. Mr. Bazely was the kind of man who drew mystery about himself like an empty house. People spoke of him in the tones used to recount tales of corpses found contorted in their opened graves long years after they were buried alive. And children, hovering in the winter dark at the edge of firelight, watched the flames lick over the logs and saw Mr. Bazely leading cavalry charges into the red embers and heard the call of bugles in the crackling wood. For some reason M. G. Galyon's tale about Mr. Bazely was the only one of his stories people believed. It was all they had about Mr. Bazely, and they could not give it up unless they had something better to take its place. But if Mr. Bazely ever heard the story, he ignored it, and so the story itself fell into a cloudy limbo of formless imagining where it did no harm.

Now he raged against the jailhouse wall in high and hypnotic fury while the mute crowd stood with bare heads and in sober reflection and believed for the moment that the preacher spoke with the voice of God. In the meantime the sun steadily became more fierce. The dry air with its fine teeth of dust chewed down into the raw skin of the crowd and made them ache with misery.

After a while John Wesley Campbell came out of his house and stood on his porch, looking out over the square. He was a large man—hulking, you might say—now gaunt with sixty-one years of age. His face was still strong and sharp, stamped with a keen and steadfast expression which made you look at him with immediate respect. But the skin under his neck sagged in dewlaps of aging flesh, and the lines in his face were unredeemably deep. People in the valley told impossible stories about Mr. Campbell, for in a way they held him in an awe as profound as that they felt for Mr. Bazely. From all the stories about him you might have expected a monster breathing smoke and fire and blasting the world with every stormy breath. Mr. Campbell was indeed a plain-spoken man, so blunt in his speech that he could shatter pretension and hypocrisy with a word. He could attack with such a sudden fury of truth that those so assaulted could rarely forgive him, and once years and years ago he had fought a duel and killed his man. The circumstances were almost entirely forgotten by now, and the incident had passed into the dreamy realm of folk memory where such things have their rest. It was the only duel he ever fought, but it was enough for certain lessons to be drawn, and injured men drew them and let their anger rot into hatred. Mr. Campbell was a well-hated man.

Knowing all this you would have been surprised to see him for the first time. He was quiet in his ways, almost courtly in his gestures, and the natural set of his face was not ferocious but sad. You might have called it an aloof expression, perhaps a moody arrogance, but then you would reflect on it and decide all at once that it was sadness. The discovery would strike you as an unexpected insight. You might look after him as he strolled on down the street, probably trailing a wisp of cigar smoke over his shoulder, and you would shake your head and wonder what made him that way.

Mr. Campbell dressed in unassuming grace. You never saw him in anything but an austere black suit, flaunting a white handkerchief in the pocket of his coat. His pants were cut slim and clung to his long legs in the best style of the day. His clothing always looked as if it had been tailored by somebody who knew what he was doing and was sent into Bourbonville from another state. He wore a neat black tie threaded through the high collar of a shirt as bleached as snow. In the midst of the sullen, tired shabbiness of the crowd on the square that day you would have looked at Mr. Campbell as something striking and vaguely out of place.

Mr. Campbell had been in the Mexican War when he was very young, and he had been in the Civil War when he was approaching middle age, and now he was growing old in Bourbonville. Once his hair had been raven black. Now it was white, and a thick mane of it fell in a tangled heap over his head almost to his shoulders. So there he was in Bourbonville, a little like a contemplative lion observing a strange world of drifting ice and eternal snow.

He had been much different in his youth. A very few women in the valley remembered when he made female hearts flutter as he strode along the street. He was new in town in those days and possessed an easy, ingratiating laugh. They remembered his sprightly step and the smiling gallantry with which he swept off his hat in the presence of ladies. But that was ages and ages ago. The women who did remember laughed like harpies at themselves when they thought of what they had felt then. They imagined that passion was one of the sicknesses of youth of which age had graciously healed them.

Now Mr. Campbell took a cigar from the inside pocket of his coat, struck fire to it, and looked narrowly through the sudden cloud of smoke to the preacher and the jail and the crowd. He saw the young Sam Beckwith leaning in tense idleness against a tree on the edge of the square, listening, watching, absorbed in the sight, his face crossed with a scowl so deep it might have been hatred. Mr. Campbell saw all this and rubbed a curious hand over his chin. He hesitated a little longer, then stepped down and walked casually over and greeted the youth. The young man returned the greeting with a quick look and an air of vague friendliness and then turned back to the preacher with that absorbing hostility. Mr. Campbell followed the youth's eyes out to where the preacher's ecstatically uplifted face shouted on against the blank tier of cells high in the jailhouse wall.

After a time Mr. Campbell spoke in a low, emphatic mutter. "The man is mad. He's as crazy as Simson ever was."

The younger man snapped his head around. "I think he's just bad. He's the most evil man I ever knew."

The two men stood for a moment looking at each other, the younger man with that fierce glare of anger, the older man with wondering surprise. "He is evil," Mr. Campbell agreed slowly. "But what's got into you? What's he done to you?"

"Nothing, I don't want to talk about it," the youth said bitterly.

"I see," Mr. Campbell said in a tone which meant that he didn't understand at all. He took a deep and thoughtful breath from his cigar. All the while he watched the youth's face, and something stirred uneasily down in the cellar of his own memory. "Well, he has something. Look at them, those poor bastards! If he wanted to lead a lynch mob right now, he could just snap his fingers and do it. It's a strange power he has. He could have made a fortune in my business. He'd have made a better lawyer than I ever thought about being."

"I would not want him to defend me."

Mr. Campbell uttered a short, cynical laugh. "You don't know what you'd want if your neck happened to be on the line. Bazely might have got Simson off."

"I'd rather die!" The youth spoke so vehemently that Mr. Campbell was again surprised. The uneasy thing down in his memory shifted again.

"He has always been a strange man," Mr. Campbell said carefully. "You know, he disliked your father very much. Did you know that?"

The youth only shrugged. "I'm not surprised. I think my father must have been a good man."

Mr. Campbell agreed with a slow, wary nodding of his head. "The preacher there stopped at your place the first night he ever spent in the valley. Your mother fed him and put him up in the barn." The older man's voice was gently prodding, but Sam Beckwith did not seem to notice.

"She fed a lot of stragglers in those days," Mr. Campbell persisted. "It was a dangerous thing for her to do, but she didn't care about that."

"Well, it's how she met my father. I guess it didn't hurt her," the youth said shortly.

"No, no, of course not. And how is your mother, Sam?"

"Very well, thank you. She's fine."

"I guess she's taking this pretty hard. Your mother doesn't forget things. Simson came to your father's funeral. I remember it like yesterday. He wore his old foraging hat from the Rebel Army. It was in honor of the occasion. Nicest piece of clothing the man ever owned, I guess. Your mother is very sentimental about things like that. She doesn't forget."

"No, she doesn't."

"You know, your father was one of the few people in this valley Simson ever called a friend. He'd come all the way across the street to shake hands with him, and you'd have thought he was shaking hands with a god. He'd take his hat off and put out his hand, and your father would laugh in that hearty way of his, and pretty soon they'd be swapping yarns about the War. I guess your father was the only man who ever made Simson feel like a human being." And after a short, nostalgic pause, Mr. Campbell said with a whimsical sigh: "Everybody liked your father."

The youth seemed not to hear. His eyes were again fixed on the preacher.

"Your father *was* a good man," Mr. Campbell said insistently. "He was one of the best men I ever knew."

"I don't remember him too well."

"No, of course you don't. You were so young when he died. Five years old?"

"Not quite."

"That's right. He married your mother in 'sixty-five, and he died in 'seventy. So you were four."

"Yes." And after a fretful hesitation the young man exclaimed: "My mother talks about him all the time, night and day, day and night. She can't speak ten sentences without mentioning him. I swear I'm worn out with his memory. I can't remember much about him at all. I wish I could." The youth's voice died away to a dejected murmur.

Mr. Campbell smiled slightly to change the mood. "He would have been proud of you. I can tell you that."

Sam Beckwith assumed a look of fatigue or indifference, and he looked away. There seemed to be nothing left to say. They both looked up at those blank cells on the jailhouse wall against which the preacher directed his fury. The barred windows glared darkly out into the scalding day, empty and wretchedly forlorn in the heavy sunlight. Nothing stirred behind them.

Mr. Campbell lingered a while longer in reckoning silence. Then, feeling vaguely rebuffed and still uneasy and curious at the youth's belligerence, he turned with a grunt and went back to his office. Sam Beckwith remained in his place, looking on with that sober watchfulness, enwrapped in his own thoughts. The furor of the preacher's voice rose in a cloud of sound and spread over the courthouse lawn. There was no place where it could not be heard. Even around where the gallows stood, the sound of the preaching saturated the air, and slowly, like particles settling to the bottom of a deep pool, the other sounds sank away, and the preacher's voice was all that was left.

Mr. Campbell went back into his house and shut the door behind him. It was a gesture of dismissal. His office was to the right of the hallway. The kitchen was out back. Steps led from the hall to his bedroom upstairs. There were other rooms up there, but they had all been closed off for years. Mr. Campbell's office was the cradle of his life. The high walls were lined with books, mostly law books. People said he had the finest personal library between Knoxville and Chattanooga. That was one of the stories they told out of their awe for him, not out of any real knowledge of how many books people owned between Knoxville and Chattanooga. Most people in the valley had a rough faith that there was something magical about the written word, and because Mr. Campbell had a lot of books they could think there was something halfway magical about him.

He sat down now in his customary place, stewed in an effusion of sweat from his short walk into the square, sat in his old chair so worn that the stuffing was creeping out around the faded leather upholstery. He sat moodily smoking his cigar, elbows on the desk, nudging piles of paper and a litter of books, and he looked indifferently out the window onto the courthouse lawn.

He could hear the preacher, but at this distance the harsh words had fallen into the incomprehensible essentials of the voice, and Mr. Campbell could hear only an irregular rasping of sound. He sat pondering Simson and Mrs. Simson and their meaningless lives. He had fought hard for Mr. Simson. He had dredged up precedents. He had lectured the court on the nature of criminal responsibility. He had discoursed on the treasure of equity in the law. He had been calm. He had walked slowly and thoughtfully before the jury and looked every man in the eye and shown them all his listless client, showing them the insanity which hung over him like a nimbus, expostulating with them over the quality of mercy. But at the end, as if it had not heard anything he said, the jury spoke its quick and adamantine word, and now Mr. Simson must die. To Mr. Campbell the law was the only rational thing in the universe, and sometimes the law was absurd.

But now in the breathless torpor of his office, he thought that perhaps it was not so bad, this hanging. Mr. Simson had descended into a vaporous pit of homicidal madness. He would never emerge from it again, even if he lived. Mr. Campbell was well enough acquainted with madness to know that. So the hanging became nothing more than a vain flailing after a presence already departed. It was really a kind of solemn joke being played on those foolish people who stood out there waiting for the grand triumph of justice.

And after the hanging the thing that had been Mr. Simson could be hidden in the ground. At least it was a better fate than that of poor M. G. Galyon—now a toothless, red-gummed idiot slobbering at the edge of the crowd and making low and happy guttural noises in response to that torrid flow of words. Death was a blessing compared to some things.

Mr. Bazely was in full run now. He had taken off his coat and flung it onto the dusty ground, and in spite of the dry air, dark stripes of sweat widened down his back along his galluses. The Bible was like a rod gone to a writhing snake in his hand, and he waved it violently at the vacant jailhouse windows and called down the curse of the damned upon the lone prisoner within.

The crowd had become absorbed in his words. Every motion of his hands and every slashing gesture of his diabolic index finger made them move. From a distance they seemed entranced and enraptured, like a woman ravenously hot and enveloped by male force and feeling within herself the savage pounding of alien flesh and the delicious rending of the most delicate fibers of her body. They were all one out there—a trinity amalgamated of preacher and people and voice and bonded together with an ecstasy beyond worlds and death.

There is no telling how long the thing might have gone on, except that suddenly something happened to stop it. Mr. Simson jumped up at the window to his cell. When he leaped up, the crowd gasped and swayed back as if touched at the fingertips by an unexpected jolt of electricity. His galluses were off his shoulders and hanging at his sides. His shirttail was out. He looked wild, and the crowd tingled at the sight of him, and Mr. Bazely caught in his breath with a wet sucking which was as if he had just swallowed a slimy word too big for his throat.

But the preacher did not stop for long. His voice had become something distinct from himself. It blew out again—words spouting upward like liquid tongues of fire. He and the condemned man glared at one another. Mr. Bazely held the Bible over his head, prepared to fling its implacable message bodily into the cell, where it would flame up and devour the wicked as fire had devoured the priests of Baal. Mr. Simson grasped the bars of the window and peered down in simian befuddlement. He seemed to be trying to perceive something indistinct in the dancing liquid shadows wavering below him in the world of men. The crowd cringed backward. Mr. Bazely kept dashing the stream of his words in furious pulsation at the inert coverlet of flesh drawn down over Mr. Simson's face.

Then Mr. Simson laughed.

It was a low, velvet chortle at first, and the startled onlookers did not recognize the sound immediately as laughter. But it grew in volume, lapping up from the abyss of Mr. Simson's madness. It poured out the barred window and flooded the lawn and trees and fell upon Mr. Bazely and put out his fires and nearly drowned the astonished crowd in its strangeness. For an instant they looked at one another in stunned silence.

M. G. Galyon recognized it first. He stooped in the back of the crowd and heard the familiar sound, and lifting his head like a dog he answered it. He howled in rolling whoops of laughter, and Mr. Simson howled back. The maniacal laughter of the two men slid across the space which separated them and fused in a single, rushing torrent of hysteria. Beneath that deluge of mirth, the crowd felt its surprise dissolve first into dismay and then into bluff humor, and the spell was broken. Somebody finally took M. G. Galyon by the shoulders and led him away and shouted at him till he caught his laughter and cowered at the backdrawn arm which shadowed his face. The crowd untied, slipped into its looser self, and the fantasy was over.

Mr. Simson laughed on for a little while. In the loneliness of his voice under the bright day, his terrible solitude lay open to the world. Eventually his laughter died. He hung limp and gaping on the bars and looked like a foolish animal, unaware either of present or past. And Mr. Bazely tried to resume his sermon.

Only when he spoke did people notice Mr. Campbell. He had charged out of his office and come rushing across the square, and when Mr. Bazely started to preach again, he was there, towering over him with a savage threat in his face and something deadly in his voice. "Bazely, that man is still my client. I want you to leave him alone. I want you to get your stinking little ass on that horse of yours and get the hell out of here."

Mr. Campbell's voice was shaking with wrath. But Mr. Bazely merely looked up at him with a cold, dead fury stamped on his bloodless mouth. "I am doing the will of God."

"Then *damn* your God!" Mr. Campbell cried.

And then a voice still more quiet and still more deadly spoke at Mr. Campbell's side. "Let's just kill him. He isn't fit to live. Let's just kill him." It was Samuel Beckwith, and the look on his face was as set and terrible as the words he spoke. A shock spurted through the crowd.

Mr. Bazely turned a look of ridicule and scorn on his new antagonist. "*You* want to kill *me!* Do you think that will make *you* pure? Oh my boy, I could destroy you with a breath. A single breath, and you would be no more. I know more evil about you, my boy. I know more evil about you than anyone would dare to guess." There was a lilting mockery in the preacher's voice, a wild and disturbing happiness.

The youth took a menacing step forward, but Mr. Campbell quickly restrained him with a strong hand and leaned in on the preacher. "Listen here, Bazely, I'm telling you to get on that horse right now and clear out of here, or I swear I'm going to cut your balls off."

At that somebody standing nearby tittered, and the titter became a general chuckle, and when the preacher looked around, the crowd was looking back at him in ridicule, and it was grinning in brutal anticipation. All at once he knew they hoped to see him obscenely humiliated. He also knew that Mr. Campbell was not joking.

He cast a black, frustrate gaze upon them. For a moment longer he hesitated. At last he turned once more toward the jailhouse and lifted the Bible and pointed it at the window. "Then damn you to hell!" he cried. And whirling around at the amused crowd he shouted, "And may his blood be on your heads, forever and ever!" Then he snatched up his coat, untied his horse and threw himself into the saddle, and lashed the animal out of town.

The silence poured in after him, broken after a few moments by the quiet murmuring and softly raucous laughter of respectful men. The women were shocked at both Mr. Campbell and the preacher. Sam shook off the bemused questions of people around him and stalked off to himself, his face swollen with silent rage. Mr. Campbell looked frowningly after him. But then he shrugged with a habitual gesture and went back across the square to his office. It seemed to be the signal for lunch.

People were just spreading their meals when the clock on the courthouse cupola ominously tolled twelve times. Many of the men on the courthouse lawn squinted up at the clock and checked the sun, and some made a ceremony of hoisting watches from pockets and snapping open the cases for yet another confirmation that it was noon. People with lunches called up their children with petulant shouting and impatient handclapping, and some hair was pulled, and some young arms were cruelly yanked. The food was laid out and devoured with self-conscious concentration. People kept their eyes fixed on their own meals. They were afraid to glance at their neighbors' food. Someone might think they hadn't brought enough, that they were poor. So it was a nervous meal, and here and there a mother paused once in a while to slap a fretful child, and lunch went grimly on to the punctuation of sudden outcries from abused children.

The people who hadn't brought lunch milled around on the edges of the lawn and pretended they weren't hungry. It is a little embarrassing to stand around like that when everybody else is eating, and most of them were a little ashamed and disagreeable, and that is probably why one of them jumped on a couple of niggers and beat hell out of them. It was a substitute for lunch and a cover for the embarrassment of not having anything to eat.

The man who did the beating was named Quillen Bradshaw. He looked a lot like a flabby bear somebody had poked out of a den in the woods and made to walk on his hind legs. He had a malicious face, and his eyes darted suspiciously out from under the shade of an indescribably greasy felt hat. He had found the hat years ago along the railroad. He still wore it proudly, hoping somebody might overlook the rest of him and take him for a banker. Quillen Bradshaw had been slouching in the shade of a tree, cussing the intolerable inconvenience of a two-o'clock hanging when somebody casually jerked a thumb toward two niggers shambling into town, and that set him off.

The niggers bore a distinguished name—Bourbon. Jackson Bourbon was the father, and Beckinridge Bourbon was the son. Once they had been slaves of the family which had given the town and the county and themselves its royal name, only now the niggers were free because the War had come along and made them that way.

Jackson Bourbon was getting old, and he looked feeble and bent. His scraggly hair was a dirty white with a yellow stain running through it. His beard seemed to have grown out on his face years ago, exhausted its energy, and died. It was dirty white, like his hair, showing the taint of rust. On one side of his face the beard curled around an ugly scar cut deep into the jaw about the place where the jawbone slants sharply up to the ear. The scar was the memorial of a long-ago brawl at night in the musty dark of a slave cabin over possession of a woman's crotch. The woman was long dead by now. Only the scar remained, a sturdy monument to an obscure war. In Bourbonville no one knew or cared how he got the scar. People took it simply as proof of his evil heart. When he was young and hard with ridges of muscle standing out all over him, the scar frightened white people. He was a mean nigger, or that was his reputation. But now that he was old and disjointed the scar simply gave people something tangible to hang their scorn upon. Like most fearful things he had become merely ridiculous with the passage of time.

His son Beckinridge was tall, frail, and angular. He had dark, intense eyes burning in an emaciated face. The whites of his eyes were yellow and unhealthy. His shoulders curved over his skinny chest, and his bones were so sharp they looked like knives under his skin. If he hadn't been a nigger people might have pitied him. Not long for this world, they would have muttered, and perhaps they would have pulled their children away. Consumption, a fearful contagion. They would have recognized it at once. It would have been easy in another skin, for then his face would have been rosy pale, and his sick flesh almost transparent. As it was, he coughed all the time—a tearing, profound hacking of air and phlegm—and the coughing brought up blood, and when he spit you could see the blood shine quickly on the thick red spittle. A jewel-like liquid beauty to it flying through the air and catching the light, except that it was blood, and it meant Beckinridge was dying. But because he was black, people didn't see much of anything. All niggers looked alike, sick or well. People did predict he would come to a bad end. He didn't jump when you spoke to him, and he was surly. Surly niggers, sick or well, generally ended poorly, and besides Beckinridge possessed an unnatural and craven appearance which made people instinctively hate him. He had large, overgrown hands hanging at the ends of his wiry arms, and when he walked they flapped comically like stiff pieces of cloth tied to him with string. He was splayfooted. Now as he plodded along behind his father, the dust flared up behind him in sheets. Hot dust in the hot air. He seemed barely able to lift one foot after another.

When Quillen Bradshaw saw the niggers, he took his hands out of his pockets and knotted up his fists and yelled at them. "Hey, you niggers! *Hey!* Where in hell you think you're going?" His voice grated over the slick quiet of midday, and people all around turned to look at him. The nigger Bourbons seemed not to hear, and they came on, and when Quillen Bradshaw saw that, saw them ignoring him, he became completely enraged.

"*Hey!* You fucking niggers! Ain't you listening to me? *Hey!*" Quillen Bradshaw quivered with rage and the delight suddenly provoked in him. Now the blacks did stop and looked blankly at the man yelling at them. Jackson Bourbon let his old face go in a slack grin, as inoffensive as he could make it. He was frightened.

"I said where you going, you goddam nigger!" Quillen Bradshaw spit the words out. The men around looked on with folded detachment—indolent, mute curiosity. More lunchless onlookers picked up from their trees or got up from where they had been crouching on their heels and leaned into the excitement coming.

Jackson Bourbon stretched his face in his scared smile. It was the only thing he knew to do. His smile looked fit to break off his face. He knew something bad was going to happen. Something that would hurt. Bad hurt looming up in front of him, and he was too old, and it was too hot for him to run away. This was 1885, and niggers were free—free to get their ass whipped by anybody who wanted to. Quillen Bradshaw wanted to whip a nigger. Jackson Bourbon saw that, knew he was the nigger who was going to be whipped, and there wasn't anything he could do to stop it.

"You think you got the right to see a white man *hung!*" Quillen Bradshaw leered at him in outrage. "You ain't *got* no right like that, nigger."

"I reckon this here ain't private property," Jackson Bourbon said. He was trying to make somebody laugh. Nobody even smiled.

"Ain't no white man's neck property of no nigger," Quillen Bradshaw said. He was stalking the niggers now.

"Why son, I've seed lots of white men hung." Again the falsely jovial voice of the old black. He was struggling to find something—*anything*—to make the white men laugh. Just one of them. Just one little snicker. If a nigger could make a white man laugh, he was safe.

So he searched for a quip, but before he could start his brain Quillen Bradshaw drew his hand back in a flicker of light and got the old man a good one in the mouth, mashing his lips back against the broken teeth and making the blood spurt. The men standing by watched in silence. They were always amazed at the way you could hit a black nigger and draw red blood.

"He didn't mean no harm," Beckinridge said timidly. He didn't move a muscle except to speak. Jackson Bourbon somehow stayed on his feet. He stood there trying to get his head to stop roaring, trying also to keep from falling dead in the street, and he drew his shocked hands up to his mouth and pressed them hard against his bloody lips. He didn't understand what had happened to him or why. The blow had addled his brain. All he knew for sure was that he was in terrible trouble, and he hurt.

Quillen Bradshaw turned around slowly when Beckinridge spoke. He had the venomous, rattlesnake hatred in his eyes. "What did you say, nigger? What'd you say to me?" His voice a toneless menace.

Beckinridge couldn't say anything. He could only grin the same foolish grin his father had tried. But Quillen Bradshaw was already moving, so Beckinridge was still grinning when the angry white man smashed him flat in the face with a hard fist and knocked him sprawling on his back in the street. The blow shook Beckinridge down to the end of his bowels. It fell so suddenly, like a wall collapsing in a fire. He rolled over like a dying dog onto his stomach and lay with his face in the storming dust, and the street under him heaved and went wildly spinning, and slowly at first and then with gathering momentum he began to cough, and he coughed in frenzy from his sickness and from the poisonous dust sucked deep into his thin lungs, and you expected his lungs to come up like gray, fibrous vomit. He put his hand up to the hurt place and opened his eyes and saw the white men, inverted in his vision and closed around him. He saw their big hard shoes, and all at once he remembered what white men did to niggers with their feet. He got his senses back enough to start scrambling to get up. But it was too late. Somebody kicked him in the chest, and he felt a rib pop. The quick pain made him suck in his breath, and that nearly choked him, and it was as if that first sudden pain were a match setting his whole body on fire with unbearable agony. But the horrible thing was the bone, *his* bone inside *him*, the bone that popped like a dry stick and scraped inside his chest. He toppled back into the street and fell into another fit of hysterical coughing, and all the time he could feel the bone ends snapping against one another like something that had broken down in a machine, only the machine was himself and his life. The circle of men pulled tighter around him, and high overhead he could see the clear blue sky.

"I swear to God I didn't mean nothing," he tried to say, did say some of it in sobs of pain and terror which nobody understood as words. And in the middle of it somebody kicked him in the balls, and in spite of the fire in his chest he bounded up and over himself and grabbed himself with both hands and screamed. Meanwhile the dry bone churned inside him, and he could hear somebody laugh in the crowd.

"No nigger ain't got no right to see arry white man hung." The nerveless, judicial voice of Quillen Bradshaw came from somewhere far off in the dense heat, booming and booming at him. A few of the white men laughed at the nigger holding onto his balls, heaving and gasping and crying the way he was, but most just stood and watched, indifferent, seeing what there was to be seen as if they were watching a train come in or seeing a fire. Jackson Bourbon cowered and looked down in abject helplessness, seeing the man-shaped thing he had helped create now trampled like a lumpy bag under the feet of the white men.

When Beckinridge was born, it was a chilly day in March. There was still cold, unpleasant rain like wintertime, and at evening sharp winds blew up and came in the cracks in the wall. There were long sad days of gray cloud, but there were also sunny days when the earth lay under a fragile warmth, and there were mornings when you could step outside just at sunrise and smell spring coming up from the south. Beckinridge was born on one of those mornings. Day was still a red glow in the east when he entered the world and cried. Mr. Will Bourbon himself came down from the Big House to the quarters to look at the boy. *He* decided what to name the child. He ran his hands over the downy, squalling form and said he'd make a stout field hand. Real stout . . .

The white men squeezed in on the niggers, Quillen Bradshaw in the midst. What he wanted was to get his hands on the sweaty, soft neck of the nigger and break it. He could already anticipate the crunch of breaking neck bone in his hands. He was panting now. He tapped the toe of his shoe against Beckinridge and spoke softly, so softly that the black could barely hear him, and the people on the edge of the circle could not hear at all. They only heard the tense mutter, sensed the mortal threat, and they pushed in through one another to see better. "Get up, nigger."

Beckinridge managed to get his head out of the dust. He could see children peeping through the forest of legs around him, and he hated them. He wanted to yank them up by the hair and dash their little heads against the stones and send their bodies, speared like pigs over a spit, home to their mothers. He wanted to tear trees out by the roots and flail the white men with them till the blood ran in the streets. But he couldn't do anything. He couldn't even get up.

And above him Quillen Bradshaw spoke in a coaxing tone. Some of the parents ran some of the children down and pulled them back because they thought children shouldn't see anything like this. Beckinridge watched them hauled away—protesting, whining little forms—and he began to plead for mercy. The big wet tears rolled off his sunken cheeks and made insignificant globules of mud in the dust.

"God, God, white man, I ain't done nothing! I ain't done nothing to get kilt over. Please let me go home. I didn't even want to come. I just come with my daddy. I ain't done nothing, honest I ain't."

"Nigger, you was born," somebody above him said. "That's enough right there to get a nigger kilt. You was born." The voice laughed—a cruel, obscene laugh, intended to make others laugh too, but it fell without response into the tense expectancy of the silent crowd.

"Git up, nigger."

Quillen Bradshaw was just putting out his hand to strangle Beckinridge on the spot when Hub Delaney arrived on the scene. He came on the dead run. He had been napping in his office when he was roused out of sleep by a hawkish little woman with a voice like an outraged alarm clock. She said it was a shame and disgrace for him to lie around on his lazy behind and let people fight in the streets, especially no-good white trash and niggers. And what did the sheriff think of the children in this country? Did he want them to see things like that? Good God Almighty, why didn't he get out there and earn his pay!

For a man of his girth Hub Delaney could move with surprising speed once he made up his mind, and once he got up steam he was pretty hard to stop. He was plowing full speed ahead when he collided with Quillen Bradshaw, announcing his arrival with a flying right fist on the back of Bradshaw's neck. Bradshaw went down like a stack of stovewood dumped in the street. But instantly he roared back with a snarl and sprang at Hub Delaney with his hands out like claws and his mouth wide open to bite. The sheriff coolly took a little choppy step backward and put his weight on his left foot so that with his right leg he was free to deliver an arching kick which got Quillen Bradshaw directly in the crotch. At which Quillen Bradshaw became deathly pale and began to think seriously about going home. He was still sucking in his shocked breath and fixing his mouth to say something important when the sheriff pounded him in the left ear with that hard right fist and knocked him cold. He raised a fury of dust when he fell, and he lay in the midst of it as still as death.

The sheriff turned hotly on the rest of the crowd. "All right, break it up! Break it up, or there'll be more than one hanging this summer!" And to Jackson Bourbon who stood there yet with his hands pressed over his bleeding mouth, he said: "Now you get the hell out of here, you goddam black son of a bitch. Pick this one up, and you get out of here before I take a belt buckle to you both." With that he stalked off toward the jail without looking back, worrying at his right fist with his left hand because he had bruised it against Quillen Bradshaw's head. The sheriff was out of sorts because he hated to be waked up from his nap.

Jackson Bourbon helped his son arise, and the two of them went hobbling off, the younger man at first leaning heavily on the older and both of them looking as frail as matchsticks in the sun. The crowd of white men slowly fell back into the drowsy shade and began to argue over the fight. Everybody despised Quillen Bradshaw. But did the sheriff have the right to be so hard on a man who hadn't done anything worse than beat up a nigger? That was the question, and everybody had an opinion about it.

Naturally nobody tried to help Quillen Bradshaw. He had lost. So he lay in the street unconscious for a long time. When he got his senses back, he got slowly to his hands and knees and vomited on his hat. He fell back into the mess with a sticky flop and tried to get his breath. After a while he managed to get to his feet, but he vomited again, and it was a long time before he could redeem his precious, preposterous hat and stumble off to find his mule and get home the best way he could. By that time the crowd had lost all interest in him because it was one thirty.

Just at that moment Hub Delaney re-emerged from the jailhouse. This time he had a new manila rope coiled loosely around his left shoulder. New rope in all its prickly yellow virginity is clean-smelling and fresh. You can hold a piece of new rope in your hand and smell it like a flower, and that was the very kind of rope Hub Delaney was going to use to hang Mr. Simson.

When he left the jailhouse, he walked purposefully up a side street to the home and office of Dr. Jeremiah H. Cogill. Doc Cogill took care of Bourbonville's ills, pulled a few teeth when he had to, and now and then yielded to the importunities of a worried farmer and looked at a sick hog. He had to be present when somebody was hanged because the law required a doctor, and he was the only doctor in the county.

The crowd surged with a low, intense murmuring. People called quietly to one another. Men napping in the hot grass were shaken awake. The swelling talk rolled in dull waves against the restraints men put on themselves in the hour of death. Tense, staring people poured over the street where the doctor's house stood and lapped expectantly around it.

The sheriff mounted the steps to the porch and rapped at the door and went in immediately. In a minute or two he and the doctor came out, the doctor fitfully rubbing his eyes from his after-dinner nap. The crowd opened for them and engulfed them. The walk back to the square was a murmuring whirlpool sweeping slowly through the ubiquitous dust. And so they came all in a wad to the gallows where the crowd around was already as thick as lard.

The scaffold was complete down to the thirteen rude steps which led from the ground to the platform under the arching gallows tree. The sheriff had supervised its construction. It was strong and sturdy, but it was his duty and the doctor's to inspect everything for one last time before the hanging, and this they set about to do. They went over the corner beams and the steps and the plank flooring. They gave special attention to the trap and the apparatus which would spring it at the correct time.

It was all as simple as salt. A long, heavy beam was bolted in the middle to the underside of the platform. Both ends swung free. One of them was set under the trap. The other protruded from under the scaffold to one side. When that end was kicked, the other end swung away, the trap fell open, and the job was done. All honest workmanship without frills or pretensions. But it produced all the justice the law could require.

Two or three times the sheriff kicked the trigger and let the trap fall, and with the trap closed he tested it with his weight to see if it would hold. A long time ago a man had been standing, strapped and bound, on the trap of a gallows waiting for the noose to be put over his head, and the trap broke open and dropped him through and broke his leg. It was all pretty messy, so the old hands said. The man's name was Duncan, and he was white, and he was hanged ten years before the War for some trivial offense that everybody had forgotten. But people talked about him still and came to every hanging hoping vaguely that something like that would happen again.

When he had inspected the gallows, the sheriff made the noose. He did it quickly and skillfully, and the deadly shape grew in his hands like a nightmare rising from the chaos of dreams. The great hush which had begun to fall around the gallows became more profound. He made thirteen turns in the knot—the traditional way—and when he was done he held it out in front of himself and worked the rope to see that it would slip and the knot hold. He was satisfied. He took the other end of the rope and looped it carefully over the gallows tree. He made several loops and secured the rope with a half-gainer knot and tested it with his weight. Finally everything was in order, and the sheriff went puffing back to the jail to bring Mr. Simson out to die.

High overhead the sun was leaning almost imperceptibly into the west, and shadows were beginning to inch outward. Not a breath of air. A quartz sky locking the world in thrall. Fiery sunlight blazing into the unprotected street by the jail. The fine dust suspended like a faint haze in the immense heat. Every face turned toward the door of the jailhouse office. The world struck dumb. Time itself pending in expectation. The light so vivid it made sight hurt. And when Mr. Simson stepped out into the street to begin his march to the gallows, he blinked hard at the incandescent brilliance laid down across the helpless earth by the invincible sun.

They had put Mr. Simson's shirttail into his pants. They had pulled his galluses up over his shoulders. They had taken off his shoes. The skin of his feet baby-pink, quickly rusted by the dust. When his eyes adjusted to the light, he looked straight ahead—blank, emotionless, unconcerned, untroubled, unhesitant. Bright blue eyes, watery and distant in the assaulting light. No deputies now. There was no need. Mr. Campbell fell in beside him, walking with a powerful, deliberate pace, his own head high, his face aloof, scornful, sad. The crowd flared out to let them pass, gathered in behind them again, and some men took off their hats, and some moved their lips without sound in what might have been prayer. Women looked on with the stolid, imperturbable watchfulness of country women who will see it all silently and comprehensively and afterward will talk about it for months and make judgments and lament that things like this must happen in the world. Through it all Mr. Simson walking, walking, not seeing the crowd but not bewildered, not dazed—just not interested. And over all the square the silence was like an invisible blanket of snow fallen suddenly in on the torrid day, and the only sound was the measured tread of slow feet and the shuffling of other feet to let the treading feet go by.

At the foot of the scaffold, Mr. Simson paused. He looked vaguely upward, seemed to locate the gallows, seemed to remember vaguely what it was for, but still his predominant expression was blank uninterest, boredom. The sheriff had a hand on his elbow. He nudged him gently, and Mr. Simson climbed the steps and took his place unhesitantly on the trap, his tender neck beside the noose of coarse new rope. He looked briefly at the noose, then looked away, gazed southward into the sun-blasted countryside where the great green forest loomed darkly against withered fields. Everything out there as rapt as the silent square, the wide earth fixed in stifling calm. Mr. Simson gazed out on it all, lost in a trancelike revery, indifferent to the sweating sheriff who worked over him, preparing him hastily for death.

First the sheriff tied Mr. Simson's arms tightly behind his back with a small cord. Then with another he tied the pants legs firmly against Mr. Simson's ankles. The last physical act of a man being hanged was generally pretty nasty, and it wasn't pleasant for the people hauling the body off if the pants legs were loose. At last the sheriff tied the ankles themselves together. Mr. Simson had been standing with his legs slightly apart. The sheriff tapped him to make him put his feet together. Mr. Simson did so in the same obedient indifference with which he had come across the courthouse lawn.

The sheriff was just finishing with the ankles when the clock struck deliberately above them. It was already two o'clock, and now the hanging was late. Mr. Simson was living longer than the law allowed. The sheriff was a law-abiding man, and he was flustered at the delay. Mr. Simson turned his head in slight interest when the clock struck. He looked up at the cupola, paused a vague moment, and with supreme detachment raised his eyes onto the huge sky. He was still looking dreamily upward when the sheriff slipped the noose down over his head and fixed it about his neck. Everything was set. The crowd stood stock still, locked in its breathless hush.

Now the sheriff searched out over them with his eyes. In a quietly concerned voice he asked, "Is there a preacher here? Is there somebody who'd like to say a prayer?" Immediately hands shot up all over the lawn. There were preachers everywhere, frantically waving their hands so they'd be seen. Hub settled on one who was better dressed than the rest. The man looked around self-importantly to make sure he was indeed the chosen one, and when he was certain he came swaggering out of the crowd and with stiff decorum came up the scaffold steps as if it had been the Mount of Olives. He appeared to ignore the people, but his thoughts were pasted on them, and with chin-puffing pride he calculated the grand impression he was making. Hub leaned over and respectfully asked his name, then announced to the still crowd: "This here's Preacher Sizemore. He's a Baptist from Knoxville, and he's going to pray."

The Reverend Sizemore looked indulgently at the sheriff, a superior smile playing at his fat cheeks. "*Doctor R. Vernon* Sizemore of the Main Street Baptist Church," he pronounced in a measured, exquisitely artificial voice. Having paused for effect, he lifted his mellow eyes devoutly over the multitude, and in tones dripping with unction he said: "Let us pray." At once there was a flurry of respectful motion. Hats came off all over the square. Heads inclined in reverent bowing. The preacher waited dramatically until everything was still once more. Then he prayed.

He intoned his gratitude to God for the power of the United States, for the Christian men who were its leaders, for common people who did not hesitate to do their duty. He called God's attention to the fact that the command was writ large in the Holy Bible,

"Thou shalt not kill." And he thanked God profusely that the same Bible ordered capital punishment to restrain the wicked. He called up the example of Achan and his sons, and he went through the Old Testament dropping other vigorous illustrations by the way. He penetrated the New Testament then and drew God a gory picture in words of Ananias and Sapphira who were struck down for something less than murder. Leaving his introduction, he plunged into the body of the prayer and slogged onward through a labyrinth of swelling words so thick with proud muck that everybody got lost. All the while the sweat beaded up and rolled off his drooping jowls, soaking the collar which had been so starched and immaculate in the morning. On and on he went until even *he* gave out in the heat, and finally he stopped on a rumbling "Amen" which rolled through the dense air like the end of the Hallelujah Chorus. With stately self-congratulation and a smiling nod at Mr. Simson, he went down off the scaffold in a radiance of affected humility, listening to inaudible applause.

The sheriff was almost beside himself with impatience. Yet he appeared very calm. Now he stood next to Mr. Simson and cleared his throat. "By the authority vested in me by the State of Tennessee and by the voters of this county, it is my bounden duty under the law to carry out sentence against you as pronounced by a jury of your peers and by a duly elected judge of this state. Have you any last words?"

The loud, bookish sentences rang out over the silence and carried to the edges of the crowd. They were not like Hub. He had stepped into his official capacity. In a wild and silent way people admired him for rising to the occasion.

Nobody expected Mr. Simson to say anything. For a moment the stillness was so deep that the sound of birdsong jangled in the smothering atmosphere like the chiming of irregular bells.

But all at once, for the first time since his arrest, Mr. Simson's eyes flickered with attention, and he took note of somebody, the somebody being the sheriff, and he cleared his throat and looked around in the most natural way in the world. An invisible veil had been snatched away from his mind.

The sheriff was startled by the sudden change in the man, and he bent anxiously forward, asking "What! What!" before Mr. Simson even had a chance to speak, and hundreds of people were pushing and shushing one another and straining to hear.

Mr. Simson said: "Hey there, Sheriff, well, I see we're going to have rain by tomorrow night." He spoke with the casual assurance of someone who has just read a surprising but irrefutable fact in the morning newspaper.

The sheriff was dumbfounded. He gaped at Mr. Simson and tried to form the words after him, and finally he just said, "*What!*" with more incredulous emphasis than he had said it before. The crowd mumbled and murmured, and people passed the word, got it all mixed up and had to be told again and told it wrong, and nobody could believe it when it was told right, and those who were partly deaf had it shouted at them, and somebody yelled up, "What did he say, sheriff?" But Mr. Simson had fallen back into his sedate madness. His eyes went blank again, and he peered aimlessly out into the fiery sunlight where stony shadows oppressed the day.

The crowd stirred and subsided. The sheriff sighed and made a sign with his head, and Doc Cogill came laboring up the steps onto the platform. He was unrolling a heavy black hood made of wool, and some in the crowd shuddered when they saw it. No eyeholes in the hood. No plaything. He smoothed it out against his body, lifted it, and slipped it down over Mr. Simson's head.

Mr. Simson moaned.

Mr. Campbell called up from the foot of the steps—a loud, angry voice: "Take it off! Damn it, take it *off!* Let the man die in the light!"

The doctor looked at the sheriff with raised eyebrows. Hub was ruffled and perplexed, but Mr. Campbell was his friend. So he nodded, and the doctor took the hood off. Mr. Simson stood there blinking in the sun. His face registered relief. High overhead the long hand on the courthouse clock was sinking toward the ground.

"Ready?" The sheriff spoke anxiously to the doctor. The doctor looked professionally at Mr. Simson and then down at his own feet to be sure he wasn't standing on the trap. He nodded.

The sheriff hooked his boot over the makeshift trigger. He shoved at it. It resisted because of the weight bearing on the other side. But before he could back up and try again, a dozen hands reached up for the end of the beam. The sheriff swore at them and ordered them off in a fury of profanity, but they did not care for that. They did not even mind when he bloodied their bare knuckles with his hard boot in kicking at them. The reaching hands laid themselves to their work and pushed with all their might. The trigger gave way suddenly. Mr. Simson dropped neatly through the obscene space sprung into being beneath his feet, and the rope caught him with a jerk and broke his neck. Many caught their own breath when they saw his precipitous fall, and so his death was punctuated with a long sigh blasted into the air around him.

He could not sigh for himself. He did not struggle with death. His neck was pulled up and stretched like a stiff piece of India rubber, and his head tilted crazily over the clasping rope, and his face turned bluish-white and ghastly. Yet there was a serenity to the face, the calm of a long-troubled man in repose. His shoulders heaved once, and he drew his legs slightly up in a reflexive and arduous gesture of choking, but that was all. In a moment his limp body swayed ever so slightly at the end of the rope so that it looked like a pendulum clock running down.

When he had been hanging for a couple of minutes or more, the doctor took one of his wrists. "He's still got pulse!" he said, mostly to himself. "Like a galloping horse." (When a man is hanged it takes a little time for the heart to realize what has happened, so it beats wildly and frantically trying to catch up the air which has been blocked out of the lungs. That was what was happening to Mr. Simson, and it went on happening for awhile.)

"It's going now," the doctor said in a few minutes. And at last, after a long, straining pause: "It's gone." He stood stiffly up and reported officially to the sheriff: "I pronounce this man dead." It was twenty-two minutes after two o'clock.

The sheriff had been standing very still and watchful, not even moving to wipe the oily effusion of sweat off his face. When the doctor spoke, he looked suddenly around and quietly called up a few of the men to help. Then he went over to the trap and cut Mr. Simson's body down. It tumbled through and fell like a sack of grain onto the grass below. The men picked it up and carried it back to the jailhouse. Mr. Simson's head flopped so loosely that his skull might have been a weight in a limp bag of bluish skin hanging off the end of his body. The rope had gouged into his neck. His soft flesh lapped over the new yellow hemp, and a trickle of blood seeped out of each of his closed eyes and rolled down his face like tears. He had fouled his pants in death, and he stank. Urine dribbled through the coarse fabric and made a glistening little pencil stream of yellow which left a spotted track in the dust.

The crowd lingered awhile afterward, discussing things. Finally it slowly began to come apart and to break up. The heavy sunlight beat silently upon the earth. The light had a despondent slant to it, and it thrust the crowd more deeply into a cheerless mood. Nearly everybody was disappointed and dissatisfied and didn't know why. The day had suddenly become like late Sunday evening with work tomorrow or else the last night of campmeeting or the day after Christmas. Mr. Simson's enigmatic words circulated among the parting clots of humanity, and they discussed them and weighed them and looked at the sky and shook their heads in a weary negation of the strange prophecy.

They did not think they would remember this hanging. As it turned out, they were wrong. But at the time nearly everyone agreed that there had been better.

1

THE YOUNG SAMUEL BECKWITH was sensitive to smells. His mother said it was a legacy from her side of the family. She said her grandfather could smell a nigger in the dark and got himself quite a reputation in his day by hunting down runaway slaves. Her father could stand in a field of strawberries and by sniffing the air tell if they were ripe. Her brother Matthew, dead like all the rest of them except her, could stand at the entryway to his room (Sam's room now) and smell clean sheets on his bed.

Sam's sense was not that acute. But when he walked close to the scaffold as they were carrying Mr. Simson away, he had smelled the corpse. He had not expected this. The heat had burned all the smells out of the air except the hard, dry smell of itself. But suddenly over that withered baking came pouring the rotten toilet odor, making the air rank and putrid. Now, riding along in the barren dust once more, the young man mused over things. In his moody discontent with the world he thought there was something indecent and corrupt in making Mr. Simson do this private act before the gaping crowd.

The sun pressed down on his back. He was disgusted at his own filth, and the heat undulating off the young corn and the oats and wheat and pasture land of the starveling fields was stuporous and terrible. The earth smelled tired, and he felt disagreeable and at loose ends.

It was after three thirty. He had waited around until the crowd was thoroughly dispersed before riding out himself. He did not feel like talking. He regretted his outburst against the preacher because it was so useless. He dreaded the prospect of questions flung at him by meddlesome people who had seen and heard. Somebody was sure to tell his mother about it. She would be shocked. He dreaded in a dull, spent way the thought of another dreary confrontation with her sweetness.

She waited for him now. Doubtless at this moment she sat dreamily before the great picture of his dead father in the sitting room of the house. The solemn, military portrait of the young Confederate soldier loomed over the room and dominated their lives. Ordinarily an offering of flowers reposed in front of the picture. But all his mother's flowers had been killed by the drought. So now there was nothing but the empty vase, white and forlorn on its small table. Nearby, as if on an altar, reposed the ancient family Bible.

The Bible was a treasure. It had been printed in England more than a hundred years before, and all the *s*'s looked like *f*'s unless you looked close. Sarah Crittendon Beckwith, his mother, said the Bible had been in the saddlebag of the first brave Crittendon to cross the Appalachians and settle here in the valley. The Bible was a repository of the family chronicle—births, marriages, and deaths carefully inscribed by various devoted hands on the pages at the front. And at the last: "Samuel Atkins Beckwith, born in Virginia, March 17, 1840, and died in his loving wife's arms on September 9, 1870."

That was the stately and delicate hand of Sarah Crittendon Beckwith, written down that very September morning fifteen years ago. She had inscribed her own tragedy in the family book.

Perhaps it wasn't proper, putting the solitary Beckwith at the foot of that long line of Crittendons. Sometimes she granted that in a forensic way as she justified herself to her son. But there were no more Crittendons left. Not a one. The family succession fell to its end or perhaps to a new birth in the marriage of the last daughter to the tired young man who set out walking home from where the War had abandoned him in the Deep South.

He didn't make it. That was part of the golden legend already spun about him after only fifteen years. He came sick to the Crittendon house, worn out from the miles, starving, feverish, near to death. "The burden of the Lost Cause was on his shoulders," his widow was to say again and again. The burden which finally killed him five years after the war when his noble heart quit beating under the strain it had endured.

She did not weep when she spoke of him, nor did her voice waver. She spoke softly and with stalwart calm as if breathing into a fragile world of gossamer images. She awoke that morning early and found him stiff and cold beside her. It was the end of a world of heavenly sweetness, she said. Fifteen years afterward she still spoke of him in the whimsical, sad way of ancient grief. Fifteen years after his death she still loved him. And she was faithful to his memory. "Our love passed the love of earth," she said, gravely smiling whenever anyone suggested that she might marry again. "There could never be another one like it." Her whole life, she said, was to make the father real to the son and to make the son the kind of man who would be worthy to carry on his heritage.

She was not old. Just in her early forties. And yet in her life an aged past somehow survived and blew across the present with a gentle, dreamlike mustiness. Sunday by Sunday she appeared in church, and as she passed through the churchyard on her way to the door men instinctively reached for their hats. People marveled at her because she held to a past which most of them could not retain—the present alone was too much for them.

She was mistress of the ramshackle old house built by her ancestors in flush times at the turn of the century. It should have belonged to her brother Matthew, but he was killed in the War, so the house came to her along with the responsibility suspended in it like a soul. She was faithful to all this in the same way that she was faithful to her husband. She nursed the frail blossoms of memory plucked from the noble line of her ancestors, that line which ran across the American Revolution and over the great, green sea to vanish in an auburn haze in the vales of Yorkshire.

An old family story held that one of her ancestors came galloping southward to succor his suzerain against the usurper at Market Bosworth. He arrived too late. His king died, and history changed for England and for her family. She loved to read aloud to her son of an evening. She liked history best of all. And occasionally she lifted her eyes from some melodious page and dreamed aloud of what might have been. If her ancestor (she did not know his name) *had* arrived in time, the tide of battle *might* have turned, and then . . . Well, who could tell? But God moved in a mysterious way His wonders to perform. She was born *here.* When she talked like this she inevitably concluded with that gentle, whimsical laughter so typical of her, delicate and clear like her gentle voice. She said that five years of her dear husband's love had been worth the loss of empire. Besides, they had their own empire here, on this good land, and she was as much a queen as she ever wanted to be. Her husband had been king. Their son was the prince who would someday kiss the sleeping beauty and restore everything as it had been.

So she was exalted in the mind of the valley, she the gallant Southern woman female novelists would later dream over and recall with magnificent sentimentality. She was the guardian of memory and hope for people who did not have the time or the imagination for such things, and they were grateful, and they admired her and loved her in the abject and distant way that saints are loved. Strange that memory and hope alike were, for young Samuel, dried flowers hung motionless in the still air of their house. They waited like an exotic garden of beautiful dead things to receive him whenever he came in the door. They waited inevitably for him on this afternoon, and in a tired renunciatory apathy of feeling he hated to go home.

A mile out of town the road forked. Ahead the pike went winding on toward Sweetwater and Chattanooga and the great, inscrutable South which lay muttering under its blanket of heat far beyond. To the left a smaller road dipped into a creek bottom and strayed through fields and woods to the old Methodist burying ground near the river. The Methodist Church was there, keeping its quiet watch over its faithful dead. Sam's father was there.

He had been a Methodist. He went to the Baptist Church in Bourbonville because that is what his wife wanted. Her people had been Baptists, and she could not become what they had not been. Nevertheless, in death she recognized her husband's religion, and she had him buried in the Methodist graveyard. People admired her for that. All the rest of her people were buried in Bourbonville, on the green and sloping hill behind the Baptist Church. "It is what he would have wanted," she said firmly. So he lay there, quite alone in a corner plot, faithful forever to the exuberant faith of his fathers.

"They were big Methodists up in Virginia," Sarah Beckwith said. When she said it, one imagined the vista of a great house set in rolling fields with noble carriages lined up at the columned porch and music ringing in the lighted rooms and beautiful women coming and going with dark, handsome men. All with the Methodist church somehow in the background.

Sam cherished that fantasy for a while as he did the picture of his father on the wall. He had let it drop by now.

For he was old enough to let some things drop. He knew that his mother never had heard from his father's people, really knew little about them. He had told her so much, she said. His mother and father were dead, she did know that. But she hadn't paid much attention to the rest. She was drunk with love and happiness, and she thought they would have years together, time enough to return to his home, to meet his kin. And there were no brothers and sisters living. But someday they would have gone back, and Sam would have played with cousins, laughed and sung. Her husband would have towered above them all, looking down like a smiling god.

But he had died. Her husband had died! A wonder how much sorrow, how much crushing fact, could be contained in those few words. He had died. A heart attack struck him down. Exhaustion reaching up for him five years after the war. Only then did she realize she had nothing of his past. "People should write such things down," she said woefully. "If *only* I had!" So it didn't matter much to Sam if his mother painted things in the way she thought they had to be. Fantasies about dead men never hurt anyone.

He went with his mother to the grave every Sunday after church. In season she scattered flowers before the tombstone. There the inscription was carved deeply into the rich, pink granite:

SAMUEL ATKINS BECKWITH, SR.
March 17, 1840 *September 9, 1870*
Asleep in Jesus
Faithful Husband *Loving Father*

Beneath were a cross and a crown twined in a symbol of victory over death. It was a triumph in stone, the most impressive monument in the cemetery.

So now Sam paused at the fork in the road and shaded his eyes with a hand against the raging sun. Then he gave the horse a nudge, and they went slowly down the fork which inclined toward the cemetery.

The road was crooked and immoderately steep in a place or two. The Methodists all grumbled at their ancestors for building the church out there and planting the graveyard next to it so that nobody could move it until Christ raised the dead. But the ancestors had had a glorious revival there around the turn of the century, and they put the church up in this place because it was holy ground. Besides, there was a spring nearby, and if you were going to have campmeetings you needed a spring, and the Methodists held campmeetings every year because you couldn't be a Methodist without them.

The spring at the church made a creek, and the creek ran across the road near the fork and had to be forded. The horse paused to drink in the middle of the stream. The water was running shallow and sick with the drought, and there was a white fringe of slime waving along the creek bank. The water made a gurgling whisper in the vast heat. Sam dismounted into the water, felt it run around the ankles of his boots. The cool running felt good and eased his burning feet. He bent, upstream from the horse, and splashed water into his mouth until he was satisfied. He scooped water onto his face, ran it through his hair, and felt the water run down his back under his sticky shirt, and he sighed with contentment at the feeling. Then he mounted his horse, and they went on.

The road climbed sharply away from the creek. There was dust here, but not so much as on the pike because this road was not so frequented. Trees came down close along the water and grew awhile on each side of the road which went beyond it—a forest of chestnuts and tall oaks and hickories, dogwood and blackgum, cedars and straggly pines. A brooding and heavy silence lay over the woods. The woods soon gave way to fields of corn. Corn on both sides of the road, laid out in precise rows, child high, thirsty and wilted with the heat and the drought. The slender leaves hung motionless, caked with a fragile veneer of dust. Nothing moved in the fields anywhere except the pulsating waves of rising heat, and far beyond, the heat made the steep horizon tremble. The heat waves intensified the solemn stillness of the day. Noise and life had been sucked out of the air by the impending sun, and Sam and the horse moved across the huge land like a single dark speck beneath the glaring sky.

A mile or so from the creek two Negro women lived in a rotting shack beside the road. It had been slapped together with rough lumber years ago by a white man. He had planned to live in it until he could afford a mansion. When the news came of the gold strike in California, he packed up his slatternly wife and left, and his shanty was left abandoned in its weedy fields. His land wasn't worth anything. Nobody claimed it when he left. At least not for a while. The house weathered and sagged and looked fit to rot away. Finally the Negro women, sisters, moved in. They were whores, or at least they had been when they first took over the house. Now people in the valley called them the nigger hags, and nobody bothered them. Not even the county, which in theory owned the land since no one had ever paid any taxes on it.

The old hands also said the nigger hags had been beautiful once. At least beautiful for niggers, and you'd be surprised how pretty a nigger could be if you saw one in the right light. They were ugly now, thin and cronelike, with screeching voices like wounded waterbirds. When they had nothing else to talk about, the women of Bourbon County chattered about the nigger hags over teacups and at quilting parties and in the steam of canning times. They concluded, comfortably enough, that the nigger hags were so wretched looking now because of the uncounted whoredoms of their youth. It was like M. G. Galyon's babbling idiocy. God was pretty smart, the women of Bourbon County thought, because he knew just how to contrive the right punishment to match a particular sin. In fact, if you took a man's calamities you could reason backward with fair certainty and figure out the sort of sin he had committed to deserve that precise punishment. On that train of thought the devout women of Bourbon County could ride all the way to ecstasy and back.

A long time ago some of the women had tried to get the law onto the nigger hags. But for twenty years the law in Bourbon County had been Hub Delaney, and people said when he used to go out there it wasn't to tell the hags to shut their house down and leave. Now it didn't matter any more. The only people who visited them came to get warts taken off or to find where something had been lost or to inquire about the best time for planting potatoes. One of the hags read palms. And they both knew something about curing both man and beast. Their practice was probably as big as Dr. Cogill's.

The nigger hags were in the yard washing clothes when Sam came up. The clothes were boiling in a great black caldron of iron. The red fire licked up around it, and white hickory smoke mingled with steam rose savorously straight upward. One of the hags was stirring the clothes with a long wooden stick. She was going at it with the regularity of a grotesque machine. The other one was looking on. Both of them wore shapeless clothes blacker than their skins, and their figures were frail and insubstantial against the enormity of the day. When Sam came into view they turned to look at him. The one stirring the clothes took her stick out of the caldron and leaned on it, and they both shaded their eyes to stare.

"Hello! Hello!" they called. Their voices clashed inharmoniously together, seemingly unaccustomed to much speaking.

"Lord, it be the Beckwith child! Orphan boy," one of the hags said piteously.

"To see his pappy's grave. You gonter see you pappy's grave. I know." The second hag spoke with a significant nodding of her head.

The first hag, the one who had been stirring the clothes, stepped hesitantly toward him. "Can I read you hand? Boy, can I read it? For a nickel I look into the future. I shows you what is to be." She held out both her hands, beseeching. They looked like thin, black claws, and the sunlight gleamed on the black fingernails.

Sam drew back. "No, I don't think so."

"Just a nickel. A nickel ain't much for rich folks. I can tell you the future."

"No, no thank you." His horse drew a step back in response to the recoiling pressure on the bridle.

"She read the hand of you pappy," the other hag shrieked.

The first one nodded vigorously so that her ragged clothes shook. She spoke more quietly. "That the Lord Jesus Christ truth. I did. I read the hand of you pappy."

The youth leaned forward and looked at the grinning hag who had come up close to him. She stank of must and sweat and urine—old woman stink—and when she came up under his nose he found that her breath was so foul that his stomach almost heaved from the reek of it. "I read you pappy's hand. Right here, right where you be sitting, now onto fifteen years ago." The rancid breath came up like gas out of a stinking pit.

"He was hunting," the other hag said.

"With Mister Campbell. They ride by here, like you is riding now," the first one said.

"She tell him he gonter die," the second hag said, and she looked solemn.

The one nearby nodded sorrowfully. "I don't want to do hit. To tell him. When I seed what was wrote there in his hand, I don't want to do hit. But if'n somebody gives me a nickel, I has to tell 'em the truth. If'n I don't tell 'em the truth, I'll lose the gift."

"Mr. Campbell laugh. He don't believe," the other hag said, very sadly. "If you pappy had listen to my sister, he might of got his heart right with God."

"Mayhap he done hit. Mayhap he done hit," the hag near Sam said. "He look awful serious when I tell him. *He* don't laugh."

"But Mister Campbell, he laugh. And *then* you pappy laugh too," the other hag said reproachfully. "But he die in a month just the same. Like that, he die in a month."

They nodded together in a mute and dolorous chorus.

"Just a nickel, please boy? A nickel? Enough to buy two old nigger ladies a sack of tobaccy?" The first hag looked up in yearning and stretched her hands even farther toward him. They were right under Sam's face.

"I never heard that about my father," he said.

"It be the truth! It be the truth!" Both the hags affirmed it at once in a sad, unoiled grating of their voices.

Sam looked down at the ground and saw withered grass and dust and small rock, and he tried to imagine his father there. The two men, on a sunny day, riding down this road, perhaps with their guns. He knew about the friendship, did not understand it. It was the only thing his mother held in reproach against his father, the only reproach from the years of happiness, the friendship of a Southern gentleman with a traitor to his country. John Wesley Campbell, veteran of the Federal Army, a man who had killed his own kin. She ascribed the fault to his father's goodness. He could forgive. Goodness blinded his judgment. She was not so good, she said. She was a realist who judged men for what they really were, and she judged John Wesley Campbell to be evil. She swelled up with anger and grief whenever she heard that Sam had spoken to him.

"Some folks is scared to know what's coming," the second hag said in a tired voice. "Let him be, sister."

"It ain't gonter be no good for none of us," the first hag said. "Might as well know it and get it over with, boy. Might as well know. It gonter happen anyhow. You gotter be brave. You can know it and get ready."

"Ain't but a nickel," the second hag said.

"It's cheap for the future," said the first. She looked up at him with a crafty grin. Sam bit his lip and looked back at her, squinting reflectively in the heat. He felt a chill in the sweat under his wet shirt. He shrugged it off, and with one impulsive gesture he plunged a hand into a pocket of his pants and drew out a few coins. He picked out a nickel.

The sisters cackled with glee and looked triumphantly at one another. The one nearest him put out her hand and snatched the coin away. It vanished into the ragged folds of her dress, and the youth thought of a hawk carrying off a tiny mouse or a baby chicken.

"He brave, this boy. Like his pappy," the first hag chortled. "The boy ain't afraid."

"It don't hurt now nohow," the second sister said. She spoke philosophically. "You can know it and it don't hurt now. It's later that it hurts."

"You has to get down off you horse," the first sister said. "You has to come sit with me on the porch."

He hesitated a moment and conjured up a fantasy of the sisters swarming over him with knives. Yet he pushed the thought aside, and he swung down and tied his horse to a sapling. The first sister hovered nearby, and when he came she went off on her fluttering way to the porch. Behind him he could hear the ragged breathing of the other one straining in the heat. He tried to imagine anyone copulating with them, and his mind reeled. In the midst of the absurd little procession he found himself musing over the quiet way that time could do terrible things.

The first sister sat down on the edge of the porch. She was puffing with exertion, and for a moment she couldn't say anything. She motioned Sam to sit opposite her, on the other side of the broken steps. He did and was enfolded in an invisible steam of odors—decaying wood, unwashed humanity, stinking breath, and the pungent, clean smell of mint growing there, under his feet, in the deep shadow of the house. Over everything lay the massive presence of a world ablaze with drought, sun, and hanging fire.

"Now give me you hand," she said when she had caught her breath. He put out his right hand, palm up, and the old woman took it. Her skin was cold and felt dry and scaly. Her fingers were like the tails of snakes, rustled stiffly up from some dismal winter's sleep. She peered intently at the lines in his palm, laboriously tracing them out with a hard fingernail and spelling things to herself in a wheezy mumbling of trembling lips. Her sister leaned over her, a sharp, distorted form splayed in eerie black against the brilliant sky. Neither of them was smiling now. They each followed the probing motion of the finger with their intense dark eyes.

Suddenly a rain crow began softly to croon far off in the woods. Sam jumped at the sound as if it had been gunfire. But, when his hand moved, the fingers of the nigger hag closed more tightly around it and held it fast. The rain crow went on, and every note fell like a requiem over the silent land. Sam could imagine his father sitting here, and in the languorous waves of heat shimmering over the road he tried to pick out the figure of a younger John Wesley Campbell, sitting his horse there, smoking his cigar and letting the thin white smoke encircle his head while he laughed. But he could see nothing but the ordinary things—his own horse idly cropping at the withered grass, the road, the seething fields, and far beyond, the giant mountains.

"Well?" His tone was impatient and harsh. He was afraid.

"I can't see it clear," the nigger hag said. She wrinkled up her skinny face in perplexity. But almost at once she brightened. "Wait, it's coming. It's coming. See? Look!" Her eyes were abruptly so alive with their vision that both Sam and her sister bent with her. He looked at the meaningless crossing of the lines in his skin and felt uneasy and ridiculous. But the nigger hag frowned again, and whatever it was she saw puzzled her. She shook her head. "They's something I can't make out. Something in the dark."

"Am I going to die? Like my father?"

She shook her head, apparently mystified. "No, you ain't gonter die. You gonter go on a trip." She raised her face and looked him directly in the eyes. He could smell her thick, foul breath, and looking steadily back at her he saw with repugnance how yellow the whites of her eyes were, how the matter clotted around the edges. She gazed at him with a worn expression of bewilderment. "You gonter go West. I don't understand it. You gonter go West."

He took back his hand. The nigger hag passively let it go. He stood up with an unhappy smile on his face and looked scornfully down at the old woman. "So you think I'm going to go West."

"You gonter go." The nigger hag sat still. Now she would not look at him. "I can't tell you no lie. You give me a nickel, and I has to tell you the truth."

"I am not going to go West," he said flatly. "I have made up my mind. I am not going to go West." He wanted to slap the old woman.

The nigger hag shook her head solemnly, still looking at the ground. "You hand say you gonter go West. It's writ down there plain, and if it's writ there you got to go."

"When? When does the hand say?" He made his voice cruel and mocking.

"I can't tell you that. I just sees you gonter go. I can't even see why."

"You can't even see why."

"No suh, deed I can't. I don't know why you gonter go, but you gonter go."

"I see."

She looked up at him and squinted against the light. "I'd tell you if'n I could. I has to tell what I knows." She shook her kinky head again and looked woefully down. "Sometime I think the spirit's leaving me. I can't see things like I used to. I just can't. I don't *know* why." Her words were sluggish and miserable.

He turned quickly away. The anger which had come up in him had gone as quickly as it came. "I hope you like your tobacco," he said. He tossed the words back over his shoulder and hastened toward his horse. But suddenly he thought of something and stopped. He faced the two women again. "Tell me one more thing: Is it going to rain? Will it rain by tomorrow?"

The nigger hag on the porch got stiffly to her feet. She looked at her sister, and they repeated the single word incredulously: "Rain! Rain!" Their voices were a shrill scraping in the enormous day. They peered inquiringly upward. The second one looked then sharply at her sister, who still searched the sky. Finally that one looked blankly back at Sam and shook her head. "Rain! Boy, I don't see no rain up there till the end of the world." The two of them stared at him, full of puzzlement, and that was the expression they had when he turned again to his horse.

"You remember we tell you," one of them cried after him. "When you go West, you remember. You'll see."

But he did not look back. He mounted his horse and rode on toward the Methodist cemetery. "Niggers!" he said, taunting himself. For a moment he felt as if he had been stripped naked and shown off to a crowd, and all alone on the road he felt a sensation of public shame.

But like the anger, the shame soon passed. He was too worn out with everything to retain feelings. He was like a glass, turned upside down and emptied of all its contents and left to dry in the fiery air. His thoughts moved unhurriedly in his brain. He felt curiously detached from them, and they were free to do as they pleased, and they turned West, to the great land which spread out there, full of promise and despair.

The West! Nobody could be alive in the South these days and

not think of the West, the wide and vacant land where dreams lay piled like the treasure at the end of the rainbow. Almost the instant the guns were stacked at Appomattox Southern men began to slip Westward. Like an avalanche of shadows they fell away from defeat. Not *just* Southern men. But Southern men had a special impulse. Sam had grown up seeing them driven by it, seeing them disappear with grimly expectant eyes into the great, bright void. You could get a new start out there. You could find something.

The West had swallowed Emilie up. The nigger hags knew his love affair. How could they *not* know? Everyone in the valley must know by now. You couldn't keep a secret like that, not something so obvious as their love and her abrupt departure. The nigger hags expected Sam to go after her.

But he had no illusions. He knew he would never see her again. She had been gone for more than a month, she and her bizarre family. If he started now and sought her from St. Louis to California, he knew he might never find her. It would be like tracking a ship through the sea under a sky without stars. No sense to the quest. Like the sea, the limitless land out there had opened and closed behind them, leaving no more trace than a track in the ocean. He was left here with his memories of a shining springtime and his loneliness, ridden with guilt. And he would not go West.

When he came into the churchyard he tied his horse at one of the hitching rails under the trees near the road. He jumped down and looked around for a moment. Before him the rectangular frame church reposed amid a grove of trees with its squat steeple rising through the branches. The sun was falling against the windows of the church, and they took the light and broke it into four glassy, rectangular suns he could not look at. The afternoon was well along, and the deserted church, the slanted light, the tall, still grass in the graveyard among the scattered stones all spoke quietly of sadness. Sam's free-turning thoughts went tumbling back to Emilie and picked their way gingerly over the sharp little pieces of memory which were all there was left to their days together.

They came here on one of the first mornings they rode abroad. He wanted to show her the things dear to him and important. To share something. The first thing he thought of was his father's grave. Letting her see it was to let her into his own heart where deep feelings lay. He had cried at his father's grave, felt the world halt here, felt the bottom wrenched out of his life and his soul plunged into the pit. Oh, long ago. Long ago. But he wanted to put the two strong feelings together. He wanted to bring Emilie and his feelings for her to this place, and he wanted her to understand something. He did not know exactly what. But *something* about himself.

So they came, and they stood together and looked down at the granite stone. All in reverent silence. Standing beside him, she slipped one hand under his elbow, and the other she laid softly on his arm. The first time she had ever touched him with affection. And when they walked away she kept her hands there and walked gravely along in step with him, her head thoughtfully bowed. The warmth of her clean young body surged at him. It was a chilly morning, glistening at the edges with frost. He took in the chill and the cold brightness of the day, and he felt something joyful bound inside him at this spot where he had always been so lonely. It was all a very quiet thing, and something he did not try to express. And surprising, surprising to him that he reached out for someone like Emilie and felt in return her reaching for him. He remembered her rough hair. Her long yellow hair with its marvelous coarseness, brushing at his cheek. He would never forget that rough hair.

Because he did remember, his father's grave nowadays was more desolate than it ever had been. Much worse than childhood, for he had long ago got accustomed to that feeling. In those days he came to the grave remembering the funeral. The somber people shuffling about in their stiff Sunday clothes, uncomfortable in the late summer heat, the red dirt shoveled out of the earth lying in an ugly mound, the gaping hole descending to shadows, the black coffin with its peculiar shape. His mother's piercing cry of mad grief, and the high, dark memory of nameless birds sharp against the September sky. Then the leaden amalgam of all these things had bludgeoned him from the grave, and for a long time (he could not remember *how* long), he could not visit it without crying. Hopeless, unrestrained crying. But in time he got used to the absence, and in time the life he lived with his mother seemed to be the only life he ever had possessed.

So the first grief lifted a little, and fantasy came in under the cloud. He roamed with imaginary companions over the woods and fields, and he made his father one of his company. Together they beat back Indians and Yankees from fence line to creek bottom, and they held the old barn fort for hours against overwhelming odds, shouting heroic things to one another, raising the invincible courage of manly love.

At the end they were decorated for gallantry on the field of battle. They were always victorious. They never faced the surrender which brought the stately dreams crashing down. And to rest they sometimes lay together in the tall cool grass of summer and looked into the lazily changing clouds shifting overhead, and they talked. He told his father things, and he put understanding words into his father's mouth for response. They whispered to each other like schoolboys under the blankets at night, and a world of bright stars and watching moon cupped itself over them, and they slept secure. The grief thinned and faded and fell into a roseate fantasy of companionship. In a way the grave was a dear thing. He and his mother loved it together.

And now? Well, now it was just another grave in the churchyard. He did not usually think much about his father when he saw it. He thought of Emilie. "You've changed, Sam. I knew it would happen. You're different. You don't care about things any more." His mother's reproachful voice murmured sadly at him. And she was right.

He came to the stone. The high grass swished at his legs. He stood there looking, his arms folded loosely across his chest. He supposed there was nothing in the grave now except the strong bones. No man there. No person. Nothing.

Did he love me? The question had once been desperately important to him. He saw other fathers, other sons, and he wondered. He got his mother to repeat the evidences of his father's love again and again. "He used to carry you on his shoulders down through the fields in the evening, and I would be sitting here, and through the open windows I could hear you laughing together. He was forever snatching you up and kissing you." He wracked his memory to dredge up incidents to prove that love to himself. A hand on his head. The memory of lips brushing his cheek at night when he lay abed, almost asleep.

Well, like so many other things, that was not so important any more. If his father had loved him, where was that love now? Into what part of the dust had fallen that collection of cells which, when knit together by life, had made up this bizarre substance called love? And a hundred years from now, where would be the feeling that Emilie had had for him or that he had had for her? What did it really matter if the combination had been love or hate? In the grave they all sank alike into the base of an emptying skull and lay inert and beyond redemption, and soon the skull itself was gone, and nothing mattered about the feelings that dust had known.

"I'll get over it," he said aloud to himself. "You get over things."

It's going to be me or her, Sam. Don't you see?

You don't understand what she's been through.

I understand that I love you. I understand that you love me. If a woman knows a man loves her, she has some rights.

A woman. She was very tall for a woman. As tall as he was, in fact, and when the two of them walked down the streets together they made an impression, and that was probably why the gossip about them spread so rapidly up and down the valley. Eyes followed them whenever they were in town with each other.

Her eyes were clear and very blue. A sharp glint of intelligence in her eyes. A kind of twinkle, only more than simple cheer. Very blond, the way Germans from the North are. Hair like bleached straw hanging around her neck. Remarkably straight, not the slightest hint of curl. High cheekbones. Maybe too sharp a chin, for she said that when she was old she would look like a crone. But now, in youth, the precise cut of her strong features made people look at her and say she was beautiful. Everybody said that, even his mother.

She spoke to him first. A Saturday morning in early March. He was in town on Saturday because everybody came out of the country and went to town on Saturday. Yellow water stood in the muddy streets, and she passed slowly, looking at the day and then seeing him, and she said something in innocent exuberance about how early the spring was coming. "In New York it doesn't come until April!"

He was taken aback by her. Strange girls did not speak first to men in the streets, and nobody in Bourbonville said anything about spring coming to New York. He mumbled something in reply and felt so embarrassed that his mouth seemed to fill up with clay. He couldn't remember what he said. Two minutes after he said it he couldn't remember. It was just something to make her stay there, to get her to keep talking to him there on the street. Whatever it was did not suffice, for she went on in her slow stride down the boarded sidewalk, looking and wondering and apparently forgetting him as suddenly as she had noticed him. He gaped foolishly after her. The knot of farmers, whittling and chewing, leaning on a storefront nearby, smiled knowingly—big, broad, broken-toothed grins accompanied by slyly nodding heads—and one of them said something which made the others laugh. The laughter made him see them, and he got hold of himself and went speedily off in the opposite direction from the girl feeling his ears and cheeks burn in the crisp air.

He frowned at himself and leaned back against the gravestone and surveyed the cemetery. The woods came up on two sides of it, and on another an unkempt field bristling with tall brown sage grass went over the brow of a slight hill. Beyond that, he knew, lay the river cutting its idle way toward the southwest. Sometimes you could be here, in the graveyard, and you could hear a steamboat hoot, and if you ran fast you could see it plying its way upstream or down, moved by its stately paddling wheels. But there was nothing now. No sound at all except the shuffling his own feet made in the grass and the almost inaudible buzzing of life in the hot forest nearby.

Memory is choking this country to death. Memory is a rag in our throats. And we hand it on when we die. Memory is the principal possession of our estate. That, my young friend, is the supreme injustice. We grub around in the garbage and unroll memory, and we choke on it, but at the instant we expire we manage to jerk the damned thing out of our own mouths and stuff it down the throats of our children, and we die secure in the knowledge that they will choke on the same crazy thing that killed us.

That was John Wesley Campbell in a talkative mood, when Sam stood by. Mr. Campbell, indulging himself in one of those black monologues which sounded like a whole chorus of doom. It was Mr. Campbell telling him that some memories were best forgotten.

But Emilie brought memory to him in a way he had never felt before. It was something he worked out very carefully to himself. Before her there was a settledness to his life. Today was so little different from yesterday that there wasn't much room for memory. No need for it. Life turned on its regular pinions, marked by the seasons and by Sunday mornings, and only very slowly and with an immense accumulation of years did you begin to put memory into one box and today into another and to see that they really were different. Life was a broad pool, dented with tiny wavelets, ultimately calm and nearly timeless.

Then Emilie turned up and all the body of life went rushing off into something totally unexpected and completely new. And then there was something new to every day. When he rode with her through the countryside, he measured off the little things. Not that he wrote them down. But he pegged things in his mind. *On Monday I gave her the iris, and she laughed and twisted it into the bridle of her horse. And on Tuesday we sat by the river and saw the boat pass and talked about how green the water was. And on Wednesday we tied the horses and walked up to the abandoned little church, and because it is on a hill we could see for a long way. And Thursday we went to the clearing where the sawmill used to be on the ridge.* And on and on. The days became distinct. When that happened, you realized all in a rush that life was passing and you were getting old. Yes, before you were twenty years old you realized you were getting old if you fell in love.

"Oh, we won't stay here long." The lightly spoken words drove dark clouds scudding across his happiness, even on that first morning when they were together and everything was new. "I know my father. We were three months in Virginia, and my mother and I thought we might stay there. But we didn't. I guess we'll go West someday. My father has a brother in California somewhere. I forget where. I met him once a long time ago. A *very* long time ago, and he told my father we should all go West. I don't remember that part of it, but my father talks about it. He and my uncle do not get along very well. My uncle makes money. My father just makes clocks." She laughed gaily, and now he thought about the way she talked about clocks whenever she mentioned her father. But the exact things she had said were sinking into that thick sediment lying at the bottom of human consciousness which gradually and inevitably absorbs the sharp things out of most memories. He held on to what he could with an almost frantic and hungering desire.

The beginning was still clear enough in his mind—like the end. He would live it over and over again as long as he possessed life. The beginning was all sunlight and morning. She turned up down there riding nonchalantly along on the road which edged the farm on that side. And when she saw him looking over his handiwork, measuring with his imagination the yield of his crops, she called out, "Why *Samuel!*" Her voice had a shrill, piercing quality. But it was a good voice for the expression of glad surprise, and that was the way it was that first time, whipping over the cool morning like a cheer. She had got up to see the sun rise in the open fields, bundled in a blue woolen jacket knit by her mother, and over the collar of her blue garment her yellow hair fell long and loose and shone in the sun like spun light.

She wanted to learn the country, she said, explaining her appearance. If she got up each day before dawn and rode for an hour or two, in time she would have it all fixed in her mind—the roads, the woods, the churches, the fields, and the scattered houses, even the people of the valley. "When I leave I want it all to be a part of me because the more you have in your heart, the bigger your life is." It was a winsome and particularly female logic which made Sam smile at first and then think about it more seriously and agree, to himself, that she was right.

If she got up at dawn, she said, she had the whole waking country to herself, and there was something about dawn in the valley with its languid mists and soft light which made her remember the fairy stories she loved as a child. She could ride along as objects were disengaging themselves from the gloom of night, and she could imagine trolls lurking in the tangled vines beside the road or else see elvish dwellings half hidden in the trees, and she could hear the wakening of the birds and pretend they were talking about her and debating, perhaps, whether they should induct her into the special realm of enchantment which only birds knew. The enchantment which made them sing. So she had ridden abroad on this spring morning, and she came upon him without knowing just where she was.

She had such vitality that Sam believed her on that first day without a qualm. Later on they laughed over her little deception. She had come to look at the countryside, but especially that part of the land where he might be. She was as struck by him on the street as he had been with her. "You don't know what a fine looking man people think you are," she said with delight. She made some discreet inquiries in the most casual of ways, and she had come out there on the narrow dirt road, and she had sat there all bright and expectant, hoping to catch a glimpse of him.

They were both in luck. That day, after the morning chores, he came down to survey his fields. And when she saw him she rode in and called, "Why *Samuel!*" And they were both sitting there on their horses, beaming at one another with pleasure and surprise. Later on she said, "I thought I might have to ride into your yard and pretend to be lost," and she smiled warmly with her fine mouth, and in the look that passed between them at that moment there was a confidence. Yes, a *confidence*. That was the word which somehow locked up all the things which were so hard to explain. Their love had been a *confidence*, and now it was all lost and broken. All gone. Departed, West.

He talked with her more and more as the days went on. Part of being in love was to share things and to discover more things which they could share. His mother talked endlessly about the way she had shared things with his father. "And at night we used to sit by the fire and see you sleeping there and *talk!* We'd talk about the future and about what you'd be and what *we* would be and all the good things that had come and would come. *Oh Sam!*" So he did not think it was out of the ordinary for him to have talked to Emilie in the way that he had. He accompanied her on their morning rides like a warrior going on crusade with his lady. He found himself when he found her, and that was not an unimportant thing. Only . . . all that he found was broken and ground into a ridiculous paste of memory when their love failed.

It was true what she said about being up before dawn. She loved that, the early morning with its fog and dew and the sun rising in a storm of light, trailing fiery vapor up the sky. She loved the serenity of the fields when they had had them to themselves, and sometimes, when they had been riding awhile, she would stop and take his hand, and they would look on the unfurling day so rapt in its loveliness that they could not speak. And sometimes when their ride was over she would slip away from him without a word or backward glance, reluctant (as she explained later) to break the spell with her voice.

She and her family had lived a long time in New York City. She said they lived in a house on Manhattan Island, just behind the busiest part of the port. Her father made clocks for ships, and that is why they lived where they did. He was skilled at his trade, and they were comfortable except for the dirt. He could listen to the plaints of first mates and sea captains in a dozen languages, peer with his sharp blue eyes into the mechanical complexity of their malfunctioning clocks, right the wrongs like a god, set the wheeling little motions in order again—if that was what was required. Or he could (also like a god) mount his own flawless creations in the elegant wood paneling of captains' cabins. He guaranteed his work, not simply by words which in any case were useless to a voyager bound away on the ocean main, but more convincingly he conveyed unquestioned trust by his silent and rapid skill. Yes, they lived well in New York, but her family did not like the city. It shut them in with its toils of smoke, its twisting streets running with dirty water, the miserable squalor of people pushed up too close together competing for the very air they breathed so that the city was like a tired, hot animal panting for breath. Emilie said they were fleas on the animal's back almost suffocated by the grime and the sweat.

They were from a little town called Flensburg up on the Danish border of Germany, though they had spent most of her life in Kiel. Kiel was a port, but frequently they made the trip back up to Flensburg where the family household was. Flensburg was really home, she said. And there the fertile soil and dark woods came close to the town, and the sky shone like blue crockery newly scrubbed every morning. In the spring you could stand in the market square of Flensburg and smell the fresh-dirt smell of new-plowed ground in the surrounding fields. When there was wind you could smell the saltiness of the Baltic Sea, a gloomy, forbidding sea which punched a finger of water inward towards Flensburg and made the town seem all the more like a comfortable fortress on the edge of danger. In winter the snow came and made all the world shine with a radiance so bright you could scarcely look on it, and a single voice would carry for miles across the expanses of frozen white. It was not like New York.

While they lived in the metropolis, her family took the tram up the island to Harlem every Sunday. There they could see green gardens and stroll along country lanes and breathe clean air. Harlem was the clean part of Manhattan Island, the uncorrupted part. She explained that carefully to him, like a schoolteacher giving a child an important lesson in geography, and then like a little girl she scrunched up her shoulders and sighed with pleasure at the memory of walking there. In autumn, she said, the skies over Harlem reminded her father especially of Flensburg and the unsullied atmosphere there, the refulgent melancholy afternoons which portended winter. "My father says that people in Flensburg are very hard and realistic about things," she said. "The air is so clear, and most of the time it's chilly enough so that you can't stand around dreaming about things. You have to keep busy. He says that if he'd been born in the south of Germany he would have been a philosopher. A professor. But in Flensburg he became a clockmaker." She laughed, bemused.

Sometimes she left Sam behind on those flights of hers, those explanations of herself and her family. He would be riding along beside her, silently, listening, calm in the calm morning, and all the while his mind would be racing and struggling to keep up with her words. He worked at understanding what Harlem was like, and Manhattan. He almost cried out in his frustration at trying to imagine Flensburg, how the skies there could be different from the skies here. "It *is* different," she said stubbornly. "I can't remember enough to explain it, so you have to take my word. We left there when I was ten years old, and that has been seven years. But you could see what I mean if you could see it one time, Samuel. Just *one* time, and you would know."

And she was off again, racing through those sparkling galleries of recollection, and right there beside her he was left in a puzzling kind of loneliness and a self-reproach at how little experience he had had, how insipid his life must seem to her. She never really knew how he felt in those times—the emptiness, the frustration. It was the only thing he just couldn't tell her.

Why didn't her father go back to Flensburg since he loved it so much? The Prussians were there now. Sam only vaguely knew who the Prussians were because once, on a lark, he went to Knoxville to hear the United States Marine Band, and they wore stern, spiked helmets, and someone told him they were helmets like ones the Prussian Army wore. The Prussians had been in Flensburg a long time now. Her father had fought in their army, but he hated it and them. She did not believe he could kill anybody, but maybe he had. He never would say. Something happened to him in the army. "My mother says it changed him. He won't talk about it. He's not political, even now. But he told my mother that something bad was happening, and he could not change it or stop it. He didn't want to be a part of it." She shrugged happily. "So here we are!"

The trouble was that her father never felt at home anywhere but in Flensburg. He was like so many people who are deeply attached to one place. Once he left it, he never really could put roots down anywhere else. He became a wanderer, Emilie said, a nomad resting here and there but always moving on. He did not try to explain himself or to apologize. He simply was the way he was, and in the quiet independence of his own being he stood aloof from the judgments of others.

In time Sam met him. He was short and gray, stocky you might say, with his hair cut very close to his scalp. He wore a thick, rectangular mustache, and the effect was bristling and military. He carried himself with an unsmiling, thoughtful dignity. Still, there was something unsoldierly about him. It was hard to think that he had done the things Emilie said he had—marched across the landscape of northern France in the Kaiser's army for a promenade through Paris in the spring.

Only Mr. Campbell ever seemed to penetrate the invisible cover which Emilie's father drew about himself. They were seen on occasion, talking seriously, quietly, smoking together, and nodding with exaggerated courtesy to one another when they parted. Otherwise he stayed close to his house and apart from other people except when he appeared in church on Sunday mornings. The town wondered at him as it might wonder at a cargo of elephants suddenly dropped in its midst by a bankrupt circus.

Emilie's father came South and brought his family because he was looking for something. For some part of America he had heard about in the old country, but something he had not yet found. The spaciousness, the freedom, the enthralling beauty, the substance of the indefinable dream.

Her mother did not like all this moving. She had not wanted to leave Germany. She did not think the Prussians were bad or good. As long as they stayed out of her tidy kitchen, she was indifferent to them and could ignore them. She had not wanted to leave New York. There were other Germans there. She looked forward to the weekly adventure of the ride up to Harlem and the strolling in the fresh air. But she was resigned to her destiny. Her only complaint showed in the hard little lines of frown which arched above her nose and lost themselves in her forehead. She looked sharply out on the world. But she would go where her husband went, serve him, and make his gods her own without thinking about doing anything else.

He came South because he wanted to find something different from New York. He thought the South would be the most opposite place in America to the oppressive city, and there might be something here . . . Emilie said she thought he expected to find Flensburg perched on the bank of some Southern river. She knew the way her father's mind worked at things, and she knew also that he had awakened from this dream at least. For he had not found his Flensburg or the fields which rolled blackly in on the German town like the waves of a fertile sea. Instead he was startled in his quiet way at the sweep of the great, tree-mantled land broken only by the ragged fields and an occasional primitive town. "He thinks it's uncivilized," Emilie said. "I don't know what he means exactly, but that's what he thinks. Mark my word, we'll go West someday, the way my uncle said. My father doesn't want to do anything his brother says, but you wait and see. He won't stay here, and he won't go back to New York. We'll go West."

But for a while he did stay and rented a house in Bourbonville and set about making clocks. Even the South had to tell time. He could have made a living at it if he had stayed. And if he had settled in Knoxville he could have made a better one. Yes, Emilie's father could have made a good living, but instead he picked up and went West—the way they all did. And when he was gone it seemed like a little miracle that he had stopped in Bourbonville in the first place.

Emilie said it was the courthouse. She said it with such laughing conviction that Sam never doubted it. It was the first thing her father had seen of Bourbonville. There it stood with the clock gleaming out of the cupola like a cyclopean eye, rising through the bare trees of the declining winter. The courthouse was a squat affair, made of red brick drawn from local kilns by slaves long ago. In time the bricks had weathered to a dark, moldering maroon flecked with thin green moss, and here and there tentacles of ivy had crawled up the brick giving to the whole building a stately ugliness which was almost beauty.

The only bright things about the courthouse were the brass cuspidors, the brass dome over the cupola, and that gleaming white face of the clock. Emilie's father saw the sunlight burning in the polished brass dome, and he saw the round clock below. The clock had works in it that had come down from Connecticut. It quietly measured off the hours of the war, and Connecticut soldiers passed under it without suspecting that it was their kin. Not that they would have cared. But Emilie's father saw the clock and was instantly taken by it. He said the building reminded him of something in Germany. He didn't say much about it, then or ever. He just pulled up the double team he was driving, and the wagon with their trunks of baggage stopped, and he sat looking at the courthouse for a long time, his chin sunk into a supporting hand. And that was how Emilie realized that they would stay here for a time.

She laughed affectionately at her father. "He has spent too much time with his clocks," she said. "He thinks about time too much." That was true enough. Time was his passion. He could measure it almost as precisely as the stars. Emilie said he would make a clock and sit watching it for hours. He never seemed pleased with his creations. He always frowned over them in oblique disappointment and in the end pushed them away and was glad to sell them. He was a clockmaker, but there wasn't a clock anywhere in the house that the family could use. He wouldn't buy a clock from anyone else, and he would not permit his family to use any clock he made. Emilie laughed with a gay toss of her yellow hair and said she thought he was trying to make a clock to make the universe slow down. Sam listened to her without amusement because he thought it might be true.

Once or twice he watched her father at work. And he came away shaking his head in a dull, puzzling uneasiness because the clockmaker was so absorbed in his craft, and there was something to it all which Sam could not quite fathom. When the man looked into the works of his clocks, there was something far away in his eyes. It was discomfiting to see. That vague air of abstraction for a man doing work so close and so precise. Yes, there was something singular about Emilie's father, something cryptic and eccentric. She loved him dearly. "He might settle down if I marry. He couldn't leave me."

Sometimes when she talked about him, Sam felt jealous. Emilie's love was so precious that he wondered if there were really enough for both himself and her father. In the end, he realized, there was a cruel irony to that worry of his, and he could not remember his thoughts without shame. But at the time he dreamed his own dreams. In them he saw little children with clear faces and shining yellow hair watching their bizarre grandfather pluck gently at the strings of time stretched there in the recesses of his endless clocks. Futile dreams. Unfashioned clocks and unborn children, all the wild hopes vanished Westward leaving phantoms. A bright death in the midst of this ordinary life which remained here.

He sighed in acquiescence and stood up from leaning against his father's monument. He had to be going. The sun was far down the west now, transformed already by the dusty air into a blood-red disk floating in the thickening twilight above the forest. He was tired from much standing, and his mind was weary from feeling and thought. The shadows of the gravestones reached out across the still grass, and he and his own long shadow went slowly across them as he walked back to his horse. The empty road stretched itself away from the church, darkly crimson in the queer light. He looked around once more in apathy and dejection. Then he climbed stiffly into the saddle and, nudging the horse, turned for home.

2

THE FOUR MEN met every night at the railroad station except when it rained, and even then they all came except Brian Ledbetter, and that was because he lived out in the country. In the summer, when it was fair, they sat in hard chairs gathered in a semicircle on the platform, and in the winter they sat in the same chairs propped up around the potbellied stove in the station master's office, just off the room where white people could sit down and wait for the trains. People in Bourbonville called them "the bachelors" because they all lived alone.

But a couple of them had been married. Mr. Campbell had had a wife and a son, and Brian Ledbetter had taken himself a wife after the War. Mr. Campbell's wife died young, almost forty years ago. His son went off to the War and never came back. Everyone knew he must be dead. Mr. Campbell had probably admitted as much to himself a long time ago, but he was always given to the musing contention that nobody really knew for sure. The boy had vanished like so many others, and one could only suppose that his corpse had rotted to dust long ago in an unmarked grave somewhere. Still it was not certainty. The boy just might come back someday. You never could tell. And in the meantime Mr. Campbell lived alone in the old house which fronted on the square in Bourbonville.

Brian Ledbetter came home from the War with a wooden leg and a pension from the United States government. He married the first woman he slept with and took her out to his farm to cook and keep things clean and to toil with him in the shaggy fields he inherited from his father. Her name was something common—Josephine. Brian always called her "Woman," and truth to tell he sometimes forgot what her true name had been. She was a hefty girl with hair the color of horse manure and a face like something cut out of a slab of lye soap by an idiot child. Brian himself had a big, leathery face which looked quite a bit like the tanned piece of hairy cowhide people hang up as the door to the outhouse. People said it was a marriage made in heaven. He and the girl together were so ugly that only God himself could have made the match, and there was a great deal of expectant interest in the valley as to what sort of children might come from the union.

Alas, the girl did not give the valley dwellers enough time to find out. She took about three months of Brian, and then one evening when he came in from plowing, all dirty and hungry, she was gone. Somebody said she ran off with a traveling fruit-tree salesman out of Chattanooga. Such a man had been in the neighborhood, and people remembered him because he plastered his hair with something that made him smell like an oversweet cherry blossom dipped in grease. He had seemed to have all the imagination of a mollusk, and people said he was just dumb enough to run off with Brian's wife or just weak enough to let her run off with him. But of course nobody ever really did know for sure. Her clothes were gone. So was Brian's pension money for that month, and she had taken his best clay pipe and smashed it to pieces against the stones of the fireplace. Brian said he got over his heartbreak at losing her in just about two minutes, but he sure as hell hated to go to bed that night without his supper. He also regretted the business about the broken pipe. It made him think his wife might have been truly unhappy living with him and not just swept off her feet by the novelty of a fragrant man from faraway places. But he couldn't do anything about it after she was gone. He had other pipes, and after trial and much indigestible error, he learned to cook for himself. He got to be quite good at pinto beans and hard-boiled eggs, and he had breath-taking talents for boiling coffee. At least that's what Mr. Campbell said when he drank some of Brian's coffee one day and nearly choked to death.

The other two men were bachelors without qualification:

Clarence Wilbur Jackson was the station agent in Bourbonville for the railroad. You might have called him a carpetbagger because he had come down from Maryland after the War to make his fortune, and he had been in Bourbonville ever since. But he wasn't prosperous—and everybody knows all the carpetbaggers got rich sucking Southern blood. When he first arrived it seemed that he might marry. But the father of the girl he dared to fall in love with didn't approve. It wasn't that Clarence was a carpetbagger. The girl's father thought he didn't have any roots, and he knew he didn't have any money, and since he was from Baltimore he didn't really have any family. You just didn't take chances with a man like that, even if he was a good telegrapher and had a steady job. So the girl married somebody else (who beat her), and Clarence took his defeat, and never fell in love again. He was left to watching the trains steam in and out of Bourbonville and to sitting at night with his friends and to drinking more and more whiskey as countless trains roared down the gleaming rails and the years clicked away under their driving wheels. Now his eyes were always red and raw-looking, and his thin mouth tended to gape beneath his prominent nose, giving to his face a habitual expression of harrowed mystification.

Hub Delaney came over from the jail. He had come back from the War with nothing to do, no land to speak of, and he ran for sheriff because the thought struck him one day when he was looking at an election poster. He was elected. He was a little surprised at that, but then his only real opponent was a Rebel, and most of Bourbon County had been Union in spite of people like the Crittendons and the Bourbons. Not really too many more than a majority, but a majority just the same, and the Union people voted as a bloc, and Hub was elected.

He lived at the jail in a room behind his office. He didn't seem to want more than that. All in all he made a pretty good sheriff. He had a kind of intuition about what people wanted in the way of law. That might be just another way of saying he knew what people he could kick in the ass and what people he couldn't. He was elected again and again, and now, twenty years after the War, nobody really thought anybody else could be sheriff. He hadn't even had any opposition in the last five elections. It was beginning to look as if he would hold the office until he died.

Sometimes he said that being elected so many times was like having a long jail sentence. Sometimes with his friends in the evening he would get to talking about doing something else. Sometimes when that mood was on him he would draw Mr. Campbell out about the West. Mr. Campbell had been there and come back (a rare bird, Mr. Campbell). Hub would make detailed plans and figure on how long the little nest egg he had in the bank would last if he started out on it and what he would do once he got to wherever it was he was going. Montana or California or somewhere.

Hub was a ponderous man, slow-moving and slow-talking, and unless he was in a fight it took him a long time to make decisions. Just when he was on the point of saddling up his horse and saying goodbye, election time would roll around again. And he would run again "So I'll have a little more time to think it over," and he would win. Then it was all to do over again—the planning and the wondering, the waiting for courage to come.

He had never married. It wasn't that he had planned it that way. The right woman just never had come along. He didn't have much to offer, he reflected aloud, and he was particular about what he got. Brian said the women who wanted Hub were all whores and the women Hub wanted were the kind who wouldn't look at a sheriff unless they were being robbed or raped. It was an uncomfortable paradox. And now, Lord God, he was forty-five years old! The thought struck him of late with the sort of amazement that comes on a man when he learns that a dear, young friend has suddenly died. Only Hub was amazed about the dear, young friend that was himself, knee-deep in middle age. He supposed he couldn't really change his life now. Too old.

About once every month or so he took the night train down to Sweetwater and visited a fancy nigger whorehouse there. It was fancy because it had a cracked mirror in the vestibule and smelled of cheap perfume, and none of the whores was over forty years old. It wasn't really the sort of thing a sheriff could keep secret. But the people of Bourbonville paid him the respects due a man discreet enough to do his sinning in another town. Besides, he was back on the milk train which got into Bourbonville before dawn. Considering that was the only time he ever took off from his job, people thought he deserved it.

Anyway, sometime after the War the four of them had got in the habit of sitting around the station in the evening, and now it had become a rite. They couldn't think of *not* doing it. Every once in a while others came. The four did not exclude anybody. Yet most of those who came at any time were Union men. Not that the four discouraged the other side. They did not seek to carry on the War so long after the last forgotten wind had blown the smell of gunpowder out of the country. But the other side simply chose to keep to itself, nursing its wounds and envying the Federal pensions and the nice gravestones which went to all those men who had chosen the blue and Union.

But always the four formed the center of the crowd, and often they sat by themselves while men with families stayed home. They smoked or chewed or talked in grunts and half-murmurs. Sometimes they did not talk at all. After twenty years they had exhausted all the more profound subjects. They knew how they all felt about all things, and they had stopped arguing about it among themselves. They voted Republican because it was the only honorable thing to do. After all they had endured in the War they wondered how in hell anybody in his right mind could ever vote for a Democrat. But then they had all concluded that the world was made up mostly of fools. They had told their war stories to one another. They had told the tales of their loves, or at least of all those which they could ever tell anybody. They had mingled their sorrows and their disappointments in the embarrassed and jocular way that men share the things that touch them deeply.

When someone married or died or gave birth or fornicated or killed, they turned it all over in the dark for two or three evenings. They went back over the ancestry of the people involved. They made calculations based on the experience of dead men, and they assigned responsibility with the careful precision of men moving checkers on a board. They talked about the weather and the crops, and at times they marveled over the imperceptible changes of days which, with the years, turned the world into something they had trouble recognizing as their own. They lubricated their talk with a jug that they passed from mouth to mouth.

All the while the window behind them was open on the telegraph key inside. The murmuring talk, the mastication of tobacco, the sloshing of liquor in the jug—all went on against the background of the clattering brass points of the telegraph. Clarence Jackson kept one ear cocked at it. Several times each evening he would get up suddenly and march with deliberate speed to the key and throw the switch above the desk and pound out a response and sometimes scribble something on a pad of paper and return.

Clarence Jackson had a remarkable hand. His slim fingers played the telegraph key with the mastery of an artist. The drunker he got, the more steady he became, and other station masters up and down the line wondered at the metrical precision of the operator in Bourbonville. In their own little enclaves of loneliness along the line they admired his performance and built fantastic pictures of him out of the colors of their solitude. They thought it would be an honor to meet him, for because he was a great telegrapher they imagined him to be a great man.

By ten o'clock the four had usually lapsed into silence, an expectant waiting, and at last the first richly mournful tones of the night train dropped lazily over the valley calm from far up the tracks toward Knoxville. Clarence Jackson sprang into action then like Grant at Shiloh or in the Wilderness, sure of himself for the only time in his life, in his own world of action and purpose. The others lingered until the drama of the roaring train with its thunder and its bell, its smoke and hissing speech of the vast land, was enacted before them and the train was gone toward Chattanooga and its long departing wail shivered over the night and dissolved in the dark. Then they stood up and stretched and scratched and belched and dismissed themselves and went off to their beds.

Only Brian Ledbetter had far to go. He clambered aboard his stout horse and gave the animal its rein and let it take him home. And sometimes as he passed the hulking courthouse standing black against the moon and rode by the scattered and quiet houses shut up against the night, he felt within himself a devouring loneliness. On those occasions he raised his voice in song and bellowed to the sky roaring ballads of bloody fields and lily loves and the wasting of roses and the flow of water and the silence of graves.

Inevitably he was answered by a chorus of dogs, greeting him as he passed and raising their own voices and sending the message on to their kind who took up the cry as he came on. So his passage was a bursting of noise in the dark, flowing like a ball of compressed liquid through a narrow tube of silence. People wakened with the noise and lay grumbling in their beds. Sometimes the man of the house (and sometimes the woman) was so incensed at the impropriety of it all that he came raging to the door shouting curses into the dark and obscene comments about the Ledbetter clan to the uttermost bitch from which the line had descended. But it did no good. Brian rode on, oblivious to all but his song and the night and his absorbing loneliness.

And often when he had gone, and men found themselves uneasily awake, they turned to sleepy copulation. Suellen MacComber told the women of Bourbon County that the last three of her children were born because of Brian Ledbetter. Ordinarily her husband Mayhew was a precise sort, a pretty good hand at pulling it out before things went too far. But when he was half asleep and bored with it all, he sometimes miscalculated or sometimes just didn't care. Mrs. MacComber dearly loved all her children, but she did at times feel that there was something imperfect in a universe where a man like Brian Ledbetter did not have to take responsibility for his acts.

Brian Ledbetter was large and soft-looking in spite of his ugly face. He laughed more than anybody else in Bourbon County, and there were big, crowfooted laughter lines around his eyes and his mouth. He loved to spin yarns and to drink whiskey and talk about God and ghosts and magic and religion and things like that. His peg leg was a memento of the War, its predecessor having been sawn off below the knee to save him from gangrene after he was shot in the foot at Cold Harbor. By that time he had been through so many bloody fights he was convinced he would die in battle. Probably no man in the history of soldiering ever greeted the loss of a leg with more jubilation. It was like having a baby in reverse. He never got over a jolly disposition which people who knew him before the War frankly couldn't remember his having then. He became as proud of his wooden leg as he had been terrified by cannon fire and the blazing Minié balls around his head. It was walking evidence, you might say, that he had done his duty. And that was important to Brian Ledbetter because it allowed him to believe that in spite of his terror he had been brave.

"They could of shot me in the balls," he said in glib deprecation of his wound. "And I tell you, you can get along right smart with a wood leg, but a man ain't going to get far in life with a wood prick."

"Aw, I don't know, Brian," Hub Delaney once said. "You might make some woman mighty thankful with a wood prick." Hub sat there musing after that, in that slow way of his, and then he said, "Course, if it wasn't no bigger than your real one, you'd punch it right through her butt."

Brian always laughed about that. It became one of his favorite stories. He loved to tell stories on himself.

On the evening of the hanging, Brian rode into town a little late. The others were already sitting on the platform. The listless calm of the day had stretched itself into the heavy twilight, and behind the emerald stillness of the evening the threat of the drought crouched like a monstrous and waiting cat. The three men who were already there sat resigned and indifferent to the heat and the threat and hardly looked up when Brian came in.

"Christ, it's hot!" he rumbled. All the faces were passive, almost inert. "I hope I haven't broke up the party," he said.

There was a slight, tired shifting, and Hub muttered, "Hello, Brian," and that was all.

Brian sighed and caught his breath and for a while did not disturb the uncomfortable silence. Then he cleared his throat and said, in a low voice, "Well, is there any news? Have you heard anything?

How's Grant?" Ulysses S. Grant, their old commander, was dying up in New Jersey.

Clarence Jackson spoke: "No, nothing new. I don't know anything more than what I told you this afternoon. He slept well part of the night and then woke up. He was hurting. Then they gave him something, and he went back to sleep again."

Brian shook his head sadly. "I know he's going to die, but I can't get used to it."

"He isn't God," Mr. Campbell said.

"No, I guess he ain't. But there was a time when I might of believed he was," Brian said.

"That's true enough," Hub said, nodding.

"It just shows how time is going by," Brian said with another sigh. "It's foolish to say, but you don't realize how it's getting away till somebody . . . Well, you know."

"Till somebody like him dies," Mr. Campbell said.

"Eat up with cancer! It ain't decent." Brian spoke with a quiet outrage.

"You think somebody ought to have shot him?" Mr. Campbell said ironically.

"Brrrrrr," Brian said, shivering. "Now I ask you, J.W., why can't they do nothing to stop things like that? Things like that ain't even civilized."

Mr. Campbell barely shrugged. "It's just something they haven't done yet. They can cut it out of some places. I guess you can't cut it out of a man's throat. I guess they'll lick it someday. I don't know. I don't know anything about it."

"I wonder if he's afraid to die," Hub said thoughtfully. "He was right down with the troops all the time, but he couldn't stand to see people suffer. Somebody told me he couldn't look at blood. That's a funny thing that a man like him couldn't look at blood."

"If he was afraid of dying, *I* never could see it," Brian said. "And I seen him, too!"

"You've told us a million times," Clarence said. "Two million."

"Well, it's true," Brian said. "In the Wilderness. I marched right in front of his face and looked him dead in the eye, and I swear to God he looked right back at me. We'd just got all hell beat out of us. You know how it was, J.W. But when I seen him sitting there, I knowed it was all right. I can't explain it. I just *knowed* it!"

"I remember that very night," Mr. Campbell said. "I was so tired I was going to sleep in the saddle, and I'd start to fall off my horse, and that'd wake me up. And I remember thinking that the horse would probably fall down dead because he was tired too. And when he did that I could crawl off somewhere in the bushes and go to sleep. That was all I wanted. To go to sleep. But the horse kept on going, and after a while somebody said we were going south. It was just a whisper. We couldn't believe it, but it was a fact. It woke me up for a while. We'd got our guts torn out, and instead of laying a hand on our bellies and running the way we'd done before, we picked up and went south. That was the night the Rebels were whipped. They didn't know it, but I knew it. We *all* did."

"You've said it all before," Clarence said, his voice thin and tight.

"It was some night," Brian said grimly. "And I'll tell about it two million times more, Clarence. See if I don't."

"I never saw him," Clarence said mournfully. "When he was in Mississippi, I was in Nashville, and when he was in Virginia, I was in North Carolina. I missed him every time I turned around."

"Well, he wasn't nothing to look at," Brian said.

Hub Delaney nodded and nearly smiled. "He looked like a little quarter horse. I seen him a lot between Shiloh and Vicksburg, and I swear to God if I'd ever walked up on him in the dark, I'd of thought he was some poor old Billy that needed somebody to button his coat! Damnedest man I ever seen to be a general!"

"I saw him on that last day," Mr. Campbell said quietly. "Lee rode off looking like Jesus Christ, and he stood there on the porch of that house and watched him go. He said something to somebody, and we all wondered what it was. I think we expected something great. You know, something to *end* things. McClellan would have made an oration, and it'd be in all the schoolbooks now. But not *him*. It turned out that he'd ordered the commissary to feed the Rebels. That was the way *he* ended it. Well, I guess it was a good way. About as good a way as any."

"I wish I could of seen it," Brian said whimsically. He reflected for a time and then spoke in a lowered voice. "You know what it means? We're getting to be old men."

Mr. Campbell laughed without humor. "I've been old for a long time, but I tell you something else. The century's getting old. Eighteen eighty-five! Lord God! I remember looking back, thinking it hadn't been any time really since the century was new. When I went off to the war in 'forty-six there were people right around here who'd been born under the king! And they're gone now. Now it's Grant that's going. When a man like Ulysses S. Grant comes down to die, then you know you're going to die too! It's a piece of us that's dying up there. We're being thrown out of something. I remember the time when I thought I *owned* youth, and a couple of days passed, and I looked in a mirror and saw an old man looking back at me."

"I think we could use the jug, Clarence," Brian said, a little too loud. He always got a little uneasy when Mr. Campbell talked that way.

"The jug? Yes, the jug!" Clarence scrambled unsteadily to his feet. "Here, inside. It's inside. Right where I put it last night." With exaggerated concern he went to the open door and brought out the jug. Mr. Campbell drank first, lifting the jug to his mouth and taking a long swallow.

Passing the jug on, he took a cigar out of his inside pocket and struck fire to it. The night had grown quite dark by now. The match made a meteoric arc of yellow flame away from the end of the cigar and fell lifeless over the edge of the platform. Brian took the jug, drank from it, smacked his lips and passed it on, and when it had made the circle they all sat without a word for a long time. The world around them was very quiet. Even the insects were not as loud as they usually were.

Finally Brian said: "Where'd you bury him, Hub?"

"Simson? We put him in the nigger graveyard at Choto Bend. It ain't been used much lately. I didn't know what else to do with him."

"It wouldn't of been right to put him with decent folks, I guess," Brian said.

"I just didn't want no trouble," Hub said. "The niggers ain't likely to complain."

"Did you put him in lime? Did you bury him in lime?" Clarence Jackson asked. His voice stammered over the word *lime*. It was a horrible word.

"Yes, we put him in lime. They ought to be a good stand of grass on that grave come next year. Simson ought to fertilize it real good. We covered him up in it and wet it down before throwing the dirt in."

"Why do you do that? Put the lime in? What does it matter when he's dead?" Clarence was plaintive in the dark. He had gulped at the whiskey like water.

Hub shrugged indifferently. "I don't know, Clarence. It's just what's always done. A man's hung, and you put him in lime. That's all I know. It ain't my business to go 'round changing old ways."

"How long do you think he'll last? In the lime, I mean?" Clarence couldn't let the subject go.

"Good God, Clarence! I don't know, and I don't give a diddle-damn," Hub said. "I do what the law says, and it don't tell me to go 'round digging up the dead to see how long they last in lime."

"I guess it gets to his face pretty fast." Clarence lifted a hand to his own nose, realized what he was doing, and swiftly let the hand drop.

"And his prick! I reckon lime don't do nobody's prick a bit good," Brian said. He meant to joke, but nobody laughed. He could not find it in himself to laugh either. Once uttered the idea was too frightful. The men were silent again.

"Well," Hub sighed at last, "I'm glad it's over. I've been dreading it since I went out there that morning. I knowed how it'd end. Not that I was selling you short, J.W.," he said apologetically. "But I knowed." He reached for the jug, drank, and wiped his mouth with a hand. "That's how I know *I'm* getting old. I can't take messy things no more. They didn't bother me once, but they do now. I know how Grant felt. I feel that way myself."

"It sure was messy this afternoon," Clarence observed quietly.

Hub nearly gagged. "It sure was," he said.

"There ought to be a better way than hanging," Clarence said in a prickly voice. "Why don't we shoot a man like that? You shoot a man, and it's all over quick. It isn't so *messy*."

"Ah, but then you shed blood," Mr. Campbell said.

"I don't see what that's got to do with it," Hub said.

"Well I'll tell you what that's got to do with it," Mr. Campbell said, as if giving a lecture. "The law is made by people who want everything done decently. With decorum. You hear a lot about decorum in the law. The people who make the law decided a long time ago they didn't like the sight of blood. You shoot a man, and you get blood all over the place. The law disapproves of that."

"So you hang a man and get shit all over the place," Hub said.

"It is not the same as blood," Mr. Campbell said.

"Boy, lawyers sure are smart!" Hub said. "I'll sure remember that next time I cut myself."

"Christ Almighty!" Brian said. "You're both drunk on two swallers of whiskey."

"It is a very serious topic," Mr. Campbell said. "The law does not like blood. Gentlemen, I present that as a fact. The law is willing to accept other things because you cannot print them in the law books. If you cannot print things in law books, the things do not exist."

"Lord!" Hub said.

"There is a sense, you see, in which Justice has a blindfold over her eyes."

"She would be better off if she had a clothespin over her nose," Hub said.

"Well, he's dead, and it's all over. I guess we all survived it," Mr. Campbell said.

"I can't understand why you took his part," Brian said, blurting the words out. "You just make people that much madder at you, J.W.! And Lord God! You've already got enough enemies to do a couple of lifetimes. He killed the woman. He didn't want no help."

There was a tense silence which slowly relaxed because Mr. Campbell did not respond. He sank back into preoccupation with his cigar smoke, as if he had turned down a lamp inside his brain and no longer heard anything or cared to talk.

"He was crazy," Hub Delaney said carefully after a while.

"That's a fact," Brian said. He laughed bitterly. "That's why he killed the woman, and that's why he said that about rain."

"He did look like he seen something up there," Hub said uncomfortably. "He might of seen a sign."

"The heat made him more crazier than he already was," Brian said.

"God knows, it's awful," Clarence said, again in a plaintive tone. "Yesterday there was a little nigger kid that came by here barefoot. And he stepped on one of the rails. He hollered out and took to crying, and I went out to see what the matter was. You know he'd burned his foot! It was blistered. I couldn't do anything about it. He went off crying and hopping on his good foot. That's how hot it is."

"Well, it ain't going to rain," Brian said firmly. "Damn it, it *ain't*," he said, more belligerently. But none of the others said anything, and as he looked around at them again his own voice became suddenly subdued and earnest. "If you start hoping it will rain, it *won't*," he said.

"I wonder where his girl will go?" Clarence said halfheartedly. "She was a pretty thing. Do you think she'll stay in Knoxville?"

"I bet she goes West," Hub said.

"Well, I guess if her daddy was crazy she could be crazy too," Brian said.

"It ain't crazy to go West," Hub said. "I swear I'm going someday."

"Christ, we're back to *that* again," Brian said. "You'll go West the day after they run a railroad to the moon."

"Just wait. You won't laugh when I go." Hub looked a great deal like an overgrown child who has been offended.

"Hell," Brian said in contempt. "I don't see why anybody in his right mind wants to go West. The West is the asshole of this country. The people that go West are the people that have been run through the bowels of this country and can't find a place to set."

"You've said it all before," Clarence said. "You've said it time and time again. Why don't you say something different for a change? I'm tired of it. I'm sick and tired of it."

"If we would quit talking about what a great place the West is, then I would quit talking about what an outhouse it is," Brian said, being self-consciously logical.

"Simson should of gone West," Hub said. "He wouldn't of killed his wife if he'd gone West."

"He was a strange man," Mr. Campbell said slowly, returning to the talk. "You know he lived over in North Carolina before the war. He fought with a North Carolina outfit. He told me once he was at Gettysburg. He was with Pettigrew, and he said a funny thing. He said he ran all the way across the fields the day of the charge until he could have talked with our gunners if they hadn't been so busy."

"It would of saved us a lot of trouble if he'd tried to do that," Hub said.

"Yes, well, he said that day was a nice day for talking. All hot and lazy. Like a Sunday afternoon, he said. You didn't want to be killing people on an afternoon like that."

"Well, they was lots killed," Brain said. "I was right there, and I know."

"You've said it all before," Clarence Jackson said mechanically.

"Clarence, will you shut up!" Brian said.

"You have," Clarence persisted. "You've told us all about Gettysburg. A million times or more."

"I'm talking about Simson," Mr. Campbell said. "He was saying how sleepy that day was. And there *he* was running up a hill with a gun in his hand, and after a while he turned around and ran back down again, and the only thing that happened to him was that a bee stung him in the leg."

"A *bee!* It's a wonder he didn't get his ass shot off. I was *there,*"

Brian said. "If I'd of seen him, I'd of done it for him. Shot his ass off and used it to hold my pipe."

"Well that's all that happened to him at Gettysburg. He really thought it was funny."

"Jesus Christ," Brian said.

"You see, he kept thinking about the way he would have looked running across that field if there hadn't been any battle. Think about it. A grown man (only he wasn't really grown), but a man old enough to know better, out there running around with a gun in his hand, shouting his head off, and then turning around and running back and getting stung by that bee."

"Lord God," Brian said. "To think the man was that crazy fifteen, twenty years ago and didn't get himself hung till this afternoon."

"It's an interesting thought," Mr. Campbell said. He paused reflectively. "You know, the way he laughed today, at Bazely . . . It sounded crazy, but maybe he thought the man *was* funny. Maybe he looked out on that collection of half-wits and imbeciles who listen to Bazely, and maybe—just *maybe*—he thought they were so funny he had to laugh at them. Maybe he wasn't crazy after all."

"You said he was," Hub said painfully. "I heard you say it till I believed it. I believed it this afternoon. It didn't make me feel good."

Mr. Campbell laughed gently. "I'm sorry you weren't on the jury, Hub," he said. "I guess the man was crazy from a *legal* point of view. But that's the trouble with me in my old age, my friends. Just because the law says something isn't good enough any more. It's a bad way to be. It's like wondering if your wife is faithful just because she *says* she is. But I see somebody like Simson, and I don't *really* know what's crazy and what's not. The jug, please gentlemen. The jug." They handed him the jug, and he drank.

"He must of been awful young at Gettysburg," Hub said. "He wasn't an old man."

"He was eighteen years old the month they fought the battle," Mr. Campbell said. "I asked him."

"Forty!" Clarence said after a gloomy moment. "He was younger than me! Good God, he was younger than me!"

"About the same age as your boy, J.W.," Brian said after a quick calculation. He dropped the words as soon as they popped into his head. They fell crashing into the midst of the little group of friends and lay there, almost glowing in the dark. "I'm sorry," he said hastily. "It was just something I thought of." Then, feeling the disapproval of others, he said, "But you know I *remember* your boy and how old he was. They's lots of people that's forty. I was forty myself once. I ain't saying you took his part just because he was the same age as your boy."

"Goddammit, Brian, shut up!" Hub Delaney said only half under his breath. "For God's sake, let's talk about something else," he said more loudly.

But instead of talking, the men fell again into silence. Behind them the telegraph key sputtered on the desk by the window, and the warm light of the kerosene lamp threw an oblong patch of brightness over their heads and into the full darkness of the night. After a time they began to mutter again about the heat—all but Mr. Campbell, who sat with his long legs thrown out before him, his face turned slightly and thoughtfully upward to some indefinable point in space. But the others rumbled on about the day and the painful weather and the baffling words of Mr. Simson on the gallows. Moving from the fact of his prophecy, they speculated about the chances for its fulfillment. They leaned back and considered the sky.

From somewhere behind the station toward town a feeble wind sprang up and blew a scrap of paper through the falling light from the window and out over the tracks and into the darkness. The thoughts of the men, like their talk, fell moodily into the slap of the whiskey in the jug, the smell of tobacco floating heavily on the night air, and the impassive contemplation of the moon-blanched fields.

Mr. Campbell sat very much alone. There was no longer any doubt in his mind: Mr. Simson's death was a relief. Now he could stack the whole miserable affair on a shelf in his mind the way he stacked the record books in his office, and he could forget about it. He had found, to his comfort, that there was much he could forget about life. As long as Mr. Simson had been alive, something tugged anxiously at the corners of Mr. Campbell's precise and dutiful mind, something commanding him to consider the case again and again so that he might see the light shining dimly at the end of a tunnel of absurdity and work Mr. Simson through it to freedom. It was a wrestling and a probing within himself, uncomfortable and contradictory. With Simson alive, Mr. Campbell lost his peace of mind. With Simson dead, Mr. Campbell had merely lost another case. And lost cases had to be forgotten because that was all you could do with them.

He pulled deeply at his cigar and savored the rich smoke on his tongue. He had been carried through two wars on the narcotic of cigar smoke. Now the smoke and the biting taste called up memory like a jinn to bear him into other days. Only now he knew his memory was different from the days themselves. And it was a special kind of memory. The days of years past played before him like a scene enacted upon a distant stage where he might contemplate events without any fear or responsibility. These things had happened to him, but now the happening was wound in its own strange world of lifelike shadows, and he could view it all with tranquility. It might almost have happened to someone else, though then he would not have known it all so well. On looking back on the past one discovered an irrevocability and a fatality—not only about others, but about oneself.

Without any self-pity or bitterness, Mr. Campbell supposed he had lost more than most men. He accepted the loss as his part of the shaded sadness which was any life. The cigar smoke, shifting like some inconstant spirit to mingle with the air and vanish, was like the past itself, blown impulsively outward and forever unredeemed. In the swirling motion of the smoke, in its fragrance, and in its burning taste he moved without moving his body.

To Mexico at night and in reedy youth, where stars shone brilliantly over the sky as they did now in the clear, dry air. Only, he noted in that factual way of his, the Big Dipper hung much nearer the horizon there than it did here. To the sound of dogs howling off in the dark, that bloodcurdling sound of Mexican dogs perpetually starved and akin to wolves, and there was always the fear that the sound might be a signal. Santa Ana's vile little soldiers creeping up in the night to slit the throats of pickets stationed out there. You smoked then and wondered in passing if the flare of light at the end of the cigar might attract a bullet flung from the dark.

To Virginia, when the rain fell in soft whispering, and you sat up in your soggy blankets and felt the earth dissolving into mud underneath, and the rain on the tent roof and on the leaves in the forest kept monotonously drumming as if it would go on forever, and the sound incarnated a war which might never end. On those occasions he puffed at his cigars, and he buried his thoughts in the smoke and in the mechanical motions of his lungs.

For he had really thought of nothing in those times. That was the real gift of cigar smoke then—to think of nothing. And now in the long retrospect of the years all those half-remembered occasions brushed and danced together like the white smoke in the moonlit night. The smoke assuaged both his fear and his loneliness. So he sat with his cigar and did not grieve for time or age or for those he had lost.

The train was on time. As always they heard it far up the line, blowing mournfully in the night, and in the still gap of silence which the whistle tore into their musing talk, they heard the distant pounding of the engine and the throbbing of the pistons on the air. Up the way the new semaphore went cranking down to signal the train's proud rolling onto the block at Martel, and three of the men turned to watch for the stately gliding lamp on the head of the locomotive to appear at the bend in the track up there beyond the edge of town. Clarence Jackson stood up and went into his office.

Clarence is drinking too much. The sharp thought broke into the torpor of Mr. Campbell's mind. The same thought, every night at this time. Every night, like so many other things, it broke on the flinty resignation of Mr. Campbell's soul. A shoal of rock in the deep stream. It did no good to worry. In the end it didn't matter. Nothing mattered.

The train lashed out of the dark and came in with a hiss of steam and a clank of steel, a roar of fire, and the banging crash of its bell. There was rushing movement, and there were calls in the night. And then it was gone, and the quivering silence flooded in after the sound dying toward Chattanooga.

The men parted without goodbyes. Mr. Campbell walked up the street from the railroad station, crossed the square in front of the courthouse, and saw the gallows still standing there. He walked on around to his house and let himself in through the unlocked door. The quiet mustiness of his books, a pleasant smell and welcome to him, encircled him as he entered. It was almost like moisture in the air. He walked down the uncarpeted hall and through the door into the kitchen. It smelled vaguely of wash water and stale coffee.

The kitchen seemed lonelier than the other rooms in his house. It was because at one time this had been the place he had begun his day. Here the tuneless matins were sung—a kiss and coffee, gay laughter, talk of common things and great dreams—now all dead and gone and lost forever, leaving only a crust of memory like the stain of coffee evaporated long ago from a cup.

From old habit he latched the door, tried it experimentally with a strong hand to see that the latch would hold. Satisfied that it would he walked through the darkened hall which he knew by heart and swiftly mounted the stairway, through the absolute darkness, which led to his room. Somehow the darkness seemed heavier upstairs. Blank doors gaped at him, and he sensed their blank gaping though he could not see them.

He pushed open the door to his room and passed from the closeness of the hallway into the stirring of the summer night drifting through his wide-open windows. He struck a match to the lamp on the table, and the yellow light blazed up and made the shadows fall crazily on the walls. The slight motion of the flame made him aware of a breeze which he could not feel. He stood for a moment with the glass lamp chimney still in his hand and listened with cocked head and sniffed the air. But there was no sound of wind, and he could smell no rain. He shrugged and chuckled cynically at himself and put the chimney in place so that the flame stood straight up on the wick, a hard simplicity of pointed light.

He sat down heavily on the bed and began to undress. He was tired. His bones ached, and the weight of his fatigue pressed on every muscle in his body. "I'm getting old," he half muttered to himself. The statement was without melancholy or rancor. It was a bare fact, reflected upon until the gray gloom of it had been squeezed into his soul, and now his announcement to the silence was a perfunctory acknowledgment to fate.

He undressed slowly and painfully and hung his clothing over a chair beside the bed. He got up, naked, and found his nightshirt in the closet. He slipped it on over himself and blew out the light. He started to throw himself onto the bed at once. But on impulse he walked to the window and pulled the tall curtains back and looked out.

The street below was unbearably still. The moonlight shone on the rocks in the street and in the boards of the railroad station and showed softly luminescent on the steel tracks. The silence was close and pressing, menacing like the furry blackness there in the hallway outside. His mind jerked backward to nights in the field when men feared the crackling of sticks off in the dark but feared the silence more. In the distance a dog barked. The barking went on and became more rapid and frenzied and turned into a long howl, a baying at the moon, a canine intoxication with light. The foreboding menace of the night lay heavily over the countryside beyond the town and filled him with a melancholy that was close to fear. He swallowed and tasted the stale leavings of whiskey and tobacco in his mouth.

"Good God, I'm *drunk!*" He grumbled the words aloud and shook his head to clear it. Usually he had had enough sense to stop in time. But tonight he had not, and he was drunk.

He fell into bed. The torpor of fatigue reached up around him. He had time to grumble again and to feel the fear seeping softly into the back of the night somewhere. He thought with curious detachment of the trap springing and Mr. Simson dropping through it with his eyes bulging just as the rope çaught him. He had time to reflect that life and death alike were jarring indignities. Then he was asleep.

Later he heard the hoofbeats. They began far away, like the barking of the dog, and they came on and on until they filled the night. He rose up from his bed and floated to the window where a soundless wind was blowing the tall curtains back, and he peered out into the night where the distorted shapes of trees stretched crazily into the amber sky, stabbing upward like black claws, broken against the moon, and he looked, and he saw his son.

There was no doubt. It was his son. The boy rode wildly down the empty street with a slim hand held high above his head, and he was shouting against the shut houses, crying above the eerie treetops, words Mr. Campbell could not understand.

"My son! My son!" Mr. Campbell cried out over the hoofbeats. His voice was caught up and wafted away like a tiny shape in a storm of wind, but he cried again: "My son! My son!"

The horse stopped. The wind stopped. The huge silence dropped over them like a shroud. The boy sat his horse on the street below and looked up.

"My son!" John Wesley Campbell called again, and this time it was his voice that shattered the silence and filled the night. "My son!"

The boy looked up, white-faced and still. They stared at each other through the amber light descending from the moon. "You filthy old man!" the boy called at last. "I despise you. I came back to tell you I despise you and always did. When the War ended, I went to Texas. I died there. I came all the way back to tell you I despise you." And jerking cruelly back on the reins of his horse, he spurred the animal with his heels. The horse reared dangerously and pawed the air with his black hoofs, then took the rein and thundered away.

Only then did Mr. Campbell realize that his son was naked.

"Come back!" he cried. "Come back! Come *back!*" His last call was a scream which rang against the walls of his room, and he awoke.

He was sitting up in the bed wrapped in a blanket and shivering with terror, and the blanket was soaked with sweat. The night was still. The dog had ceased to bark. The sky had resumed the iridescent dark of star and moonglow. He struck a match and looked at the old clock ticking beside his bed. Midnight! The booming of the courthouse bell just past. Most of the night lay before him. He sank back onto the mattress and lay looking toward the ceiling, which he could not see. A hard, round knot of longing pressed under his ribs and against his heart, and there was nothing he could do.

3

JACKSON BOURBON LAY in the dark in the pile of greasy rags which passed for blankets and savored the smells of the night. He was most comfortable at night—almost peaceful. Then he could lay his body down like a sack and escape from it, and his mind could rove out into the dark of time and caress memories—all jumbled up in his head, it is true, but still more real than the present he endured.

Sometimes he didn't know which was worse, to be black or to be old. Now he was both, and it was pretty bad. So it was good to lie back in the covers, in the peaceful warmth, and not even to think. He did not have a great many words to think with because he had never learned many, and now that he was old, the words he did know were slipping away. He had always been a pretty good talker, but last year Beckinridge had hit him with the flat of his hand and knocked him cold. Since then his throat had been stiff, and it was hard to say anything. So what he liked best now was to lie abed and feel nothing.

Beckinridge! The boy always made him afraid now. The first time Beckinridge had slapped him down, the old man had been half blind with rage. He stumbled to his feet and made for his son with both fists wildly flailing. Beckinridge simply knocked him down again. That was the time Beckinridge broke his teeth, his good front teeth. Jackson Bourbon couldn't understand it. He could only rage and curse and feel the cowering fear inching up his spine afterward.

That first night he lay in bed with his body aching all over from the blows and his mouth pulp and blood, and he tried to puzzle it out. It did him no good at all. He could not understand. Bewilderment took possession of his brain, and for all the twisting of his mind and the raking of thought through the sieve of his clumsy intellect, he couldn't figure it out. He couldn't understand why his son hated him.

The fear became constant in the old man. It was like his poor eyesight or his rheumatism. He could only dimly recall what it had been to live without the fear. Not that Beckinridge beat him every day. They would go for weeks with hardly a word between them, and some of the fear would recede. Jackson Bourbon would begin to talk to his boy again. The boy would respond in grunts and half-words and then with words, and everything would seem to be all right. Jackson Bourbon knew his son was sick, and he kept hoping (for that is what it *really* was—hope) that his boy would get so sick that he would need the old man to take care of him. But he didn't. And in time something would always happen, and frail, skinny, sick Beckinridge would beat him nearly to death.

When the two of them left Bourbonville on the afternoon of the hanging, Beckinridge leaned for a while on his old father. His father liked that. But eventually the son detached himself and went plowing on alone, driven by the energy of fear and hate. When Jackson Bourbon at last got home, his son was waiting for him. Beckinridge stepped out the door before the old man could even speak and slapped him till his ears rang. Jackson Bourbon lay down in the dirt and cried. He cried until the tears made mud of the clay under his face, and he slobbered and made bubbling noises with his mouth, asking for mercy. And after a while Beckinridge got tired and went off somewhere. Jackson Bourbon didn't know where.

But when his son was gone, and when he had lain there in the humiliating dust, he pulled himself inside the shanty. He couldn't stand for long, and several times he fell gasping to his knees and spitting blood. Finally he made it to the bed and collapsed on it in a heap of sodden old flesh. The pain and the numbness fought for possession of his body. Then the numbness slowly won, and the pain fell into a dull throbbing which was almost pleasant. He felt a sleepy peace. Let Beckinridge come! Let him find him in bed with his shoes on! It would only mean another beating. Nothing more than that, and he had had so many beatings from his son that another one wouldn't matter. Beckinridge . . .

Beckinridge! In a curious way the old man's mind kept skipping back lately to the morning Beckinridge was born. Jackson Bourbon couldn't have told you how long it had been. It wasn't "long ago" because long ago Jackson Bourbon himself had been a child, but it was "a while ago" which meant that it was sometime before the War, before freedom. Not long before the War because when freedom came Beckinridge was still a somber little boy who greeted the blue-coated Yankee soldiers with wide eyes and childish fear. But Jackson Bourbon remembered the day of his son's birth a lot more clearly than he could remember distinctly the sunlight that morning, burning off the spring mists which had accumulated on the hills during the night.

There was something about the birth of a male child at dawn. Jackson Bourbon would never have been able to say exactly what it was, but he felt the looming shape of a great thought, and the feeling remained after all these years and all this trouble. The sound of the baby crying lifted out of the cabin and stirred through the chilly dawning over the slaves gathered outside. They were standing around in little expectant groups, and they had been standing for a long time, seemingly only partly detached from the thinning darkness of the night. When the baby finally cried, they laughed and shook their heads, and when Jackson Bourbon called out that it was a boy, they were glad.

One of the men there that morning was fresh out of Africa. He could not speak English yet. He could grunt and speak in a language no one could quite understand. And all by himself he could sing a quiet into the tumult of evening after supper. A wild, incomprehensible chant of song which stirred something strange in the slaves. He had been bought off a slave boat over in Charleston, beyond the mountains. The white Mr. Bourbon had started raising tobacco—acres and acres of tobacco—to bring fortune back to his land. He needed new men, and he bought the African because he got him cheap.

The African was a solitary man, befuddled by what had happened to him—the way slaves sometimes were when they first discovered they were slaves. He was confused by the rattling discord of strange voices. The Connecticut sea captain who transported him from Africa to Charleston was a solid Congregationalist, upright to the marrow of his pious bones. He read the Bible every afternoon to his white crew and led them in prayer. He tithed all the income from his slaving expeditions and was convinced that the Lord's benevolence lay at the base of his prosperity. He even badgered his only son with his prayers until that unfortunate young man went to the Divinity School at Yale to study theology. Anyway, this sea captain hated the African. He talked it all over with Mr. Will

Bourbon, explained all the details of his own devout life and its fatal coincidence with the life of this black devil. He told all about the black's unbearable pride, the sure mark of Satan. He tried to flail the pride out of him with a whip on the voyage from Africa. But the more he beat him, the more arrogant and dangerous the African became—which meant that the sea captain beat him all the more to keep him in line.

So Mr. Bourbon bought the African cheap because he had big open cuts running all over his back, and they were infected and dripping with pus. The man himself was so bleary from all the beating that it seemed he would die. In fact, the sea captain said he honestly believed it was God's will that the man die as an example to the others. But Mr. Bourbon said he would take a chance on God's mercy, and after the sea captain had made elaborate protestations of his own good will and desire not to cheat anybody, they arrived at a price. Mr. Bourbon gloated for the rest of his life about getting the African. He used to make the man strip down to show his scars, and Mr. Bourbon would laugh and carry on over the way he had got the best of the sea captain and maybe of God himself. It was a good bargain, a lucky stroke.

So the African became part of the Bourbon place. When Beckinridge was born he stood in the grass outside and puffed at his pipe and heard the crying child. When he heard, he grunted with satisfaction. It was a primeval, throaty rumble of contentment accompanied by a string of incomprehensible words. Jackson Bourbon stepped down into the other slaves from his cabin to receive their congratulations. He saw that the African was crying. He never forgot that. He turned it over in his head with the years and weighed it, and now as he lay in the warming numbness he wondered whatever had become of the African. When the Yankee soldiers came, he disappeared. For no good reason Jackson Bourbon had an idea that he had tried to get back to Africa. Now he was more than likely dead, and nobody but Jackson Bourbon was alive to remember the tears on the morning Beckinridge was born. It was like yesterday, only so long ago, and nothing was right any more.

He turned slightly in his bed. His arm was numb, and the turning stirred alive a chiseling pain in his head. So he eased himself back to his original position and breathed carefully until the pain subsided. Where had all the people gone? To heaven? He hoped so. He hadn't heard any good preaching lately . . .

The white Mr. Bourbon came down to the quarters when

Beckinridge was born. Mr. Will Bourbon was a hard man. Nobody could tell whether he liked better to beat nigger men or fuck nigger women. He did them both with a fearsome regularity, though he knew when to stop beating a man before he had ruined his investment. All his hands were afraid of him. That was the way he liked it. He was so thin that his clothes hung on him as if he had been made of wire. He carried a slim little rod of peeled hickory wood, nice and smooth, and if any of the niggers gave him sass—man or woman—he would make the others strip the offender naked. Then he would beat the twitching black behind with his stick. And almost always after he had whipped a woman that way he would call her out into the barn and give her a good stout fuck. There was something about that he liked.

He was in good spirits the day Beckinridge was born. He laughed when he saw how dark the baby's skin was. It was an obscene old man's laugh, vile and whispery. "I guess he's your'n," he chortled at Jackson Bourbon. "If he was mine, he'd be a lot lighter than that. He's your'n all right. Leastways he's *some* nigger's child." He laughed some more after that, and Jackson Bourbon had to laugh too or else celebrate his son's birthday by getting a beating. It was a cloud on his happiness, the laughter of the old man in the March morning. "He'll make a good field nigger," Mr. Bourbon said, and this time he was more serious. "If things keep on the way they is now, I'll need to raise me some good field niggers for the market. We might get a price out of this one. A real good price." He cast a greedy eye at Jackson Bourbon, and his voice turned stern. "You remember he's my property, you hear? He ain't your'n. You didn't do nothing but fuck his mamma. See you take good care of him now!"

Lying there in the festering dark, Jackson Bourbon mused over that day. Sometimes he still wondered if he'd done the right thing afterward. But there wasn't any help for it. Old man Bourbon brought it all on himself, and Jackson Bourbon did what he had to do. That very afternoon Jackson Bourbon slipped off and went up to the corner of the chicken lot and caught a black hen. The hen squalled something awful, and Jackson Bourbon thought sure he'd be caught and whipped. But he ran off as fast as he could into the woods, and when he was far out of sight and sound, he worked his terrible spell.

He had carried the nails and the hammer in his pocket. It was an uncomfortable load, for the nails kept sticking him through his pants, and he was afraid somebody would see him yet. But he did it right, took the frantically squawking hen and nailed her wings to an oak tree. It had to be oak. The hen almost tore her wings off trying to pull loose from the nails and the pain, but before she could, Jackson Bourbon got his knife out and expertly de-gutted her so that the blood and the entrails came cascading down the tree trunk, and the hen died. All the time he was weaving the curse in a frenzy of words: "Mr. Will Bourbon! Mr. Will Bourbon! Mr. Will Bourbon!" He was careful to get the "Mister" into the formula because he knew how literal-minded the spirits were. If he didn't say "Mister," they might hear him saying something like "Will Bourbon do something?" or "Will Bourbon die?" He would get a sign out of that, he knew. But he wasn't very good at reading signs, and he wanted to be sure Mr. Will Bourbon died. So he said the words passionately and did his best not to think of any other thing, not to contaminate the curse. And when the hen was full dead, he repeated his formula a few extra times and went off and left her hanging there, crucified and empty of her guts.

And it worked! Praise God, it worked! Mr. Bourbon died before the year was out! Down in the quarters the slaves nearly laughed themselves sick with joy. They rolled on the cabin floors laughing and singing. For a while they talked about burning the Big House down to celebrate. But somebody said Cranepool Bourbon, one of the old man's sons, was perched up there in a window with a shotgun just waiting to see a black face draw near. So they stayed put and took an unauthorized holiday and lolled happily about while Mr. Will Bourbon was being planted in the cold ground.

Jackson Bourbon picked up his baby boy and held him all that afternoon. He thanked the spirits. He put milk out for them that night, high up so the dogs around the quarters couldn't get at it. He thought about Mr. Will Bourbon poking at little Beckinridge with that stubby and unsteady hand and smiling through those rheumy eyes. The father muttered to the baby in self-justification: "He brung it on hisself. He brung it on hisself." Everything was really all right now. Jackson Bourbon only hoped old Mr. Will knew who it was that'd put him in hell.

Later he wondered if he shouldn't have let Mr. Will Bourbon live a little longer—at least till the War. It would have been a good thing to let the old man see the Yankee soldiers tramping over his land as if it were theirs. It would have been a good thing if Mr. Bourbon had seen his niggers go free. Oh it would have been good to see the old man's rage, his helplessness! Maybe a Yankee captain could have taken Mr. Will Bourbon and made a slave out of him, a human stool maybe to help the captain get on his horse, and the captain would be a big fat man with sharp spurs . . . But back then, when Beckinridge was born, nobody could understand that something would happen to set all the niggers free.

Afterward there were a lot of stories. Aunt Hannah Scarbrough was Jackson's age, only she belonged to the Scarbrough family which lived down near Sweetwater, and she'd been dead for years. But before she died she used to tell about being over at Kingston ten, fifteen years before the War. She'd been waiting for her mistress to come out of someplace, and a tall white man with a beard and sad, hollow eyes walked up and said to her, "Tell me, chile, you is a slave, is you not?" And she said yes because she was, and he said, "My chile, my name is Abraham Lincoln, and I'm walking all up and down this here South seeing how bad things is, and someday I'm acoming down here to set you free."

Aunt Hannah said she didn't think much about it at the time. She couldn't figure out why any white man would take the trouble to set her free, and she'd never heard tell of Abraham Lincoln. That's why she didn't say much about it before the War. But, Lord God, how she talked about it afterward! She told the story again and again, and Jackson Bourbon believed it because he'd heard her tell it so much. But he hadn't heard much about freedom before the War.

Then the War came, and the niggers in the valley whispered about it, cogitated over it, murmured and argued, and got stuck in the persistent conviction that the War had something to do with them. *That* was a novelty! The niggers even felt proud of themselves for the War. In a manner of speaking. They knew that white people went off to fight each other every once in a while. But wars didn't have anything to do with niggers. Wars were something white people did for some fool reason niggers never could understand. But in this war the talk got around all over the place that it was being fought over the slaves. Jackson Bourbon was skeptical. He wasn't really persuaded until that day the Yankee soldiers rode in and told them they were free.

Freedom! For a while freedom was the grandest thing on earth. Jackson Bourbon (his wife was dead) took Beckinridge, and they went all the way to Sweetwater with the Yankee Army. Some trip! Best he'd ever had. They picked corn off the stalk and roasted it in the fire when they were hungry, and nobody said anything about it. They slept as long as they wanted to in the morning, and all the niggers yelled themselves hoarse with joy every time they saw a Yankee uniform. Then the winter came, and the corn gave out, and they had to go back home.

Only there wasn't any home any more. Henry Bourbon and Cranepool Bourbon held onto their daddy's place. They were about as mean as their father had been, but they didn't have his experience. Both of them were long and lanky, dry in the face so that they looked as if they had been hung up in a tobacco barn to cure and been forgotten. Jackson Bourbon and his son wanted to work for them just for food and a place to sleep. But the Bourbon brothers shook their heads. This wasn't real nigger country, they said. Never had been. They were glad the niggers had been turned loose. It saved them the trouble of looking out for a lot of worthless field hands, saved them having to kill off slaves they couldn't feed. Niggers were free now. They would have to look out for themselves.

And that was a pretty bad time! No food, no roof—winter. They barely managed to keep alive. They were human scavengers. They ate some terrible things. Some nights they slept under the railroad bridge in Bourbonville, huddled together for warmth. They learned to steal. But they made it. A lot of niggers they knew just died, but *they* made it, and the next year was better.

The old man lay in the dark and grinned. They had made it by themselves! He felt a torpor of peace come with the descent of the night. He would lie in bed to the end of time and think about nothing but himself and Beckinridge and how much they had done together. The peace inside made him want to cry. The night was black; he was black. He and the night had something in common, and now the night was all around him like a mother hugging him. The night could hide him. He would love the night.

The door opened. He heard the creaking of the hinges and the wood pop and heard the freshened sound of night noises let in. He did not move. But the small sounds brought him down from the dreamy clouds. The fear strove with him. He remembered the shoes on the bed. He heard Beckinridge stumble against a table and groan. When Beckinridge groaned like that, he was drunk. And if he was drunk, he might have some whiskey with him. Jackson Bourbon ran the premises of the syllogism through his head. He licked his lips and yearned for the taste of the good, white whiskey he had not drunk for so long.

"Beckinridge?" he spoke timidly.

Beckinridge did not answer. Instead he struck a match and lighted the lamp on the table, and for a moment the sudden blaze of the fire affrighted Jackson Bourbon's eyes. Then the flame settled on the wick, and the old man's eyes got used to it.

"Beckinridge? Has you got any whiskey?" He spoke like a little child.

His son turned slowly to look at him. Beckinridge still did not speak, and his bruised face was blank. He had one hand resting lightly against his chest. With an effort he bent down, and when he did Jackson Bourbon saw the clay jug and with great difficulty Beckinridge brought it to the table top. The light shone on the glazed clay in a steady and profound richness. Jackson Bourbon looked at it with aching desire, and his tongue darted over his lips.

"If I could have a lil' swaller? Just a lil' swaller, to wet my tongue?" He propped himself up on the bed. He had forgotten all his own pain in the ecstasy of the jug.

Beckinridge looked down at his father without expression. His face was like the leather of an old saddle, blackened by use and age, swollen along one side from the blow he had taken in the afternoon. Very slowly he understood the old man. His pendulous eyelids flickered briefly, and he looked at the jug and pondered it. The old man sat higher in the bed and put out his hand.

"Please, boy. Please!"

Beckinridge reached for the jug and meditated over something.

"Jes' one swaller. I won't drink much, *honest!*" The old man's voice rasped in the still air and stopped. The corn-shucks mattress scraped, and a wordless pleading filled the quiet of the room.

Beckinridge deliberated. Then he smiled, making up his mind. It was a slow-breaking smile that showed his teeth and sent folds of skin breaking along his cheeks where there were no dimples to receive a smile. Jackson Bourbon had not seen his son smile in so long that he was startled. His astonishment became a rising joy. He swung his feet down onto the floor, heedless of the shocking pain. He reached out with both arms to receive either the jug or his boy to himself. Something hammered to get into his mind, something of long ago, something scented with the mysterious sweetness of younger days and forgotten springtimes. Whatever it was would not come to him plainly. Instead there was a dreamy peacefulness, and ageless tranquility which like whiskey itself drowned the alarm ringing inside. He held out his arms and smiled gratefully up at the smile of his son.

"You're a good . . ." He was going to say more, something about the goodness of his boy and their common victories over the past, over life. But before he could speak, Beckinridge slowly and carefully drew back the whiskey jug and methodically brought it down with all his force on the back of the old man's head. Like someone smashing an unsuspecting bug.

Jackson Bourbon smiled on. He did not have time to alter his expression or even to feel pain. The warm glow of peace burst in his astonished brain and went out like a match in the wind. A single instant of memory came back to him, a flash of garbled light like the reflection of the lamp fire against the descending jug. He remembered a day in the spring of ages ago when he and Beckinridge had found a rabbit in the trap they had set in the garden, and the boy reached inside the rough wooden box and caught the squirming rabbit and strangled him to death. That was the flash of memory in the last second of Jackson Bourbon's life—the sight of the ferocious grin of a little boy clutching a shapeless thing of fur. The memory was gone before the old man's face crashed against the board floor. He did not feel the impact. Nor was he aware of the splinters of wood driven into his face by the force of his fall.

Beckinridge stood over his father looking at him. Some of the whiskey had spilled out of the jug. It ran down his arm and wet his shirt. In a minute he stumbled back to the chair by the table and sat down. His chest was on fire. The spilled whiskey on his hands was sticky and cool. He licked at it, licked over his fingers and down the smooth side of the jug until he tasted the blood mixed with the whiskey. Then he spit on the floor and made a face. He lifted the opening of the jug to his mouth and drank deeply. Again and again. After a while it was empty. He sucked at it until he was sure there was no more. Then he hurled it from him. It struck the stones of the fireplace and fell in ringing pieces on the floor. The warmth from the whiskey inside him raced out through his blood and reached up to absorb the pain in his chest. He sat hunched over the table. He stared glumly and without thought at the body of his father, twisted in a long heap amid the blankets on the floor. The lamp burned steadily, sending a thin wisp of smoke to vanish in the darkness overhead.

4

AT NIGHT, when Samuel Beckwith lay down to sleep, the cavernous house around him muttered with the ghosts of his ancestors. He supposed that they were not really there. He had never felt the warmth of spirit breath on his neck in rooms once inhabited by the dead. He heard no clanking in the dark. If things were as they seemed, the Crittendons all lay in their quiet graves and troubled no one. Still, there was something beyond the seeming. And just before sleep the "something" always haunted him.

He supposed later on that it was nothing more than a childish acceptance of his mother's sentimental devotion. She said she thought they *must* be there, somehow, in the house with them. It was not a fearful idea. She thought it was something like the Catholic saints. And it comforted her to think she had witnesses to her suffering, to all that she had endured. She and her son had won a great victory. It would be a strange universe, she said, if the people in whose name the cause had been won did not know about it, did not perhaps help in the winning. The cause of preserving their heritage, of making their land live and their memories survive. What mother and son had done was not for themselves, but for a whole line of men.

So as a child Sam had thought of the ancestors lurking still about the house, watching over things. He became accustomed to the presence of the dead. And like his mother he accepted the house as the place where the worlds of the living and the dead were knotted together in some quietly glowing mystery. The house was a shrine filled with relics, a monument to a glorious past and the source of a shining future.

He slept in his Uncle Matthew's room. His mother insisted on that. The cherry bureau in the corner still held the clothes of Matthew Crittendon. Shirts with lacy fronts and soft collars. Broad-legged pants of flannel and hard-spun wool, clothes a proud young man had worn on the hunt and to church and to laughing parties. Great days which rang like giant bells through the valley of other years, now tinkling softly in the memory of the woman who remained devoted to a dead past.

Sam had never worn the clothes. He had never even tried them on. They lay neatly folded where they had lain unmoved for twenty-five years and more, and now they were riven with moths and turning silently to dust. Sometimes in a pensive mood Sam pulled one of the drawers open and ran his hands over the fabric of the things that lay on top. When he did so, the cloth exuded an odor of age and time and forgotten things.

He had never known his uncle. His picture was there, hanging on the wall over the bureau. There were pictures of ancestors all over the house. Faded tintypes, photographs, portraits sketched in crayon by traveling artists, crude things, some of them, in bold colors once—all now slowly bleaching out to grays and browns and sinking inevitably into hazy shadows. There were even two portrait samplers hung in the hall at the head of the stairs. Two primitive attempts at life in needle and thread, and sewn into the bottom of each of them was a name—Promise and Gisela Jane. They were both daughters of the first Crittendon who crossed the Appalachian Mountains and settled here. They had both died in childhood.

And the pictures of all the ancestors were on view throughout the house. Naturally the portrait of Samuel Beckwith, Sr., was most important. It was also the largest and it stood in the most impressive place, in the great parlor downstairs over the fireplace there.

All the ancestors lived in the mind of Sarah Beckwith, even those she had never known. But excepting her husband, Matthew was probably more alive than any of the others. They had been so close, she said. He was younger than Sam's father, maybe by five years when their pictures had been made. There were other differences. Matthew held himself more erect, seemed far more imperious. His face was not fleshy, though it would have been someday. It was a full face, strong and marked by the haughty assurance of its own worth. It was a face that could get along in the world. No doubt about that. No room for any doubt about anything in the face. Perhaps no room for love either, Sam thought at times. He never said that to his mother. He would not have dared. But he thought vaguely that he would not have liked his Uncle Matthew.

Matthew fell at Bull Run in the first thundering of the War. He raised a troop at the news of Sumter and tore off to Virginia. All in frenzied haste, by train and on horseback. "Pray that God will wait for us." He went off on the sluggish train, cursing the fate which kept him five hundred miles from Washington where, as everyone knew, the victorious armies of the Confederate States would shortly march down the broad avenue that led to the Capitol. Bands, pennants, roaring crowds, horses, gorgeous women, fame too full for history to hold. All waiting there in the green distance of Virginia.

He was hardly out of sight on his frantic journey before his father was writing to Governor Harris, urging the governor to use his influence in Richmond when the New Nation was triumphant, influence to get Matthew Crittendon a "position"—if possible in the Department of War. Perhaps even as Ambassador to England. The boy was young, but Benjamin Crittendon called up the English connection of his family. He wrote in the confidence of blood and in the wild haste of a man fearing that each beat of the telegraph presaged the announcement of total victory.

The Lord God of Hosts answered many prayers that summer. He gave Matthew Crittendon's men their battle and their victory, though in the perverse way of God he unaccountably did not give them Washington. But Matthew himself was killed, cut down in a headlong and desperate charge for glory moments after the first volley of rifle fire rolled off the brooding hills. A solitary bullet, half an inch thick, punched directly through one of those imperial eyes and out the back of that noble skull. He never knew what hit him, probably never had the mortal consciousness that life was over. Sam's mother liked to say that Matthew went galloping with drawn saber into the gates of heaven. She liked to tell her son that she thought Matthew must have been surprised when he saw the heavenly city around him with its golden battlements scraping the sky, and heard the choirs. With the years she would laugh over her little celestial fantasy, like a grandmother recounting infant sayings, and she supposed that he must have brought his saber down in bewilderment as the angels came and perhaps Jesus himself to tell him that his wars were over, his battles done, to put down his sword and take up the shining crown of righteousness.

But that was all long after Matthew's death. When it happened it fell on the Crittendon house like a storm of wind and fire. Everybody knew that people got killed in battles. Everybody knew that the first cannonades and rifle fire were meant to kill and did. When the young men went off in pursuit of their glorious and inevitable victory, everybody knew that some of them would never return. But Matthew . . . Well, it was something nobody was prepared for. "At least he was spared defeat," Sam's mother said with dignity. "He couldn't have stood that. God was merciful to him. He never knew, and he's happy now. He's happy in heaven."

When he was a child, Sam absorbed his mother's speculations. He waited for death and his introduction to his esteemed uncle as if waiting for the train to Knoxville and a delightful visit with someone he could love. His Uncle Matthew and his father! They would all be brothers in heaven. Death would be a sweet passing in the night, over shadows of darkness to the eternal sun.

But now . . . Now he was older. The incongruity of Matthew, crowned and singing, thrust itself upon him. And he was brought to compare Matthew's haughty expression with the quietly solemn portrait of Samuel Beckwith, Sr. It struck Sam that the two men would not have got on well together. Even in death their presence in the same house seemed a little uncomfortable.

In the moonlight Matthew's proud picture was muted, gray and almost indiscernible against the flat wall. Sam possessed the room now. He wondered if Matthew would begrudge that. He supposed that his uncle would order him out if he could. By right of inheritance, no son of Sarah Crittendon should possess this house. It should all have gone to sons of Matthew Crittendon, but there were none. Matthew himself was but a picture and a bright figment of Sam's mother's mind.

Sam could not sleep on this night. He threw the covers back and got softly out of bed. On tiptoe he went to the window. The slightest sound was likely to bring his mother rushing from her room to see what was the matter. An old habit of hers. He did not like it. She apologized for it time and time again. But it *was* an old habit. She listened for him when he was a child. And he was still her son. "Can I get you a glass of milk? Can't I do *anything* for you? Do you want me to read you something, Samuel? Oh Sam, don't push me away. I only want to help."

Carefully he sat down in the chair before the window. The wood creaked with his weight. He held his breath, listening for movement in his mother's chamber beyond the wall. But nothing stirred in the house. No sound but the soft, irregular popping of the cooling joists and beams, and so far removed it was barely audible. He stretched his legs in front of him and looked out the window.

The earth outside was bright with moonlight. He studied the moon-splashed lawn, the trees, and the wooded ridge on the other side of the valley. Not a hint of breeze moved the foliage. The world was locked in a spell which only rain could break. The moon stood out in the sky like a blister in carved glass, bone-white and stark. The night smelled of the baking days. No fragrance to the smell. The charred reek of a furnace whose fires have burned out. The roses in the garden below the window were dead. Every green thing drooped in the deadly calm of the drought.

The youth puzzled over Mr. Simson's prophecy. He did not know what to make of it. It was a day of prophecies, but he did not worry about the contrived wrenching of the nigger hags over the stuff of his life. Mr. Simson's word was different. There was a mystery to that and almost a hope. He wished that there might be some realm open to the eyes of a man before death. A world of rain clouds stacking over the mountains, fresh water filling the thirsty land. But it was not likely. Not likely at all.

He turned idly to the picture of Matthew. The shape of the face and the dark eyes stood more than half concealed in the slanting moonlight. All the hope of the house had been fixed in Matthew. Behind Matthew stood the ambitions of Benjamin Crittendon, Samuel Beckwith's grandfather. More blurred by time even than Matthew. A strong man. Pious, as all the Crittendons were, but in an Old Testament way. The piety to slay the Amalekites. A hard man. A hard scratch across the years his legacy.

Benjamin Crittendon was born in 1810, here, in this house. The record was in the family Bible. He was the third child of the family, the oldest to survive the smallpox which ravaged the valley in 1817. In 1833 he married a woman named Young out of Chattanooga. She began having children in 1836. The progeny of that year and the next, two sons, died before they were able to walk. Died together. Diphtheria. A terrible death for little boys. And what might they have been? Sam knew their graves and their names. Jonathan and David. Strong Biblical names like all the male names in the Crittendon line. They were his uncles. It was a strange thought. His uncles, dead before they could do more than blink at the world, crawl, and point at things.

Matthew was born in 1839. He lived. That was the most important thing about Matthew. His father kept him by the bed, on *his* side. He stood over the nigger housegirl who changed the baby and washed him. He watched over the feeding, and he supervised the first steps the child took and marked them with a knife in the floor. The steps were from the cherry table in the dining room to the wall. The deep-cut X's were still there, carved triumphantly in the wide pine planking. Then, incidental to the pageantry of her brother's childhood, Sarah was born, and killed her mother by coming into the world. She told Sam she believed her father blamed her for it. She said it matter-of-factly and without bitterness, though with a little nostalgic sorrow. Her father needed a wife. A wife was a requirement for life in the valley. And he was a passionate and restless man, not able to bear up too well before the affronts of circumstances he could not control. It was not his nature to accept defeat without reacting to it. So he turned his disappointment and his grief into a sulking reproach which kept his daughter at a distance from him all the rest of his life. "I couldn't help what I did, and he couldn't help what he did," she said. "Every woman who gives birth to a child almost dies, and a lot do die. I almost died when you were born, Samuel. Don't ever forget that. I very nearly almost died."

So in a way she had a grievance against her father. But, as she told her son, Benjamin Crittendon had suffered enough. He did not need his daughter's rancor to follow him beyond the grave. She swore she held nothing against him. She had had enough sorrow of her own to understand what he had borne. Only she was lonely as a child. Hesitantly she would admit that. It was almost a confession of sin, this halting admission that all was not entirely golden in that happy world snatched away by the War. She was lonely. She missed the mother she lost in the way a girl would miss a mother she never knew. An uncertainty and an indescribable longing for *someone* to teach her how to be a woman. "I was a poor, silly little goose when I was young," she said. "I had to teach myself everything I know." The smile again, nostalgic and memorable, and in that slight expression she became the warm embodiment of something men believed they had fought for. A tragic, sublime gentleness rising out of the losses of time.

Matthew was good to her. Better than she could ever have asked, she said. Good, strong, solid, virtuous, brave, handsome Matthew. He was mother, father, brother, and dearest friend—all at once. When he died she wanted to follow him into the grave.

But it didn't work out that way. Her father died instead, and then it was all up to her. Benjamin Crittendon died under the shock of his son's death. It was the night of the same day that the telegraph brought the news down of "the glorious victory of our arms at Manassas." And after the report of victory a throng of expectant, jubilant people stood cheering and singing in the summer afternoon and darkness outside the railroad station waiting for the report of the entry into Washington. Instead the news came about Matthew.

The telegrapher at Bourbonville in those days was a gabby old man named Josiah Condon. He said afterward he didn't know or couldn't realize what the key was telling him until he had written it all out. His own handwriting confronted him. The dreadful message squeezed irrevocably out of the wire like acid from the glass-encased batteries in the corner. He couldn't leave the station himself, so he sent a boy from the crowd, a boy named Elwood McCarter, and when Elwood McCarter set out a storm blew in.

Rain that night and thunder boiling across the sky and pale lightning breaking like fire in the trees. Elwood McCarter whipped his horse through the dashing rain to bring the news. Sarah Beckwith hated him to this day, or hated his memory. He went West afterward, and nobody ever heard from him again. But that night he came galloping into the yard shouting, "He's *dead,* Mr. Crittendon! Your son's *dead!* He's got hisself kilt at Manassas."

"He could have knocked first. He could have done anything but what he did. I woke up. I thought it was the thunder, but then I could tell there was a human voice out there. The fool! The murderous fool! He killed my father just as surely as if he'd put a gun in his face."

So Benjamin Crittendon took the news sitting stark upright in his bed while the announcement of death surged at his window between the blasting of the thunderclaps. He got up from the room two doors down the hall from the room where Sam now sat. He went wildly groping down the dark steps to where Elwood McCarter pounded furiously at the door, still shouting. Benjamin Crittendon opened the door to the youth, who repeated the news at the top of his lungs and kept on repeating it until Sarah arrived on the scene and slapped him as hard as she could across the mouth. "I told him to hush or I'd kill him!"

But it was too late. Benjamin Crittendon pushed gaping by them. Sarah Crittendon Beckwith always said she thought he was already dying at that moment. He went across the porch with his hands thrown incredulously forward and down the steps and into the blinding rain. She ran after him. Elwood McCarter came stupidly behind. The three of them trailed into the yard, and a flash of lightning exploded over their heads. In its blue light she saw her father fall.

Elwood McCarter helped her drag him back into the house. "I didn't have anything on but a nightshirt, and I might as well have been naked, I was so wet. That young McCarter fool kept looking at me. He couldn't take his eyes off me! I wanted to kill him! That was what I was thinking all the time we were getting my poor father into the house. I was so angry. And then I wanted to die!"

Sitting in the dark by the window, Sam looked out into the investing night and tried to conjure up the rain and the lightning and the storming of Elwood McCarter's horse in the lane. He tried to imagine the tumult, the dazed old man who was his grandfather, and the lightning burst which illuminated his death. But it was like standing over his father's grave. Nothing rose out of the earth but the subdued night sounds and the dry heat of the rainless days. Behind him along the black hallways and in the moon-dappled rooms of the house the ancestors stood quite still. He thought of wagons moving in the wide land beneath the towering clouds. He thought of lonely settlements crouching in desolation on the great savannahs of the West. He thought of Emilie.

For the tranquil night was a field where memory strove with memory, and in that silent battle his own heartsick memory prevailed. Like some comfortable parasite he had been content to live on his mother's recollections of days he had never seen. She recounted her bittersweet tales, and he took them for his own. "I want you to carry it all on and never forget it, and I want you to tell it to your children. It's what we are. You must remember it, Sam. You must remember it all." He never dreamed that he could forget. But now Emilie's figure bestrode everything else in his mind. Everyplace he looked on their land, and in the sweep of the valley he saw her image and heard her voice. The past his mother lived to preserve became a confusion of dying echoes falling to dreamy rest beyond a haze of distance. Now, out there beyond the dull gleaming of the river he saw not his mother's past but his own, and they were more different than he ever imagined they could be.

On the first morning, when Emilie came on him in the field, he took a horse and went riding with her through the countryside. He would show her the land, he said with pleased authority. She smiled complacently, and they went off together on the first of many idle jaunts through the greening valley.

Spring came early that year. From almost that first morning the air turned soft and fragrant a little after dawn with only a suggestion of departing chill, and there was no hint of the terrible drought to come. They rode easily and talked of unimportant things, and he observed her closely, saw that she was tall and awkward. She was loose-jointed like a child and flopped with the motion of her horse. His mother always said that the first rule in riding a horse was to keep the backbone stiff, but if Emilie knew the principle she happily ignored it. Still there was a beauty to her.

That first day they went down the valley to a place called Grizell's Store. There was a tavern there, and Sam had coffee made for them, and they sat at an oak table by the window and watched the irregular traffic pass on the pike. The room where they sat was dark and comfortable, and the sky in the upper half of the window was solid blue. It all made for a quiet and comfortable appreciation of the world, and they sat for a while looking out, arms folded and elbows resting on the table, talking in random spurts of thought.

The keeper of the tavern was named Eaton, and his wife was large and red-faced, talkative and cheerful, with plump, pink arms. She came breezing out of the kitchen to meet Emilie. The two women smiled at each other warmly over Sam's nervous introductions, and Mrs. Eaton said, "Sam, you don't know how glad I am to see you courting. It's time you courted." And she said to Emilie, "He's a good boy, Miss. A little on the quiet side, but them's a good kind. My man Floyd is that way, and there ain't a solider man in the country. I hope you young folks come back. You stay as long as you like, you hear?"

Her invitation was almost a command, and she looked at Sam in merry boldness. Her burst of intimate hope embarrassed him. He could feel his face turn red. When Mrs. Eaton had vanished into the kitchen again, he made a faltering apology. Yet he was pleased at what she had said. And Emilie was pleased. She laughed at him for his apology. She held her coffee cup with both hands, and her blue eyes twinkled at him over the white crockery. "She's very sweet," she said. "People are so nice here."

So in that artless way, their spring began. Afterward it became a regular thing, their riding together. Something they lightheartedly agreed on that first day and then accepted as something they would do every day. They rode up the season as day trailed in on languid day, ranging here and there throughout the valley, and they began to have breakfast together in taverns like the Eaton place and others scattered in villages around Bourbonville. Around them the spring came on in a splendor of sunny mists and gentle warmth. The air grew sweet with sunlight and the smell of growing life.

It looked to be a good year. Everybody said it and read signs to prove it. Women talked flowers and laid aside their quilting. Men packed themselves into town on Saturday mornings and whittled and spat and talked and felt themselves to be very wise and prosperous. The peach trees sprang into pink bloom, and almost miraculously the bees appeared droning from their winter's sleep. The woods were sprayed with patches of dogwood, and one day the martins came back and possessed their gourd nests. It was good luck to have a colony of martins on the place, and there were martins darting all through the valley, and it did indeed look to be a good year.

For Sam everything became more intense. The hard, smooth feel of the brass doorknob on his palm when he went out at dawn. The clean smell of the cool morning air as he walked toward the barn. The quiet novelty of the unused day. The peculiar expectancy with which he looked for Emilie's blond head near the green river where they met. Even the scrape of sound the horse made when the iron-shod hoofs moved down the lane which wound through the fields toward their meeting place.

He tried to explain it to her. They were always trying to put things into words, as if by doing that they could better understand what was happening to them. Or perhaps to make what was happening more real and more enduring. So on this day they were cantering their horses side by side and talking above the hoofbeats, and he tried to tell her how the world had opened up to him. And she said in that exuberant, admiring way of hers, "Why, you're a *poet!*" There was a special wonder to her voice when she said that, a happy surprise at something unexpectedly and freshly discovered. In that instant he half believed her. It was a sharp little moment, and he knew that the memory would always be there in his brain, as if framed in glass, the words sculptured somehow out of air: "Why, you're a poet!"

But there was a darkness in it all. He could see that from the first. He thought, in looking back, that he had sensed the hopelessness on that very first day. Each day behind the facade of their joy, the hopelessness deepened just a little. It was like an indistinct spot, only faintly seen at first, but darkening gradually until it drank up all the brightness. Now the shadow hung over the memories.

He managed to put a discipline on himself because he did have work to do. He was always back home by ten in the morning. But this year, for the first time, he had to do some of his spring plowing by moonlight. Occasionally she came out there with him, and for a little while they would stand talking and looking up at the glittering sky. He came in late, humming as usual, happy in the balmy dark. He washed himself before the kitchen windows, which were thrown open onto the melodious night. And then to bed.

Inevitably on those evenings his mother stood holding a candle for him at the head of the stairs. With one hand she kept her long robe clasped about her. With the other she held the candle aloft so that its soft light spilled over the steps and lighted his way. It lighted also the hard lines of disapproval in her face.

At first he laughed at her admonitions, patted her affectionately, and kissed her goodnight with a bantering good nature unusual for him. But that did not soften the frown in her face. And eventually he went off to bed in a weir of guilt and hope and fell into sleep thinking with surprise that his mother was aging. She was still what she had been, but . . . And there was something hard and somehow unforeseen about the set of her jaw and the look of her eyes.

But he was up again when the sunlight came brimming over the edge of the world. His worrying doubt of the night was dissipated by the new morning, and his mother's stern glance seemed less important. Still, it lingered in the back of his mind.

He took to dividing the mornings up into halves and quarters. At eight or thereabouts he would say morosely to himself and sometimes to Emilie: "Today it is half over." She laughed at him for that. At first she did not understand. And there were times when they sat in the grass on the slope of a hill somewhere and idly watched the day rise, holding hands. He felt the warm texture of her skin, the light resting of her fingers in his, the brush of the cool grass under their hands. All they were, enfolded in a snug embrace of feeling. And it would strike him that this solid present was passing away and that it would be gone and that perhaps he would yearn all the rest of his life for the return of this careless moment. He did not share these thoughts with her. He brooded over them by himself.

For the truth was he was afraid to share them. Very early after they realized they were in love, she told him that she knew he would let her go when the time came. She could see the way things were. He denied her quiet charge. He protested the power of his love with quiet vehemence and sincerity and ardor, and he swore on his honor. "It will work out. You wait and see!" He hammered the words down and looked as firmly at her as the hero in a Walter Scott novel, and sometimes he persuaded himself of his own gallantry to the point that he wished he had a picture of himself the way he looked at that moment. So he could not admit his brooding. That would have confirmed her doubts. Then there would be no pretense left, no illusion, no enchantment—only the barren ribs thrust skyward from the skeleton of a love affair.

In time they kissed. The first time startled them both. It was a wonder ever afterward when they talked about it. A confirmation of something. A sudden, breathless seal of a unique attachment. It passed quickly, but later on it filled hours of their meandering talk and days of their thoughts. He never forgot it. The memory remained so strong in him that at times, years later, he felt foolish about it and wondered at such innocence which could make a kiss so overwhelming.

It was very early on a Sunday morning. All the land was calm, and the valley lay in the clear air, open like a hymnbook, and they were climbing a low hill through a woods along a narrow road. They were side by side, talking on horseback. At first their legs brushed slightly against one another. Then again, a longer brushing, and they were closer. Her body, his body against one another. Their words began to break up in their throats, and abruptly they fell into a self-conscious and expectant silence. He never quite knew how he kissed her or how they both knew at the same time that they would kiss, how the sudden inspiration prepared them both for what came.

He only remembered the way that waiting silence came on, how he clumsily and haltingly reached for her, and how she eagerly came to him. He remembered that while their mouths were pressed together, while their eyes were closed and she embraced his neck and he felt the warm flesh of her arms around him, he could hear the hollow, far-off ringing of a cowbell, throaty and peaceful on the morning calm. He remembered how his whole body trembled. And he remembered also the rich, wet taste of her mouth and the way that all their past and all their future were there with them in that compressed instant. All that and the fact that he wanted to say something beautiful to mark the moment, could think of nothing, and so kissed her again and again.

She was afraid of death, as he was. That made her begin to understand a little about dividing the morning up. At least she understood in a general way how he hated to let dear things go. And she had a conviction about herself . . .

"I know I'll die by the time I'm twenty-seven years old," she said. "It's something I've always been sure of."

"You shouldn't say things like that," he said.

She paused at the edge of a bleak thought. "To think that it all *ends!*"

He took up her thought silently and wrestled it over in his mind, and then he slowly nodded. "Yes, sometimes in the middle of something I'm doing, something that takes a lot of work . . . I'll be feeling good. Like I could work the world down. And I'll think, 'I'm going to die.' Just like that! I think about my father, you see, and the way he died, so suddenly, and I'll think that *I'm* going to die, and . . . And it makes me afraid."

"The same thing happens to me," she said in a start of recognition. "The *very* same thing. Sometimes right now I'll be in church, and that awful preacher will be shouting at us, and everybody is sitting around nodding. But I'll be thinking about how hard the seat is, and I'll think, 'The hard seat is really what life is!' That's what I'm doing most of the time I'm in church—looking around at the people and thinking this is really what life is and that we're all going to die. Do you believe the preacher? I don't see how anybody could believe him."

"Well, it's hard *not* to believe when he's shouting at us the way he does."

"I think he's talking to himself," she said quietly. "He tells us about hell and all that stuff, but I think he's talking to himself."

"He saw a lot in the War. I guess it made him like he is. You know what they say about him?"

"He rode with Quantrill. You've told me all about it."

"If it's true, he saw a lot."

"You don't know that it's true. It's something somebody said."

Sam sighed. "But if it *is* true he saw a lot, and it made him different. That's what makes him a preacher anyway. He's different from the rest of us."

"So you have to be inhuman to be a preacher. You have to hate."

The youth shook his head wearily. "He was good to my mother when my father died. I remember the way he came to see her. Several times. They talked in the kitchen." He fell to his recollections. "It was good of him. He doesn't do that kind of thing much."

"I don't know about that. All I know is that there's something . . . Something wrong!"

He laughed to dismiss the subject. The laughter had a little twitting to it, a gentle mockery, and he hugged her and caressed her, and finally made her laugh too. But later the preacher would come back to them. All dark and spectral, a monstrous presence inserted like a snake in the garden of their happiness.

But for the moment there was a great light and only a small shadow, and that one blot of darkness was his mother. She seemed slim and manageable. But she was indomitable. Throughout all the stress that came afterward she won her victory without ever raising her voice.

She saw Emilie for the first time in church. The girl's strange, distant father and her grimly reticent mother came to the Baptist Church because there was no Lutheran Church in the valley. Emilie said her father was spellbound by Mr. Bazely. Emilie's father seemed to take an interest in the preacher like the interest he might have had for some exotic clock with strangely functioning works. Anyway, they came, on the next day after Sam had passed his first clumsy words with Emilie in town, before he even knew her name, and that is where his mother saw them for the first time. Of course, afterward, people gathered around them in a cordial and embarrassed murmuring of welcome, and hands were shaken, and names were exchanged. But Sarah Beckwith was in a hurry to get to the graveyard, and she pulled Sam away.

On the way to the Methodist cemetery, she sat on the wagon seat with a wandering, abstracted mind and mused over the girl's appearance and the bearing of her father and mother. "What an odd-looking girl she is. She's so *tall*. I've never *seen* a girl so tall! Such strange people. Do you think they'll stay here, Sam? I *guess* it would be all right, but you know they really don't belong. I don't think they'd be happy. To think of having real foreigners here in Bourbonville!" There was already a premonition of worry around her thoughtful eyes.

So he was prepared, in a way, for her reaction when he told her about their first ride through the countryside. His account became an apology of sorts. He ended by recounting his meeting with Emilie and their jaunt together as something casual and unimportant. All the time his voice was affecting calm detachment, his mind was racing ahead to the next day when he would see her again. His mother smiled warmly at him and saw through his deceit. He tried to keep up the fiction of unconcern. He said she wasn't really strange, that she was a perfectly natural girl. He said, with a laugh, that he liked to be with her.

His mother was condescending and gentle. "Well, of course I understand you had a good time. I haven't forgotten what it is to be young. There's always something attractive about a new face. You just have to forgive me, Sam, but you are my only son. I've lived my whole life for you since your dear father died." She laughed softly. "I hate to admit it, but I don't like it because they're Germans. It's *very* foolish, but when her father talks it gives me a chill. I've heard that some of the worst atrocities committed against our boys in the war were by German mercenaries."

"Mother, her family wasn't even here then! They were still in Germany!"

"I know, Sam. Don't smile like that. You look so *superior.* You shouldn't act superior around your mother, Sam dearest."

"You shouldn't judge them until you've met them."

"I'm sorry. I can't help the way I feel. You have feelings you can't help, and so do I."

He tried to laugh away her prejudices. She herself treated them so lightly at first that he thought he must succeed. The things she said seemed so unrealistic to him. But behind her misgivings about Emilie lay her own memories and her imaginings of days gone and lost. She was given to talking about the girl and to lapsing almost without transition into reminiscence about the past. "I think about you and what I want for you—what I want for *us*—and I think about all the things our men fought for. *Purity,* Sam! Don't dismiss it. They fought for a certain *purity.* Oh Sam, it was a noble thing. The noblest thing anybody ever dreamed of. It makes me want to cry when I think you never can see what I've seen. I remember how grand it was to see them go off to war. It still sends chills down my spine when I think of our flag going by and the bands playing. All we can do now is hold on to what's left to us and try to be true to things. We have to be true to those people who died, Sam. Can't you understand, Sam dear? I have my responsibilities. A responsibility *to* you and *for* you and for all the things my family loved. I wouldn't be living up to my responsibility if I didn't care about the girls you saw. Please try to understand. Please."

Such were his mother's thoughts. Out of them came her swelling disapproval. Of course she had to know he was seeing the girl every morning. It was useless even to try to keep the thing secret, and there was a long time—two weeks or three—when they hardly spoke a word to each other. His mother knew that he and Emilie were ranging into the ridges and along the river and as far afield as Sweetwater, twelve miles away. Gossipy women came riding in to tell her what they or their men had seen and in the telling, perhaps, to catch some glint of thought, some expression, which would tell them what was going to happen. At first she only laughed and dismissed the whole episode as a youthful fancy which would pass. She went about in her firm, uplifted dignity and was as good to her son as she could be. Only they did not talk much. There was so little to say.

But then she seemed to take stock of the situation and reconsider her tactics. One night she floated to where he sat, deep in thought, in a chair before his father's picture. Kneeling in front of him, she took his face in her two soft hands and with her eyes near his looked tenderly at him. Her expression was love and devotion, tinted with hurt. "Sam, I think that girl has come between a mother and her son." He pulled back, and she let her hands drop, but she remained kneeling before him and looking at him, seeking his eyes with her own.

"It's beginning to worry me, Sam. The things people are saying! Suellen MacComber was here today. She said people in town are expecting a *wedding* soon! Oh Sam, I didn't know what to say. But people are talking."

"Does it matter what they say?"

"Yes, it does matter," she said dropping her smile and letting her voice grow fierce. "I don't like it."

"I'm sorry."

She smiled again. "I told Suellen I thought you were riding around with that girl just because you felt sorry for her."

"Mother!"

"Please don't look that way, Sam. I sincerely believe it's the truth. You may not realize it yourself, but I know what kind of boy you are. You're so kind, and the girl's from a long way off, and at first you were attracted to her. But now you see how different she is from us, from you, Sam, and you can't tell her. I think you want to break off with her, and you hate to hurt her feelings."

"Mother, mother." He smiled in amused exasperation.

"Please, please don't look at me that way, Sam. It's so *degrading* to me. I'm just a feeble woman. You need a father. How I wish your dear father was alive! *He* could talk with you. And you'd listen to him. But believe me, Sam, I knew him almost as well as I know myself, and I know he'd agree with me. You'd get the same advice from his lips that you are getting from mine right now. Oh Sam, I'm *counting* on you. Without you I don't have any future, and the past would be all silly and useless. I'm getting old. I know I am, and every line you see in my face is because of the care I have taken of you. When your dear father died, you were all I had to live for, and if it hadn't been for you I don't think I *could* have lived. I think I could have killed myself. That's a terrible thing to say, but you don't know how much I loved your father.

"You don't know a *thing* about that girl! You're so young and innocent that you can't judge people the way I can. She may seem nice. But it's so *easy* for a girl to *seem* nice. You have to know a girl for a long time before you can know whether she *is* nice. You have to know her family. No, I'm not going to say a bad thing about her. But you know I'm right. You *know* I'm right."

He was overwhelmed by the devoted power of her attack, the flashing look in her desperate eyes, and the physical pressure of her body leaning in on him. He nearly pushed her onto the floor in his struggle to get out of the chair. Then he walked back and forth, pacing in an abstracted way until his eyes fell on the stolid face of his father looking out of the solemn picture. He stopped and pointed at it and blurted out: "You didn't know *him* well! If your father had been alive, he wouldn't have *let* you marry him!"

It was as if he had slapped her. She had remained on her knees. But now she stood gracefully up and glared at him in almost complete discomposure. She was angry and hurt and shocked, and she could barely control her breaking voice. "Then you are trying to compare *me* with *her!* I see. I see what you think of *me*. Or are you trying to insult your father? He was the dearest, sweetest, kindest man on earth, and everybody who saw him loved him the moment he came. You go into town and ask! Just *ask!* Everybody thought of him the way *I* did! *Everybody*. There wasn't a soul in this county who ever believed a bad thing about your father. Not a soul. And let me tell you something, young man. Just hear me out! You cannot say that about this girl! You ask. If you dare, just *ask!* They'll tell you. Nobody trusts her. *Nobody!* She's different, and how you can carry on this way with a girl people don't trust is . . . is more than I can *see! I* couldn't have done it. *I* couldn't have married your father if I'd thought people felt the same way about him they feel about this *German* girl. To *think* you'd drag her name in with your father's! It's . . . It's so *wrong!*" And with that she swept up to her bedroom trailing the frenzied hurt of her injury like the long train of a diaphanous garment, and he was left alone in his guilt and regret before the stern, unblinking picture on the wall. Over it all a jagged astonishment. He had never seen his mother lose her self-control. But her response to his stinging remark was almost hysteric. It *was* hysteric.

He thought his mother saw Emilie as a rival to his father's memory. Later he understood how utterly wrong he was about that. But at the time this was the most plausible explanation he could think of for his mother's resistance. The most striking thing about his mother was the firm loyalty she bore his father after all these long years as a widow. That devotion made people in the valley worship her. People treated her with reverence and a little warm pride in themselves. For here in *their* midst lived this woman who was the living remnant of the Lost Cause. As long as she lived on in her quiet love, no one could really believe that the fight had been in vain. And wonder of wonders, her power was such that even some of those men who had worn the blue thought, when they saw her pass, that they might have been wrong. There was no one like her to embody *their* cause, and in the quiet glory falling from her devoted life, their own side seemed, to some of them, to diminish and fall to canker and rust.

Somehow Emilie with her curious and unfamiliar ways, her sturdy joy and exuberance, was an abrasion on the surface of those roseate memories and delicate accents. Sam should fall in love, but with someone his father would approve of, someone who would fit better into the memories and the dreams of his mother and all her household of past witnesses. He knew that. Somehow Emilie did not match that past.

He thought he could see his mother's fears in the endless, hopeless conversations he had with her in the days that followed the outburst of that evening. He would be making some attempt to reason down her resistance, and she would be piecing out her gentle but inflexible remonstrance. And suddenly she would break off the conversation about the girl and sink into a trance of talk about Samuel Beckwith the Elder and the Dead.

"Oh Sam, you used to clap your hands when he came in from the fields at night. I remember it like yesterday. Just like this morning. You would hear him whistling in the yard (your father was always whistling), and you would run to the door and clap your little hands, and I have never *seen* the expression of joy on a child's face. Rapture, that's what it was. Pure rapture! All innocence and joy. You would smile your eyes almost shut, and your father would pick you up and kiss you, and you would cling to him with arms and legs. It was a wonderful thing. I can't even describe it. Every spring I think of the days he used to work late over the plowing and come in just when the sun had set. He was so happy then. And I was happy. I used to stand in the kitchen and watch you both and think that everything in my life had worked itself out and all was well. And I used to imagine how happy my people would be if they could only *know!* My father especially. He thought everything was over when we lost Matthew, and it wasn't. It wasn't.

"And then your father was dead! I still almost cry sometimes to think about it, about you then. You used to ask me all the time when your daddy was coming home. It was *years* before you really understood. You'd be sitting at the supper table, and you'd look at me and say, 'Mamma, is Daddy *really* not coming back *ever*?' And you'd stand here in the door and look out toward the barn, and I would know you were secretly waiting to hear him come whistling up from work. He was so real to us he just *couldn't* be dead. But finally you'd have to give up and go off to bed, and sometimes you'd cry out for him in your sleep. Oh Sam, I don't see how I lived through those nights! I'd bury my head in my pillow and cry so you couldn't hear me because I thought if you saw me cry it would be more than you could bear, and I thought things would just break up. Sometimes the sky is going to fall in on you like a broken bridge, and the only thing that holds the sky up is your *will* not to cry. At least not in public. I used to wonder what I had done to make God angry with me." She laughed with a sigh of wondering recollection. "It was sinful to think that way, but it was a hard time, and I think God understands our weakness.

"But the worst part of all was when you would see other little boys and girls with their fathers. You and your father had *so* much fun together. I remember how you looked at the little Atcheley boy after church. His father used to pick him up and put him into their wagon. They were always laughing together, the way your father laughed with you. Horace Atcheley was a good father. You wouldn't say a word. Not a word. You would just stand there and look at them both and fold your hands together. That's all. Not even a sigh. It nearly broke my heart. I got to the place where I hated for you to see other fathers. I wanted to put my arms around you and hide you whenever I saw a father with his son. But I couldn't do that. You had to see, and you had to try to understand why your own dear father would never come back again.

"And Sam, I promised your father over and over in my prayers that I wouldn't let you forget him. I told him I would keep his memory alive, and I have! But now, what can I do when you lose your head over a girl you don't even really know? A foreign girl. Your father would grieve, Sam. He really would. You're forgetting your love for him. I have the sense to see that, if you don't. And it's out of my hands. I see that, too. It's out of my hands."

Her voice melted into a melancholy sigh of offended helplessness. On those occasions there was nothing Sam could do. Nothing, that is, except to give up with a weary shrug of his shoulders and slip out into the yard for fresh air and relief from the smothering affection and sorrow which his mother draped over him like a winding sheet for the dead.

Finally he asked Emilie to come see his mother. Later he reproached himself for that, as he did for so many things. He believed it had been an act of abject weakness. And Emilie refused at first. While he pleaded with her, she sat—not frigidly—but coolly detached and said he had to make his own decision. There was nothing she could do, she said, if he didn't do the only thing he *could* do, which was to tell his mother flatly and finally the way things were going to be. "A woman likes to be told things by a man," she said. "If you beg, a woman likes to refuse. Your mother will give in without another word if you march in and tell her how things are going to be." She added, ironically: "Your mother will get used to me. I can be a good servant around the house. She might even love me some of these days."

And sometimes when Emilie talked like that, resolution took hold of him. He would decide, and he would set his shoulders and his face. But in a little while the soft memory of his mother's ancient sadness would settle over him. He could not free himself from its folds. He felt imprisoned by her love, tangled up in her devotion, and he felt also that Emilie was asking him to do something that was not really right. He couldn't just destroy his mother after all she had done for him. So he kept on begging *her* to say something on their behalf, and reluctantly she gave in and came.

But it did no good. His mother received them in the great parlor. She even hugged Emilie, and for a moment both women stood beaming at each other through shining eyes, and afterward they had tea. It was hot, served out of a silver pitcher, one of the treasures of the house, and the two women and the youth sat painfully fastened to the little white cups, and the talk flowed like glue in which everyone felt mired down and uncomfortable.

His father was a witness to the proceedings. The somber eyes looked out of the youthful face onto Samuel Beckwith the Younger during all that difficult interview. Sam looked hopelessly back at the face there. He tried to snatch some laughing word of encouragement from the light-struck memories he retained from the world where his father had lived. But nothing came. Only a far-off rustle of forgotten things like something moving in the dark so stealthily that you only sense its presence. His mother spoke for both the living and the dead, and the word she spoke was a refusal.

It was all bathed in remorse and held aloft on the cushion of loving grief on which all her jewel-like decisions reposed. She was genuinely vexed. "I don't want to be mean," she said. "We just don't *know* you, my dear. You may be the finest girl in the world, and I hope you are. And you know, if you two insist on getting married, why, there's nothing I can do to stop you. You could run off, or you could get it done right here in the county, and I couldn't do a thing about it. I'm just a feeble woman. You can see that. But I cannot give my consent. You are asking me to do something which I cannot do as a mother. You can do what *you* want, but I can only do what I *must*." And she looked intently at them in her own splendid strength. Her eyes were darkly framed by her long hair. They were calm and unflinching.

Sitting alone in the hot dark of his room, the youth pondered the weight of that afternoon, resting as it did on the fragile white cups. The staggering mass of its importance reposing in gloomy stillness on something so flimsy as the teacups. The miracle that the tiny cups did not explode in a tinkling crash of porcelain under the silent pressure of that day. He half reclined in his chair and dropped his chin moodily upon a supporting hand and wondered if the memory of that day would be forever down there in the yard, fighting a noiseless battle for precedence with the other phantom remnants from the past which lurked there. On that day the world outside the house was alive with the songs of birds. There was a blooming fragrance on the sweet air, and the sunlight lay like a gentle arm over the teeming earth, but inside, in the parlor, everything was so strained and tense that Sam felt his own voice constricted in his throat.

Emilie eventually put her cup down, half full. She lifted a hand to block the motion of Sam's mother, who lifted the silver pitcher to pour again. "Don't you like tea, my dear?"

The girl looked startled, started to reach for the cup, but then drew back and murmured, "No, no I really don't."

"I'm so sorry."

So instead of drinking tea, Emilie sat fumbling with the lap of her dress. Sam looked anxiously at her. He expected her to respond with some argument, like a lawyer. But she did not. Instead she nodded slowly as his mother spoke, her own eyes set in deep thoughtfulness. When his mother had finished, she said, "I guess you think I'm strange because I love your son. I realize it is hard for you to think anybody could love him as much as you do."

"Oh my dear, *everybody* loves Sam. I don't think it's strange at all."

The retort, sad and understanding as it was, robbed Emilie of the point she had been about to make, and she fell back. After a time she gathered herself up again and said: "I can tell you all about myself. It wouldn't be like knowing me. But . . ."

"As you like, my dear." Sarah Beckwith looked at the girl with sympathetic interest.

Emilie looked back at her for a long moment, and Sam could see her hesitate. But then she dropped her eyes to where her hands picked nervously at the cloth of her dress, and she began to talk. A very quiet soliloquy spoken to her own mind more than to anyone else's, a sort of fumbling and picking with the stuff of her life. She began with her birth. From time to time she raised her head, and always his mother sat there, politely returning the girl's glance and listening.

Emilie did not flinch. She did pause when she looked up. It was a momentary thing, a hesitation which was really an end and a new start. Perhaps that is why her story was finally a chaos of things fetched out of her memory and strewn across the invisible plain which separated her from Sarah Crittendon Beckwith. She talked about growing up, moving, her father. She spoke of how uncomfortable he must have been in his blue Prussian uniform, and she recoiled only slightly when Sam's mother remarked that the Yankee Army had worn blue.

She told about the countryside and the sky in the north of Germany, the cleanliness of Flensburg, and the way people went about all bundled up in the wintertime. Ice skating there with people trailing vaporous breath across the frozen waters and sounds themselves so thin and delicate that they might have been carved out of the most fragile ice.

She talked about the ocean voyage, the ship, the wind whipping through the rigging at night when she and her father walked on deck, the great belching of gritty black smoke thrown out like a storm over the Atlantic. "I wondered where the smoke went," she said with a quiet laugh. "I was a little girl, you see, and I thought it was so lonely for the smoke to have nowhere to go, nothing to do but to fall into the sea so far away from people and life. And I used to wonder how much smoke it would take to fill the sea up. I thought that if boats went over the sea for millions of years, all the water would silt up and be like oatmeal."

His mother laughed with the girl's smiling reminiscence. It was a sweet and sympathetic laugh, like water gently bubbling at a rocky spur in the bank of a river.

And Emilie went on and on. The same trivial things. Disconnected memories, becoming more scattered and chaotic as the moments slipped by and her account of herself lengthened. It bothered Sam. He sat restlessly listening and watched her. She seemed to have passed into her own insulated world like one in a trance of speaking. In it she did not notice his discomfort. He wanted now to end the whole thing as decently as he could and to get them both out into the open air and away from his mother. *She's making a bad impression.* The thought was painful and irritating, and it made Sam impatient and almost angry. He wanted Emilie to show his mother how much like any normal girl she was. Instead she was showing how distant she was, how far removed from all the girls anyone in the valley had ever known. Sitting there as the afternoon softened in the tawny descent of the sun, he made a disquieting discovery. Emilie was more different than even he had dreamed.

And not only different but perhaps superior. Frowning, he entertained the glum suspicion that this was what Emilie was trying to prove. Confronted by his mother's unbending pride of family, the girl was seeking to demonstrate a pride of her own. She was saying to Sam's mother, "You may have read about these things, but I know them. You will never know them as I do. You will never even imagine what they are. But I know them all, young as I am, and I do not have to stoop and kiss your feet."

So in the end he was relieved that she stopped, for she did stop at last, and they went out together. He left his mother's serene strength with something close to an apology. "Well, we must be getting back. It's getting late. Mother has her work to do. I'll ride you to the pike, Emilie." He spoke with forced nonchalance. A strained, disappointed, and woeful conclusion to his great hope.

His mother went with them to the door. She stood for a moment on the porch and spoke tenderly to the girl. She looked directly into Emilie's eyes when she spoke. "You are a *remarkable* girl, and *so* smart! I know you cannot understand my feeling. But I would be dishonest with myself if I said I approved of your marrying my son. I have to be true to some things." She swept an encompassing and lordly hand out over space. "I was left this land as a trust. You must *try* to understand." Her eyes shone with pride and triumph. Sam saw both moods and admired them even as something else inside him settled to despair. And as they rode out on the lane together his first words were in admiration of his mother. "She's a great woman. It's like she says. You have to try to understand what she's been through."

Emilie glared angrily back at him and fought with her tears. But she could not contain them or herself. She broke into loud, wracking sobs. Her long face was contorted with rage and grief. "I don't understand . . . I can't see . . ." She bit her lip, not daring at once to say anything more. But Sam looked at her so pensively and in such self-doubt and wonder that her anger boiled over: "You're just like jelly! All you have to do is a simple thing, and you won't do it because you're just like jelly with her. I don't know if I love you or not!" And without looking at him again, without waiting for response or explanation, apology or recrimination, she kicked her horse violently with both her long legs and left him sitting there. He did not try to follow her. He watched her horse pound away, bearing her around a bend in the road where a copse of trees hid her from view.

He got up from his chair and for a moment longer stood gazing out into the night where the flooding moonlight poured silently over the great world. Only the subdued warbling of the insects disturbed the baking silence, and the trees beyond the lawn and on the moonstruck ridge across the river stood gaunt and still in the tropical heat. He felt ashamed. That and the heat nearly suffocated him, and he wanted to cry out for relief. But he only frowned in the dark and slipped noiselessly back to his bed and lay down to an uneasy sleep.

5

THOMAS BAZELY paced the floor of the single room of his cabin and fought the fantasies of the night. Outside, the enormous moon shone on the trim fields and neat fences, onto the thick woods standing like a dark wall near the house, and flooded through the window on the southern side and slid a yellow smear of light across the floor. It was past midnight. Still he paced fearfully back and forth, and still the boards rumbled in complaint at his frantic step, and he could not compose himself to go to bed. Mr. Bazely strove with torment.

Torment because of sin, his ancient sin which would not lie down in the dark and be forgot. The most terrifying mystery of his life was this mystery of sin—how sin committed in an instant, without thought, without premeditation, could like some accidental battle stamp itself in stone and remain forever for God to read. And God's devil was there to remind Thomas Bazely of that sin which God now read like a report commanding attention.

The face of John Wesley Campbell leered at him from the dark, and Mr. Bazely started back from the apparition in terror. Judas Wretched Criminal! The beast portending God's judgment on the world, the beast which stood as the incarnation of the futility of striving, the beast who jeered and mocked and threatened and damned. Cloudy horsemen riding down the roaring sea. And I stood upon the sand of the sea, and saw a beast rise out of the sea, having seven heads and ten horns, and upon his horns ten crowns, and upon his heads the name of blasphemy. And I saw one of his heads as it were wounded to death; and his deadly wound was healed; and all the world wondered after the beast. And they worshipped the dragon which gave power unto the beast; and they worshipped the beast, saying, Who is like unto the beast? who is able to make war with him?

Thomas Bazely was not able. After all these years, that was

finally clear. The beast must control an invisible web reaching from man to man in the valley, where people moved in concert to the beast's will, and all that will was directed against the striving of Thomas Bazely, and it was more than one lone man could bear, and he was enmeshed in the web and on his way to being drowned in perdition. To him that overcometh will I grant to sit with Me in My throne, even as I also overcame . . . But Thomas Bazely was enmeshed in the web and could not overcome. And I saw the woman drunken with the blood of the saints . . . The supreme irony—the woman *he* had killed, drunk with his blood; years and years afterward her spirit was intoxicated on the fiery blood which coursed through his tormented brain.

It was in Kansas, and he remembered every stark detail as if it had happened last night. Red flames shot upward from a blazing town, and horsemen charged demonlike through the fire. Shouting and gunfire, an occasional wild scream, and as a backdrop to the swirling motion the hellish flames went roaring up into the sky's black mouth. He went to rob a house of food for his troops and found the woman. She was crouching there in the dark and whimpering like a frightened child—not crying aloud, but whimpering—and he heard that faint sound and went to investigate because he thought it might *be* a child, and he was touched and wanted to steer the child to safety.

But there was the woman, wrapped in her bed clothes, whimpering, and looking at him with those large, soft eyes which were imploring and sensuous in the reflected glare from the fire outside. Where was her husband, or her father? Where was *some*one to protect her, to protect *him*—Thomas Bazely—who all at once realized that he could do something, and in the realizing he knew an irresistible compulsion which drove him on to do what he could do, what he *must* do. No retribution, he thought. Nothing and no one could pursue him. He and the woman were alone in this strange enclave of calm and sheltering obscurity in the midst of a storm of violence. He was strong, and she was helpless.

And did the woman perhaps *want* him to do what he wanted? That thought taunted him through the years. With it came the conjecture that he should have spoken to her, reassured her so that both of them might have relished the wild abandon of the secret liberty granted them by a war neither of them had caused. Did she not have the same sudden desire for lusty fulfillment that possessed him? For when she saw him she fell into an absolute silence. She was silent while he came pacing into the room. She was silent when he stood over her bed. She was silent while one by one he removed the blankets she had clasped around herself, silent when he stripped off her gown, lifting it above her head, over her unresisting arms, silent when he felt the soft, uplifted tenderness of her breasts, silent when he stroked the yielding lips of her moist and secret flesh. Only when he forced her legs apart so that he could enter that sweet mystery did she scream. Sobbing and gasping and shrieking in hysteric alarm, she guarded herself with her frantic hands and struggled with him. Her piercing cries rang out through the night and sounded above the turmoil of the fighting. The sound rose to an insane crescendo like a trumpet blasted into his head an inch away from his ear, a trumpet summoning others to come and see, and it nearly drove him mad.

So he killed her. He did not plan to kill her. All he wanted to do was choke the screaming off, for if he did not he would start raving himself, and if once he started he knew he would never stop. So he killed her and left her body to be consumed by fire. He went rushing off from his crime to hide with the galloping horsemen, his comrades, his friends. He thought he could hide from the thing which nobody on earth knew but himself and the woman, and she was dead. Only later did the dreadful horror overtake him. He never could hide. He could not fight the beast, and he could not escape retribution for what he had done. His life became a hopeless quest for his redemption, invariably frustrated and mocked, and tonight at last he knew the full dimension of his ruin.

Through the years hope departed from him in swells, like a receding tide. First there was defeat. The splendid hopes collapsed in catastrophe. The band, or what was left of it, was dissipated to the four winds—outlaws. He wandered in lonely fear, afraid even to show his face. In his wandering he saw the sordid thing his life had become in the War, and he saw also the stark horror of the things he had done. He repented. He wept with remorse. He begged God to forgive him. Nothing gave him peace. And then he decided to make himself God's tool. He would preach the Gospel, proclaim God's judgment, pour out the vial of God's wrath on the world. God *must* receive him then. And out of an insignificant chance, he fell upon Bourbonville, and here he stayed.

He did not find peace in Bourbonville, but he did find a vision, and the vision kept hope faintly alive within him. He encountered a woman who incarnated for him the fulfillment of every one of his longings. He loved her the first instant he laid eyes on her. After that first meeting he spent a sleepless night, and in it the conviction grew that if he could only win her love, he could restore the missing thing in his soul. The preaching then became the means he used not just to placate God's wrath but to remain close to her until she decided to love him. And if she loved him, surely God could not reject him. So he strove for her with a relentless, ardent passion, and he prayed God for her with all his might, and he failed. Failed twice with her—failed completely.

When the second opportunity came, he was sure he would succeed. He felt a great peace simply out of his joyful anticipation. He had labored in a superhuman way. God had blessed his labors. It only remained for the woman to say the word he knew she must say, and every patch of darkness in his life would be made bright. It was a glorious sense of relief, and the love which he felt for her was so intense that he vowed to spend his life showing her his gratitude. He would love her so zealously and so selflessly that the feeling she had for him would grow and grow and become as magnificent as the grand feeling burning in his own breast for her. With that would come God's blessing, and he would be like Christian in the *Pilgrim's Progress*, standing erect at last before the cross while the great unleashed burden rolled off behind him and fell into eternal oblivion.

But he lost her the second time too. And because he had expected so much, his defeat was all the more puzzling and bitter. He knew that John Wesley Campbell had somehow conspired in his undoing. It was never clear to him just how it was. He had the prize in his grasp, and it was torn away, and somehow, he thought, Mr. Campbell had had a hand in it. The woman denied it. But now, after the bitter confrontation with her son who had joined with Mr. Campbell against him on this day, he knew that she had lied. In the impotency of his humiliation, a lot of disconnected things fell magically together in his mind, and Thomas Bazely saw the truth about the woman, and he saw the truth about himself.

He should have known, when the dreams went on. There the woman lay, naked and waiting—leering at him amid the dancing red pillars of firelight in the sensuous dark. Twenty years after the War the vivid memory tore at him in his sleep and jolted him into a stuporous, passionate wakefulness. Dear God, he had tried! More than Adam. More than Cain. More than David. Could Paul himself have done more to repent, bloody as he was with the innocent he had slain? But nothing worked for Thomas Bazely. And with the years the face of the woman, which at first bore a look of indistinct generality, became something else. Something which deepened his horror and guilt and made him choke on his tears. The face of the woman in his nightmare became the face of the woman he loved so passionately and so in vain.

And there was no help for him. Nothing could halt his hands when they went to work in his bed at night after his dreams. They were as the swine which the demons possessed in Galilee. They tore at his sinful member, and with each motion of his raging fingers they drove the sweet, mad details of that moment into his frenzied mind until she was there with him in the room again, and he could smell her hot breath, and he was raping her and killing her once more. He could never tell what it was—the raping or the killing—which finally did the thing to him and let his body slump in a wet discharge of release and sent his mind reeling swiftly from relief into torment. Every night he raped her and killed her and fell off at last into a horror of darkness which was his substitute for sleep. Every morning he awoke groaning with remorse and swore to contain his lust.

In the day he and God were co-workers. He forgot his own sins in the brooding contemplation of the sins of Bourbonville. He saw in the placid faces of familiar people disguises of wickedness and premonitions of hell. What were they hiding? He knew that everyone hid something. He could think of "them" as if the radiant sun had cleansed him of all his own impurities. At times when he plodded in the furrow behind his horse and smelled the clean fragance of fresh-plowed earth, he could so thoroughly repent that he *knew* sin could never more have dominion over him. On those occasions he felt a wild joy. It was the joy of conquest, like those times in the War when he had seen the enemy flee after a hard fight which left him, Thomas Bazely, miraculously alive.

But when the light would begin to wash out of the sky and the night creep in from the surrounding forest, a fearful uneasiness would steal upon him. He would light all the lamps and turn the wicks up until the chimneys smoked, and he would gaze fixedly into the flame of the brightest. As the dark swelled and thickened, it swam with eerie shapes, and the fear grew. So on this night he pounded the floor with his bare feet, walking furiously and desperately back and forth through the puddle of moonlight swilled in by the window. He felt the house sway, and beneath the house the foundations of the world trembled. The time was come. Deceit and illusion had fallen away, and the last wave of hope went washing down the barren coasts of his dreams leaving a desert where nothing could remain alive. His hour was at hand.

For years he had expected a miracle to take place before his congregation on Sunday morning. The husband of the slain woman would appear to condemn him. He would be put into the hands of that buffoon of a sheriff, and finally he would be hanged. They would turn out in gaping droves, as they did for hangings, and his last sight on earth would be their triumphant leering. His congregation would watch him hang, and to the rhythm of his choking lungs and the frantic kicking of his bound legs they would sing, "Praise God from Whom All Blessings Flow . . ." Sometimes he suspected that some of them knew already. He pondered their expressions when he preached. Were they not secretly mocking him? Did not Joseph and Pharaoh have their dreams? Could not the God who planted the dream each night in his own mind also insidiously plant it in the minds of a whole congregation at once and reveal his secret to them all? Then all of them would settle gleefully back and wait until reality marched in and brought the dream alive. A patient Nemesis of a husband seeking over the miles and years and finally closing on the mark of his vengeance.

But now he understood that this was not his fate. The congregation did not know. But God knew and had prepared things in Bourbonville just for the coming of Thomas Bazely. God, for His own secret purposes, had predestined Thomas Bazely, late of Kansas, to be damned. Long, long ago, before there was a war, before any human being dreamed of what would come, God set His divine plan in motion, caused people to be born and to move in their carefully directed courses until these crossed in one insignificant town, a place Thomas Bazely had never heard of until the afternoon he rode wearily into it for the first time, a lonely and despairing fugitive. God had carved the actors and arranged the scenery, painted the broadsides of false hope and set up a puppet show where one man must appear—himself a puppet—to complete the play and bring the drama to its climax. And out of all the places on earth where he might have fled, Thomas Bazely came here, to Bourbonville, where God had planned everything in anticipation of his arrival.

Thomas Bazely understood the role he played, small as it was. The knowledge overpowered him. He locked his eyes against the burning moonlight, cried in lonely terror against eternity. The laughter rang in his brain. High above in the cool black gallery of space, God and the hosts of angels were laughing at him. He threw himself onto his bed and wrapped his head in his arms and began to curse bitterly. But the laughter filled the room and drowned his cursing. Every still thing in the night took it up, and the house itself roared with it and shook. God was laughing. The terrible world laughed in echo to its maker. Out there in the dark the jaws of hell opened wide, and hell was laughing in chorus to the laughter of God.

6

I *loved* HIM, SAM. You can never know how much! Never. Never! You're only a boy, and even if you were a man you couldn't know how much a woman can love a man. Even *he* never really knew how much I loved him. I lived every minute to show my love for him. But I think he died without knowing how much I cared for him. Yes, I think he did.

"You see, I was alone. It's a miracle I even had the house. You remember the Robinsons, the old man and his wife? Their house was down there. No, you can't see anything now. But before the War the roof came up through the trees. It was a big house. A *beautiful* house. Well, I stood up here in my own window and watched that house burn! You don't *know* the fear, the loneliness! All up and down the valley you could see houses burning. *Every-where!* And I was here, just waiting for something to happen to me. The niggers were all down in the quarters. They knew I was here by myself. It got so I was afraid to go down there because of the way they looked at me. You could tell what was on *their* minds! And when I quit going down, they quit working. They just *quit!* Try to *imagine* what it was! Sometimes it even escapes me, and I lived through it.

"I knew what the Yankee soldiers had done. Oh, there were some terrible things. I had your grandfather's pistol on the bed, and when the Yankees came for me I was going to shoot myself. Yes, oh yes. I can laugh now. It *is* funny when I look back on it, when I consider what a poor silly little goose I was in those days! But it wasn't funny then. I had *practiced* shooting the pistol so I could blow my brains out. *Imagine!* I think that put the fear of the Lord into the niggers. They heard me shooting that pistol out back. ka-BAM, ka-BAM, ka-BAM—Oh, it made an awful noise. And the niggers didn't know what I was doing. They couldn't understand. I was all alone with only my honor and Yankee soldiers filling the valley until you thought there'd never be an end to them.

"And they came! They rode right up into the yard there. I heard the horses on the road that afternoon before I ever saw them. They came right in *there.* Sometimes I wonder that you can't still see them there! And I walked to the window with the pistol in my hand and the hammer pulled back and with the *muzzle up against the side of my head!* Right *here,* Sam. Oh it's a wonder they didn't kill me the minute they saw the gun in my hand. I called down to them, and I said, 'If anybody sets one foot in this house, I'll blow my brains out, and my blood will be on your hands. The blood of a helpless woman will be on your hands.'

"And I meant it, Sam. I swear before God as my Maker. I swear before the memory of your dear father, I meant it. I still think I would have done it. They could have my life and burn the house, and I couldn't stop them. But they could not have my honor!

"Well, an officer rode out of the rest. Oh, that *was* funny. He was so *young!* He looked like a frightened child before *me,* a defenseless woman. The officer was taken back, I can tell you. *He* was frightened. *I* was calm at that moment, as calm as I have ever been in my life because I *knew* I was doing the right thing. He had a saber in his hand, and he saluted me with it. There *he* was, right down there, holding a saber with the handle drawn up against his chin, and here *I* was, in this *very* window with a loaded pistol in my hand pointed at my head. Oh my! Now it really almost makes me laugh. But I didn't think it was funny then.

"And when this officer could get his breath, he said, 'Lady, be careful!' That was all he could say. 'Lady, be *careful!*' It was *comical!* I was calm. I swear before God I was calm because I was ready to do what was right, and I have never flinched before doing what was right. Don't forget that, Sam. I have never flinched.

"And I said, 'Sir, I am deadly serious. If any of your beastly men touch this house, I shall blow my brains out.' They talked among themselves. I hadn't convinced all of them. They were a very low sort, Samuel. A *very* low sort. Some of them wanted to try a defenseless woman. But the officer knew better. *He* knew how serious I was. I could see him shaking his head at them. *He* knew.

"So then he looked up at me, and he said, 'Lady, don't you worry. We're not going to touch your house. We're not going to bother you. We know you're alone. Now you be careful. We're not going to hurt you.' And with that he led his men out of the yard. You would have thought the yard was going to explode! *Oh,* he went carefully. Down to the quarters. They went down to set the niggers free.

"I didn't even know what they were doing at first. I thought they might try to sneak up on me from behind, through the back door. So I sat here, with the pistol in my lap, waiting. Pretty soon I looked out and saw the niggers running off, and I came here, to this window, and I shouted at them: 'Where in God's name do you think you're going?' And one of them, a little hussy named Pearl shrieked with laughter, and she shouted, 'We's been set free, Miss Sarah. We's all been set free. We ain't gonter be you slaves no mo'. We's all been set free!' The little wretch! I had the pistol in my hand, and I could have killed her, but it would have only been trouble. And that wasn't the worst. Some of them called nasty things at me. I won't repeat the things they said. I wouldn't dirty my mouth. But do you know something, Samuel? It was a blessing. I was glad to see them go. When they shouted at me, I realized how terrible they were. It was a relief to see them go.

"*George* stayed. You know that. The old fool! He didn't have much sense, but he knew enough to know he wasn't going to get anything out of this freedom business. He knew it was a bunch of foolishness as far as the niggers were concerned. I have to give him credit for that and the way he helped out while you were growing up. That didn't stop him from being an old fool, but he was a good nigger. He knew his place. I'm grateful to him. You know for weeks he slept in a blanket down there on the front porch with a loaded shotgun on the floor beside him. I was always expecting the old fool to roll over on the thing and blow his head off. I expected every night to wake up to a bang. Yes, it was a good thing for us that he stayed. But it was good for him, too. You mustn't forget that. He didn't have anywhere else to go. I don't think he gave us any more than we gave him.

"So we lived through the rest of the War, George and I. From the late summer of 'sixty-three to April of 'sixty-five when your father came.

"Oh Sam, I'll never forget it. *Never.* When I think of it after all these years it seems a miracle that it happened. It *was* a miracle. There were so many people on the road. I slept every night with the loaded pistol under the pillow. We even got a dog. I never liked dogs, but that's why we had Jiggs when you were a child. George got him so he'd smell prowlers. And we did the best we could. We tried to help our own men. So many of them, getting home the best way they could. I thought they were like your Uncle Matthew, and we let them sleep down in the quarters and shared what little we had. Turnips and sweet potatoes mostly. I can't stand turnips and sweet potatoes to this day because we ate so many of them then. No milk. The Yankee soldiers took away almost all the cows.

"And your father came in one afternoon. Old Mr. Kirby brought him up in the back of a wagon because he was lying along the road, too sick to walk any more. Sam, he had big rags tied around his shoes to hold them together, and his feet were bloody. He had a piece of little rope run through his pants for a belt. And he stank! Dear boy, how he stank! He was one of our poor boys, and I made myself do what I had to do. But I didn't think it'd do any good. He couldn't even talk, he was so tired. All he could do was lie there and follow me with his eyes. I think every bone in his body must have been showing through his skin, and when I put my hand on his head I thought it would scald me. The minute I looked at him, I began thinking about how we'd get his grave dug. I didn't think he'd live through that first night.

"And if it hadn't been for me he would have died. We all expected him to die. And I guess I never would have thought much about him. He'd be buried hereabouts somewhere, and I'd pass his grave and think to myself, *Oh yes, that was the one who died. I wonder what he was like.* It was that close. But I took care of him, and thanks to me he lived. He owed his life to me. He knew it. Your father wasn't a man to forget things like that.

"We never did let the travelers sleep in the house. You never could tell. But we brought your father in and made a bed on the floor in the kitchen. The stove was down there, you see, and I had this silly idea that if you were going to have a sick man in the house, you needed to have him close to hot water. George and I took turns looking after him. I sat up at night and put wet towels on his head until the fever broke, and then I fed him with my own hands. Soup. Awful soup! Made out of turnips! Dear Sam, you can be thankful you've never had a spoonful of turnip soup in your life! But I should be thanking God. It brought him through. He got his strength back little by little. It was so slow you could hardly see it, but it came back.

"And then we fell in love! I can't explain that. It's always an accident, I suppose. You don't plan to fall in love with anybody, and you never can explain it. I didn't even think about wanting to fall in love with anybody. Only he was so helpless. A big, strong man, and he was like a baby because of the hunger and the fever! I brought him back from death you might say, and I fell in love with him. He fell in love with me, too. He was a very gentle man, Sam. When he was sick I thought that was the reason for it, his gentleness. But when he got better I saw that it wasn't. It was his nature. Oh he laughed all the time, and that's what people around here remember. He could tell stories all day and all night, and he'd have people rolling on the floor. But underneath it he was gentle. And I loved him for that, and he loved me.

"He said he'd come all through the War thinking that if he lived through it, he'd meet somebody like me and marry and go West and get a new start. He was always talking about getting a new start. But I couldn't go West because I had to stay here and guard my father's land. I told him all about the way my family depended on me. And he understood, and he laughed and said it was good to feel that way. Anyway *this* was a new start for him, this place. He said he never even dreamed that he might have a place like this one, so rich, so big.

"It wasn't the kind of wedding my father would have had for me. He used to grumble about it before the War. It was going to cost him a lot of money, he said. He didn't know whether he could afford it or not. I'd killed his wife for him, he said, and now I was going to take away his money. That's what he said, and I didn't realize how short cash was getting. I didn't realize what a bother it was going to be.

"And it *was* expensive to get married. Back then you expected a girl's father to give her husband a dowry. That's what you men think about us. We're so worthless that somebody has to *pay* you to take us off your hands. My father didn't like that. He wanted to leave everything to Matthew. Times were hard, you see. All those Northern interests were trying to squeeze the South to death, and times were hard. He thought Matthew would be the one to carry the family on. He said I'd get married and move off someplace, and then I'd belong to somebody else's family, and he didn't like to think of giving money away like that. My father really wanted me to be a school teacher, and some of it rubbed off. If I *did* get married, he wanted it to be a credit to the family. Something *worthy*.

"But it wasn't that kind of wedding. Your father was just able to get along, to get up and get around. He couldn't even ride a horse yet. I was afraid of what people in the neighborhood were going to say. You know how people talk. Two people like your father and me can be absolutely innocent, but gossipy people can still talk. So I insisted we get married right away. He didn't think much of the idea at first. I mean he was worried because he didn't have anything to offer on his side. He said he wasn't worthy. But it didn't matter. His family had lost everything in the War, and we were deeply in love. You know what they say about love and war. It makes everything fair, and nobody can ever know how much we loved each other. It was something that could just happen one time. It never could happen to me again if I lived forever and stayed young.

"But it was a simple wedding. I guess my father would have been ashamed. I sent George down to get Preacher Henck. He had just come in from the War himself. He went through the whole war with Lee, and when it was over the Methodists sent him back here. Why didn't we have Mr. Bazely? Well, we didn't know Mr. Bazely so well. *I* didn't know him, and your father *was* a Methodist. It was one of those things. I really don't remember. You see I was so wildly happy, and it just worked out that way.

"Your father still wasn't very strong, and that's why we had the wedding here. "It wasn't a big wedding. But it was the biggest thing in my life. I was *so* proud and happy. Suellen MacComber came over with her mother. She was just a little thing, and of course she wasn't married then, and her name was Suellen Hicks. We had two men who were passing through and sleeping in the quarters. One of them was named Majors and he was a big, friendly somebody. But for the life of me I can't remember the other one. On their way back to Virginia, like so many others. They went on the next day, and I never saw them again. Then there was Joe Morrison. He came out with his wife in a wagon pulled by a couple of mules. They both died within two years, the old man first. He was retired when the War broke out, and he had to start farming again to live. I guess it killed him, but maybe it didn't. Their farm was so far back up in the hills that the Yankee Army passed by without ever seeing them. I think Mr. Morrison said on the day of our wedding that in the whole war he hadn't seen a soldier on either side. It was like living in another world.

"So we were all here in the house, in the parlor where your dear father's picture is now. We stood right up before the fireplace, and back then there was a picture of *my* father hanging there. You know the one. It's the big picture of him that hangs up in my bedroom now. Excuse me, Sam. I'm not going to cry. I promise I'm not. But your father looked just *like* his picture on the day we got married. Only he was a little thinner. It was the fever that had made him so thin, and he still couldn't stand up for a long time without having to sit down and take a rest. He was just beginning to get better. He could walk around for a while without getting dizzy.

"Now I'll tell you something about our wedding supper. George went to get the preacher on a mule he'd tied out in the woods so the Yankee soldiers wouldn't find him. You remember that mule. Well, the only reason we had him was that George took him out at night and hid him when he heard that the Yankees were in the valley. So George got back before Preacher Henck could get here. And he had *two* chickens! *Two* fat hens tied across the back of that mule and still alive and squawking. He'd tied their feet together. *Two* chickens! I knew he'd stolen them. I said to him, "George, tell me, *where* did you get those chickens?' I was going to take them back. But he wouldn't tell me. He absolutely refused. He said, 'Miss Sarah, de Lawd has done provided dese chickens fo' you wedding, and you mus' take what de Lawd gives widout askin' no questions, 'cause de Lawd don't like folks to ask questions.'

"*Oh*, your father thought that was funny! He clapped old George on the back just as if he had been a white man. And your father said, 'Well, Lawd, now that I see you face to face I have to say I never did realize you were a nigger.' It was *terribly* irreverent, but we laughed. We all laughed, and George looked so pleased. He was like a child around your father. And he had those chickens killed and cleaned and in the stove before you could say Jack Robinson. I guess Preacher Henck doesn't know to this day that he ate stolen chicken for our wedding supper.

"Chicken, turnips, and sweet potatoes! And honey. We had a little honey. I didn't even mind the turnips that night. I was so happy I wouldn't have minded clay. Preacher Henck led us in singing some hymns. I don't remember what we all sang, but I remember how clear and strong his voice was, and how we were all caught up in it. We sang and sang. It was as if we'd locked the whole world out, the defeat, the disappointment, all the deaths, everything bad, and we were all here together and safe, and we loved each other. There was such a feeling of *love* in the room that night.

"The two soldiers that were here had some whiskey. They weren't drunkards, you understand. But they had some whiskey and brought it out, and everybody had a little. Even Preacher Henck had some. I guess that was the only drop of liquor he's ever drunk in his life, and he was sweet about it. He said it was against his principles most of the time, but then he said the Lord made wine for a wedding. He said if the Lord made it, then maybe we ought to drink it. And when your father said this wasn't wine but whiskey, Preacher Henck just laughed and said the Lord had made several pots of wine but that we only had a jug of whiskey and that it amounted to the same thing. And it *wasn't* wrong, Sam. The War was over, and we'd lost a lot, and we were still alive. Still able to be happy about something. Still able to look *forward* to something. The little drop of whiskey we drank didn't hurt a thing.

"The last thing we sang was 'Dixie,' and that made us so sad we had to stop. I guess we all cried. Yes, even *I* cried. I didn't cry when Matthew was killed or when my father died. You'll be surprised at that, but I couldn't. But that night when all of us stood around the living room and sang that song . . . I cried. I just had to cry, and your dear father took me in his arms and kissed me. It was all so . . . so *noble!* We'd fought hard, and we'd lost, and things would never be the same again. I *had* to cry.

"So your father and I were married, and we lived together from the twenty-sixth of July, 1865, until the ninth day of September, 1870. Five years, one month, and sixteen days! Long enough to get over the honeymoon feeling. Not that we ever *had* a honeymoon. Long enough to understand how much in love we really were. And I want to tell you something, Sam. In all that time we never had a cross word. Not *one* harsh word passed between us. We lived and loved, and when he died we were still in love. Oh, forgive me. Forgive me. I know you don't like to see me cry, and I promise I won't. You're not the way you used to be. Time was when *you* would cry, Sam. Don't you remember? I'm sorry. It's just that . . . that I *loved* him.

"But it was enough, I suppose. The Lord gives, and the Lord takes away. We must bless the Lord for what He does. He let us live together long enough to have you, Sam. You were born on the morning of the fourteenth of May, eighteen hundred and sixty-six. It was the answer to the prayer I made to the Lord—that I'd have a son. And I did! God gave you to me, Sam. You were not just an ordinary child. You were a gift of God.

"Oh, how I wish my dear father had lived to see the day! He never thought I was good for much of anything, you see. And I'm the one to carry on the line. In *you,* Sam dearest. In *you!* My father thought it would be Matthew. He never *dreamed* it would be me. He had a right to think that. Nobody could tell about the War then. We couldn't see the future, and it was the most natural thing in the world to think the line would go on in Matthew. But it didn't work out that way. *I*, a feeble woman, was the one appointed by God. His ways are mysterious, Samuel. We cannot understand them. But we can see what He does. Oh, I know you're not named Crittendon, but that doesn't matter. You're in the direct line, and anybody can look at you and tell you come from our family. You *are* our family! I'm laughing because I'm so happy. My father would shake his head in wonder. *My* son is our whole family! Don't ever forget it, Sam! Don't you *ever* forget it. Oh, Sam! I love you *so* much. Try to understand. Please try to understand. I know you're there, so close to me, asleep. Dreaming. Dream about God's will, Sam. Dream about your duty."

7

BRIAN LEDBETTER came slowly to himself in the early dawn. He did not want to wake up, but he was roused by a strange knocking in the room with him. At first it seemed to come from some distant and obscure point in his consciousness, and he thought it was a dream. But as his mind rose sluggishly from clinging sleep, the knocking, a steady, rhythmic pounding which went crack-crack-crack without end, became more clear and more demanding.

Finally, and with horrifying abruptness, he realized that the knocking was causing small tremors in his own body, emanating from his leg. With a mighty roar of indignation he opened his eyes and lunged out of bed. In the process he knocked a skinny little boy onto his bottom on the floor and thus made the child stop the rhythmic pounding with a knife against Brian's wooden leg.

"What the hell are you *doing*?" Brian sat on the edge of his bed and stroked his wooden member as if it had been skin and muscle. His face gaped with sleepy unbelief and injured shock.

The boy looked up in brave fear. "I was chopping on your wood leg," he said. He looked ready to cry.

"But *why*, goddammit? Why was you *doing* that?"

"I wanted to wake you up," the boy said. He sat where he had landed on the floor, the knife still in his hand. He looked at Brian with large, dark eyes. A painfully serious face.

"Well, you sure done that," Brian said. He rubbed his finger gingerly over the fresh scars in his wooden limb. He looked so distressed that he might have seen blood.

"I guess you're going to beat me up now," the boy said. He seemed even closer to tears.

Brian forgot his leg and leaned forward, openmouthed. "Beat you up!"

"I guess you're going to beat me up for chopping on your leg like I done. Go ahead. I knowed you'd do it."

Brian got up and stalked slowly around the seated child as if contemplating some new and fantastic variety of wild bird come to roost in his house. He was completely bewildered. "What the hell are you talking about, you little son of a bitch?"

The boy followed Brian with a defiant twisting of his head. A large, solitary tear trickled out the corner of one eye and rolled down a dusty cheek. "Go ahead. I reckon I can take any beating you can give me. I reckon you ain't man enough to make me cry."

"God Almighty," Brian roared. "Stop that! I ain't going to beat you up. You didn't hurt nothing."

"You ain't even going to hit me?" The boy relaxed just a little.

"Hell no, I ain't going to hit you. I don't go round beating up little children. I ain't sunk *that* low."

"They's lots that does," the boy said cautiously.

"They's lots that fucks sheep, but I don't," Brian said. "Now you get the hell up from there."

The boy got up slowly, still hesitant and eyeing Brian with a great deal of open mistrust. "That's right hard wood," he said. "My knife's pretty sharp."

"It's chestnut," Brian said. "Good God!" The day had not exactly begun on a pleasing note. He still had his clothes on from the night before because he had been too tired to get out of them when he got home. They stuck to him in uncomfortable places and made him tug and scratch to get himself into shape, and while he was doing that he belched and farted with great, sleepy vigor and muttered about the oily heat.

"Don't you even lock your door at night? Somebody could come in and kill you dead." The boy looked at him reproachfully.

"Hell no, I don't lock my door. Why would anybody want to kill me?" Brian walked over to his water bucket and splashed water on his face and rubbed it vigorously with his two hands. Then he put the dipper into the water bucket and took a drink. The water was warm, and he sloshed it around in his mouth and spit it out the open window above the sink.

The boy watched him gravely. "Well, then they might come in here and steal something."

Brian guffawed.

"Well, I ain't as poor as I look. Ain't *nobody* that poor. But what

I got ain't here. It's in the bank, in town. I ain't no dumb dirt farmer that keeps his money in a sock. I know what banks is for."

"What if somebody robs the bank?"

"Then I lose my ass. Look here, child. What in hell do you want?"

"I don't want nothing," the boy said. "It's mamma. She wants the loan of your bull. She's got a need."

"My *bull!*"

"We've got a cow that's in heat, and Mamma wants it put with your bull."

Brian shook his head sadly and in the choking weariness of a sage encountering unbelievable idiocy. "So your mamma sent you over to get my bull! Just like that! You've probably got a little rope outside, and you want to lead him home like a dog. Or maybe you want to drive him along like a sheep. You little shit!" he roared. "That bull'd tear you and me both to pieces if we even got close to him. He'd eat me up for the meal and have you for dessert, and in two day's time you and me'd be a couple of piles of bull shit out there in the pasture. Goddam! G–o–o–o–o–o–ddam!"

It was quite a rage on Brian's part, and the boy waited unruffled until the smoke had cleared away. Then he said, with condescending patience: "That ain't what Mamma said. She sent me over to fetch *you*. You come over to our house and fetch our cow back to your bull. You don't have to be afraid of our cow. She's real gentle. And when your bull gets done, you can bring the cow home."

Brian sat heavily down on the bed and sighed. "Goddam," he said. The day was not getting better.

"Mamma said if you come on right now she might give you some breakfast. We better not be late. Mamma don't like to feed people late. It ain't good morals."

"It ain't good morals." Brian dully repeated the words.

"Jesus always eat his meals on time. Good children does what Jesus done."

"And if you ain't on time for breakfast . . ."

"Then you don't get none."

Brian nodded in deep, worn understanding. "I see. I see." The idea of breakfast did interest him. He doubted that the boy's mother would serve up hard-boiled eggs and pinto beans. That was what he fixed for himself every morning. And every noon. And every night, too. Brian stuck to things he was good at. It was safer that way. So the thought of another kind of breakfast stirred that part of his humanity interested in new and exciting experiences.

"Thing is," the boy went on, "you'd be cheating me out of my breakfast, too. I ain't had none yet myself." He looked at Brian with solemn reproach.

"All right. All right. I'm coming," Brian said. He stirrred around, looking high and low for his shoe. He *had* taken it off before falling into bed, and he found it at last, under his pillow. He put his bare foot into it and knotted the laces.

"Your house sure is dirty, Mr. Ledbetter. Mamma says you live like a pig. She says that's the *worst* thing wrong with you." The boy spoke as if there were a great, manifest catalog of the faults of Brian Ledbetter which everyone knew and argued about, trying to determine the most awful ones.

"Which one are you?" Brian asked helplessly.

"I'm Virgil," the boy said. "I'm the oldest. My daddy always called me the firstborn. Then there's Caleb, Joab, Aaron, Gilboa, and Clyde. Clyde's the baby."

"I'm glad to hear it," Brian said. He finished with his shoe and stood up.

"You really ain't going to wear no sock?" Virgil asked, showing considerable interest.

"No, Virgil, I am not going to wear no sock," Brian said. His voice sounded funny, coming as it did from nearly clenched teeth.

"You sure are a dirty man," Virgil said wondrously. Then he looked at Brian with a start of curiosity. "Ain't it awful hard to buy just one shoe?"

"No, it ain't so damned hard. You don't think everybody got his *right* foot shot off, do you? God ain't that orderly, boy. They's lots of folks that got their *left* leg took off, and them and me can split our shoes."

"There ain't nobody around here that's got his left leg shot off."

"I get my shoes down from Knoxville when I get them."

"I guess Knoxville's filled up with people that don't have nothing but right legs," Virgil said in a factual way.

Brian did not answer for a moment. He gave the boy a hard, perplexed look and went back over to the sink and looked in the scrap of mirror hanging on the wall. He examined himself carefully, stood back a little and assumed a stately, portrait pose. He turned his head from side to side, trying out the view. He drew one hand across his fuzzy chin and frowned. "I guess if I'm going to see your mamma I'd better shave."

"Oh, that don't matter none," Virgil said. "Mamma says there ain't no helping your looks. It's something we'd all have to get used to." The boy looked at him comfortably.

"Something . . . You'd get *used* to . . ." Brian all at once received one of those sudden, unexpected visions of life which come to men when they are shot in the stomach.

"I tell her it don't make me no mind. Our own daddy always used to keep hisself shaved. But Mamma says *her* daddy used to go round looking like you do. He didn't live like a pig though."

Brian sighed. It was barely audible. His face was blank with thoughts too great for wrinkles to express.

"Me, I think it'd be something swell to have a man with a wood leg around the house," the boy said. "It ain't ever feller that's got a daddy with a wood leg—even a stepdaddy, which is what Mamma says you'd be. It'd sure be something to talk about. Maybe you'd let me borrow it sometimes to take to school. I'd like to show it off. I'd be *real* careful with it."

"God Almighty in the outhouse," Brian said.

"You sure do use bad words," Virgil said. "If you get married to Mamma, she won't let you talk that way. She'd put a mop in your mouth."

"Listen, you little shit! I ain't going to marry your Mamma. You get that out of your head, you hear? I wouldn't marry your Mamma if she was the last woman on earth."

"She wouldn't have you if she was the last woman on earth," Virgil said calmly. "She could get something better. Mamma says she has to take what she can get now."

Brian only glared at him. He went back to the sink and spilled some water into a basin.

"What are you doing!" Virgil cried out in alarm.

"I'm fixing to shave, damn it! What does it look like I'm doing!"

"We'll be late," Virgil wailed. "We won't get no breakfast!"

"That's just too damn bad," Brian said.

Virgil dropped listlessly onto a stool in the corner. Brian got on with his shaving. He made lather by agitating a shaving brush against a yellow bar of greasy-looking soap. "Ain't you going to heat the water?" Virgil asked petulantly.

"I thought you was in a hurry," Brian said. "If I heat the water, we'll *really* be late. Now shut up while I get on with this." He leaned in close to the mirror.

"You sure do everything in a queer way," Virgil said.

"When I cut throats with my razor I do it real normal," Brian said.

He tried different poses of overwhelming dignity and examined each of them in the mirror. He applied the lather. Carefully. Exquisitely. Like an artist touching up a masterpiece. A great, frothy lathering of creamy white all across his face from ear to ear. "Damned if I don't think I'd look real good in a beard," he muttered softly. He surveyed himself once more and turned to give Virgil the full, glorious benefit of a face-to-face view. "How'd I look in a beard?"

"You look a little like Sandy Claus now," Virgil said. "Not that I think there *is* a Sandy Claus." He added the last with suspicious haste.

"Damn it, Virgil, it's *Santy* Claus! Not *Sandy* Claus. God Almighty! You can't even talk right. How you going to amount to anything if you can't even talk right?"

"*You* don't believe in Sandy Claus, do you Mr. Ledbetter?" There was mostly a sophisticated scorn in Virgil's voice, but also just a drop of hope.

Brian made a serious gesture wtih his large head and bent his shoulders slightly in a speculative way. He wielded a long-bladed razor, keen and shining, which he stropped from time to time on the heel of his shoe. The balancing act he performed on those occasions was worthy of note. Virgil admired him for it. But something vastly more important had got the boy's attention.

"You *don't* believe in Sandy Claus . . . Do you?"

Brian shrugged indifferently. "It ain't for me to say."

"You ain't never *seen* Sandy Claus."

"We–e–lll, I ain't never exactly *seen* him, but . . . Oh look, just forget it, Virgil. It ain't important. A boy smart as you are ain't going to be interested in what a old man like me has seen." Brian had paused thoughtfully and turned again to look at Virgil. He was about halfway through his shaving. He turned back to the mirror as if to break off the conversation. "Course I've *heard* things. I ain't never really *seen* nothing. Anyway, you wouldn't be interested."

"I ain't going to know if I'm interested lessen I hear what it is," Virgil observed.

"No, no. I know you wouldn't believe it," Brian said. He went on shaving himself with hurried dedication.

"You don't know no such thing," Virgil said.

Brian puckered his face. He appeared to be worried, trying to make up his mind about something. "No, you wouldn't believe it," he said finally. "I *know* you wouldn't believe it. I'd be wasting my time talking about it." He made the last few strokes with the razor, wiped his wet face vigorously with a grimy towel, and looked sadly at Virgil. "I'm a honest man," he said solemnly. "And there ain't no honest man on earth that like to have people believe he's a liar."

"Well, I ain't saying I *would* believe you, but then I ain't saying for sure I *wouldn't*," Virgil said carefully.

Brian drew himself up into a thick tower of melancholy resignation. "All right, I'll tell you on one condition. You promise you won't tell nobody on earth. You promise?"

"I promise," Virgil said.

"You won't tell your brothers. You won't even tell your Mamma?"

"Cross my heart and hope to die." He crossed his heart with both bare arms.

"Well, I believe you, Virgil. Honest to God I do." Brian spoke with sudden relief and cheer. "And I'm going to tell you what happened to me once. What I heard. It was back in the War. It was the night before Christmas in eighteen hundred and sixty-two, and that was a long time before you was born. Now you believe *that*, don't you?"

"Yep," Virgil said, nodding. He was leaning so far forward that he seemed likely to fall off the stool.

"Well, like I was saying, it was the night before Christmas." He paused for effect. "We was lying in camp, and they was singing that night. Christmas songs. You know any Christmas songs?"

"I knows all that is. My daddy used to sing 'em all. 'Silent Night,' and 'Good King Winchester.' "

"All right. We was singing them songs, and we was outside of Washington City, and it was *cold!* My fingers still just naturally get blue ever time I think of that night. Here, look for yourself." He stretched out his hands. Virgil eyed them curiously.

"I don't see nothing."

"It's because we're inside. If we was outside in the sun, you'd see. My fingers is blue right now. Well, it was cold. And we quit singing along about midnight, and I rolled up in my blanket in my tent on a cot. You listening?"

"I'm listening."

"All right, I was rolled up in my blanket, and I heard bells go by in the sky. I was in my tent and couldn't see nothing, but I got up and run outside. Only by the time I got there, they was gone. Now what do you make of that!"

"It might of been a train," Virgil said.

"Oh hell, Virgil," Brian said in disgust. "You ain't never seen no train go by in the *sky!*"

"It might of been a unusual train," Virgil said.

Brian shook his head dolefully. "I knowed you wouldn't believe me. I just knowed it. Now you'll probably go tell your mamma."

"No I won't," Virgil said stubbornly. "I made a promise."

"I guess you'll have to tell your brothers though?" Brian looked sadly at Virgil from beneath questioning brows.

"No, honest I won't. I said I won't, and I won't."

"Course it'd make me look silly." Brian cleared his throat confidentially. "They wouldn't understand it the way you and me does, Virgil."

"That's true," Virgil said hesitantly.

"A man says he's heard bells go by in the sky, and pretty soon folks'll be saying he's crazy. I thought so at the time. When them bells went over and I went running outside, I said to myself, 'Look here, Ledbetter, what do you think you're doing?' But it'd make me look pretty silly if you was to tell, and I'd be bounden to you if you wouldn't."

"I won't tell," Virgil said firmly. "I crossed my heart and hoped to die."

Brian relaxed with a wide grin of pleasure. "We'll be all right. Yessir, it'll be our secret, and we won't tell *nobody* else. I swear I heard them bells, and I swear to God I believe you, Virgil. Your word's good enough for me. Now I ain't really asking you to believe *me*. But I believe *you*. What do you think of *that*?"

Virgil really didn't seem sure what he thought about it, and he weighed it all for a few seconds. He looked at Brian with an expression of puzzled gravity and tried to make out just what it was that Brian was all about.

Meanwhile Brian fetched his large straw hat from a peg and looked at himself again in the piece of mirror before putting the hat on. He fixed his features in a stern expression and threw his shoulders back. He contemplated the effect with a certain rigorous satisfaction. "I don't reckon I'm as ugly as some," he said bravely. "How old's your mamma, son?"

"Mamma's twenty-eight. She's good-looking, too."

"And how much land you got?"

"I can't say exactly. You'd have to ask Mamma. It's a pretty good piece."

Brian nodded sagely to himself and smacked his lips. "I bet it is. Yessir, I bet it is." He put the hat on and picked up a clay pipe, which he stuck in the bib of his overalls. They went outside. Brian left his door standing ajar, and Virgil went back and shut it.

"Somebody's going to steal everything you've got," the boy said, scolding.

"Well, I ain't got nothing, so that takes care of that," Brain said. "Come on. I got to run up my horse."

They went down to the barn. Brian went through the gate and out into the lot behind. He whistled the horse up to running distance, then put on a surprising performance of lunging at the animal, throwing the bridle over his head and leading him back into the barn to affix the saddle.

Virgil was greatly impressed. He'd never seen a man with a wood leg run the way Mr. Ledbetter could, he said. He sure wished Mr. Ledbetter would take off and run around the house a couple of times when they got home. His brothers sure would like it since it wasn't something you saw every day—a man with a wood leg running that way.

Brian glowered at him and got to talking about what a good club a wood leg made. He'd used his own to club the brains out of a lot of pestiferous little boys in his time, he said. He'd be glad to beat the living shit out of the whole litter of Virgil's brothers. But at the end of this fearful pronouncement his eyes twinkled, and he grinned, and Virgil's apprehensive stare was slowly replaced by a shy smile. They set out for Virgil's place in a companionable mood, and Brian secretly enjoyed a silent feeling of victory—which he laid by just in case he wanted to make something of it. He wasn't sure yet just what that might be.

The sun was well off the horizon by now. It loomed there above the mountains like a huge, tremulous blob of jellied fire. The sky was glassy blue, looking fresh-blown and incandescent from the furnace. The sunlight blazed on the sere land. No reflection of sparkling dew. No drop of moisture anywhere. The world lay exhausted and panting. As Brian contemplated things, his cheer left him. It evaporated slowly like water in a pan under the sun and left him empty of feeling.

The road, passing through fields under the bare sun, left Brian's place and wound lazily upward through banks of trees. There was an ominous quiet to the forest. A dark silence, portentous and grim. The thick air settled heavy and still under the treetops. Fumes rather than air, hanging explosively over the dying earth. For a long time they rode along without speaking.

Finally Brian remarked: "You and your folks wasn't at the hanging yesterday."

"Nope, Mamma wouldn't let us go. She said it wasn't fitting for us to see it. I cried and took on something awful, and the others howled pretty fierce. But it didn't do no good. Was you there? I bet it was fun."

"Fun! Jesus Christ! It ain't fun to see somebody get hung!"

"Well, if it ain't fun, why'd you go?"

Brian felt Virgil's dark eyes on him, and he had another discomfort added to the heat. "It wasn't to have me a lot of *fun,*" he said. "I'll tell you what. It was to . . . Well, I'd knowed Simson in a manner of speaking. We always spoke. I mean *I* spoke. They was lots of times when he'd pass without saying a word. But we knowed each other. It wouldn't of been *right* if I hadn't gone."

"I guess he'd of missed you all right," Virgil said.

"That's not what I mean, dammit. I mean that when a man's hung it's a kind of responsibility on folks to go. It ain't right to make somebody do it by hisself. The sheriff, I mean. It wouldn't mean nothing if we all didn't go. Dammit, it's . . . It's like going to church."

Brian gleamed with the wisdom of his sudden thought. But Virgil merely shook his head slowly and reproachfully from side to side. "I ain't never seen you in church, Mr. Ledbetter."

Brian spit wearily into the road. "Virgil, you don't understand nothing."

"Mamma said she felt sorry for him. For Mr. Simson. She said you could just take one look at Mrs. Simson and tell she wasn't fit for no man. She said it takes a real bad woman to make a man kill her."

"That's crazy talk."

"Mamma wouldn't like it if she was to hear you say she's crazy."

"I suppose if your mamma was married to Mr. Simson he wouldn't have killed her."

"Nobody'd dare try to kill Mamma," Virgil said with lazy confidence. "She'd of busted Mr. Simson good with the churn dasher. That's why we ain't got no bull."

They came out onto the pike. In the open road the vengeful sun fell on them with all its force. The sweat which had been oozing beneath Brian's clothing came flooding through and darkened his shirt. He wiped ineffectually and hard at his face with a handkerchief, succeeding in stirring up more sweat by his grunting efforts. "What in hell's a churn dasher got to do with a bull?" he asked irritably.

"Well, we had one. A bull, I mean. And a churn dasher too. Wasn't as good as your'n, maybe, but he was good enough to get in there and try. He was mean too. Maybe meaner than your bull. Because one day Caleb got in the pen with him. He was going to try to ride that ole bull, and I bet him two cents he couldn't. But the bull took one look at him and knocked him flat down and was stomping and pawing and rooting and trying to get a horn in Caleb. And Caleb was howling something awful, and we was all jumping up and down and crying for Mamma. And she picked up a churn dasher and come running and cleared the fence like a chicken with one jump. And she hit that old bull between the eyes and knocked him dead. He didn't even grunt. He just fell down dead. Mamma sat on his carcass and cried. She liked to of beat Caleb half to death. The meat was tough too." The boy laughed. "It was really something, and now Caleb owes me two cents."

Brian laughed too. "I would of liked to seen it," he said. He rode along for a little while with a grin on his face, trying to imagine it. But the grin died in a moment. "God, I feel dirty," he said. The thick dust muffled the slow plumping of the animal hoofs. It rose in grainy clouds behind them. "And Simson said it'd rain today. Good God Almighty! It'd sooner rain in hell." Then, reflecting: "Maybe that's what he meant."

"What was Mr. Simson talking about rain for?"

"Oh Lord, Virgil, I don't know. It was the last thing he said. The heat got his brain, I guess. It didn't mean nothing." He glanced up at the silent and sinister sky. "No, goddammit, it didn't mean a thing."

"Mamma said Mr. Simson was a brave man. Him and my daddy and my granddaddy all fought for the 'Federacy."

"Yep, that's true enough," Brain said. He looked off ahead where the burnt road wavered dizzily in the sunlight. The dust lay so finely ground by the heat and the traffic that it assumed an almost liquid character, coating the pike with a thick brown meringue. If you stepped into the dust it would cover your ankles and fill your shoes, and Brian rode along helplessly thinking of Cold Harbor and remembering how there the blood ran into the bitter dust and made it clay. Cold Harbor! Back there, a world ago.

"Mamma says you fought for the other side," Virgil said cautiously.

"That's a fact."

Virgil lapsed into thought. His sandy hair flopped gently with the motion of his mule. The sweat streaked his face and neck, droplets of sweat quivering and shaking and shining in the blistering sun. He asked with even more delicate caution: "Why'd you do that? Why'd you go and fight for them?"

Brian came out of his own hot reveries and looked frowning at the boy. For a while he didn't say anything but looked away again, into the trembling heat waves on the road. "It was one of those things," he said laconically.

"Was it for the niggers? Was you a niggerlover? Did you want to make the niggers free?"

"Well," Brian frowned uncomfortably, "in a manner of speaking. I mean it wasn't *right* that niggers was slaves. But I guess that didn't matter much to me. I didn't own no niggers myself. And I didn't see no sense in fighting for somebody else's niggers. I don't give a damn one way or another about niggers lessen it's . . . Well, I just don't give a damn." He was about to say he didn't give a damn about any niggers except for the pleasures of nigger whores, and he was on the point of giving Virgil a lecture on the joys of nigger whoredom. But he decided in midsentence that the subject wasn't delicate. Not on this day.

"Mamma says the Yankees wanted all our money, and that's why we had the War."

Brian fought manfully with his first impulse. But the effort of choking down what he wanted to say was so great that he couldn't say anything.

"Mamma says if we'd of won, we'd all be rich now, and we wouldn't have all this trouble we're having in the world."

"Virgil, let me tell you something. If you folks had of won, you'd be living like a nigger right this minute. You'd have yourself a little shack, and it wouldn't even be yours. And some big-assed rich man would be hollering 'Boy' at you all the time, and you couldn't do nothing but say, 'Yessir!' You'd live on the weedy ass of some rich feller's place, and that's all you'd get out of life. The ass end of everything."

"Mamma says we'd of all been rich, and we'd have lots of parties, and we'd all have us a horse to ride."

"You'd be poorer than a church mouse."

"Mamma says if we'd of won, we'd all have a slave. Only . . ." He hesitated in some confusion.

"Only *what?*"

"Only she says she's glad we don't have a lot of slaves around the house." He brightened suddenly, an innocent, sure cognizance breaking over his tanned face. "But if we'd of won, we'd have us *good* slaves. We wouldn't have no *bad* slaves—the kind that steals and does sinful things. And we wouldn't have a lot of other things." This last he said with such bold insinuation that Brian's dander was raised.

"What, for instance?"

"Gambling and drinking for instance. Card playing and . . . And folks like you not going to church on Sunday morning. Mamma says our side was awful strong on church. If we'd of won, we'd make everybody go."

Brian sighed in profund contempt. "Jesus H. Christ! I reckon you think the whole Rebel Army was one big floating Sunday School."

"Mamma says Stonewall Jackson prayed ever time he drunk a glass of water. You can't show me no *Yankee* general that done that."

"Jackson was crazy," Brian said darkly. His words were a subdued muttering, an uncomfortable reflection over a horror. "He loved to kill, that man did. If the War hadn't come along, that man would of ended up just like Simson yesterday. He was a fanatic, one of the worst men that ever was." He uttered a malicious laugh. "I wish he'd seen the end. Lord God, I sure as hell wish he'd knowed he was whipped."

"What makes you *say* such things?" Virgil asked in a hurt tone. "You done all the awful things you done, and you ain't even sorry!"

Brian guffawed with deliberate cruelty, shaking the notes of laughter out like a whip over a raw back. He looked at Virgil with a sneer. But again something walled in his words. *He don't even know.* The amazing thought jumped into his brain. Again the something thoughtful and terribly serious came back. "Virgil, I'm going to tell you why I done the things I done and why I say the things I say. I remember it all like it happened yesterday. Fact is, it's hard for me to remember sometimes that it *wasn't* yesterday. Time's getting away so fast. So *damned* fast.

"I was in town the day we heard about Sumter. I remember what it done to people that ought to of knowed better. Sumter was like a big drunk. It made a lot of folks foolish. Maybe the whole goddam country got drunk on Sumter.

"A feller named Condon was the telegrapher. You don't remember him. He's been dead for many a year. But I remember just the way his voice sounded. Like yesterday. I remember him singing out the news all day long, and I remember the way the news shot out into the country and made people come into town. And they come! Lord God, they come! Everybody was pushed in around it and listening to the news, and it was *some* thing.

"It was spring. And I'll tell you something. You'd be surprised how I remember the way things smelled on that day. And I seen J. W. Campbell that day. That's something else I won't ever forget. Him and me wasn't good friends back then. He was a lot older than me. I guess I knowed his boy better than I knowed him. His boy was four or five years younger than me. His boy was a quiet sort. Not like J.W. It was a strange thing when I think on it. J.W. can always be so calm about things. You figure he's got everything under control. His boy wasn't like that at all. His boy was always sitting around and watching his daddy and listening, but the only time he'd say anything was when you spoke to him, and then he wouldn't say much. He'd grin and shake his head, and he had a big, loud laugh. He was always breaking out in that big, loud laugh. Only it wasn't *funny* laughing. He wasn't laughing because he thought things was *funny*. It was sad to hear him laugh thataway. Oh, I can't explain it."

"You was talking about the way the War begun," Virgil said.

"I know it, damn it. I know it. I was just thinking about things. Well, J.W. was standing on his porch with his hands folded behind his back, and his boy was sitting on the porch with his feet hanging off the edge. Neither one of them was saying anything, but they looked like grim death! So *still*. All that noise and commotion, and them two was so *still*. J.W., he look at me. His eyes caught on me for just a second and then moved on, and he looked off like he didn't want to talk. So *still*. But I could tell what the look meant, and I went off and thought about it.

And you know the next time I seen J. W. Campbell? It was way up in Virginia. Out in the middle of nowhere before Cold Harbor where I got my foot shot off. He come in to where I was, sitting at a fire, and it was raining. Well, we seen each other, and we stood by the fire with the rain spitting in it, and we talked for five, ten minutes. He asked me right then if I'd heard anything from his boy. Course I hadn't, and hell, his boy wasn't going to write *me*, and if he had, I couldn't *read* it. So when I said I hadn't heard a word, he lost interest and went off. Next time I seen him was back here, after the War, when it was all over.

"But that day, the day of Sumter, all them fools like your grandpaw was standing there yelling and cheering and slapping hands when they heard Old Man Condon sing out the news. We was all standing around there, and everything smelled like the daffodils, and it wasn't like blood at all. But we was making up our minds which side we'd kill for. They was a lot that made up their minds about dying that afternoon.

"J.W., he taken his boy up to Knoxville that very same night. And ever time the folks around the telegraph yelled, it made me make up my mind just a little bit more. I can't explain it now. But after a while I knowed I had to haul my ass out of here before it got too late.

"I went on home. Didn't say nothing to nobody in town. I just went home, and I told my mammy and my daddy what I was going to do. My mammy didn't say nothing. She didn't cry, didn't give me no argument. I never seen her again after that day. I always used to think about her dying and me crying by her bed and all that, but she died before I got home. My daddy said she cried ever night for a week after I got gone, and she went down to her death worrying about me. She didn't say a thing that night, except she asked what I wanted to take.

"My daddy said he guessed I'd need a horse. I said I didn't want to take none of the horses. I knowed stock'd be hard to come by in the War, but he said the place was mine as much as it was his, and he said he'd be damned if he'd let a boy of his'n go off to war without a horse.

"We was sitting around talking all of a sudden like I'd growed up that afternoon. Lord God, I was twenty year old! We was most all children that foughten that war. Oh, they was folks like J.W. and lots of others that was older, but most of us was children. We was the kind of boys that you expect to stay home and watch their short hairs curl except on Saturday night. But we was the very ones that went off and foughten the goddammedest war that *anybody* ever fought! It's a wonderful thing when you think on it. War's so big you think it ought to be fought by bankers and presidents and senators and railroad men and preachers and school teachers. But it ain't. It's fought by a bunch of poor dogs like me.

And we was all just children back then, and we didn't know to say excuse me when we farted. We was the ones that foughten that war! I tell you, it makes you think!"

They rode along, and Brain reveled for a few moments in the grand thought of what he'd done, an expression of full wonder and satisfaction on his beaming face.

"Get on with it," Virgil said. "Go on and tell me about it."

"Well, I was pretty well packed up, ready to get when it got dark, and my daddy was fixing to run me up a horse when up in the afternoon Matthew Crittendon come riding into my yard. Right where you rode this morning. You never did know Matthew Crittendon, that son of a bitch!"

"Mamma says he was one of the biggest heros that ever was!" Virgil was hurt and anxious.

"Matthew Crittendon was one of the biggest sons of bitches that ever was! He was the kind that would of run this country if you folks had of won. He had him a uniform on already when he come to see me, and you know something! It was *white!* He looked like a goddam admiral of the ocean sea! He rode up with a bunch of young piss ants, little bastards willing to eat his shit so's they be near to that *white uniform!* He had long greasy yellow hair, Matthew did. It was all the way down to his shoulders. He was getting a troop up to fight the Yankees, he said. They'd elected him captain, and they was out looking for more men.

"I tell you what's true. He wanted to kill me right then. He smelled like whiskey, and he was mean. He run me off his place once. I tracked a deer onto his land and killed it, and he come when he heard the gun and cussed me out and run me off his place. Wouldn't even let me take the deer. Said I was a trespasser, and I eat beans that night instead of deer meat. I ain't never forgot the taste of them beans to this day. I think he wanted me to say I was going Union, and he was going to kill me and maybe my folks too. I can't prove it. He's dead now. But I got my thoughts on it. It was the look in his eye. He was all set to see blood. And there he was with them friends of his, and they wanted to start the War with me.

"Damned if it don't make me laugh yet! I pitched a fit. I talked about Abe Lincoln like he was a dog. I said I'd had my doubts, but this was too much, too damned much! I had wanted the Union, I said, but I didn't want no killing of brave Southern men, and by damn now I'd made up my mind, and I was going to give them Yanks hell, and I'd be honored to fight with Captain Matthew

Crittendon. I said him and me had had our differences, but now I'd be right proud to shake his hand, and we done it. We done it, and we swore brotherhood forever.

"Matthew Crittendon didn't know what the hell was going on. He had a lot of sense, that boy did! Like a burned stump. Like my wood leg. *God,* was he dumb! And he was real surprised and pleased. He smiled. The kind of smile you see on a idjit's face when you rub his back. I said them mean old Yanks wasn't going to come down here and rape *my* poor old mammy, and I put my arms around her and give her a big hug. Lord, Virgil, you ought to of seen it! My mammy, she nodded her head like she was scared to death of being raped, and my daddy took it from me and got cussing mad at the Yanks and the Republicans and Abe Lincoln. I said that if Captain Crittendon would let me stay this one more night with my dear mammy and daddy, I'd be out to meet him first thing in the morning. So him and his shitty friends went off, and he was smiling all the time, and we must of shook hands ten times before he got going. Matthew and me was about the same age, but I called him 'Captain' most ever other word, and it tickled his ass. He couldn't hardly sit on his saddle his ass was tickled so much.

"But I tell you the truth; we was scared. I didn't know what he'd do to my mammy and daddy when he found out the truth. But I had to do it. I had to do what I done, and it worked out all right. Even Matthew Crittendon couldn't go round killing old folks. Not if they was *white.* We waited till it got good and dark, and then my daddy run me up a horse, and I lit out. I went north, to Kentucky, and that's how I went to the War. And I'm glad I done it." Brain sighed heavily and wistfully for something lost and shook his head in ponderous wonder.

"I was scared shitless. When I rode out of here, I had a knot in my chest. I could almost put my hand on it and feel it. It was so big I thought it'd stop me breathing. And I'll tell you something, Virgil. On the road to Knoxville that night, I cried. Oh, you needn't look at me that way. Men cries sometimes. On the road that night, out under the sky with the air smelling fresh and clean. I cried. I never had even been away from home for a night in my whole life, and I was twenty year old and going to fight a war, and you try to do that without crying! But I'd do it again. I'd do it all just like I done it if I was young and the War was to come again. I can't tell you why exactly, but I'd do it. I made history when I was twenty years old, and

I'll never forget it. No, I'll never forget it." He shook his head again with that profound, blissful, nostalgic wonder.

"So you was a Yankee horse soldier," Virgil said.

"Hell, boy! I wore my poor old horse out on that trip. I rode him all the way up into Kentuck, and he was lame when I got there, and they put me on a train and hauled me to Washington City, and I was in First Manassas. We got cut up pretty bad then, and after that they stuck me in the Sixty-ninth Pennsylvania Infantry. It was a Irish outfit, and with a name like Brian Ledbetter they thought I was a goddam Irishman and belonged with them." He chuckled in reminiscence, and his fleshy face glowed with pleasure in the dark shade of his hat brim. "That was what they call the fortune of war. I fought out the whole shebang with a bunch of men that couldn't even talk right. Yep, Virgil, it was a great thing. I'd do it again. Damned if I wouldn't, if I was young."

"You really had it," Virgil said in admiration. Then his voice dropped and became abruptly mournful. "I ain't never going to have nothing like you had. We ain't never going to have no more wars. It's all over for me. All over before I even begun."

Brian burst out laughing. "Shit," he said.

"If you'd only fought on the right side," Virgil said with a flat note of condescension.

"I *did* fight on the right side," Brian said.

Virgil looked pugnaciously at him. "Mamma says you knowed better than you done. She says that's why God taken your leg off."

Brian pulled violently back on the reins of his horse and stopped the animal dead in the road. "She *what!* She said *what!*"

Virgil stopped too and looked alarmed. But he held on bravely to his original utterance. "She said you knowed better than you done. And God punished you for it by taking off your leg."

"Well, I'll be a goddam son of a mongrel bitch in a nigger whorehouse," Brian said.

"You're mad," Virgil wailed. "I've made you mad!"

Brian's face went from purple to a hideously enraged vermilion the color of sick wine. He expressed himself for a great while with boiling, swelling eloquence. He called up words he had not used since the War. He invented words never before heard by man. He juggled words which never in history had been thrown into the same fantastic sentence together. It could not last. The high intensity of the moment burned him out. Suddenly—quite suddenly, in fact—Brian Elisha Ledbetter toppled backward and, flailing silently, fell into the deep of exhausted quiet. He glared speechlessly at Virgil. After a long time he spoke with a calm as frozen as the Arctic void: "I done what I done, and I'm glad!"

Virgil snicked with his tongue to his mule. The animal flicked his ears back in the way of mules and went plodding on ahead. The boy looked around at Brian as if peering remotely at some remarkably bizarre object cast suddenly down from the sky. But he spoke as he passed by, saying, "That's why Mamma says God taken off your leg."

Brian closed his eyes tightly and put a hand over his tortured face. His features were contorted in a fearful grimace. The crushing sunlight was on his head. And he was hungry. Good Lord, he was hungry! Helplessly he kicked at his horse and went on behind Virgil toward breakfast.

8

SAMUEL BECKWITH AWOKE when the sunlight came sliding down the wall over his head and stung him in the face. He got out of bed and stood spiritlessly collecting his wits. He had a dull headache.

He had not slept well. All through the night his dreams lighted the slack figure of Mr. Simson plunging through the trap in the scaffold to be strangled by the innocent rope. In some of the fragmentary dreams Emilie stood by the gallows. She looked at him in silent reproach. He drew near to touch her, put out his hand, and woke to the upper levels of sleep. There on the margin of wakefulness she melted away in the stuffy dark. He would fall back into his deeper sleep. The spasm of Mr. Simson's fall would again flicker across his mind. If Emilie were not there, he was searching for her in the crowd, not knowing what he sought. And so the night had passed away.

He went slowly to the window, sniffing for rain. But looking out he saw that the earth languished still in its slow and suffocating death, and there was not a cloud in the sky. His headache was worse from the motion. He turned to dress with the blood throbbing at his temples. Clean clothes lay neatly piled on the bureau. Every afternoon his mother put them there. He scowled at the thought of how soon they would be sodden with sweat and the grime of the miserable day.

He dressed slowly. He thought glumly of Emilie and the blundering haste with which he had thrown his clothes on himself in other mornings, so recently; she would be waiting for him, and he must hurry. The thoughts came back with the regularity of the mornings, and he was exhausted by his feeling about the thoughts. He could sweep his mind into their hidden crannies without passion and without remorse. Without remorse? At least without the palpitation of his heart, the shattering sadness, the urgency of those first days.

Such remorse as he had was a stale heaviness, a little like his headache.

The drought added its own massive weight to such dead grief as he felt on this morning. It was time to think of threshing, for there would be threshing in spite of the drought. Like his thoughts of Emilie his thoughts of the work to be done were heavy with resignation. The pitiful oats were yellow. Mayhew MacComber would be up now, perhaps already tramping over his own stunted fields and looking at his grain with a careful eye, measuring time, tending stolidly to his business.

Mayhew MacComber owned a threshing machine. He owned a large place. He threshed the fields of the men who helped him thresh his own. Wherever his thresher went it harvested the grain and left piles of clean straw to bake in the sunlight. The children would frolic in the straw, and it would be for bedding down the stock in winter, and the grain would be for feed and flour. Yes, you could believe there was a God in threshing time because you could see the neat working of things, the regular grinding of the little geared wheels against one another in the mysterious machinery of nature. You could believe there was a God because of the usefulness of things.

He went down the steps and out the front door and made a circuitous course to the outhouse behind the house. The outhouse reeked of lime and disinfectant and the strong fragrance of the perfumed block his mother bought at the hardware store to drown the other smells. He emptied his bladder with a grunt of relief, and the pungent smell of urine rose out of the pit under the toilet hole to mingle sharply with the other odors. It made his headache thicken, and he was glad to escape into the open air. He went into the house through the back door and into the kitchen.

His mind still played idly with the events of the day before. He knew he would dismiss Simson. It was the first hanging he had ever seen. He went partly out of ordinary curiosity, but underneath that he was driven also by a compulsion to witness horror when horror was available. That part of it was a disappointment. The horror was not so horrible. Simson fell like a sack of wheat and died, and it was an effort to make yourself think that anything important had happened. Nothing dramatic about something so common—a sack of wheat, a man, falling.

His mother was in the kitchen when he came in, and she had everything prepared for him. She was always bustling around, always busy and athletic about the house. She combed her dark hair carefully back and did it in a bun at the back of her head so that her bearing was already severe though she was not old. And she did not look old—merely businesslike and capable, a woman in full command of her life. Her greenish eyes flashed warmly still out of that pure-white skin unblemished by a single flaw. The perpetual loving smile was fixed to her full lips. She was always up before dawn to prepare his breakfast. Lately she performed this task with special pleasure. In the days when he rode mornings with Emilie he had not eaten breakfast at home.

"Did you sleep well?" she asked cheerfully when he came into the kitchen.

"Oh, all right. It was hot."

He dutifully lowered his head, and she kissed him lightly on the cheek. He went over to the sink. Hot water was already steaming there in a pan. His mother had poured it as soon as she heard his footsteps nearing the kitchen. That was something she started doing when Emilie left. A new service. He hoped she would eventually stop it and leave him alone, but he doubted that she ever would. It was a token of her devotion, one of the unexplained but perfectly evident little ways by which she showed him he had made the right choice—her over Emilie. He reached for the razor above the sink.

"What do you suppose he could have meant, Sam?"

"Who, mother? Simson?" He had told her about Mr. Simson's prophecy. He had not mentioned the prediction of the nigger hags.

"*Mister* Simson, Sam. Yes, what could he have meant?"

The youth shrugged indifferently. "It sounded to me like he meant it would rain today."

"*As if* he meant, dear," his mother said. He had taken her corrections so often that now he hardly noticed, and he only muttered in response: "The man was crazy. The heat got him." He began to shave, splashing hot water onto his face. With his soaking fingers he rubbed hard at his eyes and relieved the stickiness there, and he felt the headache gently recede before the pressure.

"I guess he doesn't feel the heat now, poor thing," his mother said with a melancholy sigh. "I guess he's in the ground. His first night under the ground! That's always the saddest moment about a death, I think—when you realize that. How fast life changes! who would have thought three months ago that both he and she would be in the ground this morning!"

The presence of her own unexpected sufferings charged the air in the room. Sam bent studiously to his shaving and made an effort at ignoring her. She went on in her cloudy sadness.

"I guess he took just as much as he could of being poor. Mr. Simson had a very hard life." And then with sudden vigor she exclaimed, "And who are we to judge? Maybe he did the right thing!"

"The *right* thing!" He glanced sharply around at her.

"Well, we don't know," she said defensively. "He was a good man at heart. I knew him. He fought on our side in the War. He came to your father's funeral. He was a good neighbor. I can't forget all that."

"He killed his wife," Sam said drily.

"It might have been an act of kindness."

"Mother, what's got *into* you!" Sam was thoroughly startled, and he looked at his mother as though she had changed to somebody else before his eyes.

"We don't know what his intention was," she said with cold force. "You have to judge people for their intentions."

"The law judged him for killing his wife, and yesterday he was hung."

"Hanged, Sam. Pictures are hung and men are hanged. Don't talk like an illiterate."

"Mother, you're changing the subject. The man killed his wife, and he was . . . he was *hanged* for it yesterday because he committed murder, and you're apologizing for him."

"I just say we don't know his intention, and if we did maybe we wouldn't be too hard on him. Man looks on the outward appearance; God looks on the heart." She averted her face and went busily stirring over breakfast.

Sam stooped over the sink, his face half shaven. He felt like mocking his mother. He had that kind of reaction more often lately to her pronouncements on things. But he could not frame a response, and he bent back to his shaving.

"Mrs. Simson was very odd," his mother said, gently taking up the subject again. "You couldn't get her to talk about anything. And she got worse with the years. I think it was because they were so poor. Why, the woman couldn't even think to want anything. She didn't have much to do at home. You know, you have to have good land before you can do any work."

"They had a hard time, all right," he said indifferently.

Her voice took on a romantic brightness. "Now, just suppose he saw she was going crazy, and they were so poor he couldn't help her.

Suppose he worried about her night and day. Once he loved her more than anything else in the world, and it was all going to turn out shameful because she was going crazy. He couldn't stand for their love to end that way, so he killed her."

Sam did laugh now, though not unkindly. "Mother, you sound like a female fiction writer! Simson never looked worried about anything to me. He just got angry at the world and took it out on her. Why not leave it at that?"

"Don't mock, Sam," she said reproachfully. "You've killed animals to put them out of their misery. He could have done the same thing to her."

"He tried to kill his daughter, too. *She* wasn't in any misery."

"Maybe he thought she couldn't live knowing . . . knowing what he'd done. It's going to be a horrible thing for that girl to live with."

Sam chuckled again without mirth. "She'll get along. I saw her talking to the newspaper reporters on the day of the trial. She was pretty pleased with herself. Now she's got something to make her important until people get tired of hearing it. I'm surprised she didn't come to the hanging."

"She's just a child," his mother said impatiently. Again she looked out into the sunny morning, and her rueful gaze lingered on the stricken land. "And he said it would rain today." Her voice was flat and sorrowful as if she had been forced to admit that a wise man had said something utterly silly.

"He said it. I heard him."

"I don't see any sign of rain, but you can't tell in weather like this. You can't think it will go on like this for long."

"It's gone on now for fifty-four days," Sam said. "That's about long enough so it can go on the rest of the summer without making any difference."

"I've seen rain come when nobody was looking for it, especially in the summertime. The day's new."

Sam had finished his shaving and was scrubbing his face with a towel. He looked over it at her with an ironic smile. "Do you really think he saw something, Mother?"

"I don't know, Sam dearest. You don't have to sound so scornful. You're scornful about everything lately."

"I just think it's funny how you take up for any lunatic who came to my father's funeral."

"The world around us is full of unseen things. We can never hope to understand all its secrets until we are on the other side." She spoke these words with a serene restraint which lifted them above argument.

But Sam said, "I know, mother. When we all get to heaven Mr. Simson can give us a nice talk on the whole thing, and afterward we can have lemonade." He sat down crossly to his breakfast. His mother sat down across the table from him and looked at him with a troubled frown.

"I saw Mr. Campbell yesterday," he said casually.

"I don't see why you want to tell me that."

"Well, he asked about you."

"Why should he care about me?" Her voice was frigid and strained and barely civil.

"I don't know, mother. Maybe he's got a bet with somebody on how long you'll live."

"You're being rude, Sam. I don't like it."

"Well, you act as if I just committed the unpardonable sin by speaking to him. Maybe I should have run off screaming."

His mother sniffed. "He didn't do well by Mr. Simson."

"Oh mother, everybody says he did as well as anybody could have done."

"His client is dead."

"His client would be dead if Jesus Christ had been his lawyer!"

"Sam!"

"It's what everybody says in town."

"I never taught you to say what everybody else says about anything."

"Mother, why do you hate Mr. Campbell?"

His mother gave an incredulous little laugh as if astounded that anybody on earth would ever suspect *her* of hatred. "Hate Mr. Campbell! I don't *hate* Mr. Campbell, Sam."

He grinned at her. "Well, if you don't hate him, you don't exactly love him like a brother either. Why? He was one of my father's friends. From what people say he was the best friend my father had in the valley. You take up for a crazy man like Mr. Simson just because he showed up for my father's funeral. But you dislike Mr. Campbell. Why?"

She tossed her head in disdain. "Don't listen to what other people say about your father. I knew him better than anyone. I loved him, Sam. I . . ."

"Mother, please don't change the subject," he said with exaggerated patience. "Everybody says my father and Mr. Campbell were good friends. Now, why do you hate him?"

"Your father had a forgiving spirit. We've been through all this," she said in a curt tone intended to dismiss the subject.

"We've been through it all, but you've never given me a reason." He looked at her again with that ironic grin and went on with his breakfast. For a moment a tense silence settled down over them, broken only by the rattling of his knife and fork against the plate. Then he said with studious unconcern: "Mr. Campbell had a run-in with the preacher yesterday. It was something to see."

"What? What did you say? With Preacher Bazely?"

He looked at her in quick surprise. "Why Mother, what's wrong?" The look of distress on her face was so evident that he grew anxious. He stopped eating and leaned forward, peering at her intently.

"What do you mean? What did that man do to Mr. Bazely?"

"Why are you so excited?"

"Sam, I'm asking you a question!" Her voice was almost shrill. But her son merely laughed.

"Well, he nearly beat him up. But he didn't."

"Beat him up! That man nearly *fought* the preacher? *Please* tell me what you are talking about!"

"All right, mother. You don't have to get so huffy. I'll tell you." He spoke with a low, wondering caution, gingerly looking at his mother to measure the expression on her face. And in that strained mood, he told her how it was—about the preacher and Mr. Simson's insane laughter and the indignation of Mr. Campbell, who rushed across the square to drive Mr. Bazely off, and the preacher's sullen departure. His mother sat listening, her face tight and still. And at the end he composed himself into a brutal calm of his own, and he said: "I offered to help whip the preacher, mother. You'll hear about it. I wanted to fight him, and if I had fought him, I would have killed him."

"Oh Sam, Sam!" Her words were a hurt and despairing wail. "Leave the man alone. For my sake, for *your* sake, leave the man alone!"

He looked at her in grim discernment. "You're afraid the man will tell what he saw? About Emilie and me?"

"I don't know. I don't know anything!"

"If he does, I swear I'll kill him."

"Sam, the girl is gone! The preacher did not make her go! Can't you just leave him alone? He could hurt us both."

"He couldn't hurt *you*. You and he must have been on the same side, remember?"

She shook her head as if to clear something away. "I don't want to talk about it. I haven't talked about it, have I, Sam?" She looked earnestly over the table at him, and her eyes seemed near to tears, they were so glistening and sad. She put out a hand to take his, but he quickly got up to avoid her.

"You don't *have* to talk about it, Mother. You won. Emilie's gone."

His mother looked sorrowfully up at him. "Did I win, Sam? I may have lost you."

"I'm still here, Mother. You can see for yourself."

"Oh Sam." His mother sighed and stood up to face him. She had reduced the troubling thing in her mind, and looking directly at him she assumed an almost frigid self-control. "There is one thing I want to say."

"Then say it."

"Your father did not have a blind admiration for John Wesley Campbell. In his own sweet way your father saw the man for what he is."

"I guess we all see that," Sam said curtly. "He's a smart man, a good lawyer. It's what people say."

"The man is a weakling."

"Bazely didn't think so yesterday."

"*Mister* Bazely, Sam. You don't believe me, and I can't make you see it, but it's true. Your father knew it. Behind all the swagger that man puts on, he's a moral weakling. Why do you think he came to Bourbonville?"

"I don't know anything about that."

"Well, I do. He didn't think he could be successful in Knoxville or anywhere else where there were *good* lawyers. So he had to come down here where he could lord it over all of us. Why do you think he sits around at night with those *friends* of his? Why, that Ledbetter man's an illiterate! But that's just *it!* Your Mr. Campbell can look down on them, and that's the *only* kind of friend he can have—somebody he can look down on."

"I don't think you know what you're talking about."

It was her turn to laugh sardonically. "I know. Believe me, I know. You didn't see how he treated his own son, but I remember that. He couldn't even talk to the boy unless he was telling him something the poor child was doing wrong. The boy's name was Tom—Thomas Jefferson Campbell. The fancy name made a fool out of him. He was a pitiful, lonely child, afraid to open his mouth for fear of what his father would say to him. I didn't blame the boy for running off the way he did in the War. I would have run off myself." She smiled in whimsical nostalgia. "He was a good-looking boy. We were children together, and I always felt sorry for him."

Sam flicked off her digression and looked at her with the same steady and faintly mocking smile. "There's only one thing, Mother. If Mr. Campbell picked friends he could look down on, why did he pick my father? What was wrong with *him?*"

The question trampled irreverently on sacred ground, and his mother's mood hardened. "Your father was an exception to all the rules," she said in a testy voice. "Mr. Campbell doesn't deserve any credit for liking him. *Every*body loved your father."

The evasion wearied him. Arguing with his mother was always a futile charging against bastions which veered off when he drew near. "It's all over and done with now. I don't see any point in talking about it," he said spiritlessly. He wanted to get on with the chores.

"Sam, your dear father said to me one time, 'You know, John's one of the most mixed-up people I've ever known. He can tell everybody else exactly what to do, but he never knows what to do himself.' Those were his very words, the words of your sweet father before he died."

"Mother, I don't feel one way or another about Mr. Campbell. I don't see any point in hating him or being nasty to him or running off whenever he comes up to me in the street. I think you ought to remember the fact that he was my father's friend and be civil to him, or else you ought to forget him altogether."

"Sam, you *must* understand," she said, resuming her earnest and explanatory voice. "I am only trying to preserve our values. We lost *so* much in the War. I think it must have been God's way of working something out for the world. I don't know what, but there must have been a purpose in it, or it wouldn't have happened. To me our loss just means we have to work harder. We have to be like Daniel, like Shadrach, Meshach, and Abednego. No matter how hopeless it looks, we must still be faithful. If we are not, everything Matthew and your father and all the others fought for will be lost. I can't stand to think about that."

Something in her voice deepened as she spoke. Sam had heard it all so many times—the profound and delicate harmonies playing wistfully over a sublime theme. Always nowadays he made up his mind to resist it. But her tragic presence and her own powerful devotion invariably bore him down. No matter how old or how familiar, her plucking at the old melody as if on some magic harp called up a shining vision—men marching bravely to tapping drums, faces enthralled by the glory. Behind them a land of promise glowing and reaching like immaterial light into a vague realm of stormy and magnificent dreams. Gone—all gone and dead except in the hearts of those gallant people like herself who were a faithful remnant and persevered.

She put her hand lightly on his arm and gazed up at him. "I did not make her leave, Sam. Not the preacher, not me. She left of her own accord. If she had really loved you, she would not have gone. Her leaving was not my fault."

It was a serene discharge of obligation so perverse that Sam wanted to shout at her. But he could not. Instead he pulled away without another word and went out the door and down the low steps into the yard. The sunlight and the morning received him, and he felt the heat strike him like a blast of fire.

9

HE KNEW it was near dawn when the nailheads in his ceiling began to puncture the obscurity of night. He lay on his back and watched the darkness thin, heard the first waking birds take up the chorus of morning, heard a cock crow somewhere in the middle distance, undoubtedly the same cock which had crowed in the deep of night, sensing the morning long before it was there. He shut his eyes and ruminated in a disinterested way over Simson's prophecy. When he did so, he sank close to the border of sleep, and his mind drifted aimlessly.

No one would have taken Simson seriously on a commonplace day. He grunted in wry scorn at the thought and rose to a surface of wakefulness. *He was crazy.* His prophecy was nothing more than the last abject hope of a man who had choked on hopelessness. Trying to make anything else out of it was absurd. But because he had predicted rain in the moment of his death, his pathetic comment became a mysterious prophecy. With it Simson acquired something he had never once had in all his life—dignity. You had to grant dignity to a prophet! But of course he was simply insane, as anyone who claimed to see rain in this hard world of sun and stone must be insane, and tonight everyone would see the futility of his prophecy, and that would be that.

Mr. Campbell opened his eyes and looked lazily toward the window, toward the patch of whitish sky showing over the trees. No trace of clouds there. Not the least figment of a single hope. He felt a vague sense of absurd disappointment, the disillusion of a child who has hoped in vain for an impossible gift.

The dream about his son haunted him. In the nature of ghosts, the apparition was less real in the daylight. He could dismiss it as the turmoil of a spent mind. A perfectly normal dream, given his drunken state and permanent longing and self-reproach. But why did it come back again and again?

Mr. Campbell had long ago lost his faith in an invisible world which tied together all things visible. Sometimes he yearned for that forsaken faith in the same way that an adult may yearn for the Christmases of childhood. Yet he knew with a flat certainty beyond all doubt that there was no secret world. No unseen realm where a dying man might glimpse the coming of rain while ordinary men stood panting in the naked sun. No black pit from which a boy could ride to curse his father. No hell, no devil, no God. There was no pale horse but death, and Mr. Campbell knew that the world was just as it seemed.

Nothing in his dreams changed a thing out there. For all his nocturnal fear the sun now rose upon a Bourbonville which was stricken and suffering and yet quite normal, quite ordinary. The limpid air, unstained yet by the dust, revealed a world too stark and too poor for mystery. His father would have grieved for him, for the loss of his faith, for the way that each event and each object stood as unconnected in his mind as particles of dust suspended in the atmosphere.

His father. He sat up and dropped his chin against an upheld fist and gazed for a moment at the floor. His father so long dead, his body fallen to dust down there in Bradley County. All quiet the dust that had been his father, no voice there to preach the Word his father had preached. The elder Mr. Campbell expected to see Jesus return in clouds of glory. He read the Bible with passionate hope. He used to sit at night by lamplight when he was home, the great black book open on his lap, and he would lift his strong face and say with awesome conviction: "I can see the signs. I know the Lord is coming back before I die. Someday I know I'll see the heavens divided and hear the trump of God." And the youngster standing nearby could imagine the high, sharp blast of doom blown ringing across the sky by the vehement trumpet and all the heavens filled with wings and light.

But typhoid got to his father before Jesus did. God did not warn his servant of the bad water, the flooded river which corrupted the wells. He took a fever. He slipped into a deep, tormented sleep. The fever made his muscles twitch, and it never broke. No sweat ran down his face. He died with dry cheeks. John Wesley Campbell remembered that because he had laid his own face against his father's and cried, and his own tears were the only moisture there was. He was fifteen years old.

His father had been ardent for campmeetings. They were miracles. God came down and touched people there. Sometimes, when the preaching was good and the Spirit was at work, joy rained down so thick you could hardly catch your breath. Care and fear were snapped away from constricted hearts. Sinners got converted, and there was shouting, and strong men cried with happiness and release, and dim clearings in the almost trackless woodland were suddenly raised up to the shining vision of the Eternal God. In the fresh air, under the starlight, ordinary men were swept up into a divine passion.

And there was passion for something less divine. It was the way campmeetings were. Preachers knew it. They shook their heads sorrowfully about it and consoled themselves with Genesis. For there was a serpent in Eden. There was a passion for God at campmeetings, and under it came slithering this other passion, and where one was present the other seemed always to be nearby.

After all these years Mr. Campbell still thought of the girl at the campmeeting in Bradley County. She was the first to startle his slumbering adolescence awake. As it turned out, she was the first one he lost.

They walked together into the summer woods. The girl kissed him in the dark for the first time he had ever been kissed. He almost fell before the wetness of her mouth, and she took his slack hand and brought it up over her breast. He could still remember how soft her breast had been, the sharp little cry of delight she squealed into his ear when his fingers tightened over the soft mound. For a moment he was sick with love and desire.

But only a moment, for he flung himself away from her and left her giggling and taunting him for his inexperience. Yet all that night he lay dozing and waking, half mad with anticipation and tormented by regret. By morning he had resolved to sin. He had considered all the commands of God, and he had decided to violate them all—a curiously rational, unflinching process of logic for a mind in a stew of longing. He forced himself to work it all out—measure his desire, marshal the consequences, sniff the fires of hell—and he made his decision.

But the next night the girl went off with someone else. He stood at the edge of the clearing where a preacher thundered the Gospel, and he saw her slip into the darkness like a shadow. Another shadow glided to meet her, and the woods, palpitating with singing insects, took them into the giant shadow of itself. Long hours later, when the clearing was still, the lesser shadows slipped back and detached themselves. He cursed his innocence, and he never saw the girl again. Her breast and her gasping little mouth and her taunting laughter had become an immaterial memory afloat in a haze of years.

He laughed at himself, his chuckling, dry, resigned laughter which was the way he crossed himself in passing the darkened graveyards of his life. The first real failure of his life! His father would have thought it a miraculous success. The elder Mr. Campbell would have woven a providential explanation around it, and in that fancy trellis his failure would have become a garden of roses.

But his father never knew anything about it. Mr. Campbell was now more than sixty years old. His father had been younger than that when he died, and Mr. Campbell thought him to be an old man. Some time, he thought in moments of fantasy, he would go back down to Bradley County where his father lay buried and tell the dust all about it—just to set the record straight.

Was it the unpardonable sin, that decision made that night wrapped in his blankets under the stars? The rational, calculating decision to sin and to sin as much as necessary to ease his aching desire, and to hide the fact of his sin from his father's face? Was it possible that all the casual failures of his life ran in a track to that moment? He wished that it were so, for then his life would mean something.

He got slowly up and walked to the window. The glass-filled frames gaped open to the air as if the house were panting for breath, and the sill was coated with a film of red dust. The nigger woman who cleaned for him had been in the day before. She had sopped and scrubbed all afternoon after the hanging. She labored with a wheezing repetition of heavy sighs, and she left a house so clean that one imagined the wood and the glass bruised from the slapping of her hands. The house stood (except for the shut rooms) in that incorrupt state as of yesterday afternoon. Now the thin film of dust smirched the window sill. Mr. Campbell looked at it, idly ran a finger through it, looked at the mark he had made, studied distastefully the red smudge on the end of his finger. He knew that every surface in Bourbonville was coated with the dust. He knew also that the steady heat was daily working more deeply into the surface of the earth and that in time the wind would rise and blow the topsoil away. It would tear back the skin of the earth like a knife, laying bare the infertile subsoil. That inhospitable ground would be left to absorb the faith of men who lived off the land, and Bourbonville itself would wither and fall sick and nearly die.

His dead wife had loved Bourbonville. She said it was *their* town, and she made him believe it, and he came to love it too. That was the way things worked out for them at the first—his golden age, like all golden ages shining like a dream in the unbelievable past.

He had met her in Knoxville. He was reading law there. He met her at an absurd little party put on by the wife of one of the partners in the firm, a woman much given to lustful reading of the newspapers from Washington City about society in the nation's capital. Charlotte circulated through the party, laughing gaily but nervously, and she came to him because undoubtedly the two of them were the most uncomfortable people in all the uncomfortable crowd. And they were young. Yes, by God, they were young! She spoke with an accent which was very soft and more Southern than his own twanging speech, and the first words she said to him seemed to take him into her confidence. She was slim and fair with chestnut hair falling to frame an oval face. Her eyes were clear and brown, and her features were precise to the point of being delicate. He thought at the time that she was a cameo come to life. Her teeth were slightly uneven, but it was the kind of blemish which makes a woman truly beautiful because it conferred an individuality upon her which was striking and memorable. You never forgot her smile. So that is how they met.

He courted her hesitantly and stupidly. He was woefully self-conscious with her, but in his private hours he could think of nothing but her. He could spend long moments absorbed in the memory of her mouth and entranced by the mystery of the way she alternated between girlish effervescence and stately dignity. He wanted her so badly that he gave her up for lost the first time he saw her. But for reasons he could never understand, she fell in love with him. He adored her. They were married. It was January in the year of grace, eighteen hundred and forty-four. A rainy, wintry January heavy with the smell of burning wood. He loved the dreary month for the rest of his life. The world was as new and young as the two of them, and everywhere they looked there was hope.

He never quite knew what particular thing brought him to Bourbonville. It was a casual decision. He was very young, and

Knoxville had its share of lawyers, and some of them could talk so hard and so fast that a man of slow temperament like himself was bewildered by them. He foresaw himself ground underfoot before he had scarcely learned to walk in the profession. He thought he might fail before his wife, and that prospect filled him with foreboding. At the time there were no lawyers in Bourbonville, and it was really not far from Knoxville. Twenty-six miles by the Hiwassee Railroad, which was new in those days. So he came down here to get a start. He could have gone elsewhere, and he never intended to stay here. He came to get a little momentum. With that, he reasoned, there was no telling where he might go. A man could make a name for himself in a coming town like Bourbonville, Charlotte said. And in an untamed frontier state like this one, a name meant unbelievable power.

The young Mr. Campbell believed his wife. In this vast, hot world decades removed from that luminous year, the fact of his belief seemed strange to him, strange that she had been his trust and hope when now he could not quite form a picture of her face in his mind. He could still describe her if anyone inquired after her—which no one ever did. There were words which fitted her, and he could recite them. Were she to come alive from the grave, he would know her instantly from afar. And sometimes when he dreamed she appeared to him in all the lost clarity of their truant youth. Sometimes she laughed in his sleep, and he laughed with her, and there was a bright happiness in their laughter which made all things shine like a gold piece fresh from the mint. But he awoke from all his dreams to find that time had rubbed the edges off her precisely beautiful features and dulled the gold to the color of iron. She was quite gone. And it was strange to him—in the way half-forgotten things are sometimes strange—that he had listened to her and believed in himself. "We will have a great life, John. I know it. You'll see, my dear, sweet John."

She was right about the quality of the life they had together. They both erred in their estimate of its duration. They imagined years progressing into great age, when grandchildren would frolic about the knees of white-haired grandparents decades and decades hence. But it was not to be.

Within a year she had their son. There wasn't even a doctor in Bourbonville in those days. No one to deliver a baby but a nigger slave, a woman who understood such things. Mr. Campbell was afraid. He wanted her to go back to Knoxville to be with her family until the child was delivered. She refused. She would stay with him. And the baby was born, and she survived the birth—pale, tight-lipped with the pain, but she came through. They both laughed like children while the baby cried in his arms and the nigger midwife looked at them both in a dull, professional condescension at their joy.

Charlotte recovered soon enough, the baby grew and flourished, and Mr. Campbell walked firmly about the settlement, consulted by everybody, respected, admired, and he assumed the important look of a young man of affairs, a young man of promise shooting up in a green world where everyone waited for the days to turn over like the pages of a well-known book to the inevitable conclusion where good triumphed and hard work received its just reward. He did work hard. He applied himself to becoming the best lawyer around, and he labored at eloquence and believed there was a power in words. He laid his hands to the digging of the great foundation under their soaring dreams.

Days of hard work—and great nights following. A symphony of variety falling into a blissful pattern. On some nights he would tumble wearily into bed and in peaceful habit put his arm over Charlotte's lithe body and hold her hand and feel her warm little bottom slip close against him in preparation for sleep. In other nights they made love in a thrashing, delirious, and prolonged abandon up and down the bed and sometimes onto the floor. She had a streak of obscenity in her. It was one of the refreshing little surprises she presented him when they knew each other better. Sometimes she would lie in mock thoughtfulness beside him when all their passion was spent and speculate about her talents as compared with those of any whore in the country. He in turn would fondle her gently and reproach her for her unconscionable ambition. So she would laugh and snuggle down beside him, and they would drift off into an untroubled sleep.

In his precise and rational way, Mr. Campbell tried to put together a bill of particulars about his passion for her. He decided that what he loved most was the way she gave herself to him as completely as she could. He was always profoundly aware that she was not just an extension of himself but that she was a world of her own. Sometimes in the midst of their love-making, with his head against hers, he thought, *Next to me is another universe. It is her universe. And it is different from mine. I possess the owner of a private world!* It was a strangely dispassionate thinking in the frenzy of their love, but then that was the way Mr. Campbell's mind worked.

Then again—especially when court was in session—there were times when he would simply lie on his back next to her and talk—long, rambling monologues about his work, the details of some case, the character of a judge or contestant, or the peculiar temperament of a jury he was trying to convince. He would expound on the way in which some great principle of jurisprudence was related to a minor quarrel over title to a strip of bottom land near a creek, and he would define and refine the hazy issues in some particularly murky litigation. He talked on and on, interspersing his remarks with dry laughter about himself, and occasionally he apologized to her for his long-windedness. "I always feel I can interrupt if I want to," she invariably said with a quiet laugh, and he said she would make a fine judge. He went on talking, and she listened. He talked out things that worried him and things that amused him, and he ruminated aloud on choices he had to make. His mind loosened up with his talk. Sometimes in the morning he would waken with a new insight about something, and he would go off that day in a new direction and often come back that evening chortling with success. He said she created a plain of understanding and sympathy, and on that plain his mind roved at will, and he could see things with a clarity which sometimes startled him. He said once, laughing, that he would be the first President of the United States to make his wife a member of his cabinet. She laughed happily at him and said he was crazy.

There was no doctor in Bourbonville. No doctor when they came, and on the night she awakened with the agony in her side and her belly as hard as iron there was still no doctor. It was appendicitis—one of the quiet hazards of life removed from doctors. She died before either she or he realized it was as serious as it was. A very casual, undramatic death done without formal last words or farewells. She died in this room with a gentle sigh, and the doctor who came hurrying down from Knoxville to the urgent plea of the telegraph arrived only in time to tell him she was dead.

After that he went blindly off to the war—that other war so long, long ago. He took the bewildered little boy to her parents in Knoxville, and he went off with thousands of others who filed westward to win a nation from Mexico. He marched to Santa Fe and to Monterey and finally to Mexico City. He drank a lot of *tequila,* and he slept with uncounted whores trying to recapture something, and in the broiling heat of the Mexican lowlands he took sick and almost died.

He might have wished that he could die, but he could not wish for anything. He lived like something thoughtless and adrift, a piece of flotsam on a dim sea or else a lichen growing green on rotting brick, existing without feeling and without purpose, not thinking about the past because something had dropped down between himself and it—a screen of dimly opalescent glass, forbidding and impenetrable. It was not that he forgot; it was simply that he did not care to remember.

Once, in 'forty-six, in a skirmish on the way to Mexico City, he lay with his face in the dirt while bullets swirled over him. He chewed sand with the impossible sun on his back, and he thought that he would never see his boy again. The thought was large and sad. With his bare face thrust into the sandy earth, he had a startling recollection of how soft the boy's face had been against his own. The zing of leaden death stitched the ground around him, and the air above him made life seem as velvety and tender as a baby's cheek. But the moment itself was brief, and he got up after the skirmish and shook himself and went on.

After that, for several years, when he thought of himself, his home, and his son, it was as if he were thinking about somebody else, somebody mysteriously related to but decisively cut off from John Wesley Campbell in Santa Fe, New Mexico Territory (as it became), or wherever else he happened to be. He could give an account of his life to anyone who asked, and did so in saloons and whorehouses all across the Southwest. But his recitations were dry catalogs of facts culled from the history of a vanished time, strangely distant and uninteresting even to himself, and finally he stopped them altogether.

He tended bar for a while and had a part interest in a whorehouse and tried his hand at gambling, did pretty well for a time, but then lost everything he had in one night, including his interest in the whorehouse. After that he drifted north and onto the Great Plains and hunted buffalo and mingled with the Indians and thought about going to California to prospect for gold. His life was an unformed lump of clay. He was silent now for long periods of time, answering laconically only when he was addressed, a loner by habit and left alone.

But one morning he got up and decided to go home. He always said that the reason was his sudden, sharp memory that he had a son. Not just that John Wesley Campbell late of Bourbonville, Tennessee, had a son, but that *he* had a son and that that son was part of Charlotte's flesh, the only part of her he still possessed; something she had loved and granted to him as a legacy.

And he had more than a son. He had a place in the world. For there were lawbooks back home which must be riven by worms and termites, warped and in danger of falling apart. Quite suddenly he longed for them, his son and his books, with a terrible, irresistible longing. And so he came home to claim them.

To this day he had never quite understood the onslaught of desire that brought him back. It fell on him as precipitously as an Indian attack or the tumbling of a horse into a hidden ravine. He had no warning that he could remember, no early stir of involuntary nostalgia, no half-playful toying with the idea. It simply happened that he lay down one night in the same dead emptiness of mind in which he had lived for so long, and the next morning he awoke with a fiercely passionate longing to go home. In his twenty-seventh year he felt the relentless pressure of time, and all at once he gave way before it. Since that day he had never assumed that people must always be merely what they appear to be at the moment. Rather he saw the most quiescent human being much as he had seen (and was to see again) cannon lodged in their heavy iron silence just before battle. Rarely afterward was he startled by what men did or became.

He wondered later, when things did not go as he expected, if he had loved the lawbooks more than he had loved his boy. Now in the morning quiet of the time-swept house, he supposed that this may have been the case. For he did love his books. Not merely the words but the feel of them in his hands and the comfortable smell of leather rising in the stillness when he studied at night. He loved print, and he loved the law, and he had a soaring faith.

Not a religious faith. His faith was in the law. He believed that the law took all the chaotic fragments of human life and ordered them into a grand design. He imagined the law as a golden line holding nations and empires together, an almost magical force which reached over the abyss of barbarism and called civilization into being.

There were gaps in the law. He knew that. Or rather there were places where the shining cord disappeared in patches of cloud or else lay buried in ignorance. But every day, somewhere in the world, the line was being cleaned, scraped, polished, and laid bare. Out in the vast plains of whispering grass or in the shifting desert alone,

John Wesley Campbell was insignificant and invisible in the mighty order of things. But in the law his tiny life took on an immeasurable purpose. However frail his hands, they were laid on the chain which pulled the world around.

Now he recalled that youthful fantasy, and he laughed softly at himself. Not bitter laughter. The nostalgic laughter of an adult observing a child who believes fairies inhabit the forest glens. For Mr. Campbell had observed the law now for a great many years. He had labored in its commonplaces and strained at its cumbersome precedents to make them apply to Bourbonville. Now he saw the law as the decorous line of deceitful subterfuge decreed by the few to oppress the many. The law was indeed a cord, but a cord which choked the tender neck of humanity—absurd, arbitrary, cruel, and drenched with blood. There was a fascination to it, and here and there one could shift the cord to make it gouge less deeply into the soft flesh of humankind. Perhaps that was justification enough for being a lawyer. Perhaps it was not.

Anyway, John Wesley Campbell had come home. He had a son. Only by the time he got back, his son was five years old, a stranger. He hid from his father in an upstairs room of his grandparents' house and had to be hauled weeping downstairs, frightened half out of his wits—a stranger, forever a stranger. Mr. Campbell would always remember the small, fair child sitting upright in a chair in the corner of this house, here in Bourbonville, looking at him with those wide brown eyes which incessantly posed the silent question "Who are you?"

He shook his head. For a moment the memories scattered like glittering fragments of glass broken in the brilliant sun. There stood the courthouse. There was the jail. There were the wood-laced tracks of the railroad. There was Bourbonville in the early summer of the year eighteen hundred and eighty-five, and here he stood at the window like a foolish old man awash in his own past. And what was he?

He knew that his features had broken with age. And he could imagine that the strong, angular configurations of grief also collapsed with time into an aimless sentimentality which fed on itself. He supposed it was only sentimentality that made the buried hope still kick in his heart, the hope that one day his son might yet come straggling home. He knew he could not make his own life a pattern for the life of his son. And what would he really do if the boy, now forty years old, did come home after all these years? It was a thought with a high, dark edge which he could not see over. But he faced it as bravely as he could and in the calm realism with which he tried to view the world, and he waited from day to day.

It was a strange uneasiness, that thing which he felt toward his boy in those long-ago years when they had a chance together. Now in the useless perspective of age, he supposed he understood. He wanted desperately for his son to love him because his son was all he had left of Charlotte, and Charlotte's love was the support around which he had stacked his life. The desire was so strong in him that he felt humiliated, and humiliation made him cautious and reserved. So out of the caution and the reserve there grew an impassable barrier between father and son, a lethal wall of silence, which grew more solid and thick with their years together. It was something that just happened, and then it went on happening, and after a while both of them accepted it like a deformity or a chronic disease—silence, deadly silence.

At first Mr. Campbell tried. He talked about the West to his son, perhaps in some dim way remembering those nights when he had talked in his rambling, easeful fashion to Charlotte. Each night he took the boy up to bed, putting him to rest in one of the rooms across the hall—a room now long shut up, probably sticky with abandoned cobwebs in the way of unused rooms. But in those days he would sit on the edge of the bed while the boy lay there, looking silently up. It was a contrast: the hulking, awkward man towering there in the half-light above the reclining slim form of a child who was almost frail. Clumsily he tried to explain why he had been away so long and who he was. And when he could find no explanation which would make even a decent lie, he talked about the West.

He did not tell his son about the whorehouse, though he did talk of the gambling, and he told of bloody fights and aimless cruelty, and he described the sunrise, silent and huge like watery fire in the dry enormity of the New Mexico Territory. When he talked about it, it all seemed serene and beguiling, like sand cliffs seen at evening under a stark moon. It was something as beautiful as paradise itself, and his time there became a resting, when he found himself, took energy and force from the inexhaustible supply of the great West, and brought them home. "I never forgot you. I always thought of you out there. It just took me longer to get home than I planned." And the boy gazed back at him over that silent and troubled distance.

But nothing quite worked to take away the uncertainty of the little boy—the little boy who was growing larger in the silent drift of years. A slim, shy child with his mother's brown eyes set in a sensitive oval face. And in time Mr. Campbell's stories faltered and died.

When his boy vanished, Mr. Campbell took all the blame for the failure onto himself. He had stayed away too long. When Charlotte died he abandoned the child before the boy was old enough to know who he was. And when he returned from the West, it was as if he had come up out of the earth to carry the boy off. On the long trek home he worried about Charlotte's parents. *They might not give him up!* The fearful thought worked at him with the miles. But Charlotte's people were strong and businesslike. Her father took pride in his own unsentimentality. The only way to get along in the world, he said. In fact he thought Mr. Campbell carried things much too far in his grief over Charlotte's death. "These things happen," he offered in his businesslike way. "It's something we all have to bear up under, my boy. But the Lord giveth, and the Lord taketh away. Life must go on." All this uttered with a convivial, formal regret ending on a note of decent dismissal; that was the way Charlotte's father was about everything.

So there was no trouble about the boy. Charlotte's father was actually relieved to see his son-in-law back again and prepared to take up his paternal responsibilities. "Only natural and right," he said with a grave nod. "A boy ought to be with his father. Now Tom, you can come to see us any time you like, you hear? No, no don't cry! Men don't cry, my boy. Stop it!" And with that he pushed the child away, brushing him off like some unwelcome clinging insect into Mr. Campbell's arms. And that was all there was to it.

Somehow it should have been different! Easy enough to think now, thirty-five years removed from the morning he rode back into Knoxville from the West. But then the consequences seemed tame, manageable before the great proud joy he felt. "I'm your daddy, child. I've come home. Didn't they tell you I'd come home?" It was only later that the silence absorbed all the joy, and then it was too late.

The blue of the sky was hardening as he watched. His thoughts sank into the view. The brass dome of the courthouse, newly polished for the hanging, caught the blinding sunlight. In a moment the intense brightness made him shut his eyes. That act broke the spell of his terrible nostalgia.

He went downstairs, carrying his shoes in his hands. He prepared the coffeepot, pumped fresh water out of his well, unharmed yet by the drought, and he put a vessel of it on the stove. When he was dressed, he made his breakfast, whipped biscuits together with a quick expertise, poured his coffee, and sat down by the window. Two decades ago he had opened his house for the second time, sat in the same room, in the same place, and memory had ached in him so that he wondered how he could go on living. But the sharp ache had subsided into a dull heaviness long ago. *All feelings are of short duration.* It was a comforting maxim he had picked up somewhere.

And it seemed to be true. Now he recalled Charlotte's slim body bending through the breakfast chores in time to unheard music. He remembered the baby chortling on a blanket, slobbering, lifting his little head to watch the common things with such innocent wonder. At times nowadays it troubled him that he no longer choked with emotion at his recollections. But with detached, invincible assurance he reflected quite calmly on the fact that the world did not mean anything. Nothing endured the slow erosion of time. If a man lived out his span he got accustomed to things like death and loss, and Mr. Campbell had lived sixty-one years now, and he could accept some things with little emotion. He viewed the world with stoic calm, and in his resignation at the way things were, he rarely experienced either joy or bitterness.

He had not learned that wisdom when he returned to Bourbonville after his Western journey. He tried to snatch up his life and resurrect his dreams and to clothe his days once more in joy. But he could only grasp at the ashes into which everything had fallen. His son was the key to everything, and his son would not respond to him. Mr. Campbell was not a patient man. *What else can I do! Must I grovel on my back and beg him to love me? By God, I won't do that. A man has to keep his dignity!* No matter what Mr. Campbell did the boy was always reluctant, always a stranger, always withdrawn into a private, inhospitable world where there was no room for anyone but himself. *All right then, I've done my best! Damn you, I've done my best!* Mr. Campbell flung a silent curse against his son and fell back on that shallow substitute for love which is dignity.

He kept his dignity for years—the crazy, meaningless thing with its inner walls of ice, the absurd quality which made Roman lords pause to dress while Vesuvius was erupting. Dignity made him draw back so that in the end he kept his dignity and lost his son. It didn't seem fair in a way, he thought now with his ruminating lawyer's mind. For when he made the contract, he did not realize all its terms. Most important of all, he could not make himself realize how final it was, how irrevocable it would become in time. Dignity in exchange for a son—he meant it only as an expedient until something better could be worked out. But it turned out to be something different.

A decade plus one year! That was the time he had with his son. Eighteen fifty. Eighteen fifty! John Wesley Campbell at home with his son. Little children who would die in battle shouting over childish games in eighteen fifty. Villages whose names battles would brand in fire slumbering in anonymity in eighteen fifty. Abraham Lincoln a failure in eighteen fifty. U. S. Grant a failure in eighteen fifty—everything so different from what it would become.

And John Wesley Campbell at home in Bourbonville, far from everything, groping around for the fragments of a shattered life and still believing he could pick them up and put them back together again. Striving. Failing. Bewildered but not yet hopeless. The days falling one by one into the space of years. A red darkness creeping in from the horizon, where men looked anxiously for a sign. Resonant words ringing over the nation where men plowed and planted and copulated and endured and pursued the implacable routine of lives regulated by the seasons and ticking to the pendulum of birth and death. Abraham Lincoln, no longer a failure: "Slavery is an unqualified evil to the Negro, to the white man, to the soil, and to the State." "A house divided against itself cannot stand." John Brown, a lunatic near to death: "I, John Brown, am now quite certain that the crimes of this guilty land will never be purged away but with blood." Turmoil. Fury. Flags. Shouting. Secession. Sumter. Secession. Singing troops on the march through the green springtime. Drums pounding, pounding. The children of eighteen fifty grown to manhood, still playing at childish games on their way to war and the irredeemable loss of childhood. The childish innocence of a nation gone forever, already cracking and falling in that night when John Wesley Campbell rode up to war for the second time in his life.

He took the boy to Knoxville once again, to his grandfather. The boy's grandmother had long since died. Now the grandfather wanted the boy, threw trembling arms around the child that night and cried. The fierce walrus mustache all gray and dead. Age and war had surprised the old man, found him unprepared for both. He clung to the boy as the boy had never clung to anyone since his mother died. Mr. Campbell ordered his son to stay put, ordered the grandfather to watch over the boy, made the formal declaration that he would hold the grandfather eternally responsible for anything that happened to Charlotte's son. And uttering one final, profane command for the boy to stay there, Mr. Campbell fled.

As he cleared the dusky outskirts of Knoxville, passed the misshapen wooden buildings bulging at him from the dark, the loss settled over him. No matter how much he had expected it, *he* was unprepared for this war. All at once he recognized the futility of his own pride, the counterfeit worth of dignity, and he was afraid.

Somehow he had always expected time to cure things. In the end, things would work *out.* The boy would overcome something and would become something else all by himself. The son would put away childish things and become a man, and father and son would be men together. When that happened, Mr. Campbell kept thinking from year to year, life would settle down and become something rich and full and so satisfying to father and son alike that their days would be almost sublime.

But all the while ordinary life had run on from day to day, and John Wesley Campbell watched it abstractly, like an old sailor half asleep in the drowsy sun watching a hawser fall behind a plunging anchor. Four thousand lost days! Four thousand lost chances had tumbled into the deep of time, and then the war which ended time like the Second Coming, the war which halted ordinary life with an unexpected blast of trumpets and a roll of sudden drums.

And he was riding north, and Knoxville was falling behind him. Bourbonville swallowed up in the glittering dark, and the drumming hoofbeats of his horse beat a funeral tattoo to fallen hopes. He was sure of only one thing as he slipped out into that fragrant spring night—sure that he loved his son, that he loved him fiercely and passionately and miserably and that now the years of time and opportunity were a Gordian knot, hurled past him and gone, to be neither cut nor untied.

So in this war he had something simple and precious to lose—one more chance with his son, one opportunity to trade dignity for a boy. A simple, ordinary human desire so easily frustrated by a simple, ordinary fragment of unthinking metal. No surprise then that he faced every day of the conflict with mortal fear and went into every battle with dread in his bones. Some men could always find something to laugh about in war. The laughter was a rein on their fear and maybe a saddle too. Brian Ledbetter had been such a man.

Mr. Campbell was sure of that. It was the peculiar gift of the War to him, for before the War he was a slim, shy, overgrown boy who shrank from public notice. The war made him laugh, and it made him funny. He could lie behind a rock wall against a Rebel charge and be so frightened he pissed in his pants. And he could laugh about it and tell the story and make others howl with laughter until battles seemed a stage on which Brian acted out a hilarious comedy. "Rebel tea," Brian called it—laughing.

To Mr. Campbell it was just piss, and he never laughed about it. What Mr. Campbell liked to remember of the War was the smell of grass and the illusion of peace which hung like the morning haze at the beginning of the new day in rural Virginia. More painfully he remembered the elaborate plans he made to set things right with his boy when he returned home. He would not simply talk to his son, but they would *do* things together—perhaps go West as he had always planned. He vowed to make things up to his boy, to be a father no matter what the cost.

So he survived the War and came back to Knoxville to find that Charlotte's father had died and that their son had vanished. "He went off to the war, right after you," uninterested people said. "You say he was just sixteen years old? Well, he looked older than that." Why of course they thought he went north to fight for the Union. A boy wouldn't fight against his own father, would he? And that was all he ever knew.

Not that he didn't try to find out more. He tried for five years. And sometimes even yet he was tempted to try again. He wrote letters to the War Department. The War Department finally responded with frigid, bureaucratic courtesy that nobody could tell him anything about his boy. He would have to provide more information. He wrote again, and he suggested things, and a bored clerk in the War Department responded that it was quite impossible to do what he wanted. It was strongly implied in the letter that the life of one young man was not important enough to waste time on. So many had died. One more or less was insignificant. And Mr. Campbell really had no answer to that.

But he even went to Washington. There stiffly correct and bureaucratically sympathetic men told him that they really did understand. They made a career of understanding, and they were good at it. But it was all quite impossible. If the boy had not come home, he could be presumed dead. Certain conclusions could be drawn. A hard war. Men killed and buried fast so they wouldn't stink up the land. Often not buried in time. You couldn't stop work long enough to see who you were putting in the ground. Unless the dead man were lucky enough to have a comrade who knew him, he was likely to be dumped into an anonymous grave. Oh yes, hard to lose a son and an only son at that. Mother dead too? Too bad. Really too bad. And the bureaucratic men went through a ritual clucking of their tongues and shook their heads in affected sorrow. Ahem, ah, the Union had been preserved. Some real gratification in that for all grieving fathers. His son had not died in vain. Far beyond our poor power to add or detract. Government of the people, by the people, and for the people . . . The living Union a monument to his dead son. The father could look around him at this glorious nation and be proud for the noble sacrifice. And then they offered advice. Nothing he could do now but return home, pick up what was left, and go on. His son had done his duty. With that same high courage he must now do his. At this the bureaucratic men assumed expressions of terrific nobility, and you might have expected them to shed inky tears which could be caught by the right functionary on the right form and promptly filed in the right drawer under "TW" for Tragic Weeping.

So there was nothing for him in Washington, and finally Mr. Campbell took courage enough to swallow the dregs of his pride and seek help in Richmond. Five years after the War he had to visit the old capital of the Confederacy on a piece of odd business on behalf of a friend. While he was there he went around to the state authorities and explained himself to them and asked where he might find help. But they too shook their heads. Richmond had been pretty well burned out, they said. The records were in chaos. Before he could find any news of his son there, he might as well start traveling all over the country to look at every young man he could find. They threw their hands up helplessly and said they were sorry. Mr. Campbell nodded and said he was sorry too, and with that he came back to Bourbonville, and here he stayed.

At first he did think about leaving the town. He might go West again, maybe to California. This time he would be respectable, keep his eyes open, and who could tell? The great dreams of his youth were all gone, but a few small ones still hung over the wreck of his life, all like small amber clouds floating high in the blue dark of night in the hour after sunset. California law was not *that* different from Tennessee law. Practice maybe in San Francisco, in sight of the purple ocean and the whitecaps. You could smell the Orient in Frisco, people said. He imagined that smell to be salty and spice-pungent and fresh and somehow free and mysterious. And perhaps along the sidewalks of the booming town, he just might one day encounter a familiar form . . .

One night the thing took him like a fever. He got to thinking about it when he lay down, and he couldn't sleep, and as a kind of joke on himself he got out of bed and lighted the lamp and began laying out things he would take if he went. Just a sleepless joke, but in a sudden instant it turned serious and became a frenzy. Something like the great blunt thing which had overpowered him years before in the Great Plains. He began slapping things into two large carpetbags, and he got everything he really wanted jammed inside—everything except his books.

He carried the lamp downstairs to his office and held it up. There they were, glistening softly in their mellow leather bindings, row on row and timeless, bricks holding up his universe. He put the lamp down on his desk and let the steady light shine in delicate splendor on the books, and he ran his hands over them, catching the smooth and the rough with his fingertips and feeling within himself a deep satisfaction at the life tingling there. He fondled them, smelled them, and told himself that he could send them overland on the railroad. There *was* a railroad by then which knit the Atlantic and the Pacific together with steel. It would just take a little time to pack the books carefully, and then he could take time to sell the house, and that would be more sensible anyway. More fitting than to vanish like a spirit in the dead of night.

But even as he pondered, the enfolding presence of the town impressed itself upon him. It lay out there, hunkered down in the night, still and dreaming like a sleeping cow. He gazed out the familiar window at it, took in its familiar form made enigmatic by the darkness, laughed suddenly at himself, went upstairs and unpacked, and never seriously considered leaving Bourbonville again. Fifteen years after that moment he was still here. And if his son ever returned in his lifetime, Mr. Campbell would be here, waiting.

He looked out the window at morning lighting the West. Making a short, resolute gesture of decision, he took his eyes off the land and got up from his breakfast. He stood in the midst of the kitchen and rubbed his hands gently over his face. He could feel the hard lines around his eyes and in his forehead with his fingers, and in a distracted sort of way he thought of his books and likened his face to the binding of a volume closed to life like the ancient Bible of his father.

He opened the door from the kitchen into the hallway. The enclosed space was stuffy. He went to the front door and opened it onto the morning and stood for a moment in the open air. The sun glowed like molten iron and threw hot rays against his face. Today would be hotter even than yesterday had been. It was already an effort to breathe, and the day was just begun. He felt his habitual dull resignation at all that and noted in his factual way that the air did not yet reek of the dust. The dust was yet unstirred, and the day untrammeled.

But even as he watched he heard the jingle of traces and harness and the muffled fall of hoofs in the powdery streets. People and animals were beginning to move about, and the dust would be raised soon enough.

A train was due down from the north in a half hour or so. Mr. Campbell could see the blurred form of Clarence Jackson moving behind the windows of the railroad station, and he contemplated it with a sudden, human sadness. All above, the sky opened wide to the zenith and shone in the morning like hard blue glass blown just in front of infinity. The sun blazed over the crouching town. He withstood the scorching onslaught of its heat for a moment longer and then gave way before it.

He turned for refuge into the room where the law books were and settled in the chair behind the desk. He reached for the book which lay in front of him from the day before. Even as he made that slight exertion he felt the sweat break out on his back. And when he laid his hands on the smooth, wooden top of his desk, he almost immediately felt the itchy beading of moisture between it and his skin. Noticing these things, he promptly dismissed them, and opening the book, he began to read.

10

Beckinridge Bourbon awoke to dingy light hanging in the cabin, shading in the corners to gloomy darkness. The sun was up. It did not shine directly into the room because there were no windows on the eastern side. In one of those corners under a lean-to roof his father's bed squatted beneath its tumbled load of filthy blankets. Tangled in the blankets lay his father's body. The body sprawled headfirst off the bed like a rod of hardened excrement, and the blankets trailed off the bed behind it in a long wad.

Beckinridge had slumped forward onto the table. Beside the oil lamp with the missing chimney he had passed into a profound and drunken slumber. He twitched and whimpered with primitive dreams but slept on and awoke at last with the morning in possession of the earth and the lamp still solemnly burning beside him. He knew that the oil was almost gone, and he blew at the flame, muttering at the waste. When he did so another fire blazed up in his chest. Snatching his hands up with a gasp of pain he remembered all the fear and humiliation of yesterday afternoon.

The pain was so sharp he could scarcely breathe. He tried to stand. His chest burned over the broken rib. When he moved he cried out in anguish and dug his fingernails into the edges of the table and thought for a moment he was going to die. He eased himself back onto the chair, groaning almost without any sound except his raw, panting breath. Little by little the pain subsided. He sat with his fingernails still gripping the table and breathed as slowly and as deeply as he could, trying to drive the clouds from his head.

His eyes, climbing from the table, took in his father's body. Like some slow birth the dim shape of the event of last night rose out of everything else. The old man was dead, finally dead, and he had killed him. Tears swam in his eyes. They trembled softly on his ponderous lower lids and rolled streaming down his cheeks, and he felt the drops fall with tiny splashes onto his overgrown hands. He had loved the old man. Most of the time he had loved him. He had hated him just enough to beat him up once in a while. And to kill him. Enough to do that. But mostly he loved him.

Very carefully he settled back against the chair. When he moved even slightly every muscle seemed to catch fire again, and the pain was so hot he could hardly keep from shrieking. But when he tried to cry, the vise around his chest clamped itself harder over his breath, and he could not. He sat down and went on struggling to breathe and dimly and dully began trying to work things out in his mind.

His father was dead. That was the first fact he had to consider. Something would have to be done. A second inescapable fact. And tied to it a third. His father would have to be buried. Buried in the dry, hard ground. If not buried, stinking. More stink than a 'possum or a skunk because he was bigger. More like a horse would stink, and he, Beckinridge, would have to watch the rot and smell the stink, and the white men would come and smell the stink too, and their eyes would light up, and they would find the body, and then there would be shame.

So he would have to bury his father. All the other facts finally added up to this one, and it was the biggest of all. He would have to bury his father, and he could not wait to do it.

The thought throbbed at him like his pain. And at last, when the weight of it was too much to bear any longer, he clinched his teeth until his jaws ached and tried to get up. The pain threw him back. He moaned helplessly. *He had to get up.* In all the torment he had to rise somehow and get the earth over his father. Nobody in the wide world to help him. Nobody in heaven above or earth beneath. And so in spite of the cruel pain and the near paralysis of his muscles, he tried again, lurched, struggled, and did it.

He stood panting over the table. The sweat was running off his face now, pouring into his eyes, blinding him in passing shadows like gray clouds going before the sun. A foolish thought kept beating at him, almost like the pain throbbing through his broken chest. There were always whites around wanting to bury a nigger. It was a sport with them. If the nigger you wanted to bury wasn't dead yet, it was a small matter. You could always kill yourself a nigger and get one to bury. Kill him, and then have a nigger to bury. Put him under ground where his black skin would fall off the bones and leave the nigger looking like a human being. Lots of whites around just panting to bury a nigger. Only Beckinridge had him a nigger to bury right here, and he had to do it all by himself.

And he had killed the nigger all by himself. That was another remarkable thing. White people were the experts at nigger killing. But Beckinridge wasn't anything but a nigger, and he had killed another nigger all by himself, and even if it was his own father, there was a way in which it made him as good as any white man going. How could any white man have done any more? Maybe the white man could have thought up something more fanciful and elaborate, but the result was just the same. A nigger was dead.

The thoughts all came at him in bits and pieces. He couldn't think them all at once, couldn't quite make the thing out of them he wanted to. They pricked his brain, fell back, got in backward, fell into a violent cloudiness but kept rising again and beating at him like metal tips of a leather belt. And the sharpest, most incessantly beating thought of all was that he had to bury his father.

The room swayed around him and made him dizzy and sick. His mind got so jumbled up that he thought he would fall. But as he stood the room slowly settled down, and the blackness which had come crowding up from below to engulf him slowly ebbed and receded and fell into its subterranean sea. The pain remained, intense and burning, but he fought with it and pushed it back and managed to take one step.

When he did so he felt the broken ends of the ribs touch and scrape in his chest. He thought he could actually hear them—hear the abrasive grinding, the crunch of bone on bone. He almost vomited. His mouth was rank and sour from the bad whiskey he had drunk. His stomach heaved violently just once, and when that happened he really did almost faint. For in struggling with his stomach he forgot his rib, and in forgetting he hurt himself so badly that he uttered a wracking groan, animal-like and terrible. The darkness came rushing back. He let his stomach go and took yet another step, and now he did vomit all in an explosive rush. The stinking, foul-tasting vomit almost choked him, and he wanted to drop and never get up again, and a storm of hopeless wretchedness blew over him. He bent and clutched his legs above the knees with his awkward hands. *"Lord, help!"* The audacious prayer burbled out of his vomit-flecked mouth, a cry for pity to the hard sky rising out of his sight beyond the shingles of the cabin roof.

In his torment he thought of killing himself. The old shotgun stood in the corner. He shifted his eyes and saw its ancient barrel, dully gleaming in the bad light. He could do the job, blow his brains out, and in time somebody would come across the white skeletons, scoured and honed by rats and worms, and that would be the end of it. No trial. No hanging. No cheerful white faces gaping upward as the new manila rope was exquisitely fixed around his tender neck, tightened just enough so that he could still breathe until the sudden fall would take breath away forever. His salvation lay in the shotgun. Despite the pain he could load the charge, tamp the shot home, fire his redemption into his broken chest, and die. He could deprive white men of that peculiar pleasure they got from killing a nigger. There was something dimly grand about the thought—as there was about the thought of killing his father. He could not quite get all the grandeur into his brain because he was so tired, but he sensed its presence and looked at the shotgun in a momentary hunger and thirst for death.

Only momentary, for he pulled himself erect again, still biting on his teeth with all his might, tasting the filth in his mouth, and he looked into another corner and found a spade. He made for it, bent with infinite care to lift it, began to sweat again with the grinding pain, but he did pick it up, and he did walk out into the vivid light, and a short distance from the house, in an old garden where the ground had been loosened before and where sweet memories of childhood, when he did not know what he was, lay finely scattered like the dust, he found a place.

When he turned the first spadeful of earth his broken rib snapped so that he knew this time he heard it. It was no imagining. The sound was clear and sharp, even above the flump of turning earth. The foot with which he pushed the spade into the dirt burned up his leg and into his hip and tore at his chest. He looked with almost complete desolation at the pitiful result of his effort—one worthless lump of dry earth displaced from a nearly invisible hole, and he wanted to cry. He leaned on the spade, felt the sweat streaming over his whole body like warm blood, looked blindly up into the fiery sky as if nailed to the wooden handle and cried, "God! God!" Above him the empty sky burned on, and whatever gods might be refused to hear.

So he turned to his digging again, turned to making the minute impressions one after another in the dusty earth. Slowly the pain settled down to something he could bear. It did not go away. It was merely pushed to one side so that it did not seem to be as important as other things. Burying his father was now the only thing on earth he wanted to do. It was all that mattered, all that ever had mattered, all that ever would matter again.

Above him the angry sun toiled up the sky, and all around the world baked in fire.

11

SAMUEL BECKWITH had just finished the chores when he heard the wagon jouncing in the lane. He walked back toward the house, wiping futilely at his face and neck with a large red handkerchief, his slender form bent in expectation.

It was indeed Suellen MacComber. She brought her team of horses to a brisk stop at the front door. The flatbed wagon's heavy wooden brake made a tremendous scraping against the steel-bound wheel. Suellen MacComber shouted at the horses—"Whoa, there. *Whoa!*" And little children perched on the back of the wagon were tumbled over backward out of sight behind the sideboards. Immediately the children bobbed up again, leaped like dusty Indians to the ground, and rushed helter-skelter across the yard yelling and laughing, tripping over themselves and rolling delightedly in the dry grass. The arrival of the MacComber wagon was always accompanied by raucous and incredible noise.

"Hello there, Samuel Beckwith Junior," Mrs. MacComber called, all out of breath. "My man says tomorrow. Can't wait. Heat or dust or what. Oats got to be brought in. Can you come? But Lord God, ain't it hot!" All this said in fits and starts and interspersed with gasping breath. At the end her enormous body sagged, and Suellen MacComber looked wilted and tired in the morning heat, more shapeless than usual, with all her sweat looking like a great bag of flour recently hauled out of a pond.

"Suellen! You shouldn't have come over here in this heat! You should have sent one of the children." Sarah Beckwith came scolding out onto the porch like a friendly wind. She was in her habitual black, a slim figure wiping her hands in a white apron, the apron starched and bleached. You might have thought she looked like a servant, but she didn't. Her manner was too warm and confident, her bearing too completely in control of things ever to allow anyone to think that Sarah Beckwith was the servant to anybody on earth.

Suellen looked up at her in something close to rapture and smiled, and some of the visiting woman's shape seemed to come back, and her worn, hot querulousness died like a shadow lighted by the sun.

"You're sure looking good, Sarah, awfully good! Don't see how you do it!" The admiring comment was almost a sigh in the heavy air. She looked around at Sam and knitted up her fleshy brows. "You've got a fine mamma, and don't you never forget it," she said belligerently. "Ha! Send a child! Don't trust these kids to do nothing right! Nothing! They'd of told you to come in next year and make molasses because that's what they like. And if one was to come by hisself, all the rest would howl over it for a week of Sundays. Can't one of my kids leave home without the rest thinking he's got something special that all of them ought to have. You ought to be thankful to the God Lord Above that you ain't got but one child, Sarah. But Lord, Lord! I don't know what I'd do without any of mine! I love them all! I hope to die if I ever see it so hot again in my life."

"Tell Mr. Mayhew I'll be there," Sam said quietly. He was always just a little astonished at the way Suellen MacComber could fill the air with words.

"Mr. Mayhew! Mr. Mayhew! Samuel, you sound like a nigger! Sarah, you've raised this boy so polite he sounds like a nigger!"

"He's a good boy, Suellen. A real good boy. I've taught him to be polite!"

"Well it ain't polite to call my husband 'Mr. Mayhew!' Call him 'Mayhew,' Sam. That's his Christian name!"

Sam flushed. "I'm sorry," he said.

Suellen looked at him critically. "Well, how are you these days, Samuel Beckwith Junior?" Her searching gaze looked him up and down, and he felt the impact of a thousand unuttered questions.

"I'm getting along just fine," he said softly. He looked down at his feet, and only with an effort did he bring his eyes back up to face her. But instead of pursuing her attack, she broke into a friendly grin and showed her big teeth.

"My! Don't the boy look just like his daddy! It makes my heart jump to see him, Sarah. I swear to the Lord God Above, don't it make your heart jump?" And she looked at Sarah Beckwith in sweaty rapture.

"Well I've always thought Sam looked a little more like his Uncle Matthew," Sarah Beckwith said easily. "Do you really think he looks like his father?"

Suellen cocked her head and looked Sam over again from head

to toe. Then she exclaimed, "Why of course he looks like his daddy, Sarah. Look at those eyes! And the cut of his chin! The face all over. Stands like his daddy, too! Long and lean. Don't hold his shoulders up neither. Stand up straight, Samuel!" He did, at least for a moment, and she became more exercised with her conviction. "Botheration, Sarah! I knowed Matthew. He was heavy. He'd of been a fat old man if he'd lived long enough. This boy's the spit image of his father. The very spit image!"

"I just hope Sam will be as good a man as his father was," his mother said. There was a slight testiness in her voice.

But Suellen took no notice of it. "Like father, like son, the Good Book says," she said and nodded her big head in token of her perfect understanding of God and man. And then, after a short interval of silence, she sighed again, a big, loud heaving of her great lungs. "And he's been dead all these years!" she said mournfully. "Think of it! *Think* of it! I swear I don't know where times goes. It seems like yesterday. And him so healthy-looking. Nobody I ever seen could ride a horse like your daddy, Samuel Beckwith Junior! I remember when I heard the awful news. My daddy come in from town, and he stood in the kitchen and told my dear sweet departed mamma, 'You know something just terrible? Sam Beckwith died last night, in his sleep.' Oh, it was a blow! My dear sweet mamma sat right down and cried, and then we come straight over here. You remember, Sarah? My my! The days of man is short on the earth as wormwood, the Good Book says. And it sure is true. Lord, it sure is true!" Suellen sat sagging over her doleful memories and the huge sadness of life until it seemed that she might just fall into herself and turn to grease before their eyes.

But abruptly she sat up and glared at Sam. "But I tell you one thing, young man! They's lots and lots of women that wouldn't of been faithful like your mamma's done. *I* sure wouldn't of. I *couldn't!* I don't have the gift. I know my own weakness like the Good Book says. And I couldn't stand it. Better to burn than to squirm, the Good Book says. And what's this I hear about you fixing to beat up the preacher, young man? Did you hear about that, Sarah?"

Sarah Beckwith smiled. A forced smile. "Yes, he told me about it, Suellen. It didn't mean a thing. I'm sure Sam will apologize. It was a very hot day, and the preacher made him nervous. You know how it is sometimes."

"Are you going to apologize?" Suellen MacComber looked at him doubtfully. Her eyes were like hammers in her fleshy face.

"No," Sam said. He looked at the ground.

"You hear that, Sarah? He ain't going to apologize!"

"We'll talk about it later, dear," Sarah Beckwith said. Her voice was strained.

"I don't know what the world's coming to with folks looking for preachers to beat up," Suellen said. "Of course I always did say Preacher Bazely was a queer one. If you got to beat a preacher up, better Preacher Bazely than anybody else, Sam Junior!"

"Suellen!" Sarah Beckwith was genuinely shocked.

"Don't 'Suellen' me, Sarah. You know the man's crazy. I know what you told my dear sweet mamma years ago. My mamma said . . ."

"I think we've talked enough about Mr. Bazely, Suellen. He's a man of God. I won't have him talked down in my presence." Sarah Beckwith was on the edge of being angry.

"Oh, tush!" Suellen said. "What's true is true. But let sleeping dogs lie, as the Good Book says. Anyhow, the man's a good preacher. I could sit and listen to him preach about hell all day long. Ain't nobody I ever heard could do it better. You'd think the man had been through the place on a local train. You got any coffee, Sarah? I sure do need some coffee."

Something of the dazzling good cheer of Sarah Beckwith came back. "Of course, Suellen. Get down. Do come in."

"Shouldn't drink so much coffee, I guess. But I hate to sit around with nothing in my hands, and a pipe makes me sick as a dog. Children! You, *children!*" She suddenly hollered and stood up in the wagon and slapped her large hands together. The children stopped as if at a signal and looked respectfully at her. "You stay put, you hear? Don't you go running off nowheres, you hear me?" She slapped her hands together again. It made a sound a little like wet butter being slapped into a bowl. "Else I'll switch you all from the oldest to the youngest." And stooping to get off the wagon she said in her normal voice: "With seven children I have to think a minute to see which is the oldest and the youngest. I hope my child-bearing time is over, but I bet it ain't. Lord, Lord! Give me a hand, Samuel. Don't stand there like a post."

Sam, aroused from his own thoughtful calm, sprang quickly forward and proffered his hand. Suellen took it and jumped down, and he thought he could feel the earth minutely tremble. Her ruddy skin was dripping with sweat, and Sam got his own hand thoroughly wet by placing it in hers, and he thought of how dry the hands of the nigger hag had been on the day before when she read his palm. Suellen stood pulling herself vigorously into shape by means of a mighty tugging at her dress. She looked miserable, but then everybody was miserable, and days and days ago people had stopped fighting the misery. She cast an apprehensive glance at the sky.

"I ain't never *seen* it so dry," she said. She was puffing from the effort of getting out of the wagon. "Mark my words, there's going to be fire. Lord, Lord! The *dust* would burn if you struck a match to it." Her voice had abruptly descended to reverence. She looked about at the forbidding stillness of the woods, and Sam could read in her face an awed and primordial fear of fire. He nodded in agreement.

"It'd never stop if it started," he said. "I guess the grass would burn."

"You *guess!*" Suellen recovered her turbulence. "Samuel, it's so dry that every single blade of grass would blow off like a firecracker. You *guess* it'd burn!"

Sam chuckled in spite of himself. "Well, we'll all be burned up come tomorrow night. It's going to be something to harvest a crop in . . . in this." He gestured helplessly around him, and his good humor died.

"Awful, just awful," Suellen said soberly. "I could say what it's really going to be, but the delicacy of my sex forbids it. Lord, Lord! You'll all be dead by tomorrow night. Be sure you drink water all day long. I'll have a good barrel out. Else you'll have a stroke. I told Mayhew he was crazy. Course I tell him that all the time, and it don't do no good. He ought to let the oats go. But you know the man. He planted oats in the fall, and he's going to harvest oats in June. We could have a dust storm out there, and Mayhew's still going to be out there with a thresher. Oh, I guess I'm hard on the man. He's a good provider."

"He's a good farmer," Sam said. "He's the best in the valley."

"Yes, he is," Suellen said proudly. "But not for long, Samuel. You're going to be the best around. Mayhew says you're already better than anyone else but him, and pretty soon you're going to be the best. Everybody says so. It's a miracle what you've done by this place. By the sweat of your brow you'll get filthy rich, the Good Book says, and you're doing it. He's a better farmer than any of your folks ever was, Sarah. You ought to be proud of him."

Sarah Beckwith flashed a tight little smile. "I *am* proud of him,

Suellen. I am *very* proud of him, but you didn't know the place in the old days. You can't remember how it was. You were just a little girl."

"Oh piddle, Sarah! I can too remember. And my mamma, God rest her dear departed soul, told me a lot that she remembered, and I still say this boy's the best dadgummed farmer you ever had on the place." Then, without breaking the galloping stride of her words, she turned back to Sam himself. "I'll fix good for you tomorrow, count on that! But Lord, Lord! And to beat everything else, the cistern's gone dry! Mayhew's been hauling water out of the creek in the pasture. We have to boil it, and there ain't nothing tastes as bad as boiled water lessen it's worm medicine. And we had crawfish in the cistern. They're all dead. Phew!" She held her bulbous nose with a ridiculously delicate finger and thumb. "I went out there and raised the lid this morning. Smells awful! You wouldn't think it was a cistern. More like a grave. I don't know whether I can drink water out of it again or not. You remind me to let you smell it. It ain't like nothing you ever smelled in a cistern."

"Come in, Suellen. We're all roasting out here." Compared to the streaming volubility of Suellen MacComber, Sam's mother seemed even more stately and more commanding. "It's still a little cooler in the house. Are you sure you want coffee?"

And Suellen MacComber said, "Yes, Lord, Lord! I guess coffee'll be the death of me. Mayhew says I drink so much I ought to turn brown and go live with the niggers. And it makes me sweat something awful! Look at me now! You think *this* is sweat. You just wait till I have me a cup of coffee. *Then* you'll see sweat! Next to me in a good sweat the Tennessee River ain't nothing! But eat, drink, and be merry for tomorrow the deck is stacked, and the chips is put away, as the Good Book says. Smell the air! It's like fire deep down in wood. You mark my words! We're going to have fire before this is over. It'll shut out the sun. Come have coffee with us, Sam Junior."

"Coffee? Oh, no thanks. No thank you."

"Look how I startled the boy! He's got his mind on other things, Sarah. It's a pity." Suellen MacComber ran her big eyes over him in real sympathy.

"Oh Suellen, Sam just doesn't like to sit around drinking coffee with old women, do you dear?" And with her bright, sad smile hanging over her shoulder like a carelessly thrown wrap, Sarah Beckwith steered her friend through the door and into the house.

The children went on playing in the yard, the clashing sounds of their high voices making the yard sound like recess at school. They ignored Sam, and he, feeling uncomfortable and at loose ends, went back toward the barn and the pasture and looked to where the line of trees stood so still in the brassy day. He was in a lackluster mood. His mouth was dry. He went into the springhouse to slake his thirst.

Inside it was cool and dank, and the quiet sound of water pouring steadily out of the earth had a music to it. He drank deeply and ran the cold water over his face and sat back on his haunches to look worriedly at it. No mistaking. The spring was not flowing with its usual force. Somewhere deep in the ground the source of it was dying from the drought. He felt a tight strain under his neck when he looked at the spring. The whole farm rested on its strength. The stock drank from the creek it made. The milk and the butter were cooled in vessels sunk into its water. The spring meant the difference between prosperity and something else. If it died . . . In the orderly, reflective way that farmers quietly plan for bad times he began thinking about what he would do if the spring failed. Nothing gave him much consolation. Nothing would save the valley but rain. And that thought brought him abruptly back to Mr. Simson.

Mr. Simson, forgotten for an hour or so! *This time yesterday he was alive!* He formed the thought grandly, worried at it, tried to make something out of it, failed, and came back out into the open and felt once more the slap of the rising heat. His land. His kingdom. He could almost hear the land cracking for lack of water. And like the land, he was paralyzed by the drought.

For there was nothing he could do. Not today. Not until it rained, for the harvest of the next day would be a mockery, an empty thing except that in its way the harvest fitted into the ritualistic mind of Mayhew MacComber. You kept up appearances in bad times, but in reality the drought had brought the world to a quiet, exhausted halt. Nothing to do but wait until the thing started again of its own accord. Nothing to do, so he went on wandering without purpose, and the suspension of everything made him think of Emilie, and the deep ache of the lost thing came up under the heat like a knife enveloped in wool. She was gone. He was left with his land. It was what he wanted, the choice he had made in place of her.

Though in a way it was no choice at all on his part. She robbed him even of that consolation to his pride by the way she left. She simply picked up and rode away, and that was the end of it. Just as he was gathering all his cumbersome will power to make a decision, she yanked the whole problem deftly out of his hands by riding away and leaving him alone.

Not at once. For they continued to ride together after that dismal interview with his mother. But now there was a dim frame of hopelessness thrown about their days. They talked, and sometimes they laughed as they had laughed in their first times together. They plotted, they kissed as before—but all with a gloomy shade of unreality cast over everything they did.

Around them a swelling drone of interest went filling the valley. Mrs. Simson's death. The impending trial. Samuel Beckwith and that foreign girl who'd stolen his foolish heart away. An exciting springtime for the women of Bourbon County! What did those two young people *do* out there in the morning alone together! Who'd they think they were fooling! With his very own eyes G. R. Newcombe had seen them ride out of the big woods which covered Black Oak Ridge. And Mrs. Newcombe was off right away to see Mrs. Elkins Janeway, who sat thunderstruck at the account and wondered what on earth people could do to help that poor, dear Sarah Crittendon Beckwith bear up under the awful shame!

Mrs. Elkins Janeway was so concerned she got on a horse and rode right over to see Sarah Beckwith herself. She had the right to ask an honest question, she said piously. Sarah Beckwith received her coolly, said she really didn't know what Sam and "that girl" were planning to do, said she hoped for the best, sat there with a tense, grieving face and eyes close to heart-rending tears. So afterward Mrs. Janeway circulated through the valley from day to day, raising a doleful chorus of shame and sympathy from the watchful women of Bourbon County. Sympathy for the unquenchable woman who had borne so much. The dear woman who must now bear the harshest cross a mother could carry—the ingratitude of a son.

The women of Bourbon County felt obligated to do what they could to help. In ostentatious scorn they swept by Emilie in the street, muttering righteous little comments just loud enough for her to hear. They shunned her mother and her father. And Mrs. Walter Abernathy took it on herself to corner Sam in town one day and give him a tongue-lashing.

"I always say what I think," she told Sam's mother. "There ain't nobody in this valley that can say I don't say just exactly what I think, and I told that boy he made me so mad I wanted to pull ever hair in his head out by the roots. I told him if he was a boy of mine I wouldn't feed him. Starve some sense into his head. I told him he had the dearest, sweetest, most kindest, most noblest mother in all God's creation, and that he didn't appreciate it. I think he was about ready to cry when I got through with him. He was so choked up he couldn't even *talk!* I told him he was just lucky his daddy was dead and in the grave. I told him his daddy would of took him out behind the barn and took a belt to him, old as he is. I told him everybody could see that girl warn't nothing but a slut. I used the word, Sarah. It was my bounden duty to call a spade a spade! I tell you, I gave him something to think about."

His mother protected him. She told Mrs. Walter Abernathy to leave the boy alone. She told her it would all work out. And afterward she told Sam about the woman's visit and said she was sorry, said also in her quiet self-restraint that what Mrs. Abernathy said didn't matter but that if Sam married the girl he would always have to put up with talk like that. People in the valley would never accept Emilie, she said. Emilie was too different, and after a while the things people said would be a hard burden to bear.

Sam was young, and Mrs. Abernathy's blast rang in his ears like a blow. He felt the whole county reverberating with his affair. When he rode through Bourbonville he felt invisible eyes fastened to his skin. And when people saw him with Emilie he wondered what they were thinking.

Emilie grandly ignored all the gossip. She looked directly and scornfully into every turned eye. When they rode through Bourbonville together she was careful to lace one of her arms in his, to hold on to him with a calm possessiveness. And she pressed Sam to marry her. "If you love me, you just have to make up your mind to do it! She'll have to get used to it. And she *will,* Sam! She *will!* Don't you understand? It doesn't matter what anybody says, your mother or anybody else. You have to live your own life. You have to decide you're going to *do* something. Oh, Sam! If only you weren't so . . . Oh, Sam!"

And when he ate his supper in the spring twilights his mother would sit opposite him and talk with her quiet, reasonable voice. "I think I've done the wrong thing by keeping you so close to me. You should have had more experience with girls. That way you wouldn't have fallen so hard for the first new face you ever saw. You'll do what you want in the end. But I have to say this: I cringe at the thought that one day that girl may be mistress of this house. May God forgive me, but I can't bear to think of it."

There was a vehemence to his mother's voice. Saturated with

love though it was, there was a vehemence. And in it Sam could see the woman who had stood in the window with the pistol barrel against her own head, while the Yankee legions moiled in the yard.

Probably the most terrible part of the whole terrible business was that he did understand what his mother was talking about. Emilie was "different." She was from far away. She had seen things he could never see. She saw and loved a world which vanished above his world in the impenetrable haze of his inexperience, and she could even speak German. Sometimes she called him Schatz, and sometimes when they rode together she would break into songs he could not understand. She did it to please him, he thought, but it made him uncomfortable. He doubted that he could ever learn German. And why should anybody speak German in the United States! It was a foreign language! Even when she spoke English there was a faintly indefinable accent to her words, not wholly foreign, but not quite like anything Sam had ever heard. Yes, she was different, and her difference made her dangerously unpredictable, and sometimes at night he lay wide awake on his bed and tortured himself with the dilemma. He might marry her and kill his mother with grief and dismay, and still later he might waken some morning to find Emilie stolen away from his bed and vanished. Emilie was a harmony of so many things—like a fine piece of cut glass catching the pure rays of the sun and shining at every surface with a different light. How could he dare think that she would continue to sparkle once life settled down into the fixed order of farm life in the valley? How could he dare to think he could hold her love?

So he hesitated because of his mother's tender vehemence and because of his doubts—doubts about Emilie which were finally doubts about himself. His mother swept her hands in the direction of the pictures of the ancestors, a grand gesture of her splendid pride, and she demanded of him: "What would they say?" What indeed would they say?

In years to come as Emilie strode along the ever-gloomy hallways before their reticent frames, how would they regard her? He could not put the fantasy of their thoughts, their staring eyes, out of his head. And somehow he persisted in the equally irrational conviction that if his mother would only concur, the ancestors would settle down in their frames in acquiescence and peace. His marriage would be sealed by their dumb benediction. They would lapse again into their long, dreamless slumber.

But concur she would not. "Samuel! Dear, dear Samuel! Please don't be angry with me. Remember how happy we've been all our life together, and don't be angry. What do you know about that girl? Nothing but what she's told you. Nothing at all. Why, she could be a *common woman!*"

"Common woman!" In the jargon of delicacy that meant *whore*. When his mother said it, he could all but hear the mute clatter of ancestors calling to each other out of the shadowy corridors and closed rooms of the house. And later he could sense their terrible cry echoing around him as he lay abed with the lifeless moonlight shining into his room. He could feel that cry of anguish sharpening in the interior of his bones on those taut occasions when his mother marshaled the forces of her love against him and pleaded with him to recant. Through all his hours at home he could sense the uneasy grumbling of the spirits of men long vanished into the grave. He moved in an invisible cloud of uncertainty.

And then there came the day.

It was a quiet morning when they followed a tiny roadway climbing circuitously into the hills. They held hands, abandoned to silence and to thought. The horses went along with a languid plumping of their hoofs. The spring smells of life and blossom lay on the atmosphere, and squirrels jumped from limb to limb in the trees and chattered at their passing. No houses here. Only the woods, deep and dark, and the streak of brown road climbing through the trees. In the treetops the friendly sun sparkled on the new leaves already so thick that only a dappling of light flecked the forest floor. High above, the sky showed in broken patches of vivid blue.

The way they followed had been a logging road. In the lusty construction which followed the War, the road had been cut into the virgin forest on the ridges overlooking the valley, and the forest had been raped of its great trees. Only the stunted evergreens, the thin black gums, the dogwoods, and some other useless species remained. All through the woods the black earth was rutted with wagon tracks and littered with hulking stumps left nakedly squatting, white and bare.

On the crest of the ridge the road ran into a clearing. While the logging was going on, a steam-driven saw had been here. The great trees were trimmed and sliced into loads which could be managed by the wagons and the mules before being hauled below to their final fashioning into lumber. The saw and the steam engine had long ago been removed to a more profitable place. Only a high, moldering pile of sawdust remained in the midst of the clearing, surrounded by high grass and sprawling blackberry bushes and waves of honeysuckle.

He came here frequently with Emilie. From this place they could look down into the valley, see Bourbonville, see how the cupola on the courthouse and the steeple of the Baptist Church rose through the blanket of oaks and chestnuts which lay over the town. They could see the dark-green swath the sluggish river cut beyond the town, the toy railroad tracks which came down along the river from Knoxville. They saw trains pass, heard the distant, solemn blowing of the whistles, the silver tinkling of the bells, and the almost inaudible chugging of the locomotives, and they saw the black smoke pour out the flaring smokestacks to lie like a greasy smear over the river, slowly to dissipate in the radiant air long after the trains had gone.

There was always the possibility that somebody in the town might see them. They supposed that a glass, swung by some incredible chance into their place, might expose them to the curious. But the possibility was faint and gave the vaguest tint of danger to their being there, and that made it all the more pleasant and beguiling in the clearing. So they sat arm-in-arm and laughed in the warm pleasures of sharing one another and made up stories of what people were doing in the houses they could see far below.

But on this particular day they came silently and without cheer into the clearing. They slipped off the horses and tied them in the shade and came out into the warm sunlight and sat without a word at their place. For a long time they sat quietly, arms laced together, looking out over the waking day. It was still early. The day was unlived and unspoiled; the sun standing over the misty bulk of the great blue mountains to the east announced a new chance for something. There was a coolness to the air. The grass was still moist from the evening dew, and fingers of sunlight rippled the grass and made the dew shine.

She leaned solidly against him, holding her own arms around her knees, hands clasped at her ankles. He felt the warm curve of her body, and they were both so still he could feel her breathing against himself, could feel the gentle, rounded pressure of her breast come and go. He sat thinking of the great looping courses of life which had brought them from so far apart to such nearness. The very solidity of this moment impressed him with a deep unreality. He sat engrossed in the thought of her, the mystery of their relationship to one another. Often they had picked out important moments of their lives lived heretofore and had tried to imagine what the other was doing at such and such a time. Now Sam had meditating over the simple fact that there had *been* a heretofore and that chance had brought them together.

At last she said: "No matter what happens, I'll never forget these mornings." She spoke with a great, dreamy finality.

He said: "We'll always come here. All our lives we'll come. We'll bring our children." And then moving into the further illusion of concrete plans he said: "Maybe we can buy this place someday. We'll have the money. We can build a house right here, a house like we want. We can start something new, really new."

"What about your old house?" she said.

He laughed in an unsuccessful attempt at being casual. "It has too many memories stacked up inside it. There won't be room for us." He was trying to make it seem as if everything were really already arranged and that it was only a short matter of time before they would settle down to the serious business of putting things like marriage and a family and a house in order. But something in his voice, just beyond his control, gave the lie to it all.

She looked at him with a sad smile. Then impulsively she leaned over and kissed him lightly on the lips. "You can remember me here," she said. "When you are a very old man you can come up here and remember me." She lifted her eyes from his lips to his own eyes, her face close to his own. He averted his gaze.

"We'll both come," he went on stubbornly. "When we're old, we'll have this place together." Then, desperately, he threw his arms around her and hugged her so close that his arms ached. "Oh Emilie, please trust me. Please give me just a little more time."

She pulled away, sat looking at him for a moment, then kissed him again—a sad, hopeless kiss which said without a word: *I don't trust you. You are going to give me up. But I love you. I love you.* He tried to pull away, to make some other pledge of certainty about their future. But she would not let him go. Their kiss lingered and evolved into something desperate, and they were clinging to each other in the warm sunlight.

"Emilie, Emilie! I want you so much!"

"Then come away! Let's leave all this. We can go West, Sam. You and I, alone. We can go West and leave *everything* behind. Please, Sam. Leave her and go with me." She whispered urgently at him, her lips at his ear. He could feel the moist warmth of her breath. Her bare arms were locked around him.

Go West! It *was* possible. Simply to go West, vanish in one clean stroke. Abandon the past, the knots which could not be undone. Go West, and they could do it. "I have some money at home," he said tentatively. "Money I've saved back, just in case. I have five hundred dollars!"

"Five hundred dollars! Why Sam, it's a *fortune*." She pushed back and sat up, eyes shining.

"I thought if something happened to the bank I wouldn't lose everything."

He tried to convey an apology with his voice for his innate caution, but she was afire with the possibilities and did not notice. "It's all we'd need to get a start somewhere. We can *do* it! We can go right now, this afternoon. I could be ready in an hour. We can get married on the way. And when we get to wherever we want to stop, we can write your mother. Then she'd *have* to accept me. But it wouldn't matter if she didn't. She couldn't do anything then. Let's go, Sam! Let's go!" She leaped up and stood over him, gay as a child.

He remained seated in the grass, trying to think things out. "I couldn't do it today," he said hesitantly. "I couldn't just walk in and tell her I was going."

"You don't have to tell her."

"I couldn't just *leave*."

"You could."

"It wouldn't be right. It wouldn't be fair."

"Sam, do you love me?"

"Yes, I love you." His voice shook and was husky. He looked down into the grass where her shadow fell.

"That's all that matters," she said softly. "We don't even need the five hundred dollars. I'm willing to go right now, without anything but what we have this minute. If you'll just go with me, I'll get on my horse right now and start West. We can beg. We can sleep out. We can steal, Sam."

He shook his head. "We've got to make plans," he said. "We couldn't just pick up and leave without anything!"

"Yes, we could."

He shook his head again, more emphatically, and frowned. "It'd be impractical. We couldn't make it on nothing."

"All right, Sam. All right. Get the five hundred dollars. And tomorrow morning I'll be ready. I'll bring some things, and you can bring some things of yours, and then it'll be all right." Her voice was tight and strained.

"I don't know," he said. He plucked absently at the grass. They were silent again. She still stood over him. The woods noises hummed around them, and off to one end of the clearing, in the trees, there was a sudden, alarmed cry of birds. He heard it, imagined they saw a snake or a hawk, and in the midst of his worrying about what to do with Emilie he wanted to get up and go darting over to find the snake and to kill it.

"You will never convince *her,*" she said, very gently. "It's going to be something you have to decide yourself. You have to make up your mind between her and me and then do something about it."

"I don't know," he said helplessly.

"I have never met anyone in my life who suited me as well as you do," she said. "We go together. We fit." It was something she had said to him often before, wistfully and romantically. Now there was no romance to her voice at all, nothing but a fact calmly and rationally expressed.

"I feel the same way. You know I feel the same way," he stammered. "I wish you could understand. She's so *alone.* I'm the only thing she's got left in the world. I can't just destroy her."

"So you'll let her destroy you."

"No, I don't mean that," he said irritably.

"She'll never give you up of her own free will."

"We haven't given it enough time. For goodness sakes, it's just been three months! That isn't long. Things like this take time to get used to."

"We've had enough time. Haven't you had enough time, Sam?" He could feel the wry smile on her lips.

He shrugged impatiently. "I'm not my mother," he said. "Three months for her is nothing. It isn't even time to catch your breath."

"How many months do we live?" she said. She turned from him and looked out over the valley. He glanced upward, saw the thoughtful stance of her tall form, the calm bent of her head, the hands clasped serenely in front of herself. In a moment she turned back to him, and they looked steadfastly at each other without speaking.

It was one of those times he would remember with wondering clarity for the rest of his life. Probably that was because this moment came before a storm (or two storms) of such violent emotion that he could never remember what followed with any clarity at all. That tranquil instant balanced on the edge of tumult! He recalled the standing, sunny repose when the tumult was only a confused, dim roaring in his mind. There she stood, tall and womanly, with a stateliness all beyond her youth, her yellow hair shining against the bright sky, her clear eyes a deeper shade than the high, pale blue above her. A profound silence hung between the girl and himself. Only after a long while she said, "Sam, you said you wanted me. I want you."

With that she began to undress.

At first he did not even realize what she was doing. It was so sudden, so unexpected. When he did understand he jumped to his feet trembling, and stood gaping at her like a fool. All the while she kept her eyes fixed on him, looking directly at his astonished face with a whimsical little smile, perhaps a smile of undisturbed superiority—proud of her mastery over this moment. She moved her fingers without hesitation down the little white buttons in front of her dress, and one by one she undid them, leaving the slack folds of the dress draped over her full breasts. Then she stripped the dress away and stood in her undergarments—the tight shirt which bound her breasts itself quickly removed and dropped with a little swish into the grass.

At that moment he threw his arms around her. He wanted to embrace her or to shield himself from her superiority or to make love to her or perhaps to stop her from going farther. But if he wanted to stop her, he did not succeed. She squirmed against his hold and somehow released her underpants, and they fell down her long white legs to crumple at their feet with an almost silent whisper of cloth. Holding onto her he could see her bare back, could feel her naked body thrust wildly against himself her breasts at his heart, could feel her crying in his arms.

He was crying too. He did not know why. He never did really understand it. His legs trembled so violently that he did not know how long he could stand, and both of them were crying in great, wracking sobs, and they kissed each other in a frenzy of feeling and got their tears all mixed up. They kissed again and again, and it seemed that his whole body heaved and swelled with hot desire for her, but as the furious heat surged through him he was completely unsure of what he was going to do. He was afraid of what he might do. The irrevocability of it. The finality. But there she was, clinging to him, pressing herself to him, sobbing that she wanted him, that she wanted to have his child, no matter what.

He would have made love to her. Later on he was convinced of that. He was not strong enough to resist. Or maybe he simply loved her too fiercely not to take her when she yielded her young body for him to possess. And maybe it really was the best way out, the very best way to get the waiting over with, to end the pleading and the arguing, the wheedling, the killing indecision. It would have made all the difference. Fifteen, twenty minutes, and life for him would have become something so different that afterwards he had trouble even imagining what it might have been. Marriage, children, a house and land of their own—all the common little things he and Emilie had talked about, had laughed over, had sat thinking about, her hand in his and her head gently resting against his shoulder. All the things they had raised from the ordinary earth to a paradise of happiness and fulfillment. If not in the valley, then somewhere else. Some other valley, or perhaps the open land out there, somewhere West . . .

And what would have happened after that? Probably their tempestuous love would have fallen quietly into commonplaces. Bread, meat, land, children, seed, harvest, toil, weariness. Contentment or guilt? Which would it have been? Probably both, a little. He couldn't really decide. Afterward he thought that even with Emilie there would have been something unfulfilled, seeing as how that was the way life was. Still, it would have been different. And he never could shake off entirely the terrible longing to know what that difference would have been had they spent their lives together.

But he did not make love to her, because they did not have the fifteen or twenty minutes. Because when Sam was holding on to her, he glanced accidentally out to the opposite side of the clearing. To the place where the birds cried out in alarm. Because in looking at that place, without thinking about it, without at first believing it, quite suddenly, quite distinctly. Sam saw the shadowy outline of a human form in the foliage. He saw a man standing there. A man watching them.

The man did not try to hide. He wanted to be seen, for when Sam saw him and pushed Emilie back, the man emerged from the shadows and stood clearly on the line of the woods. Thomas Bazely, Preacher of the Gospel. Thomas Bazely, champion of God and the Word. Thomas Bazely was watching them. He stood with his lean arms folded, hatless, glaring up the clearing at them with gunshot eyes. He was too far away for Sam to see clearly the expression on his face. But the youth always supposed it to have been evil. A righteous sneer. Full of gratification at having discovered sin.

Emilie did not see him. When Sam first began pushing her away, she misunderstood. She tried to cling to him. She fought him for his embrace. He kept trying to disengage. She struggled with him. He cried at her: "Stop, my God, stop!" And finally he said, almost beside himself: "The preacher! Right over there! The preacher!" She turned, open-mouthed, and when she saw the man standing there with his implacable gaze, she gave a startled cry of fear and reached frantically for her discarded clothing.

They never spoke a word to Mr. Bazely. He said not a word to them. He only stood there with his arms folded like waiting death while they scrambled over her clothes and themselves and their horses and got away. As they were riding off, down the overgrown road at breakneck speed, her clothing all in disarray, her face scarlet with shame and fury, she cried: "You should kill him! Go back and kill him! You should hunt him down and kill him like a mad dog!"

And she was right. It was only a short time before he acknowledged that. Later he wished with all his heart that he had killed the preacher that morning, wished for the sweet purity of murder, to wash his hands in the blood of one so hateful and inhuman. The chance to kill the preacher then and there was another one of those decisive moments which it seemed his destiny to miss forever.

But it was too much to decide all at once. The preacher meant righteousness. Whatever kind of crazy man he was, at that particular instant he represented all Sam's childhood, all his mother's religion, all his own worried guilt. Guilt at what? At falling in love with a girl as "different" as Emilie. As strange. At doing the unexpected thing. Something not bargained for by those stern ancestors who gave him the reason for his life before he was ever born. So he could not kill the preacher, and he did not.

The thing was a numbing horror to them both. Like news of sudden death, the meaning of it all slowly grew on them. Almost at once they knew it was no accident. The preacher had not simply happened upon them. There was no road on that side of the clearing. It was far from the preacher's house. Mr. Bazely must have known their habits. He expected them to come to that place, and he had crept up the wooded slope to spy on them. He had slid through the underbrush like a snake. No blundering noises. No breaking sticks under his crafty feet. Only the birds had signaled his presence, and that was no warning at all. So he had waited there (for how many mornings?) until finally he could reveal himself in the full, furious condemnation of them both and their love.

And why? The strange thing was that at the moment Sam did not puzzle much over that question. He felt enough guilt to expect the preacher to seek them out. The preacher was God's agent on earth. God's eye and God's tongue. God's ears and God's teeth. So there was something perfectly logical at finding the preacher where anyone might have thought to find God. Enshrouded in the forest gloom at the edge of a clearing they thought deserted. Stalking them. Glowering at them. Keeping his record in the invisible and eternal book. Only much later, and in a torment of bitter regret, did he think of the preacher as a man, a wild lunatic with a pathological bent for spying.

The preacher knew and he had to tell—at least one person. Sarah Beckwith. Never a word from him to Sam. Nothing to Emilie. Nothing to anyone else on earth. But he told Sarah Crittendon Beckwith.

She almost lost her mind. When Sam came straggling in at lunch, flushed and unable to look her in the eye, her face had gone to wax. She uttered one blank sentence: "The preacher was here." Enough. More than a dictionary of violent words impacted in that terse statement. Her eyes were filled with shame and reproach and hurt. And something more tremendous and terrible—fear. Stark, anguished terror.

No doubt about the look in her eyes. The same recoiling dread she exhibited at the discovery of a copperhead under the porch years ago. The barely contained fright incited in her by the sluggish, reptilian body gliding out into the warm light to sun itself. Only now she did not lash out in alarm. Instead, with the same tingling energy she might have spent to strike him, she contained herself. She put plates onto the table and measured out his lunch as of old. No loud clattering to the plates. No slapping down of crockery in speechless rage. Rather, a taut gentleness rising from her fear, a gentleness lest she disturb something slumbering uneasily in the dark. She was terrified at something, and all at once it struck Sam that she was old.

Yes, old. Really the first time the youth had perceived his mother's age. There was a dry slackness to the skin under her chin. Grooved lines reaching for the corners of her eyes. The skin of her face like something slightly deflated by a capricious child. The sharp, carven edges of her profile going limp with time, and age heaving itself forward like an old, neglected account demanding to be paid.

He supposed then that his mother was afraid because she thought the battle lost. In the midst of the weary repetitions of their arguments, there was inserted the stark fact of Emilie's naked body. It brought shame on the house. The girl had seduced him. Or she *would* have seduced him had Providence not brought the preacher miraculously onto the scene. The preacher. The savior. Sam would certainly not have saved himself. The preacher had saved him—for the moment. But just for the moment.

By stripping herself before him, Emilie had verified the worst of his mother's fears. Who on earth could think that a *nice* girl, a lady, would do a thing like that! If she could undress herself so easily for him, how much practice had she had? What other male eyes had looked upon her naked breasts . . . And all the rest? He posed the nagging questions in his own mind on the behalf of his mother. Confused, desperate, senseless, unanswerable questions equipped with iron collars, studded with goads.

But whatever the reason, Emilie had done it. She had presented herself to her lover, and she had been seen. She could be had, and her lover was young and strong and at that instant had been half mad with desire for her. Something new was created out of that moment. Sarah Crittendon Beckwith for all her stately control of her world did not believe she could handle the new thing, and she was afraid. Sam thought she feared because she had lost. He thought he knew all about his mother just as she knew all about him, and he could read her mind. Out of that reading he fixed the explanation for her fear on Emilie and the tangled clearing—the deserted hideaways up and down the valley—and the wondrous soft nakedness of a willing female body, young and passionate.

Later he understood how much all this came out of his own mind. But he was left to imagine what he would because his mother said not a word to him the rest of that long day. She did not condemn him. She did not explain herself. Instead she withdrew, into the upper silences of the house. She emerged again to prepare his supper. But supper passed in the same wordless tension. He had nothing to say to her. He could not make a confession or beg forgiveness. And of course he could not explain. He could have explained only to someone uninvolved in the whole sad affair, but not to his mother. He thought he would suffocate before he could say anything else to her about it.

So he ate his supper in that terrible quiet. He went out onto the porch and watched the day dilute itself into a portentous twilight and subside at last into darkness. The night came down. His mother vanished into her room immediately after the evening meal. So in the dark the one yellow rectangle of light shone out over the yard from her room, where she guarded herself behind the drawn curtains. In the stillness of his own room he could hear her slow pacing, her bed creak as she lay down on it and creak again as she arose. He heard her soft walking, without pattern or plan, through the night until, after a fitful dozing, he awoke to hear nothing but the lively sounds of a normal spring night warming into summer.

The next morning he rode off to find Emilie and to make a resolution of things. He had to do something once and for all. They had to make a decision. That was the outcome of his own spastic dozing, his troubled rolling in bed among the knotted covers, his weary anguish. He decided that something had to be decided, and in the morning he rode off to the river with his mind set on that fact.

He was not certain what the decision would be. He only thought he knew. If he had the chance, he believed he would tell Emilie it all had to end.

This was the dreary light at the end of his long night of tossing misery. It was the only way he thought he could get things right again in his life. In the warm and fragrant darkness he made a decision to try to leap backward and recover something Emilie had made him lose. He arrived at his decision through a thick toiling of logic, and in that plodding darkness he arrived also at a way of looking at the world.

Before Emilie rode into his life, he lived in the valley possessed by a satisfying routine, forming a way of doing things which people recognized as his own. His life had a shape to it, a pattern, and in its orderly simplicity he was perfectly at home. He worked very hard; he slept easily. He read. He studied farming like a science. And he had an innocent confidence that life was an orderly procession of things he could control. Then Emilie came and turned his complacent world upside down. So in the way of human beings jolted by the utterly unexpected, he sought for a reason.

But the only reason he could muster was the blind working of chance, and that was no reason at all. Her father was struck by the sight of a courthouse cupola thrusting through bare trees. That single glance with its afterthought of contemplation was perhaps triggered by nothing more than the kind of impulse which makes a man shift his body while in bed asleep. An equally unpredictable chance might have made Emilie's father keep his eyes straight ahead as their wagon creaked through Bourbonville. It was a maddening thought, but from it Sam drew a conclusion as stark as ice. There was no meaning to the universe. Things simply were as they were, and there was no reason for it, and they could be any other way, and there would be no reason for that either.

So Sam went on to decide that he could dismiss Emilie. He could shrug off the love which he had for her and restore life to the comfortable old ways and make himself forget. She did not matter because nothing mattered in the end. If nothing meant anything, you did what was convenient, and when you considered the life of the younger—and living—Samuel Beckwith, it was more convenient to give Emilie up than to take her.

Had she been able to see the reasoning behind his decision, she would have recoiled in horror. If it had been "reasoning" at all. Maybe it was more a vision, an apparition of the most complete darkness—opaque, terrifying, and overwhelming. As it turned out, there was freedom in the heart of the vision. The substance of his later self-reproach came to be that he did not see that at the time. But for the moment all he could see was that he could renounce Emilie simply by deciding he would do so. And that was the thing he determined on that morning when he got up and dressed himself and grimly set out to meet her.

But in fact he did not have the chance to renounce Emilie. She renounced him. He went riding off to their place by the river, but she was not there. It was two hours before he convinced himself that she was not coming. That made all his resolution knot up and finally go slack and queer. Later he wondered if there had been any resolution in the first place. He waited and waited, and she did not come, and the river washed on in a pouring stream which mocked his waiting.

So there was nothing to do but go home. And all that day he wrestled with himself again. A maddening thing to have it all to do over, after the anguish of the almost sleepless night. Maddening almost to have his eyes so heavy that once that day when he was worn out with his thinking he sat down in the shade in the corner of a field and went fast asleep. He woke up almost immediately and felt his impotency and the foolishness of going to sleep in midday at such a time in his life. But the fact was that had he stayed there, in that cool and grassy place, he would have gone to sleep again.

Maddening also that it was such an ordinary day. It was always to surprise him a little that great things could happen on ordinary days. He never quite got over the expectation that great things should happen against a symphonic background of natural wonder. But on this day all the fields were quiet. The drought had already begun, but no one knew that at the time. The first tender green shoots of corn were sprouting in their orderly rows. The wheat and the oats were just high enough to give the land the appearance of being covered by a thick carpet. And that calm of dawn which endured throughout the day passed into a peaceful twilight. That was the day he lost Emilie, and it was a very ordinary day.

Ordinary except that twice in the afternoon he got himself on the road to Bourbonville. The last time with five hundred dollars in new bills rolled into a tight wad and secured against his breast by a purse which hung from a cord around his neck. Five hundred dollars and a fixed expression of manliness. An unshakable decision. And a vision, this a shining point of light in the midst of the blot of darkness. Treeless hills rising there beyond the great, open expanse of unlimited plain. To Emilie's reproach, to her tears, the simple, heroic question: "Do you want to count scars, or do you want to marry me?" The fantasy of her arms hugging him close and her sobs of relief wetting his shoulder. The sense of *her* victory after apparent defeat adding to her joy and his pride. The hard little wad of money like a tiny engine which fed him of its force.

And he had the force—for a while. It was his horse that stumbled to a walk, halted finally to the quick, forlorn tug he made at the bridle, then came plodding back in a slow plumping of hoofs. He could not quite bring it off. The invisible thing held him, and he couldn't quite bring it off and do something. Finally, late that night, he went off in an exhausted sleep, sunk in a weariness which came from his bones.

Then on the second morning he awoke with a start, very early, long before his mother. When dawn was still a dream forming on the sleepy eastern horizon. He left off the chores, forsook the cows bursting with their milk, left the bewildered pigs without their food. In a frenzy of haste he got his saddle onto the horse and rode off to Bourbonville. A cruel, shameful awareness nagged at him as he went.

She was already gone. She and her strange family. The little house had no life in it. He peered into the windows, cupping his hands around his face against the glass, searching beyond the thin, gaping reflection of himself. Barren rooms behind the hollow windows, shorn of their curtains. The shelves where her father had kept his clocks were all empty. In the room off the kitchen in the back lay cluttered the litter of odds and ends which families decide they don't need when they move. The doors were padlocked.

They had gone the day before. Clarence Jackson, who saw everything in Bourbonville, told him they left in the first light of morning. Told him with red-eyed simplicity and bewilderment at what the fuss was all about. They had gone West. Clarence had gone out to ask, and Emilie told him. Just somewhere West, she said. They didn't know where. He repeated that information, and looked out in the direction they had gone. Clarence full of blank, bemuddled curiosity and reeking of alcohol sweated through his pores.

Sam could imagine the old man stiffly sitting on the seat with his wife, she glancing nervously at the houses, thinking of the slumbering people within, all sliding out of their lives. She was probably relieved when they cleared the town without rousing anybody but the station agent, relieved to be rid of the women of Bourbon County. Emilie's father would have looked far ahead, searching for the dim outlines of his own mystic vision and turning West. And Sam could imagine Emilie riding out behind them, tall and proud on her horse, free to the last. Had she urged them to go? It was likely. But then again it might have been nothing but chance. It need have been no more than that.

When he heard the news, he whipped his horse out the road toward Kingston. At Varner's Cross Roads a lesser road angling north from Bourbonville tied in with the great pike which came down from Knoxville to Kingston and went on to Nashville and the West. A tavern was located at this junction. Lounging in the indolent shade of the porch was a man who had seen them go. When Sam hailed him with the question, he got up and came deliberately down into the road and slowly drawled out his information. "They passed by bout seven-thirty of a morning, and it was yesterday. I yelled at them, but they didn't say nothing. They sure looked strange to me. You ain't finding many folks that won't even say good morning. Germans, you say? Well, that don't surprise me none. I knowed they was something wrong with them three somewheres."

Sam could have gone after them. It was his last chance. They had the start of a day, but with the wagon they couldn't make good time. They probably passed the night at Kingston and crossed the river there by ferry in the morning of this day so that with any luck at all he could catch them in the westward mountains by evening.

But what would he find then? If Emilie had taken this step, she would probably scorn him should he go after her. He had never quite understood how or why she loved him. And now he thought that her departure was the final seal on something she might have felt. All at once, like lightning crashing into a forest, her love for him had come crashing down so that nothing was left of it but smoke. Perhaps he would ride his horse into the face of her bitter mockery. And he couldn't face that. The thought of it dried up his resolution. Wasn't this what he had wanted in the silver dawn of the day before? Wasn't this the substance of what he had decided?

So the apathy came back. It descended upon him like a sheet of lead. It crushed his desires, his love, his sense of time and the way time made people lose everything they had. Most of all it crushed that tiny little spark burning with wild bravery within his heart, the little flame which could make him do something as reckless and unexpected as to forsake all his past for Emilie. The invisible little impulse which set his muscles all aquiver with the expectation that he might stand and be his own man. That little fire died.

And he turned his horse without another word to the man in the road. For Sam it was the last physical motion he made in his love affair with Emilie. The slight pressure on the bridle of his horse was a period. Quite casual and normal. But it turned the horse around, and Sam rode back to his mother.

She was in the kitchen when he got there. She was standing by the stove, mechanically going through the motions of preparing the noon meal. He put his arms around her and hugged her. "Well, you've won," he said gently. "She's gone. She and her family have gone West."

His mother put her face against him without a word. But in a moment he felt her hot tears wetting the front of his shirt. He pushed her gently away and went out to sit on the porch, and that morning he looked out into the ripening spring and thought it was time to check his fences, and that is what he did. His mother cooked him a huge meal that night, and they sat together over it and talked idly of crops, and once they even laughed at some meaningless thing. Afterward he walked quietly under the peaceful stars and noted that the summer constellations were rising, and that Orion and the Dogs had trailed winter out of the sky. And then he went to bed he felt a relief in his mind. Things were restored to the way they had been. He had done the right thing. That was all he could ask of himself. His family would be proud of him. And so he fell off to sleep and dreamed of childhood and found Emilie lying in the long grass, dead and devoured by vultures.

His mother did not bring up the subject again—not until the morning after Mr. Simson died. Bad days were best forgotten, she said. She even seemed sorry for all the heartache her son had endured. She might have had her personal regrets, for she spoke kindly to him, softly, and though she tried in a host of little ways to show her love and her gratitude, she did not really thrust herself upon him. She left him to the slow healing of his own wounds. They settled down together again in a semblance of the old ways.

Except that Sam now fell into long silences and withdrew even further from life in Bourbon County. He asked his questions of himself. He nursed his loneliness in solitude. He found himself listening with more interest to stories about the West, the broad land and the slow, processional moving of tiny people in search of something under the changeful clouds.

He taunted himself with fantasies. One in particular. That of Indians raping her on the plains, where there was no one to help. A shudder of fear mingled in his mind with the uncomfortably abstract wondering that illiterate Indians might enjoy so casually the treasure he had been so near to having, the treasure he had lost forever. Violence was so ordinary in the terrible West that no one took note of it. If it happened, there was no likely way he could ever know. Realizing his ignorance, he became convinced at times that it did happen or that it would. No one could tell what Indians might do. There was Custer, and only a few years before.

But in his more rational moments he knew that Custer and the Little Big Horn and the crying Indians had all been a last shining bubble of tragic romance which burst on a hot day and left the enduring realities. The land which must be plowed and planted, the land which put forth high grass for cattle to graze upon, the land which meant toil and life and unending hardship. That was the way he supposed Emilie would end—the worn-down wife of some struggling man with all the beauty drained out of her, the sprightliness faded by the intense Western sun. Not the rape of Indians. Nothing but the slow, sad erosion of time and the land. That was enough. Entirely enough.

But finally it was the darker fantasy which asserted itself. She had never really loved him at all. He was a plaything. She was lonely and in a strange place, and he blundered into her life at just the right moment, and she imagined she cared for him. If someone else had spoken to her first, or if he had held back, then she might have passed through the same romance, but with somebody else. Perhaps now that she was gone she would have other romances, affair piling on affair until the words and the passions of one were all mixed up and irretrievably confused with the rest.

She had enumerated the reasons she loved him. It was part of that rational summation of the reasons they should be married. He was touched. He was enormously proud. He believed her picture of himself, and that was a part of his own love for her. But maybe it was all something conjured out of her own mind without any real relation to him at all. Perhaps now she saw that he was none of the things she imagined. In time she might not even remember his name.

Before Emilie left, his mother helped this particular fantasy to grow in his mind. She did not nag at him or raise her voice or assume any arrogance. No, she observed things with a flat objectivity, a detachment which gave a rueful color of accuracy to her words. She simply pointed out that her love for his father was one of the rarest things on earth. At times she spoke of it with mystified puzzlement. Almost a regret. It was as if her love had taken command of her, almost against her will. When she spoke of it she was not boasting. She was merely indicating that she too saw what everyone could see. She was humble and grateful for what had happened to her. You could think of it as a grace, an election out of God's Providence. She could not claim any pride, for it was a great gift, and she was not responsible for it. God had made her to be that kind of woman.

But Emilie was not that way. No, his mother ruminated in that wise objectivity of hers, Emilie was the kind of girl who might feel things intensely but never deeply. In one moment she was absorbed with one set of feelings only to drop them in the next. She was an intelligent girl who needed continuous drama, frequent changes of scene, a restless, unsatisfied soul who could never be satisfied.

If she won Sam, the pleasure would be over for her. In time she would want other things. In time she might want to win another man. If the circumstances arose, she was the kind of girl who could forget him. It wouldn't be her fault. It was just the way she was.

Well, now the circumstance was that she was gone and had been gone for a month.

My God, the heat!

The train of his listless thoughts finally broke up on the hard, dry edge of the heat. Nothing to do on this morning but await tomorrow. Without any real purpose he ran up his horse and saddled it and went out to ride over the simmering land to look at his crops. Anything to pass the time away by himself. He rode down behind the house, passed a fringe of woods which concealed the clearing where the slave quarters, long deserted, lay rotting in on themselves. He went down the lane to where he had seen Emilie on that day ages ago. He tried to put his mind on the standing oats and on the wheat, the stunted corn, and he tried to lose all his thoughts in the wordless apprehension of shining yellow reflecting the blinding sun in the motionless fields.

But in spite of himself he could hear the cheery call of that other morning, the eternal thing which, he sometimes thought, would linger over that field long after his death: "Why, *Samuel!*"

He ran his tongue over his mouth and found his lips cracked and dry like the land itself and the taste of dust down in the crannies of his teeth. He did not know whether to curse or to pray. In fact he did neither. He felt a profound lassitude and an emptiness. He went slowly down the margin of the field and came out onto the dusty track of the secondary road which wound around the farm on that side to the south.

Sitting his horse there in the clear, hot sunlight, he saw the man and the boy emerge from the trees a half-mile away and ride jogging toward him.

12

WHEN THOMAS BAZELY wakened on the morning after the hanging, he was quite mad. He sat up on his bed and glared blankly at the dismal light, and he could only barely comprehend it as light. For the morning swam with fantasies, and beyond the veil cast by the light lay an outer darkness. He looked about in a heightening of fear, and in the midst of the swirling things in the room he could not even force his mind to put one thought after another.

When he moved, it was in a torment of terror. Every still thing in his cabin seemed hostile. But most terrible of all was the light. Until this moment he had always relished the light. He had dropped his soul into it each morning in the way a man dying of thirst might throw himself into a pool in the desert. But now the light was hostile, and the dark was also an enemy, and the creation itself leered at him, and he was an outcast without a shred of dignity or a spark of hope.

He got up and stood for a while trying to get his bearings. The fear was almost overpowering. It was a shriek in the marrow of his bones, a wild electric shock. His senses were so acute that he had feeling in his hair, and the very pressure of light on his head made his hair burn as if every strand were an inflamed and elongated tooth. His fingernails ached, and the pressure of the floor against his bare feet was like a blistering fire.

In the daylight Thomas Bazely had always managed to keep a wall between the present and the horrors of the past. But now the wall was shattered, and the past came flooding in on him like the light itself, irresistible and overpowering. The forms which darted at his head were the people he had killed in the war—not just the woman in Kansas, but children, old men, young girls, and adolescent boys. They were all there to mock him. They swayed and danced before him in the exact form they held at that moment when he drove death home on them. A blond child with a saber wound in her head, a fleeing boy ridden down by the iron-shod hoofs of a galloping horse, a girl with a water bucket clubbed to earth in the street where she was caught going to the well. And more. Many, many more. They were like bees buzzing around his head. And above their frenetic swarming, a hearty divine chuckle rolled across the sky and filled the celestial realm where once Thomas Bazely thought he saw a vision.

In one corner of the room stood an old cupboard. It was high and dark and dirty with age, and its shelves held only a few scattered cups, most with the handles broken off, a cracked bowl and a tin mess plate. But atop the cupboard, hidden behind a shabby cornice, reposed an ancient service revolver, loaded and primed. The well-used side arm of Thomas Bazely, late of Quantrill's Raiders.

Now Thomas Bazely fixed his eyes on the cupboard. Moving with meticulous care, he crept across the room and reached up, felt for the weapon, found it, and felt a confidence of wild freedom come surging into his blood from the hard and familiar touch of the gun. He thrust it down into his pants at his belt so that the naked metal lay hard against his skin. Dropping his shirttail over the pistol, he grasped the butt with his hand as though for support. Then he plunged out into the violent sunlight, striking his shoulder against the door as he emerged into the glaring brightness and fearfully bruising himself. He paid the pain no attention at all. He went to the barn and ran up his horse.

He did not put on the saddle. He did not think of it. The bridle still hung over the horse's head from his humiliating ride home on the day before. He pulled up onto the animal's bare back, and holding the pistol butt with one hand and the reins with the other, he rode Indian fashion out the open gate and onto the rutted trail which farther in the woods became a road.

Then it seemed that in the dense trees flanking the way he heard drums begin, a rising tempo of parade drums, joined by another and another until a file, invisible and innumerable, was pounding a tattoo summoning men to death, to the long, long judgment. His head began to throb in time to the noise of the drums, and the pain was so intense that he thought he must fall to the ground and die. And once again as in those haunting years he seemed to feel a saddle beneath him on a horse ready for battle. The roll of the drums grew louder, pounding and pounding, and his head pounded with them, and he was nearly blind with pain. Phantom soldiers lined out along the trees and stood at attention and saluted as he passed by. He returned their strange salutes with a dazed motion of his hand which, when it touched his head, scorched his forehead.

And there was Quantrill riding with him, a giant of a man with a look of steel in his cruel eyes, and Thomas Bazely remembered how Quantrill had seen the vision too. A vision of the South rising like heaven itself out of the chaos of that war. Quantrill was a school teacher. Thomas Bazely was a school teacher. And in the days before the War they walked along quiet country roads together in the evening when school was done, and they talked of the glory that would be if war came and the South emerged triumphant. Those long, quiet walks in the cool of the day came back to him in this sunny brilliance spilled down on the road from the lofty sky. A world so real and yet so unreal, a world remembered beyond the fires of burning towns and the tumult of horsemen and the dying screams of the innocent.

Quantrill was rational about it all in those days—as befitted a school teacher. Some would have to suffer. Some would die. Some would perish without reason and without justice. But that was the way of the world. You fought hard, you killed any way you could, you paid any price for victory. And when victory came nothing else mattered, for then you could make all the dreams come true. And when they did, no one would condemn the midwives who brought the dreams to birth. In assisting birth, you got your hands covered with blood. That was one of Quantrill's favorite sayings, and in those long-ago walks Thomas Bazely would nod and agree and see the logic of it.

In the War Thomas Bazely still listened to his master. They sat around campfires in the open air, and Quantrill would expound his stark philosophy of history and explain their own part in it. When Thomas Bazely sat silently, his face brooding with distress, Quantrill was always ready to put out a confident hand and tap him on the knee and reassure him.

"I don't like to kill the women and the children," Thomas Bazely would say in mournful hesitancy.

And Quantrill would console him. "It's the way we'll win the war, my friend. The enemy is most vulnerable where he is most weak, and women and children are his weakest spot. If we kill enough of them, he'll get tired of the war, and then he'll talk peace. Look at it that way. Every woman and child we kill takes us that much closer to victory, when we can all go home. If we kill enough now, we'll never have to fight another war."

But it was one thing to speak of killing on those serene walks before the War, and it was another thing to *do* the killing in the helpless towns where the shrieking of the guiltless filled Thomas Bazely's head with a roaring which would never go away. He cast a baffled glance at the ghostly figure riding silently along beside him now, and he remembered what Quantrill said in those days. "Just remember, my friend, we are fighting for the Confederacy, for the most glorious ideal in all history. We are fighting to be a nation. Nobody's going to think about a few women and children when the world *sees* what we build, my friend. I tell you what I sincerely think. I think if these people could see what we're building up, they'd be glad we killed them! It'd be like they were martyrs. Don't you see it? Don't you *see!* A few civilians dead. It's a cheap price for glory! Our cause makes anything we do just. Remember that. The justice lies in our reasons, not in our acts."

And with that Thomas Bazely would smoke a pipe and stare into the fire and at last wrap himself up in his blankets and lie down to an uneasy sleep. And in the nights he dreamed—again and again. It seemed that something wakened him—a rustling noise, something scraping in mysterious rhythm. And he got up. Every night he thought he got up and went to see what was making that uncanny sound, and he found himself in a windowless building of stone. He came unerringly out to the doorway, and on the bleak threshold he saw a woman, a tall woman, very thin and bent over and dressed all in white, so shrouded he could never see her face. She was sweeping in the doorway, and her broom made the scraping sound. Back and forth she swept, and Thomas Bazely never knew who she was, never knew why she swept, never as long as the war went on. He told Quantrill about the dream, and Quantrill laughed it to scorn. But now he understood what the shrouded woman did. She swept away all their hopes. They were buried along with the people they killed. And all the crimes they committed for the glory remained mere crimes when the glory was departed. For the South lost. Quantrill died skewered with bullets from an ambush in a stinking barn. But Thomas Bazely lived to remember and to have memory accuse him in the deep of night when he could not sleep.

Quantrill said God was on their side. Thomas Bazely had decided that God was on every side, and when the flags of the Confederacy lay in the dust, God was pleased. It pleased God to bless, and it pleased God to damn. Thomas Bazely and William Clarke Quantrill and all the rest? They were God's tools, played with like something almost forgotten in His divine fingers, and then cast aside when their work was done. "Hath not the potter power over the clay, of the same lump to make one vessel unto honour, and another unto dishonour? What if God willing to show his wrath, and to make his power known, endured with much long-suffering the vessels of wrath fitted to destruction; and that he might make known the riches of his glory on the vessels of mercy . . ." Those were the very words from the Book. Thomas Bazely knew them well.

God was merciful to Quantrill. He let him die. But Thomas Bazely lived on and on with all the people they had killed, all the towns they had burned. He lived with dying children and dead women—every night for twenty years. He would not have a mirror in his house because his face was so hateful he could not bear to look at it. God had branded the mark of Cain in his forehead, and he could not die. But Cain was fortunate. He wandered to the East of Eden and found someone to love him. Thomas Bazely longed for someone to love him. Someone pure and holy and good. Even God could not damn love. But Thomas Bazely found no one to love him, and so he found no redemption.

He heard a wind rising along the road, a strange wind. He heard it howl above the drums, and yet it did not move the leaves. He thought that Satan must be passing overhead—Satan, the horse God rides. The wrath of God was going by, and the roaring would not stop, and Thomas Bazely knew that God would never let him rest on this earth. It had been God's will that they kill and burn, that they maim and destroy, that they ride over children and rape women, that they reek of blood and fire. And now God was finally done with him, and there was nothing Thomas Bazely could do.

Nothing? He squinted against the fierce sun, and the dancing shapes dissolved in the clear air and left only the unmoving trees and the crooked road. He was riding, riding, and the purpose he only vaguely perceived at first became more clear. He was riding to possess the woman he loved—to make her love him at last or to kill her. He was riding to attack his most bitter enemy. He thought he might be riding to attack God himself. And once he dared to think that thought, he sat more erect and looked more grimly ahead, and he felt that the eyes of all the universe were turned now on him, and there was a silence in heaven itself.

The cry of the windless storm rolled behind that steady drumbeat, and the sunlight had a quality of mystery and revelation to it—the light that shone down on the bloody Nile or else scorched the land of Ahab, the light that shone like a flashing sword in the chaos brooding over the cloudy dawn of time.

And now there were others riding with him, not only Quantrill's ghostly and speechless presence but others who had ridden with them in the War and died. Suddenly, from somewhere nearby, a rippling shout of a bugle slashed the air above the throbbing drums and split the hard sky in a clean, rending call. And behind Thomas Bazely and William Clarke Quantrill a long column of mounted irregulars swung into line, gallant horsemen riding easy, and the sound of hoofbeats rose on the morning and filled the day with thunder.

13

WHEN BRIAN LEDBETTER came upon Sam at the edge of the wood the youth was sitting almost motionless on his horse. Nothing but an indecisive working of his hands in the bridle leather. Brian realized that the youth was uncomfortable, that he just might turn his horse back into the lane and go away without a word. But Virgil called out in glee: "Mr. Beckwith, it's you!" And with that Sam was stayed and waited for them to come up.

He and Brian exchanged greetings in the short, noncommital way of country people meeting unexpectedly, and there was a momentarily uneasy silence. "I'd never of thought in a million years that you're be out here!" The exclamation from Virgil was so fresh and admiring, so joyous, that Brian grinned and Sam Beckwith smiled too, though nervously and hesitantly.

"I was just looking at the crops," Sam said. "I guess I'd better say I was looking at the ruin. There isn't going to be much crop. Mayhew MacComber's going to start threshing tomorrow. Have you heard? Mrs. MacComber just brought me word."

Brian shook his head and spit in exasperation. "That Mayhew! He's like a goddam machine. We'll put up about two hundred and seventy-five bushels of dust when we get to my place. Add that to a case of sunstroke and two or three heavy bellies from drinking too much water and a couple of heart attacks thrown in, and we're going to have us a damn good crop."

"It's bad all right," Sam said ruefully, glancing at the sky.

"It's hell," Brian said. "I ain't been this miserable since Cold Harbor, and then I had me a leg shot off to take my mind off the heat. Jesus! I wish I could be that lucky now." He took out his handkerchief and scrubbed vigorously at his face. Against the sticky puddling of sweat on Brian's body it seemed sadly ineffective. His shirt was stuck to his skin, and the sunlight sparkled on the heavy ooze of sweat dripping through the fabric. "Jesus God!" he exclaimed. But he scrutinized the sky and lowered his voice. "But I'll tell you something. It's a hell of a lot sweatier now than it was yesterday. The air's thicker today." He left unexpressed the rest of his thought. Sam smiled briefly. "I guess you think Mr. Simson saw something."

"I didn't say that," Brian said defensively. Then changing the subject and speaking with a rush of feeling, he said: "Sam you look awful like your daddy. It wouldn't have took me much of anything to think you *was* your daddy just now, when we come up."

"I remember you said you knew him."

"*Ever*body knowed your daddy. Everbody in this whole valley."

"I barely remember him," Sam said. His voice was indifferent.

"We're on our way to eat breakfast," Virgil said.

"You're a little late," Sam said. "It must be nearly eight o'clock."

Any mention of the time of day was the signal for Brian to hoist his fat pocket watch into the light. Now he did so and nodded affirmatively. "Yep. Five minutes past in fact."

"It's because I couldn't get Mr. Ledbetter out of bed," Virgil said. He looked reproachfully at the older man.

"What are you fixing to do?" Sam asked.

"Well, Mamma . . . That is, Mamma and me and the boys has a cow in heat, and Mr. Ledbetter's going to get a free breakfast out of it if he comes and takes our old cow to his bull."

"I volunteered to do it because I'm so goodhearted," Brian said. He laid a rough hand over his chest.

"We have a bull," Sam said. "You could bring your cow here if you want. You wouldn't have to go so far in this heat."

"That's *exactly* what I said to Mamma," Virgil said. "But Mamma said your bull ain't good enough for our cow. She said Mr. Ledbetter had the best bull in the county, and Mamma always goes after the best. I mean she goes after the best she can get. Anyway Mamma's thinking about marrying Mr. Ledbetter, and she wants to look at him up close. She wants us kids to see him too. She says he ain't near as bad as he looks."

"Congratulations," Sam said, looking doubtfully at Brian.

"Shit," Brian said.

Virgil went rattling on. "Mamma says with his land and ours we can make a real go of it. She says we can clean Mr. Ledbetter up a right smart so he'll look respectable, and he can work both places, and they's us kids to help, and we'll be the biggest farmers in the county. Bigger even than you, Mr. Beckwith. Mamma says we have to look at it like we was buying a pig. It's a business proposition." Virgil's tongue stumbled a little over "business proposition," but he made a valiant try at the words and got them out.

Sam did not quite know what to make of this conversation suddenly dumped on him like so much cement. But he could add up land and estimate value, and he nodded thoughtfully. "That'd be a healthy lot of land, all right. It'd be separated, but that doesn't hurt anything." He looked professionally at Brian. "Might be worth thinking about."

"You can see I've just swept that poor woman off her feet," Brian said.

"Only thing worries Mamma bout Mr. Ledbetter is his fighting with the Yankee Army."

"I ain't fighting with no army right this minute," Brian observed.

Virgil ignored him and looked gravely at Sam. "Mamma was talking the other night about your mamma," he said. "And how is your mamma, Mr. Beckwith?"

"She's fine, Virgil. Just fine."

"I'm mighty glad to hear it," Virgil said gallantly. "Well, my mamma was talking about yours, and she said she didn't know how she could face your mamma if she went and married Mr. Ledbetter here. She said everybody knowed how your mamma didn't even get married to nobody after your daddy died, and here Mamma's not just fixing to get married, but she's going to marry a *Yankee*. And one that ain't even *ashamed* of it!" He looked back to Brian with peevish rebuke written across his face. "It's just because you're the onliest man around. You was just born lucky, Mr. Ledbetter."

"Them's the very words the doctor said to me the day he sawed off my leg," Brian said.

"He ain't even *sorry!*" Virgil said, getting back to his most troublesome thought. "He sat right there on top of his horse and called your Uncle Matthew a son of a bitch. That's the very thing he said!"

Brian had been slouching easily in the saddle, more troubled with fantasies of water than with the prattle of Virgil's voice. But now he sat up sharply and with alarm. "Shut up, you little bastard!" The words were as threatening as a gunshot.

Virgil looked up in surprise and with sudden respect. "You said it," he said sullenly.

"I ain't denying I said it!" Brian expelled a weary and disgusted sigh. "Look, Sam. Me and your Uncle Matthew never did get on. That ain't no secret to nobody that was in this valley then. No use trying to hide it now. But it's all over and done with you, you hear? I don't hate the dead. Just don't let this little ball of shit make trouble between you and me. We're still living, and hating ain't good for us." And turning back to Virgil he said: "I've got a good mind to whip your ass."

"No, no. It's all right." Sam broke in hastily. "I'm not about to get mad at anybody over my Uncle Matthew. I never even knew the man." And looking directly at Brian he said, "From what I know, I guess he *was* a son of a bitch."

The youth's unexpected severity was disconcerting. His words were uncommonly frank and hard. Brian was taken back by their quiet vehemence and their sincerity.

"Mamma says your Uncle Matthew was a hero, Mr. Beckwith," Virgil said stubbornly. "She says if we'd won the War she wouldn't of been one bit surprised to see your Uncle Matthew get to be President of the 'Federacy. She always said he was a lot better looking than Jeff Davis ever was."

Sam looked at the serious little boy and laughed. Brian chuckled, too, and Virgil smiled because he realized of a sudden that he had said just the right thing for the moment, and he was pleased with himself. They all three sat in the clear light, smiling at each other. Brian leaned over and put out a hand. "All right?" he said. "All right," Sam said quietly and took the hand. They sat shaking hands over the necks of their horses, not knowing exactly what it was, this agreement they were making, not quite realizing all its terms, but making it just the same, smiling over it, liking each other. Yes, Brian felt that, and he was satisfied by it. He couldn't have explained it exactly, but it was a liberation of sorts, and he was very pleased.

"You got a smile like your daddy too, Sam. Just like him." Brian spoke again with that sudden flood of gentle sentiment. He took back his hand and swept it out in an encompassing gesture to the road and forest around them. "I've seen your daddy many a day, right here in this very spot sitting his horse like you was doing. *God* that man loved horses! And when I seen you just now, it . . . Well, it made my heart jump."

Sam laughed, embarrassed. "I was just four when he died. I remember him, but not much."

Brian nodded his cyclopean head. "And you missed knowing

a good man. Him and me was on different sides in the War, and for all I knew we might of swapped lead once or twice. But he was a good man."

"I remember the way he used to laugh," Sam said. "It's like something maybe I *think* I remember, and I'm not sure. We've got a big picture of him at the house. It's a serious picture. He isn't smiling. You can't imagine him ever laughing when you look at him in the picture. It's like he was thinking about death."

Brian solemnly nodded. "He probably was. It's what we all thought about most of the time. By God, there was reason enough!"

"Yesterday . . . I was going home. After the hanging. And I went out to the graveyard. The Methodist graveyard."

"To where your daddy's buried?"

"Yes, that's right. Only, on the way I saw the nigger hags. I stopped to talk a minute with them."

"Did they read your hand?" The question was natural enough to Brian. The hags had read his hand and more than once. They had told him where to look for a lost cow once, and a long time ago they had told him that his wife would never return. But Sam was startled by Brian's candor and flushed at the question.

"Yes, yes they did. And they said they'd read my father's hand."

There was a silence. Then Sam said: "They said they told him he was going to die."

Again the silence. Above them the hard, bleached sky. The woods behind thick with heat. The sleepy buzzing of forest life droned on in the foliage, and the foreboding of fire hung in the air. The sun made a dazzling lake of brilliance around them. Brian nodded in heavy, desolate sorrow. He wished he could forget a lot of things. "Well, it's true. J. W. Campbell talked about it. He was there when they done it."

"The nigger hags said Mr. Campbell laughed at them."

"I reckon he did. He ain't much for them things. He didn't laugh when your daddy died, though. I can tell you that." And then after a pause: "It was a real worrisome thing."

"I'd never heard it before," Sam said carefully. "Looks like I'd have heard something, from somebody." He looked at Brian again with that quiet vehemence. "Did my mother know?"

"About the nigger hags? Oh yes, she knowed."

"Then why didn't I hear it?"

"Why should you?" Brian demanded with affected carelessness. "Couple of niggers! Two old wore-out whores looking for some way to make a living. It ain't like it was something important. It was just something they hit on. Hell, a busted clock's right twice a day."

Brian fumbled bravely with the words, knew he was fumbling, and dropped his eyes in perplexity. For he remembered something out of the sludge that was time. An evening fifteen years before, all closed in now by the falling of years. He remembered men laughing on the platform at the railroad station and the one man unusually serious in the middle of that bright pool of gaiety. And he remembered the sorrowful procession of dilapidated wagons along the tortuous road to the Methodist graveyard. Normally he liked to recount mysteries. But this one was too close. It was a worrisome thing.

"It sure sounds creepy to me," Virgil said. He looked fit to shiver.

"You shut up, damn it!" Brian said fiercely. And then to Sam: "Well, what'd they say? What'd they tell you?"

"They said I'd go West."

Again the profound silence. Brian took out his pitiful handkerchief. He swabbed violently at his hot face and averted his eyes from those of the youthful Sam Beckwith. He looked down at the ground, saw the sickening dust choking the road at the feet of the horses and felt a helplessness. With elaborate care he swabbed at every patch of exposed skin. He ran the handkerchief down his back under his shirt. Then he took it, held it in front of himself, wrung it and watched the dirty sweat spring through his fingers from the pressed cloth and splash on the ground. "By damn!" he said in disgust. "Look at that." And as they looked at the little blot of pathetic moisture in the dust, he felt the sweat streaming out in the places he had wiped, and his skin where his clothes touched it was all prickly with heat.

"Well," he said after another moment, "they's lots of folks that goes West. You wouldn't be the first, and you wouldn't be the last. Leastways they didn't tell you you was going to die."

"No," Sam said.

"I know lots of folks that talks about going West. They's some say you can still get rich out there. Hub Delaney talks about it all the time. Ain't no nigger hags ever told him he was going West." Brian looked cautiously at the youth, but Sam said nothing.

"You can't go West, Mr. Beckwith," Virgil said, sorely troubled. "It's too far away from home."

Sam laughed. "It is that," he said.

"We'd best be getting on," Virgil said. He was reluctant to part, but he looked up at the sun and knew that the morning was coasting past the decent hour for breakfast. Brian hoisted the watch again.

"Yep," he assented. "My stomach and my watch are running right on time. Time to eat." And then suddenly to Sam: "Whyn't you go along? You could hold another breakfast, young feller like you. I could eat *three* breakfasts when I was your age."

Sam half smiled and was about to decline. But Virgil took up the suggestion with a shout. "Sure, Mr. Beckwith. Come on. Please come! Mamma'd be proud to have you. *Real* proud." The child looked up in open glee at the prospect.

"Oh, it'd be too much trouble. I guess I've eaten all I can hold."

"Then you wouldn't be no trouble at all," Brian said gruffly. "If you've eat that much, then you ain't going to trouble nobody by sitting at the table."

"Sure, Mr. Beckwith! Sure, come on! I'll go on ahead and tell Mama. Will you come? We'd be bounden if you'd come."

"He'll come," Brian said. And to Sam he spoke in mock and friendly pleading: "Come on. From what this little bastard tells me, I may need help getting out of there with my skin on. You come on. It'll be all right."

"Well, then I will," Sam said with a sudden nod of decision. He smiled pensively at Brian, and they were pleased again in the nervous, embarrassed way that they were pleased when they clasped hands.

Virgil was simply thrilled. "I'm going to tell Mamma! You all come along, you hear? I'm going to tell Mamma!" And before anyone could say another word he had kicked his mule into something like a gallop and had ridden off in a violent fume of dust.

Sam looked after him, amused and puzzled. He shook his head. "Now, why'd he do that?" he said.

Brian chuckled. "You're a hero, by God. He's heard so much about you and your folks, and now he's going off to tell his mama that the Lord Almighty is coming to their house. Come on. Let's get the hell out of here. Our brains is going to be cooked in our heads."

They rode on. "It's peculiar," Sam said. "I've never done a thing. I didn't even know Virgil's folks very well. Not till his father's funeral. We went to that."

"Hell," Brian grumbled philosophically. "Kids is going to have somebody to worship. Let him have his pleasure. He'll get over it soon enough. Then he won't worship nobody, and he'll be sorry."

"Did you have somebody like that? Somebody you looked up to?" Sam asked shyly.

"Yep. Yep, I sure did. About when I was Virgil's age. A blacksmith."

"M. G. Galyon? He was a blacksmith."

"Oh shit," Brian said in scorn. "Not that big mouth. Long before him. Man of the name of Boring. Theophilus Boring. God, he was a big man! I tell you what I seen once. I seen it with my own eyes. They was a horse that kicked him when he was putting on a shoe. And you know what old Theophilus done? Grabbed that horse by the leg—the leg that'd kicked him—and picked up and heaved, and *bam!* Goddam horse fell over on his ass. I tell you, I thought Theophilus Boring hung the moon." He sighed in sudden mournfulness. "But I got over it, I guess. Theophilus died, and hell, I don't even know where he's buried. You forget everbody after a while, even the people you worship."

They rode on silently for a little while. Above them the empty sky stretched monstrously from the glaring sun. Brian glanced up at that sky from time to time. When he did so, he averted his eyes quickly from its dreadful emptiness. But he was drawn to it again like a man feeling for a hole in his tooth with a lacerated tongue. The day lacerated his mind. Around them the hard light glinted on the forlorn landscape and made the world an oven of heat and cavernous silence.

"You think it's bad that the dead is forgot," Brian said after a long while. He had seen the thoughtful look on Sam's face.

"Well, it makes you think."

"It's the way things ought to be," Brian said sternly. His voice was quiet.

Sam turned a direct and curious glance upon him but said nothing. So Brian picked up the theme of his own thoughts, speaking levelly, without emotion, a circumlocution of thought, a halting evasiveness before something immensely grand and bleak. "You see, the trouble with the living today is they remember too much about the dead. You take this valley. It's hanted. They's a thousand hants walking around, and people ought to forget about them so's everbody can rest. Them and us. The living and the dead. They ain't got much in common when you think about it except that the living will die and the dead has lived. Course, that's something, ain't it?" He tried to laugh, nervous at his attempt at profundity, but he became instantly serious again. "Do you get what I mean? It ain't right. If we'd forget about the dead, why maybe they could rest in peace. Now, that'd be something, wouldn't it? We'd have peace, and they'd have peace. It'd work out all right."

"Do you believe in ghosts?" Sam asked.

Brian shrugged indifferently. "Well, in a manner of speaking." Then, after a thoughtful pause, he said vigorously: "Hell yes, I believe in ghosts. I ain't ashamed to admit it."

Sam did not smile. He said: "I think sometimes we must have ghosts in our house. I've never seen any."

"I've got this idea," Brian said with sudden confidence. "Long as you think about somebody who's dead, you keep him from resting. You stir him up, and he drifts around and can't sleep. You know it, too! Lord, boy! I seen ghosts enough at the War! That night at Cold Harbor, when I got shot in the foot. I taken my belt off and wrapped it around my leg under the knee to stop the bleeding, and I hollered for help, and then I just hollered for water. Then I laid me down to die. Made up my mind and laid down to do it. Lord, Lord! *That* was a night! You know something? They was a dead man laying not two foot from me, and in the night he farted! I swear to God he did. And I guess they was lots of farting that night in the dark, and lots of ghosts around. Ghosts of all the men that died that day, and ghosts pulling loose from the men that was out there dying. I swear I could feel my own ghost bulging under my skin, trying to get loose. And I thought I could see them others just as plain as I see you right now.

"And you know something? I bet I could go right back there tonight and call them up. They wouldn't like it neither." His voice sank to a near whisper, eerily resounding in the hollow stillness of the day. "Maybe I'm disturbing them right now. Maybe they's some ghost that's been asleep, and suddenly right now he's up and moving around over Cold Harbor. And he don't know what's happening or why he's out there stirring around. Maybe he's all out of sorts and 'bout forgot who he was. All rusty. But the time'll come . . ." He concluded with a significant nod of his head.

"What time?"

"Oh, the time'll come when it'll all be forgot. All of us that remembers will be dead, and then Cold Harbor, and Gettysburg, and Antietam—Bull Run—all them other places'll settle down. The men that was killed there will rest. Yes, by God, they'll rest! And we'll be all asleep and all forgot."

"I don't see how people can forget everything," Sam said slowly. "It's written down in books."

Brian scoffed. "That ain't the same thing," he said. "You take a man that'll write a book about Cold Harbor. And if he wasn't there, he won't know a damn thing. He'll have a bunch of words that don't mean nothing but words. But me! I remember it the way it was. The screaming and the dust and the noise and the way men cried all night long for their mammas and the way dead men farted. It ain't just words with me. It's something in here." He banged with a fist against his large chest. "I can't write no books. Hell, I can't even *read*. But if I was to go back, I'd remember how it was that night I laid down in a hurry to die. Oh, these fellers that writes books, they'll go, and they'll think about it, and when they do they might hear the wind pick up a little, but they won't take no notice of that. Pretty soon they won't be nothing *but* wind. A hundred years. You give Cold Harbor a hundred years, and they won't be no ghosts there. Or if they is any, they'll all be pressed together. All them men that died there nothing but that patchy kind of fog I was talking about."

Sam mused softly. "A hundred years! I guess all this valley will be at rest by then."

And Brian with equal gentleness said: "Sure, you and me and everbody else. Everbody that was in the War. We'll all be dead and dust." He looked wistfully off into the burning light. "I guess it's a good thing to rest, but then it'd be nice if somebody come and stirred me up once in a while. I'd like to see what things has got to be by then."

"Maybe you do need some grandchildren," Sam said, grinning. "To think about you once in a while."

Brian looked at him sharply. "Whose side you on anyway?" They laughed companionably.

But the laughter of the youth quickly died. His laughter was always something which flashed and died, something like a shooting star in the very dark. He said: "I wonder if my father is at rest. The way my mother thinks about him . . . If you're right, then maybe he's troubled."

"They say a woman's tears keeps her husband's graveclothes wet," Brian said.

"My mother wants me to think about him all the time. It's hard to do. Hard for me. She knew him and loved him, but I can't remember much. Mostly I remember how still the house was when he'd died."

"Your daddy filled up ever place he was," Brian said. "When he laughed it'd fill a churchhouse. He could walk into a crowd of people he'd never seen before, and in ten minutes they'd all be wanting him to be governor of the state. Folks used to wonder if he ever got mad at anything. You couldn't figure him mad. He liked to laugh too much." Brian spoke with unaccustomed sadness, something deeper than the talk about Cold Harbor, something unexpectedly somber in a man like himself.

"I remember sitting on his lap. He used to run his hand through my hair and talk. I remember that better than anything else—the feel of his hand. But it's a funny thing . . ."

"What?"

"Well, in my mind, when I think about sitting on his lap . . . When I look up, all I can see is the picture that hangs on our wall. My mother wants the picture to remind me of him. But it gets in my way. I see the picture, and I can't remember what he was really like. The picture doesn't laugh the way he did."

Brian nodded in heavy sympathy. "It's a real shame," he said. "Your daddy was proud of you. You'd of got on well with him. Lordy, it don't seem like he's been dead fifteen years."

"I remember the funeral. It was awfully hot."

"There wasn't no drought, but it was hot. September heat. That's a hard kind of heat."

"My mother cried over the grave. I remember that."

"She had a right."

"And I cried. I guess because she was crying. I didn't really understand what had happened."

"They was lots of folks that cried that day. Folks that only just barely knowed your daddy. They was lots of Union folks at that funeral. Me and J.W. was there, and Clarence and Hub and lots more. Simson was there. By God, I remember he had on his uniform hat. Only part of his uniform he had left, I guess. Maybe the only part of a uniform he ever owned."

Sam nodded. "I was talking to my mother about that this morning. She was partial to Mr. Simson all through this. She wouldn't go to the trial. She didn't want me to go to the hanging."

"He stood there by your daddy's grave and saluted. It made an impression."

The road was climbing now, and it had left the trees entirely and meandered through rolling pasture land, all withered by the heat, brown and dead and fearfully wasted by the sun. Suddenly the youth spoke with quick intensity:

"Tell me one thing, Mr. Ledbetter . . ."

"Folks round here calls me Brian. I'd be obliged if you'd do the same."

The youth paused, momentarily embarrassed. "Please, tell me this. Why does my mother hate Mr. Campbell so much?"

Brian shook his head and did not answer.

"Wasn't he a friend of my father's? Didn't he come to the funeral? Why does she hate him?"

"I don't know. Nobody really knows, maybe not even your mamma. Sure they was good friends, your daddy and J.W. You'd see them out hunting in the morning like two kids. Your daddy made J.W. laugh. I guess he ain't *really* laughed since your daddy died. It was a blow to him. Know how J.W. lost his boy?"

"Yes."

"Your daddy made him forget that for a while. Maybe not forget it, but your daddy helped him get over it."

"Mr. Campbell doesn't go hunting any more. I've never seen him hunt."

"That's a real true fact," Brian said.

"My mother loves everybody else who was my father's friend. She took up for Simson to the last. Mr. Campbell's the only one she hates."

Brian sighed in the way of a heavy man. "Your mamma's folks didn't get on with J.W. before the War. I don't know what it was, but they didn't like him, and he didn't like them. He could see what was coming, and a lot better than the rest of us. He used to say that when the War come it'd be a rich man's war and a poor man's fight. He thought folks like your'n was pushing the war on folks like him." He chuckled in dusty reminiscence. "I tell you something else that's almost forgot around here. Day or two before Fort Sumter your granddaddy challenged J.W. to a duel."

"A duel! I never heard that!"

"Well, it's God's own truth. It didn't amount to much. J.W. called your granddaddy a fool to his face, and that afternoon your granddaddy sent your Uncle Matthew around to deliver a challenge."

"Well?"

"Well, nothing. J.W. come to the door of his office and told

Matthew to get back on his horse and get the hell out of town or he'd lay him in the street dead. J.W. had a gun on his hip. He started wearing a gun when it looked like the Rebs would go for Sumter. He'd been out West, you know, and he could use a gun. He'd be a hard man to go against today if you ask me."

"And did Matthew just . . . *leave*?"

"Hell yes, he left. I guess that's something else your mamma ain't told you."

"That's right."

"He made a lot of noise. He called J.W. a 'dishonorable wretch.' Them was his very words. But he said them back over his shoulder, riding out of town."

"I'd like to have seen that."

"Well, you can't blame Matthew much. He didn't want to miss all the excitement of the War by getting killed by J.W. before it even *begun.* And let me tell you something. That's exactly what *would* of happened if he'd of foughten with J.W."

"I guess it didn't go down very well," Sam said. An odd smile played at his lips.

"Nope. So you see there was reason for your mamma to hate J.W. Bad blood boils a long time. When your daddy and J.W. was so thick, your mamma was deep in love, and she couldn't do much but go along. Not that she ever seemed to mind. I'll tell you something you won't believe. Many's the time I seen all three of them —your mamma, and your daddy, and J.W.—all three laughing over things like they was the best friends in the world."

"That is hard to believe."

"And then your daddy died. Pap! Just like that, in the middle of the night. It never was the same after that. Maybe your mamma blamed it on J.W. Maybe she thought all that riding brought on your daddy's heart attack."

"Maybe. But it does seem strange." Thinking a moment more, he shook his head with a frown of denial. "She's never said she blamed Mr. Campbell for that. She says my father had chest pains from the first time he came. She says she did her best to make him be careful, but he wouldn't pay attention. She never mentions Mr. Campbell when she's talking about that."

Brian grunted reflectively. "I heard about the pains after he died. Nobody knowed about it till then. Nobody except your mamma. But your daddy wasn't much to talk about his aches and pains. He wasn't much to complain about nothing. That's why it was such an awful shock. You know, I seen your daddy the last day he ever lived. He was in town. He come out of J.W.'s office and jumped on his horse and rode off. That was the last time I ever seen him alive, and I can remember it like yesterday—your daddy in full gallop on that horse. He never looked more alive, and next morning he was dead. It was a shock. You expect old folks to die, and in war you get used to seeing everbody die. But in ordinary times—well, it was a blow."

"I remember the night," Sam said quietly. "I remember it was the middle of the night and dark, and I remember the way my mother screamed. I used to have nightmares, and it'd all be happening again—my mother screaming and my father cold—and I'd wake up crying." He paused and added hesitantly: "I tell you the truth. I *still* dream about it once in a while and wake up in a sweat. I wouldn't tell my mother about it now for anything. She's always blamed herself for screaming out the way she did. She never talks about that night without talking about the way she found him lying cold beside her and screamed. She says she should have controlled herself better. But she couldn't help it."

The youth stopped abruptly, embarrassed it seemed by how long he had dwelt on something as sensitive to him as childhood nightmares. Brian was nodding slowly and affirmatively, and he said something inconsequential to lighten the burden of sad thought which had fallen upon them. But he poked with his mind at the worrisome thing the way somebody pokes at a dead snake with a stick, and he felt ill at ease and queer. He could not exactly explain his worriment. It was something thick and insoluble in the greater thickness of time, something better left to sink into the muddy oblivion awaiting all things.

But there was something about the death of the elder Samuel Beckwith, something that would not go away. There was something expected about that death. Call it a premonition or whatever, the intuition which steals on people who have the gift to sense the future.

Maybe that is too strong for it. Brian had not thought in so many words before the event: *This man will die soon!* Of course there had been the dark, uncanny prophecy of the nigger hags. Afterward people in the valley blew that up into witchcraft and talked of going out there and burning their house down with them inside it. At the time most people had simply laughed, and even Brian, who always took these things seriously, chuckled uneasily with the rest.

But it was something more subtle than the nigger hags. Something that fell to like a closing door when the news came, a door blown shut by the wind. Things were working up to something. You could feel a faint breeze freshening into a storm. And when Samuel Beckwith the elder died, Brian thought: *So that's what it was!* It was the expected door slamming hard off somewhere in the night where you had forgotten to pull the latch, and you were in bed and on the uneasy verge of sleep, vainly trying to remember something neglected. Then the door slammed. It fell in on the green world of Bourbon County with a jarring crash. Yes, Brian Ledbetter had had a sense of expectancy about the death of Samuel Beckwith, Sr. It *had* been there, a worriment that picked at him strangely when he saw the grave face of a man who did not see him, lunging across the porch from an office from which that man usually emerged laughing, spewing jocose obscenities, seeing everybody in town. Then the speeding horseman riding away, a moving shadow against the September light. He thought he had heard Mr. Campbell speaking in a raised, tense voice just before the elder Samuel Beckwith came plunging out that door. But when Brian entered, Mr. Campbell sat there behind the desk, completely composed as he always was, and flippantly denied that anything was wrong. Still, after all that, the word of the death came like *B* after *A* as far as Brian was concerned. There was a curious logic to it. Even an illiterate could follow it. Maybe an illiterate could follow it better than anyone else.

And now on another morning, fifteen years after the father had taken his fire and lively tongue and high-flown blasphemies off to the grave, Brian rode along with the son. They were both troubled, silent and miserable in the inexorable heat.

The youth was tall and fair with sloping shoulders—like his father. His face was deeply tanned. A somber face. More somber now that the girl had gone. Everybody knew about the girl. You couldn't keep secrets like that in the valley. And when you took a strange, foreign girl and threw her into things—well, everybody talked about it. If it hadn't been for the Simsons, the talk about young Sam Beckwith's love affair would have been a cyclone. As it was, the affair was a stout gale blowing the windmill tongues of the women of Bourbon County. Brian knew the girl had left suddenly, without a word. Behind her the boy slid back into his serious ways. As long as the girl was here he appeared almost lighthearted. Not any more. The difference between father and son. When the father was serious, you were surprised. The opposite with the son. He did laugh at times, often at quick, unexpected moments, and then you remembered the father's old and perpetual gaiety. A keen, nostalgic memory. Something like the smell of autumn a sharp wind is inexplicably likely to blow up for an instant in the dead of winter.

And now the youth and Brian rode up the morning together. Brian stole a glance at him from the side. For just a moment he thought he might try to break the uneasy thing to the youth. Might tell about the premonition, that day in front of Mr. Campbell's office —a handful of other curious things—and they might be able to talk about the strange expectedness Brian felt about the father's death. Maybe the son could understand where all the others had failed. But it had all been fifteen years ago, and that was a long time. A very long time when you thought about it, and nothing back then mattered now. Better to let ghosts settle to rest. Better on the living and on the dead. And while Brian was already composing himself to silence, Virgil returned. Then it was no good even to think of something as faded and useless as an old mystery whose very form was terribly blurred by the years.

They both saw Virgil at once. The boy was a tan point on the black lump that was the mule, moving like a pencil lead at the head of a cloud of dust. "Here comes the little shit," Brian said. "He looks like a goddam regiment." When he got closer they saw that he was recklessly kicking his bare feet against the poor mule's ribs, and the mule's brown hoofs were flailing the powdery earth.

The boy blew up in a tumult of dust. The mule heaved and shook in the middle of it, panting for life and probably unable to believe in his mulish way that he had actually galloped on a day like this. For a moment all of them were enveloped by the bitter storm. They coughed and rubbed their eyes, and Brian delivered himself of a fine and extraordinarily obscene indignation.

But Virgil paid him no mind. Almost breathless he called out: "Mamma's fixing a new breakfast. I told her you was coming, Mr. Beckwith. She throwed everything out and started all over again. New biscuits even. She's cooking them on hickory wood. And we're going to have ham! Just for you! Ham and red-eye gravy and apple stew. We're going to have ourselves a *breakfast!*"

And now Brian laughed again. "So what if God Almighty was to come down to have breakfast? What more would his mamma do? What more *could* she do?"

14

Sarah Beckwith walked out onto the porch and called: "Sam! You, Sam!" She listened. But there was no reply.

She did not really expect one. The torrid quiet of the day mocked her voice. When she looked toward the mountains she saw that they were blurred with haze, and the world seemed to have shut her in. She paused briefly and absorbed the fact of the haze. Yesterday, she remembered, the crests had been quite sharp and distinct. But quickly she let the thought drop. She muttered sadly to herself. "He's gone again." And in a despondent mood she came back into the house and sat uneasily down in a large chair confronting the picture of her husband.

Sarah Beckwith was forty-five years old, and she felt that she was losing control over things. She was deeply sensitive about her age, though no one else in the valley knew that fact. To those who admired her as the emblem of something inexpressibly grand she seemed too exalted to worry about the slow sagging of her handsome body. But she did worry. A beautiful woman could command while an old woman could only nag. So at night, as she prepared for bed, she spent long minutes rubbing at the lines hardening and deepening in her face. They would not go away. Her breasts were still full. Dressed in her severe but stately clothing, they made even yet a suggestive bulge under her dress. Naked they flopped on her chest, and the nipples had gone from pink to brown. These she sometimes contemplated with despair. She rubbed her hands over them till they emerged like dried cherries from the rest of her flesh, but they were still old, old. Age was happening to her. She, who remembered as yesterday the frightening mystery of the first swelling manifestation of her womanhood, now presided helplessly over the decay of her youth. She had not yet undergone "the change." But she expected the first symptoms to begin any day, and she was resigned to them in the same melancholy way she was resigned to death.

Lately, when she studied the great picture of her husband, she lingered over his youth. She had begun to nourish a sentimental envy for the fact that he would be eternally young. She did so long for people to remember her as the strong and beautiful woman who held a world together. She knew they would not. It was a little like the Methodist doctrine that a man's eternal state was determined by his condition on the day he died. If she lived to be a drooling old crone, that would be the way her memory would be preserved in the life of the valley. The vision made her shudder. Seeing her in that corrupt state, people would not remember how she *really* was. The thought was not only an affront and a sorrow; it was an unspeakable terror.

She felt her youth slipping away like a coast vanishing in a great dark. It was a calamity for her husband that he died so young. But in the long sweep of time, it was a blessing. And when she was not considering the immediate fact of her own age, Sarah Beckwith always looked to the long sweep of things. When she turned through the Bible for a word, her heart came most comfortably to rest in the Old Testament. She adored that fabulous world where men did their duty, harsh though it may have been, lived for the generations they begat, and were remembered for their sons. Considered in that light, what had happened to her husband had been a blessing. He would go down in the annals of the valley as a youth, and in time it would be difficult for people to believe she had ever been his wife.

And now in the morning calm of her house, bereft of her son, Suellen MacComber departed with her raucous children, Sarah Beckwith looked reflectively at the picture of her husband. The picture looked soberly back at her, and there was an electric bond between the dead and the living which tightened in the great emptiness of the house. "I have not let you die," she said quietly to him. "You can thank me for that. It's a debt you owe me. I wonder if you know how much you owe me?"

She took a feather duster and got up to tend the picture's ornate frame. That brought her own face closer to the face behind the glass there, and she looked into the unfluttered serenity of his eyes, and she felt the hot tears rise in her own.

"Where did it all go?" she whispered. Often when she was alone nowadays she whispered at her husband's face. And now her mind filled up with the sunny day years ago when a soldier was brought, sick and weary, to her house. The recollections were like glistening tears, falling interminably in a great and eternal brightness. Life turned majestically on the pinions God had ordained. The soldier might have been well. He might have stopped for the night, mingled laughter and reminiscence and the sadness of defeat over the supper table under lamplight, slept in the barn, taken his breakfast, then vanished like the rest. This one might well have continued his errant journey back to Virginia. From him she might have had one of those scrawled letters (still reposing in a casket upstairs) sent her by those who had been both grateful and literate. Smoothly, anonymously, he would have vanished like a stone dropped into the swift and muddy river that was time. All these years since would have been unimaginably different.

And now she said to the picture: "I could have given him another father, you know. I was faithful. I shall be faithful unto death. I hope you appreciate that. In whatever world you inhabit, I hope you know your son remembers you because of what I did!"

She said the last so fiercely and so proudly that she had no more thought for tears. She had endured more than most women. She had been stronger even than her own strong father. He had lost wife and son, and the loss killed him. She remembered when she thought he was a god. Yet only a little adversity had brought him crashing down. She had lost mother, father, brother, husband, wealth, and prospects. But she endured. She prevailed. And in her the family she cherished, the land which belonged to them, their station in the world, had also prevailed. In her the dead lived. The family survived which had not appreciated her worth. And in the progeny of her son—someday—they would live on. She could see the track of God's secret step, rimmed with blood and trailing sorrow across her life. A hard thing, an inexplicable thing, but then Christ was betrayed and carried his cross. She was no better than that. And there *was* a purpose to it. God had cast down the proud and lifted up the weak to confound the mighty. Only . . . Sam! A pain of love tightened in her chest. She had almost lost her son. Maybe she had lost him anyway.

She went out onto the porch again. Beyond the sweep of shadow laid down by the house, the sun lashed the earth. Everything was spectrally still. Already in the midst of the bright morning the silent heat was eating at the tender profiles of trees and grass, and you could imagine that it was eroding the minute bindings which held cell to living cell, and you could think of a time when a puff of wind would blow across the world and it would all collapse into formless dust.

Far off in that vacuum of heat she could hear a cow bell. The sound of it came throbbing over the lonely distance like a knell of disaster. She wondered what poor cow was searching for food, and she went back into the house suddenly burdened with the suffering of dumb animals who could not understand what had gone wrong with the world.

They had ten cows now. Or was it eleven? Sam raised them, mostly to sell in Knoxville. Every year he sold all the calves, grown to young beefs, and deposited the money to their account in the bank in Bourbonville. Rufus Swope Mitchell went into a frenzied rubbing of his pink hands whenever he saw Sam come in the door. He wanted to lend him money to raise hundreds of cows. He wanted to help Sam get rich. He told marvelous stories of the new day opened by the wonder of the refrigerated railroad car. But Sam resisted. He was cautious about such things. Too much money tied up in cows could spell bankruptcy if prices changed. He read the newspapers. He diligently kept up with livestock prices telegraphed out of Chicago. He knew all about fluctuations, and he explained them carefully to the banker. Rufus Swope Mitchell could not argue against such reasoning. So he merely nodded and praised Sam, feebly, for his "sound business sense." But then in his fussy banker's way he grumbled: "You *could* be rich." He said a lot more than that to Sarah Beckwith.

But she stood by her son. Rufus Swope Mitchell was given to mentioning the word *mortgage* in a sugary, inconsequential voice. But the thing was there, sharp as a pinprick, piercing like the first minute pain in a stomach presaging inexorable death. Sarah Beckwith heard it and envisioned Rufus Swope Mitchell ensconced like a rat in her house. A money-grubbing usurer without family and without principles settled in the house of her ancestors, their pictures displaced. So she was barely civil to Mr. Mitchell. She recoiled from him as if he had been a stranger who suddenly gave her breast a friendly squeeze. He was offended at her cold resolve. He thought he was slighted. He still rubbed his hands at her, but his eyes carried a look of injured pride, and when Sarah Beckwith scornfully divined what the look meant, she felt with undisguised pleasure the racy old contempt her family had always nourished toward bankers.

Sam was like his father in these things. He knew when he had a good thing, and he had a mind to work and a head for business. Not a chip out of place on the farm. Not as many fields produced now as in slave times. Acres of the Crittendon place had grown up in new pine forest, thick, unkempt. Sam looked on the spindly, loblolly pines with equanimity. When his mother pursed her mouth and recalled the fields they choked, he said they could be burned off in a week. Someday he *would* burn them. But not now. Slowly, slowly, you did what you could. Meanwhile the land rested and recovered its strength.

And the land that was cultivated produced more than all the acres ever farmed by Crittendon men and their slaves. The place fairly sparkled. Neat fences cinched the fields—rails and supports all in place, saplings and honeysuckle rigorously purged from the angles. It must be a witness to the superiority of the white man, so thought Sarah Beckwith. All the niggers they'd owned once, all the effort it had taken to keep them from running off and to make them work, and the place looked better now than it ever had in her life. It really hurt her, in a way, to admit the way the land shone and produced nowadays. It was almost a confession of disloyalty toward the past. But it was true. She still remembered the way her father talked to bankers in her youth. He might spit out his venomous mockery of them behind their elegant backs, but in their presence he cowered and held his hat tightly in his hands and made nervous jokes which were unpleasantly coarse.

In her youth bankers held sovereign chits of paper on which the past and future of the Crittendon place depended. Papers which could explode to bits in a blast of decorous legality and blow away both tradition and hope. But now her son talked to bankers with the same confident equanimity, the same methodical certainty, with which he did everything on the farm. So Sarah Beckwith salved her disloyalty toward the past by imagining that the safe prosperity she now enjoyed was a sign of white supremacy.

But then she had always been triumphant over the niggers. They had always tried to rule her, but in the end she had always mastered them. It was a game with her once, exciting because it *could* be lost, warmly satisfying because it never was. She treasured her first victory even yet, years and years after she won it. It was something that gave her the lifelong confidence that she could always do what had to be done, no matter how hard it might be. She had subdued

Auntie Jessie, the black witch, the chief house nigger who once presided right here, in these very rooms. It was a sweet and easeful victory, and it taught Sarah Crittendon a lot about herself.

Auntie Jessie had billowing white hair, a radiant, white-toothed smile, and a warm and ingratiating way around white men. She could coo and croon, roar with insinuating laughter which dripped with suggested obscenity. An older Sarah Crittendon interpreted her mannerisms as the relics of uncounted whoredoms. But that was best not thought about.

Auntie Jessie could pinch suddenly and expertly with her crooked thumb and forefinger. She never broke the skin or left a mark. An abused little girl had no evidence that she had been pinched at all. That brave child could only fight back the tears with the force of her pride and go off rubbing the pinched place and biting her lip. Until one great day Auntie Jessie kept that poor little girl in a slavery more complete than any black endured during all the years of bondage.

Auntie Jessie's harsh power was founded on her understanding of the way things stood in the house. The woman had a foxy intelligence. Even Sarah would grant her that. "I tell you Mist' Crittendon, that Matthew am one *hellion!* Heh, heh, heh! He goes *some* I mean! Ain't afeered of nothing. Nosiree! Can't do *nothing* with that boy! Miss Sarry, now, she ain't like him, but she's gonter be a pretty thing. She's a mite spiled, that's all. Wants her own way all the time like her mamma done. She don't favor her brother at all. They's sure cut off a different stick of wood."

When the men were home—Matthew and her father—the girl was treated to excesses of slobbering love on the part of Auntie Jessie. When the men were gone she was pinched, thoroughly managed by a tyranny drenched with syrup, a gushing flow of orders sticky with honey, enforced always by that demonic finger and thumb. There were times when Sarah Crittendon couldn't hold back the tears in spite of all she could do. Then she went flying to her room, and behind the security of a locked door wept bitter tears into the smothering bulk of her feather pillow. Behind her she left Auntie Jessie smiling in the smug fashion of an empress in triumph over a vast domain.

Then one morning, when the men were away, Sarah Crittendon grew up.

It was a minor battle on the surface of it, a hot little skirmish over and done with so fast that it seemed impossible to assign much importance to it. A comic side to it. In fact it was one of the few childhood memories which could make the grown woman laugh aloud in solitary moments. Sarah could laugh out of that feeling of motherly devotion she felt for the poor, lonely little girl she had been. Laughter, affectionate and understanding, full of sympathy, sharp with the recollection of the silly thing that shook the old alignments of the house all out of place and brought in a new order. The day Auntie Jessie began her swift descent into the grave.

It was a question of chamber pots.

From time immemorial the Crittendons had had slaves to take care of the chamber pots according to an ancient ritual. In the morning the male house slave would fetch them one by one from the various rooms and empty them into the holes of the outhouse bench. They were then rinsed out carefully and placed in the sun. Along about midday they were returned to their proper places, dry and spotless. For as long as anybody could remember, the chamber pots were dried in a row along the front porch.

The male house slave of Sarah Crittendon's youth was a boy named Eustus. Eustus was like a shadow blown against the wall by the wind. His scared eyes, shifting frantically in his black face, made him look like something made to step on and kick. Eustus was terrified of Auntie Jessie. She hated him the way people hate cowed dogs. Auntie Jessie only oozed coy sweetness onto Sarah Crittendon so that the poor girl was pinned up like a fly to honey, and once in a while she pinched her in that carefully barbarian way of hers. But she swore at Eustus with a vehemence unrestrained by God or humanity. When that did not ease her, she beat him with the first thing she could lay her hands on. So he walked in trembling fear. He gasped at life like a fish out of water and sucking air, and you could look at him weaving upstairs and down like an undernourished shadow, and you would just naturally wonder at the implausibility of a divine plan which allowed for things like Eustus.

One morning Eustus set to the chamber pots while Sarah lingered over her greasy breakfast in the kitchen. She was sixteen years old. Auntie Jessie was upstairs, supervising the making of beds and the dusting. The toiling female slaves bent silently and hastily to their tasks, took her irate abuse with eyes turned down in jittery fright to their work. Sarah sat imagining their fear. Occasionally she could hear the slap of Auntie Jessie's hand against a female buttock, and her own young bottom cringed in her dress. But never a cry from the women so abused. They were too frightened to make a sound.

Out back Eustus was making noises with the water and with the bucket from the well. She could see his thin, black form come and go, hear the heavy clink of crockery, laboring sighs, and strained grunting. And suddenly—like a stick breaking—Sarah decided it was a disgrace to have the chamber pots drying in front where everybody who came to the house before noon could see them. Once decided, she did not hesitate. She stepped out back and hailed Eustus.

"Eustus! We're changing things today. I want you to take those vessels out to the barn and let them dry there."

Eustus unbent and looked at her in consternation. "Whut?" he asked. He was frightened at the way things were, but he was terrified at the thought of change.

"You heard me! Carry those vessels out to the barn."

"Miss Sarry . . ." He faltered and looked near to fainting.

"Don't argue with me, Eustus! Now get on!" She heard her voice rise, felt her face turn red.

Eustus still stood there. "I don't know," he said sorrowfully. "Miss Jessie, she tell me to put these here pots out front, and if'n I don't do whut Miss Jessie say, she gonter cut my head off. She told me so."

"Auntie Jessie is not the mistress of this house," Sarah said sternly. "You will be taking orders from me from now on. Now you get a move on and get those pots out to the barn. *March!*"

"Yes ma'am," Eustus said softly and with hopeless gloom. He bent and took up one of the pots, embracing it tenderly, and slowly he set out for the barn, which lay through a screen of trees behind the house.

At that moment Auntie Jessie glanced out an upstairs window. She saw Eustus, going the wrong way with a chamber pot!

The window was open. She leaned through it until she seemed to defy the laws of gravity. Her voice was an unearthly screech, a dragon's howl out of a nightmare. "Boy! Boy! Where you going with that pot!"

Eustus turned and looked up at her. He couldn't speak. His eyes rolled white in his ebony face, and he couldn't move, couldn't turn, couldn't put the chamber pot down. He looked at her, fixed to the earth and entranced with fear.

"Don't just stand there," the old woman shrieked. "You get them pots 'round front where they belongs. *Right now!* You hear me, you black devil? *Right now!*"

Sarah stepped out into the yard where she could be seen from above. The hardest steps she ever took in her life. Her mind giddy behind the stern set of her face. "Eustus, you do as I told you. You take those vessels out to the barn. Put them in the sun. Go along now." Her tone was as mild as water dipped in a glass.

Auntie Jessie dropped incredulous sugar from her window. "Miss Sarry, honey, what you telling that nigger to do something crazy like that for? You know he ain't suppose to. Now you get on back in there in the house where you belongs!" To Eustus again, this time in naked, cannibal fury: "Get on there, you nigger. You do like I say!"

"Eustus!" The girl spoke again. A quiet note of menace resounding over the sunny morning. She stood calmly now, defiant and erect. Eustus trembled. He rolled his eyes up and down, looked upward to where Auntie Jessie loomed threatening his life from her awful perch, then down again to the rocklike, commanding figure of Sarah Crittendon. Sixteen years old, A slip of a girl. But strong! Yes, stronger than anyone had dreamed. A child, lonely and lovely, and *strong*.

"Miss Sarry, honey, I told you to get on back there in the house. I swear to God Almighty, I'm gonter tell your daddy. You ain't got no business fooling round with no piss pots! You a *lady!*" The girl could feel the old woman's sharp eyes biting into the tender skin of her soft back. She felt the skin there quiver and knot. She could feel the thumb and finger the nigger woman must even then be manipulating, pinching the air.

"Eustus, you go right along and take those vessels where I told you." Sarah gestured placidly toward the back of the place, betrayed only by her hurrying, nervous voice.

Auntie Jessie lifted her own voice again. "Now looky here, both of you. I ain't gonter stand for no foolishness this morning. Boy, you go put them pots long the front porch like we always done, or I'm gonter come right down there in this minute and lay you out. And I'll fix you too, Miss Sarry. You see if'n I don't. Don't you go getting uppity with *me*, young lady!"

Only then did Sarah turn slowly, with terrific calm, a deliberation she still gloried in after all these years. She looked up at the window where Auntie Jessie hung her black head out. "Auntie Jessie, I have given Eustus an order. He is to do what I tell him to do. If you continue to contradict me, I shall have you stripped naked, and I shall whip you myself! I shall make all the others watch while I whip you myself. With a leather belt." She turned with that same terrible deliberation to face the boy: "And if you continue to stand there, sir, I shall have my father sell you to a cotton planter in Mississippi."

Sarah never forgot that moment. The old witch who had arched over her childhood turned to butter in the heat and melted away. The sagging body, the aging face wrinkled like a rotten plum, the flaccid muscles slack around the drooping mouth—it did not even look like Auntie Jessie any more. It was still a startling thing when Sarah thought about it. The old woman changed in the same way that people changed in fairy stories when the fairies waved a magic wand. She vanished from the window.

Eustus took the chamber pots to the back. Ever afterward he came to Sarah for his orders—up to the day he left, transformed himself, flinging cackling obscenities over his thin shoulders as he walked out to freedom.

Auntie Jessie fought one last, rear-guard action. It was all futility, all loss, but she did it. She went to Benjamin Crittendon that night, honey in her mouth. And Sarah swept into the parlor, imperially firm, calm as marble, talked the nigger woman down, told her father that the foul creature was getting old and senile, that she could no longer do the work. Sarah had decided, she said, to retire her. There were three or four vacant cabins in the quarters with the other slaves, and she would have Eustus and some of the field niggers clean one up and move Auntie Jessie down there. She didn't like the idea of a nigger woman sleeping in the house with them anyway. Didn't like the nigger smell in her room. And besides it didn't look right. It was almost as if the nigger woman were as good as *they* were, and *that* didn't set well. Everybody could see that Auntie Jessie walked about with an air of pride. A sinful thing, pride, especially in niggers. Dangerous, too. You let a nigger have pride, and there was no telling where it would end. It smacked of abolitionism to her, and since she was mistress of the house it was something that she, Sarah Crittendon, could not allow. Auntie Jessie had to go. At once.

The honey drained out of the old nigger woman then. She whined. She groveled. She cried. Sarah still thought about that part of the episode with distaste. It was so mean of the old woman to take on so, so undignified. She half expected Auntie Jessie to throw herself on her knees. Miraculously she did not. But she pleaded, and she sobbed like a baby. She called up her years of loyal service, the way she had stepped in when Sarah was born, when the girl had killed that angelic woman, Benjamin Crittendon's late wife. What was her name? Auntie Jessie tried to call it, faltered, could not remember, stumbled over her lapse like a horse on a fence and went blindly on. She deserved something more in her old age than to be sent down. The field hands would kill her. Sure as death, they would kill her.

Matthew Crittendon came into the house in the midst of the commotion and stood leaning against the mantelpiece and took it all in. He began to chuckle when Aunt Jessie was making her defense. By the time she stumbled to a conclusion he was laughing so hard that she could scarcely be heard. Finally she stopped in the middle of a sentence, and he said: "For God's sake, paw, get her out of here before Sarry kills her with an axe! Sarry's right anyhow. She can't do the work no more. My sheets was dirty for a week last month, and she didn't do nothing about it. I swear she didn't do nothing."

"It ain't so," Auntie Jessie said frantically. And it was not. Sarah knew that then; she remembered it now. And she was still grateful for the way Matthew had taken her part. The old nigger woman saw Matthew's insolent grin. She was not too old to know what it meant. She saw the smile play over the thick mouth of Benjamin Crittendon. Sarah saw it too and knew that she had won. Auntie Jessie turned an evil eye onto the older man and drew up from herself the last stout reserves of her arrogance. "You told me once, long time ago, that if I let you fuck . . . !"

She did not finish the sentence because Benjamin Crittendon jumped up like lightning and smacked her across the mouth with the back of his hand and told her to pack up and get the hell out of his house. Matthew whooped with laughter. Sarah was almost in a swoon from the force of that nasty word spoken before men. Benjamin Crittendon turned furiously to shout at his son. His face was so red that he might have had a stroke right then. And in this uproar, Auntie Jessie slipped out. Out like a shade, an absence, a vacancy with form. She was holding her mouth, but she was not crying. Her eyes were sunk in a submission that was already death. That night she slept in the quarters.

She lived for a month after that. The field hands had feared her for almost as long as any of them could remember. Now she was in their power. The women would not speak to her, but they crowed with shouting gibes whenever she showed her face in the door. Children jeered her, threw stones at her, and mud and filth, and smeared chicken shit over her porch so she couldn't walk outside without stepping in it. Their ringing scorn met her whenever she emerged into daylight. At evening the men taunted her with vile names, and at night she huddled in her ragged bed while they pounded on the walls of her cabin and screamed like wolves to keep her awake. Sarah remembered the wild shrieking, softened and made weird by distance, something out of the primitive jungle from which the blacks had come, carried to her in the deep of night as she lay in her bed upstairs.

Remembering, she felt a pang of regret over Auntie Jessie's fate. Sarah Crittendon Beckwith did have her regrets. But she remembered also that she was goaded into action by events. Auntie Jessie had to be put in her place. It was for the good of the household. A hard thing, yes, but life is full of hard things, and if Sarah brooded over them, the brooding did not keep her from doing her duty. As for Auntie Jessie, the only way she could preserve herself was to die, and that is what the old woman did.

Sarah went to the funeral in the slave graveyard. She took flowers. She even wept gentle tears, and they were sincere. She was truly moved. Auntie Jessie had been something of a mother to her. Sarah was sorry for what had happened. With God as her witness she could say that she never in all her life meant to be unkind to anyone. What she did was necessary. She held no malice toward Auntie Jessie. So she wept, and the slave women observed this tenderness of affection, and it moved them. They accompanied it with frantic outbursts of their own. They all sang so mournfully that even the men cried and took on. Altogether it was a good burying. Everybody felt satisfied about it. The slaves talked about it for several days. Maybe a month. And it was at least a year before something carried off the wooden stake set in the ground to mark the grave and people forgot where the old woman was buried.

So Sarah ruled the house. Her father did not suddenly begin to love her. She did not expect that. But he deferred to her. Matthew treated the whole episode as a rowdy joke. Once in a while he would tickle her behind in a playful way and make some remark about his sheets. Then he would roar with laughter. Sarah saw that the sheets were regularly changed. She saw too that he had a clean shirt every day and clean underwear, that his room was mopped more often than it had been, dusted, scrubbed, and kept spotless. It was a kind of worship. But if Matthew ever noticed it as such, he gave no sign. Sarah did not expect him to. She did it because she knew her responsibility. And never in her whole life did she ask anything but to do her duty.

"How I loved them!" she uttered the thought aloud, standing with her hands clasped in front of her body, gazing into the haze of smothering heat which cupped the earth. "How I adored them!" The bright tears came up in her eyes, and she wept softly.

15

THOMAS BAZELY RODE into the nigger Bourbons' yard just as Beckinridge was dumping the body of his father into the fresh grave. It was a shallow hole, pitiful for a grave, but it was the best Beckinridge could do. He stumbled back in fear when he saw the white man. "Oh Lordie!" He looked up at Mr. Bazely with wide, flaring eyes. He began to babble, his voice high-pitched and confused. "He was sick, Massa. He fell, in the house against the shotgun. It liked to blowed his head off." There was hopeless supplication in the voice.

"Halt!" Mr. Bazely threw a wild hand high above his head, pulled his horse to a stop with the other. "What goes on there, nigger?" He looked haughtily down at the cowering figure.

"I'se burying my daddy," Beckinridge said. "He got kicked awful bad by our mule. Oh Lordie, Lordie!"

Mr. Bazely nodded carefully. He wore an expression of somber comprehension. "It is a burial detail, I see. One of our brave comrades." He came down off his horse, almost fell, caught himself with a wild flailing of his arms, stood then swaying dangerously at the edge and looked down into the grave. Beckinridge lost some of his fear. He saw the blanched face, the unsteady body, the exaggerated concentration, and he saw that the preacher was mad. "Killed in action, I see. A shame. A pity."

"Yes suh," Beckinridge said quietly. He glanced sideways into the grave, not wanting to take his eyes completely off the preacher. His father lay there, face up, dried blood caked over the face. Rigor mortis made the stiff hands appear to claw upward, tearing the air.

"Is there a preacher, a chaplain?" Mr. Bazely demanded.

Beckinridge shook his head. "Naw suh," he said softly. "I ain't had no time to get none."

Mr. Bazely nodded with an understanding frown. "Well, it is indeed fortunate for this man that I am a preacher. *Very* fortunate." He fixed Beckinridge with his wild gaze and spoke sharply. "Cover him up, nigger. We cannot have a funeral with that thing lying open before our eyes. It's not decent. Cover him up." He jabbed at the grave with a finger, almost lost his balance, caught himself, and all the while managed to keep a harsh, commanding look turned on Beckinridge Bourbon.

"Yes suh," Beckinridge said. He picked up the shovel. He slipped his hands along the smooth handle, holding it like a club. For an instant he looked calculatingly at the exposed flesh of Mr. Bazely's neck just where it joined his head, and he could see the quick beating of the man's heart pulsating beneath the soft, protuberant skin. Quietly his hands tightened around the handle.

"Come on, nigger! I don't have all day. I have work to do—houses to burn, women to rape, devils to kill! Don't keep me waiting. I have business with the Lord. You get on with this burying!"

At the lash of command Beckinridge responded. He bent under the stinging voice and thrust the shovel into the red dirt. The effort made him gasp in pain, but he managed to dump the shovelful of earth onto the body of his father. He bent again, grunting, puffing, and soon the last ragged fringe of his father's denim shirt disappeared. When the grave was filled Beckinridge was again wet through with sweat. For a moment he stood swaying near the preacher, leaning hard on the shovel, fighting for breath.

But the preacher waved him back with a furious gesture. "Step back, nigger!" Thomas Bazely took a commanding position at the head of the grave and looked sternly about. He blinked his eyes into the morning sun, trying to see the faces of his auditors. But the light was dazzling, and he could not make them out. Even Quantrill was hidden. A brief, blank look of perplexity flitted across the preacher's face. But he began anyway.

"Men!" he cried aloud, "our comrade is dead. He died bravely, fighting for his cause, for our cause, for our country, and for God. He did not understand that God's will was for our land to be cursed. He only knew that God willed for him to go and die. And he did. He obeyed his Maker. He heard the great command, and he answered with his obedience!"

He paused and looked about. The giant heat of the morning engulfed the words as he spoke them. He spoke so loudly, but the sound was so faint. Yet now he could see the men, rank on serried rank in the seething glare, and he could see Quantrill, and behind him where the day melted into the dark of the woods he could sense a commanding Presence brooding over him and the world. The Presence cast a motionless spell over the forest gloom and the glaring earth, and he was drawn hypnotically toward it and almost lost his voice. But the files of waiting men were stirring expectantly, and so he began again to speak.

"We may be comforted, my comrades, in knowing this one thing, that though our fallen brother may end in hell, he will be there by the Will of God. That *is* a comfort, my friends. If we burn there, we know that there is a purpose to it. We can meditate on it forever and ever. In the fire we can think and thank God for using us and thank Him that He did not extinguish our souls in an eternal night."

He looked around at the respectful multitude. His eyes fell on a nigger, standing warily at the fringes and looking up at him with no expression at all. Something about the nigger was familiar. For the life of him he could not remember what it was, nor could he recall why he felt the nigger to be significant. He was simply there.

"Now, you take that nigger," he said, groping for the thought. "He's cursed, too. We have seen his damnation as we have seen our own. He is damned, comrades, damned on earth and maybe forever." The Spirit soared within him. "The nigger is God's word Incarnate for the South. He is our sacrament, the outward and visible sign of an inner and invisible grace—our damnation! Bless the Lord, oh my soul, for niggers! If we didn't have niggers, maybe we couldn't see God's judgment so plain! There it is, brothers! The Word of God!" He pointed jubilantly at Beckinridge. "How good is the Lord to let us know!" Beckinridge said nothing.

Thomas Bazely searched the hard sky again. The sun was climbing. The horses behind him were pawing the earth. It was time to go.

"Nigger!" The voice cracked like a thin whip. Beckinridge responded with a shifting of his body, something that dimly resembled coming to attention. "See to it that this grave is kept! Do you hear?"

"Yes suh," Beckinridge said.

"Plant it with grass and flowers. I'm coming back this way, do you hear? I swear I'm coming back to see about you, and if this grave isn't kept . . . If this grave isn't kept . . . I'll tell Quantrill—and God, too. I'll tell God you failed Him."

"Yes suh," Beckinridge said. His face was blank.

Mr. Bazely looked at Beckinridge once more—a long, befuddled, and searching look. "I would like to spend more time with you," he said in sudden low solemnity. "I would like to hear what God has to say with your voice. But I must go. I must be about the Lord's business. I wish only . . . I wish I had realized a long time ago. We might have talked."

He threw himself onto his horse, almost pitched over onto the other side, caught himself on the mane with difficulty. Then he steadied himself and sat erect. He turned to the men around him, made a curt sign with a nod of his head. They mounted swiftly and in terrible silence. Not a harness rattled in all the forest. Not a voice. Not a sound of stamping hoof. The mysterious, throbbing beat of the drums had fallen mute, though he could see the drummers clear as the day itself pounding relentlessly at their unceasing tattoo. Faces blurred uncertainly. He could see the horses bending their necks, but no sound! No sound but the champing of his own horse, the musical calling of birds in the sleepy woods, the ragged sucking of his own breath. His eyes filled with sweat, and he was blinded again by the sun. He saw trees as men walking. But there was Quantrill! Quantrill would not leave him till the end. He threw up his right hand. "Column, *ride!*"

They moved out. Along the forest road Captain Bazely rode grimly forward. The troops lined out behind him, riding easy, still in that overpowering silence. The pistol jabbed at his skin under his pants. He smelled the smoke of battle, saw the wild flames. He saw men shouting and saw women open red mouths to scream. He saw the blond child struck down by the saber blow, saw the blood like some crimson fountain soar leisurely upward and splash into the ground. And he thought of all womankind incarnate in the single pure woman whose possession defied him.

He knew what the woman was now. She was the amalgamation of all womanhood to the damned. Those women of all generations with tender thighs and wet lips, alabaster teeth, full white breasts tipped with taut nipples of pink delight. Women who walked demurely through the world, bearing unseen their secret temples which the damned longed to enter, there to adore the warm, dark side of God. Women whose soft virginity was a sweet rose snatched at a million times a million times by longing men, desperately grasping for something, some enchantment of sweet love which would be salvation. Men reached for the rose, drew back mysteriously empty hands and found the hands bloody, incurably infected by the poisonous thorns. Somehow the elect avoided the thorns. They climbed out of the muck and were enfolded by the clean petals and lay eternally secure in that embrace. The damned perished for the want of the sweetness, and could not understand their failure. The woman who was the incarnation of all that, the woman he adored with desperate passion, the woman who could save his soul, was out there waiting for him to come.

16

THE DIRT ROAD entered the forest again and then emerged into the blinding sunlight. It passed over a little rise, and there was the Weaver house on a slight elevation to the left. Dothan Weaver had built it himself. He was a good carpenter, and he had done a good job. Not a large place nor a fancy one, but it had a look of tight comfort, and it was almost painfully trim. There were rocking chairs on the porch and a swing, hung by chains. You couldn't look at all that without thinking of quiet Sunday afternoons in the spring and summer and visitors sitting around in their Sunday best, swapping yarns and gossip, talking about crops and commenting on the morning sermon. And of course there would be Indian summers when you could sit on the porch and see the trees on the distant ridge standing red and gold against the blue autumn sky. Brian thought about the prospects, and he bit his lip and looked grave.

The driveway ascended to the side of the house and curved behind. It passed between tall, shady oaks and under an especially large chestnut and went out toward the barn. The barn was unpainted, but there was something unusual about it, and slowly it dawned on Brian that somebody had actually whitewashed it once, and not so many years ago! The fences seemed to be in good repair, and there was a broad pond by the barn, obviously spring-fed from a deep source because it was brimming full and the water was shining green. Brian took it all in slowly, like a man getting used to heaven when he didn't expect to make it, but what his eyes finally fixed upon was the lawn.

For the lawn was green. In the midst of the drought, the Weaver lawn was living green. The grass was so fresh-looking that rain might just have passed. Brian wanted to get off his horse and roll in the grass and sing an obscene song. He couldn't do it, of course.

He didn't want the Weavers and the Beckwith youth to think he was crazy.

And flowers! My God there were real flowers! Larkspur mostly. And roses! Green bushes laden with rose buds and blossoms, reds and whites, one bush brilliantly yellow so that it looked as if somebody had sprinkled little curds of butter through all the leaves. The whole place smelled as sweet as springtime. Instinctively he spit out his tobacco. They rode around back and into the yard and passed under an arching white trellis of red roses, and the scent of the roses made him want to stop dead so he could sit right there and smell them until he died of their sweetness.

Brian was jolted by the fragrance. He was shaken by the cleanliness. He was disturbed by the ruddy children, who came shyly out of the house to greet them. But what agitated him most was the smiling woman, buxom and sturdy, who followed the children, vigorously wiping her hands on her apron, proudly carrying herself in lively dignity. *I smell like a barn!* The thought was a hopeless recognition of sorts, but there wasn't a thing he could do about it. So he took off his floppy straw hat out of respect and nodded stupidly at Evelyn Weaver and made a clumsy greeting.

She didn't even notice him. Her eyes were all for the young Sam Beckwith. She came striding up to him and lifted a hand. "Samuel Beckwith, Junior! It's an honor to have you in my house!"

Sam reddened, put down a hand and took hers, said awkwardly: "It's a lot of trouble I'm putting you to."

"Trouble! Don't you think no such thing! A little breakfast for somebody like you ain't no trouble. It's a honor. And how are you, Mr. Ledbetter?" She did not put up a hand to him, and she did not seem overly interested in his condition.

"Right tolerable," he replied, bowing deeply over his saddle horn. He was going to say something else equally elegant, but Mrs. Weaver turned her back on him and looked again at Sam.

"Get down! Get down! It's on the stove. When Virgil come and told me you was coming, I made everything up new, and you're just in time."

"You shouldn't have done that," Sam said.

"Quit sitting there complaining, and come on. Wash up and come and get it before it gets cold and has to be throwed out."

The men got down, moving uneasily as if afraid of getting dirty feet on the grass carpet. Brian dismounted with a great sigh. His pants were stuck to his crotch with the sweat, and he went through uncomfortable and only half-surreptitious motions to free them. One of the children giggled, and Brian felt the blood rush to his face. He wanted to stamp around and get his clothes decently shaken down, but he didn't dare mess up the clean grass. So he just shook himself like an embarrassed dog and went on looking about in glum wonder.

"How is your dear mamma, Sam? I ain't seen her to talk with in so *long!*" At the mention of his mother the voice of Evelyn Weaver took on tragic solemnity, for it was accepted in the valley that no one mentioned Sarah Beckwith lightly.

"She's fine," Sam said. "She doesn't complain."

"That's the way she is!" Evelyn Weaver said admiringly. "All the trouble she's had, and I ain't never heard that woman say a mumbling word! I told her myself, I said, 'Sarry, you've got the patience of Job.' And when I said it she give me the sweetest smile! It does our hearts good just to know her."

"Nice place you got here," Brian said, clearing his throat. He was absorbed by the barn. "I ain't never seen a barn that's been whitewashed."

"I reckon you ain't seen a lot of things, Mr. Ledbetter. I reckon you don't think cows knows it when they've got a clean barn. *That's* why we whitewashed the barn. We like our cows to feel proud. It needs another coat now. It's something else needs doing around here. They's lots that needs doing."

"I've seen lots of . . . of outhouses that's been whitewashed, but never a barn."

"And we all take baths here, too, Mr. Ledbetter," Mrs. Weaver said with a meaningful sniff.

"I'm right proud to hear it," Brian said. He was ready to drop the subject.

"It sure is beautiful," Sam said with unexpected wonder. "So green! I guess I'd forgotten what real green looks like. And the flowers . . ." He chuckled nervously, as if he felt foolish for noticing. But he went on looking around at the luxuriant grass, and finally he just had to bend over and snatch some up in his hands and let it glide through his fingers.

"We've got a good spring," Evelyn Weaver said. "I get these boys out ever day before sun-up to hauling water. The Lord's been good to us."

"I guess you got people toting water from your place," Brian said.

"Yep. Wilker Edmonson was just over with his wagon and a

barrel. Poor Wilker! His spring just dried up. He said he went out there day before yesterday, and it wasn't nothing but a wet place in the ground, and today he said he could put his hand down the hole and bring up dry dirt."

Sam nodded absently. He was still looking at the yard. "My mother's flowers are all dead. There isn't a bloom on the place."

"The poor things!" Evelyn Weaver said in a fresh outburst of sadness. "Next to my children I love my flowers the most of anything on earth. Couldn't you water your mamma's flowers? Couldn't you do that much for that good woman?"

There was such genuine reproach in her voice that Sam could only drop his eyes. "I guess I should have. I've been busy."

Evelyn Weaver snorted in irritation. "I know what you've been busy about, young man! It's that girl. Well, she left you, didn't she? She run off, didn't she? You got ever reason in the world to forget about a girl like that and get to watering your mamma's flowers. And what's this about you fixing to beat up the preacher?"

"Oh, hush up!" Brian said sharply.

Evelyn Weaver looked around at him with her mouth open. "Are you telling *me* to hush up, sir? Are *you* standing right there on *my* grass and telling *me* to hush up!"

"That's about the size of it," Brian said.

She gave him a withering glare, but since he refused to wither she turned around with a huff. "Well, you oughten to do things like that," she said to Sam, but her voice was softer.

"Oh Lordie, I'm hungry," Brian mumbled, patting his broad stomach.

"Well, I ain't going to bring it out here," Evelyn Weaver said. "You can wash up on the porch." She led them through the door onto the back porch. It wasn't really a door—just an opening which pierced the plank wall enclosing the porch waist high. The floor inside was paved with unhewn flagstones and smelled pleasantly dank and cool. The air swam with the smells of breakfast wafted out the open door which gave onto the kitchen. "There you are," Evelyn Weaver said. She pointed to the water bucket and to a tin washpan on a plank table in a corner. "Help yourself. Only be sure you throw the water out on the grass when you get done with it. Get a move on, now! *You*, boys! You get in here with me."

Brian looked on with his eyebrows knotted with interest as her family trooped into the savorous kitchen behind her—all except Virgil. The smaller boys looked back over their shoulders, wide-eyed and abashed with curiosity, an innocent wonder at the two large strangers standing there in the hot morning that smelled of hickory wood and ham. Virgil lounged about looking so ridiculously grown-up that Brian had a good mind to kick him in the ass. But instead he ran a hand suddenly through Virgil's pale hair and made a loud Indian noise and set to washing.

Then leaving Sam and Virgil to their own cleansing, he marched into the kitchen like Leviathan from the great deep. Without being asked he sat himself down with a grunt at the table and looked around and nodded his great, rough head in the understanding typical of land speculators who know they have a good thing.

For it was a good thing. The house was cool and, like the yard, perfumed with flowers. There were roses in vases along the window sills, on tables, and even on the black stove which stood coldly gleaming in the parlor just off the kitchen. And with the flowers there was the demanding aroma of food—strong coffee, bacon, ham, biscuits, eggs, and the unusually spicy smell of apples cooking. Brian's stomach turned to a paper bag inside him. It rumbled so loudly that everybody in the room could hear it. All the little boys giggled, and some of the older ones punched each other with their elbows and looked at Brian in such happy glee that he smiled at them in spite of himself.

Finally Virgil and Sam came in, and Evelyn Weaver set the food down. First the coffeepot, dull metal blackened by the fire, squat and steaming its thick smell into the room. After it came three enormous crockery cups, which she poured full of coffee. "Virgil gets milk," she said and turned to set a brown pitcher of milk on the table. Virgil looked at the milk with distaste and shame and said nothing.

But Brian nodded in devout agreement. "Boy ought to have milk. Make him grow stout. Take my word for it, son. Don't never cuss, smoke, drink, carry on with women, or drink coffee, and you'll be a better boy." Brian looked so sincere that Evelyn Weaver threw him a caustic frown. But if she was about to say something she caught herself in time and went on laying down the food. White biscuits with the fragrant steam rolling off their toasted crowns. Honey, yellow butter, deep red ham stewing in red gravy. A platter of fried eggs all atremble in melted butter and laced with strips of bacon. The stewed apples. And at last—herself.

Brian was transfixed by it. It made him weak inside, and without thinking he put a hand out to the food, not even knowing where he would put it down. But he was arrested by the blunt voice of Evelyn Weaver: "I guess we ought to thank God for it first. Don't you think so, Mister Ledbetter?"

Brian jerked his hand back as if he had been stung by a biscuit, and he looked very uncertain for a moment. Recovering quickly, he managed a look of extreme piety.

"Don't reckon neither one of you men pray?" Evelyn Weaver said. Brian looked so absolutely aghast at the suggestion that she nodded in scathing agreement with her own scornful thoughts. "Didn't reckon you did. Virgil! Ask the blessing!" Her head bowed sharply at her own command. Virgil was appalled, and his eyes went from Brian to Sam in desperate embarrassment. The two men fled his glance by bowing their own heads in fervid devotion, and there was no help for the boy but to pray. He was goaded by his mother, her own head still stiffly bowed, who called out: "Virgil?"

So he bowed himself and blurted out their collective thanks: "Dear God, we thank you for the privilege of gathering ourselves together around this board to partake of this food, and bless it to the good of our bodies and our bodies to thy service, and help it to rain, for Jesus' sake, Amen." He rushed through it all so fast that it sounded like one long word passed by a freight train, and at the end he jerked his head up and looked angrily around at the little boys, daring them with his eyes to laugh.

But Brian was mightily impressed. He looked at the boy with respect. Virgil obviously had a rare talent for praying. Right then, in the tiniest of fractured seconds, Brian began to wonder if Virgil might make a preacher some day, not just some little-bitty preacher like the kind that preached in the half-assed churches all around, but a great big preacher, maybe one with a brick church in Knoxville. Yessir, Brian thought, if Virgil could do this well now, there wasn't any end to what might be expected of the boy. He himself wasn't any good at praying. He hadn't uttered any kind of prayer since that morning after Cold Harbor when the doctors were sawing off his leg and a stout nigger was holding him on the table by lying over his chest. Then he prayed hard to die. Obviously, he concluded ever afterward, his talents didn't lie in that direction. But now, all in a twinkling, he conjured up a big church for Virgil in Knoxville with buggies lined up as far as you could see on Sunday morning and big people coming for miles just to hear the preacher do his prayers. And he thought too that it might be a healthy thing to have somebody around who was a good hand at praying. On the crest of this wave of exuberant calculation, he leaned across the table and pounded Virgil enthusiastically on the back and said, very loudly, "That was a *damn* good prayer!"

At which the little boys standing around sucked in their breaths, and Virgil looked simply horrified. Evelyn Weaver drew herself up as stiff as a mountain of starch, and her face became a burning red ball that looked fit to blow up and wipe them all off the face of the earth. Brian got the distinct impression that he had offended her. She said, "*Mister* Ledbetter! You ain't been in my house *five* minutes before you start taking the Lord's name in vain!"

Brian looked at her in bewilderment. "I ain't said a thing about the Lord." He was going to add "Not a goddam thing," but he thought better of it.

"You sat right there in that chair and said 'damn!' "

" 'Damn!' Hell, woman, that ain't taking the Lord's name in vain!"

Her face became a deeper hue of red to the point that Brian wondered with alarm if a woman her age could have a stroke. "Mister *Ledbetter!* I ain't going to sit here and let my children hear talk like this! Now you make up your mind. You either clean up your talking, *or you get out of my house!*" And she pointed to the door with the commanding gesture of the Angel of the Lord beside the gates of Eden.

Brian very nearly got up and stomped out pronouncing a curse on the woman and her brood forever and ever. But he didn't. For one thing he hadn't had breakfast, and he smelled the ham and the biscuits and saw the red-eye gravy steaming richly up around the ham. And for another thing he saw the room in its blaze of flowers, and he saw Evelyn Weaver in her stormy wrath, and he liked what he saw. He liked it very much. So instead of getting up, he relaxed a little and laughed. "Lordie, woman! I didn't mean no harm. Honest I didn't. I didn't mean to get you all riled up like that. I've just lived so long by myself that I forget. I swear I just forget!" And to Virgil he said, "It was a *real* good prayer."

"It wasn't neither," Evelyn Weaver said. She was somewhat mollified, but her voice was still cross. "I've told Virgil time and time again that he prays too fast."

Brian made a hopeless little sigh and reached meekly for the ham. "Well, I admit he's got some way to go before he can catch up to my cousin Estelle. Now there's a woman that can *pray!*"

"Your cousin *Estelle?*"

"Yep, I reckon you know my cousin Estelle. Estelle Buffington? Female prayer champion of the last thirty-six campmeetings in Bourbon County!" He looked slyly up under his eyebrows to take in the effect of this revelation on Evelyn Weaver. He was not disappointed.

For she looked at him in sudden and somewhat unwilling respect. "Estelle Buffington! I declare! Is Estelle Buffington your cousin?"

Brian had his mouth full of ham, and he went on slowly masticating while he nodded gravely and the worth of his kinfolks slowly filled the room. Finally he swallowed and said, "Yep, that's what I said. Estelle Buffington's my cousin. I call her Cousin Estelle. I call her that ever time I see her." He nodded over his words in pompous satisfaction, the more pompous because he was so obviously trying to be humble about it.

"Well, I declare!"

"Course, she's my first cousin once removed. She's really first cousin to my mamma, or she was before my poor old mamma passed."

"I was sad to hear about your mamma."

"She's been dead twenty years, Mrs. Weaver."

"I was *still* sad to hear about it."

"Well anyhow, Estelle Buffington was first cousin to my mamma, but I reckon that makes her my cousin, too. Her mamma was Ernestine Letsinger, and before she got married to Coy Letsinger, Ernestine Letsinger was Ernestine Cabe."

"I know that," Evelyn Weaver said.

"Glad to hear it. So Ernestine Cabe was the sister to Maudie May Cabe that married Linard Beeler, and Maudie May Cabe and Linard Beeler had a daughter that was Lucile Beeler before she got married to good old Finchum Ledbetter, and that was my mamma! Finchum Ledbetter was my daddy. Leastwise that's what mamma always told me!" He grinned boldly across the table at Evelyn Weaver.

But she ignored the insinuation, frowning in concentration over the tangled knitting of genealogy. "Was your daddy named Finchum Ledbetter? I never knowed what his first name was."

"Naturally not. Folks always called him Hog. He was a big man, my daddy."

Evelyn Weaver puckered her face up in further inquiry. "Well, well! And does that mean your daddy was any kin to Chance

Finchum that was the daddy to Roberta Finchum that married Cory Lee Oxendine?"

Brian looked suddenly away and forked more food into his mouth, and his face took on an expression of infinite pain and sorrow, and for a long time he just chewed and couldn't say a word. But Evelyn Weaver insisted. "*Well,* Mister Ledbetter?"

So then Brian said—slowly, softly, and with immense gloom: "They was first cousins. My daddy never liked to claim that side of the family, Mrs. Weaver."

Evelyn Weaver crowed. "Well, I can see *why!* So you're kin to a bank robber, Mister Ledbetter! Some family *you* have!"

"Bank robber!" Virgil spoke out with huge interest and something suspiciously close to admiration. His mother quelled him with a look.

"A bank robber! Roberta Finchum Oxendine and her no-'count husband robbed the bank in Sweetwater back in 'sixty-six and run off with the money on two black horses. And him a steward in the Methodist Church! They had the presiding elder to dinner on Sunday noon and robbed the bank on Monday morning."

"A *lady* bank robber!" Virgil swallowed a whole mouthful of half-chewed food.

"A *female* bank robber," his mother said.

"I've heard about that," Sam Beckwith said suddenly. He had been eating silently, lost in his own thoughts. "They never did catch them."

"Well, *that* ain't no surprise, is it, Mister Ledbetter?" Evelyn Weaver said with a scornful little laugh. "Everybody knows the sheriff of Monroe County was second cousin once removed to Cory Lee Oxendine. He was Hebron Lawhorn, and *all* the Lawhorns is kin to *all* the Oxendines, and the whole bunch ain't worth *nothing! I'd* say Hebron Lawhorn knowed about it all along. *I'd* say them two paid him off good so's he'd be out of town the day they done it. And he was, Mister Ledbetter. Don't you sit there and deny it. *He was out of town when they done it!*"

"He was delivering a baby in the country," Brian said doggedly.

"A *baby!* What's the sheriff doing delivering a baby!" Sam looked at him in amazement.

"Well, they was hard up in Monroe County back in them days," Brian said.

Evelyn Weaver dripped contemptuous laughter. "*Listen* to the man!"

"Well, that baby is still living, I'll have you know, and his name is Hawkshaw Williams, and you can go right down there to Monroe County this very day and ask him if Hebron Lawhorn didn't bring him into this world."

"Oh, Mister Ledbetter! You must think I'm descended from six thousand generations of imbeciles," Evelyn Weaver said. She had put down her knife and fork to glare at him, and with all that concentrated effort she did a pretty good job of making Brian feel about as wretched as a man can feel.

"It's all water under the bridge," he said wearily. "It liked to of killed Hebron. It *did* kill him in fact!"

Evelyn Weaver delivered herself of another sarcastic laugh. "The voters throwed him out because they knowed what he'd done, and he drunk hisself to death! Demon rum's what killed him! That and a guilty conscience, Mister Ledbetter. A guilty conscience that he earned fair and square!"

"That ain't so," Brian said staunchly, but he looked quite downcast.

"Oh! Well, maybe he cried hisself to death because he didn't get as much money as he might have from Cory Lee Oxendine."

"Lord God!" Brian said.

"Mister Ledbetter, you're cussing again!"

"No I ain't, Mrs. Weaver. I'm praying for strength."

"Oh, I see," Evelyn Weaver said, intending sarcasm. But her voice relented just a bit in uncertainty. Her mamma had taught her to respect everybody's prayers, be they Protestant, Catholic, or Jewish.

"I just don't think we ought to judge," Brian said piously. He preserved an air of immense sorrow, even while gorging himself with biscuits and red-eye gravy. "I always did think myself that old Cory Lee led that poor little innocent girl astray."

"Well, he must of led her by the shooting match while he was doing it. I always did hear tell that she was the one that held the gun."

"Somebody had to count the money, Mrs. Weaver." Brian managed a look of extreme hurt and wrong. "Which was more sinful? Taking the ill-gotten gains or holding a pistol that probably wasn't even loaded while the captain of the whole terrible business was stealing the filthy lucre? I think poor little old Roberta took the best part myself."

"I might of knowed you'd defend your no-good relatives. I can read your character plain, Mister Ledbetter, and what I read ought not to be wrote."

"I ain't defending nobody, Mrs. Weaver. I ain't doing nothing but stating the truth like I sincerely see it. Look how sincere I am!" Brian looked at her sincerely.

"Well, my mamma always told me that Roberta Finchum was the greediest woman that was ever born into daylight in Monroe County! She said the only way Roberta Finchum could of been greedier was to be twins."

Brian recovered his expression of sorrow and regret. His face worked into a resignation beyond argument. "I'd just like to point out that you're speaking ill of a little girl that ain't here to defend herself," he said.

Evelyn Weaver hooted. "I *guess* not! If she was here she'd be in state's prison. My *conscience*, Mister Ledbetter!"

"I wonder what ever happened to them," Sam said. "I've heard they disappeared into thin air. Like ghosts."

"Oh, they went West," Brian said. "Everybody knows that. Where else is there for a bank robber to go? I reckon they changed their names and set up housekeeping somewheres in one of the territories. That Roberta Finchum was a good little housekeeper."

"And I bet they're sitting pretty out there someplace right this minute," Evelyn Weaver said. "I bet they've got themselves a big ranch somewheres. Oh, it makes me mad! And him a steward in the Methodist Church! I tell you they's a special place for folks like that. I ain't going to mention what that place is, but you read about it in the Bible, children. *And all bank robbers is going to go there.*"

"It liked to of killed my poor old daddy," Brian said sadly. "He couldn't eat good for a month afterward."

"I reckon it was something to bear," Evelyn Weaver said, a faint tincture of satisfaction in her voice. "Blood will tell, Mister Ledbetter. If you got some of the blood of Roberta Finchum in you, *even a little spot,* there ain't no telling how it'll come out."

"You make her sound like a nigger," Brian said in a hurt tone.

"I'm just saying blood will tell, Mister Ledbetter. *Blood will tell!*"

"Folks always did say I taken after my mamma, Mrs. Weaver. And *she* was cousin to Estelle Buffington." Brian loked very earnest over the logic of this pronouncement.

"Well, that's a fact," Evelyn Weaver said dubiously.

"Cousin Estelle's the one that can pray so good," Brian said, explaining it again to Sam. He bore down gently on the word *Cousin.*

"She can do that," Evelyn Weaver conceded. "She's one of the best hands at praying I ever seen."

"We're awful proud of Cousin Estelle in my family, Mrs. Weaver."

"I just wonder why folks like Estelle Buffington ain't out praying for rain," Evelyn Weaver said with sudden petulance. She looked out the window, beyond the green yard and the flower garden and took in the exhausted land sprawled like a dying body under the sun.

"Cousin Estelle's been feeling pretty poorly lately," Brian said. "I guess she ain't got the strength to pray like she used to. You know we all get tired, Mrs. Weaver. Maybe you've noticed that yourself. Back in the old days Cousin Estelle would of stood up and hollered till she wore God out and He give her what she wanted so's He have some peace and quiet. But she can't do it no more. She can't hardly even sing Old Hundred."

"Mr. Simson said it would rain today," Sam said softly.

"Yep, Wilker told me. He said they was a red sunrise this morning, too. Course that don't really mean nothing," she added hastily. "All signs fails in dry weather."

Brian nodded vigorously. "That's a real true fact," he said. He paused. "They's haze on the mountains today. There wasn't none yesterday. They was clear as glass." He spoke with uneasy caution.

"The nigger hags told me it wouldn't rain till the end of the world," Sam said.

"Nigger hags! My conscience! Have you been hanging round with the nigger hags?"

"I went to the graveyard yesterday, after the hanging."

"He went to see his daddy's grave," Brian said.

"That's right. They were out in the yard when I went by. I talked with them."

Evelyn Weaver sighed. "Well, it ain't good for your mamma's son to be hanging round with the nigger hags." But after a heavy silence she said, "But Lordie me! I don't reckon you'd be your daddy's boy if you didn't jolly the niggers. It was a sight in this world to see the way that man played up to the niggers. They thought he was some kind of god. John Wesley Campbell hisself said Sam's daddy could run for President on the nigger ticket and whip Abe Lincoln with a white eyeball to spare."

"He was friendly to everybody," Brian said.

"You wouldn't never of thought he foughten in our army the way he treated the niggers," Evelyn Weaver said stubbornly. She turned to Sam. "I reckon you knowed them nigger hags of yours said your daddy was going to die, and right to his face."

"They told me about it yesterday. I'd never heard it before that."

"Well, if you was to ask me I'd not be far from saying they put a spell on him. Why else'd he die so sudden like he did? You tell me that."

"They didn't *want* him to die," Brian said.

"No, that's a fact. I guess the only person in Bourbon County that maybe wanted to see Sam's daddy dead was Preacher Bazely, and maybe I judge the man wrong."

"Preacher Bazely!" Sam looked at her with a start.

"Yes, Preacher Bazely! The man you was about to beat up yesterday. He was crazy about your mamma, Sam. He was in love with her before your daddy come, and he was in love with her while your daddy was married to her, and he was in love with her when he died."

"I think that's enough, Mrs. Weaver!" Brian spoke quietly, like a man cocking a pistol in the dark.

Evelyn Weaver shot him a hot glance. "You know it's the truth! My mamma told me all about it. He stayed the first night he ever come to this valley out at your place, Sam, and he seen your mamma, and everybody says that's what made him decide to settle right down here. He wanted to marry her. He was sick for her. Everbody knows that. When your mamma wouldn't have nothing to do with him and married your daddy instead, why it liked to of killed the man. She wanted him to do the honors at the wedding, and you know he wouldn't! She had to send after Preacher Henck. And when your daddy died. Preacher Bazely was right back out there trying again."

"I remember him coming to the house," Sam said. His eyes were slitted with recollection.

"Your mamma had the good sense to put him off. The man's crazy. John Wesley Campbell's right. The man's crazier than a hen house. I don't know why the Baptists put up with him."

But Brian interrupted: "Well, let's not talk about it. We got a lot of children around here." He looked around at the boys and grinned jovially. They grinned back at him and looked at each other shyly and with great pleasure. Even Virgil looked pleased. "Looks like you and Dothan kind of run to boys, Mrs. Weaver."

"That we did, Mister Ledbetter. And their daddy left me well stocked when he died."

"I knowed you was in a family way when he passed out," Brian said, coughing delicately.

"That ain't what I mean, Mister Ledbetter. I mean that Dothan J. Weaver provided for his family. He left me an independent woman!" She looked defiantly across the table at him and elevated her head a couple of notches.

"Mrs. Weaver, I don't reckon the time'll ever come when you ain't an independent woman," Brain said. He poured himself another cup of coffee from the pot. "I guess old Dothan done all right by you sure enough. Never did hear no complaint about Dothan being lazy."

"He worked hard," Evelyn Weaver said. She dabbed in a perfunctory way at her eyes with an apron, but she did not appear likely to burst into tears. "He worked a lot harder than he had to. I told him not to go work on that barn. They was stuff to do around here, but that Stewart Scott told him he'd pay cash money for some help, and Dothan always was big for cash money."

"That's the best kind of money they is," Brian said.

"I had me a warning." She paused to give Sam a sharp look. "And I didn't need me no nigger hags to tell me nothing neither. I dropped a bag of salt on the kitchen floor the morning he went off for the last time. Even a white woman can tell what's going to happen when you drop a bag of salt on the floor!"

"Is that bad?" Sam asked.

"Bad! Honey, it's the worst thing they is! It means somebody's going to die. When they come and told me he was dead, I was sitting right here with my bonnet on, waiting to go fetch home the corpse. You may not believe it, but I wasn't even surprised."

"I believe you, Mrs. Weaver," Brian said.

"It was the saddest day of my whole life. I couldn't hardly see to milk that night. I kept crying in the milk bucket, and I had to kick the cow three or four times to make her stand still."

"I heard you was real broke up," Brian said.

"I thought my heart *would* break. Have some more coffee, Sam."

"Thank you," Sam said. He held out his cup with both hands, and she poured the coffee into it, expertly pulling the pot back with a flourish and not getting a drop on the tablecloth or even off the side of the spout. Sam drank it slowly, looking moodily out the open window onto the still, hot day.

"But I hear your neighbors all pitched in," Brian said.

"They sure did. Specially Wilker Edmonson. He come over here ever day with his oldest boy—little Sylvester—and they shocked corn. Lord, did they shock corn! Virgil helped. And I tell you something right now. That Wilker Edmonson is a Christian man. That Bessie Edmonson don't know what a real Christian man she's got. She don't appreciate him. Wilker says so hisself."

"They's lots of folks that don't appreciate poor Wilker," Brian said. "I was thinking just the other day that I didn't appreciate Wilker Edmonson like I should." He looked around again, grinning broadly, inspecting things.

"How much land you got here, Mrs. Weaver?"

"One hundred and forty acres, Mister Ledbetter. They's forty of it in good woods. They's twenty-five, thirty acres in good pasture land. They's about fifty that's in hay and grain. Good fences all around. It's a good place. You can see for yourself."

"Grows a good crop, I reckon?"

"Good as any land in the country! I always told Dothan if he'd quit working for other folks and work for hisself, we could be rich offen this land. But you know carpenters! Their hands ain't shaped to hold a crooked plow handle. They got to hold a hammer."

"That's a real true fact," Brian observed. He swung his head around again, slowly and methodically, fixed his calculating gaze on the ring of boyish faces peering anxiously back at him. "And some of these days you're going to have six good field hands." The boys grinned, and their grinning fluttered at their lips and died again into worry.

"Virgil here, he's old enough to do a good day's work now, ain't you, Virgil?" Evelyn Weaver looked proudly at her eldest, and he nodded self-consciously.

"Well, you want to save up on Virgil," Brian said. "Don't want to work him so hard he'll do bad in school. He'll be wanting to go to college some of these days."

"*College!* My conscience, Mister Ledbetter! What a thing to say!" Evelyn Weaver laughed out again. Or at least she started to laugh, and all the little boys except the baby picked up the whoop of her voice and started to laugh with her. But right in the middle of it she stopped and put a wondering hand to her mouth and looked at Virgil as if she'd never seen him before. "College!"

Virgil repeated in equal wonder: "College?"

"Sure, college!" Brian set the words down hard and straight like a brickmason. "They got a university up at Knoxville, ain't they? The University of Tennessee." He spelled the words out laboriously as if he were reading a sign off a ten-story building. "What's to keep a boy like you from going up there and getting an education? Rich land like this. You can make it. Make yourself a preacher maybe. Or maybe a lawyer like J. W. Campbell. There ain't no end to what you can look out for." Brian spoke so calmly and with such assurance that all at once everybody in the room old enough to understand such things began to believe that Virgil would someday go to college.

"The University of Tennessee!" Virgil handled the important words with reverent care, as if they might fall out of his mouth and break on the floor.

"College!" Evelyn Weaver said. She was a little dazed. "I think that's the first time that word's ever been spoke in this house."

"Well, you ain't going to tell me *that's* a cuss word are you, Mrs. Weaver?"

"No I'm not, Mister Ledbetter," she said in quick heat. "Only it does seem right strange to me that you're sitting here talking about college when you can't even read and write your name."

"Mrs. Weaver, I reckon you talk about the Virgin Birth of Jesus ever Christmas, and I bet ten dollars you ain't never had one yourself."

At that Evelyn Weaver fumed up with so much excitement that she couldn't even blow off, and while she was trying to say something Virgil got there before her.

"I get good marks in reading," he said. "I ain't too good at 'rithmetic."

"You ain't too good at talking neither," Brian said. "You shouldn't oughter say 'ain't.' "

"You say 'ain't' yourself!" Evelyn Weaver said in outrage.

"I don't claim to be smart, Mrs. Weaver. But look here. Let's get down to business. How's your oats this year? Pretty bad, I reckon?"

Evelyn Weaver turned solemn again and sadly nodded. "Like everywhere else, Mister Ledbetter."

"Dothan always worked with Claude Braysheers. Is Claude going to bring his thresher onto your place this year?"

"He said he was. He said he would even though Dothan couldn't work this year. It don't look like they's going to be much to bother with. I've give up on the oats, and I reckon the wheat ain't much 'count. But we got corn. The corn might make something if we get some rain." She looked darkly around at her boys and repeated her thought slowly and quietly. "It's got to rain pretty soon. For the corn."

"Sam and me's working with Mayhew MacComber. We start in tomorrow."

"Mayhew MacComber! Him and Dothan fought side by side. They was both with Joe Johnston."

"I knowed that," Brian said with a laugh.

"So you and Mayhew MacComber is working together." Evelyn Weaver looked at him with pursed lips. "And you was on the other side in the War."

"Yep. We've worked together for years. I ain't never shot at him yet."

Her face abruptly brightened. "Well, if Mayhew MacComber is big enough to forgive you, I say that speaks might well for him."

"*Forgive* me! He ain't forgive me for nothing. And I ain't forgive him neither. He's still as big a lunkhead in politics as he ever was."

"Then I reckon you hate each other. That ain't even Christian, Mister Ledbetter!"

"No, we don't hate each other, Mrs. Weaver." Brian's voice had a weary tone to it. "It's just that we got oats to harvest. We got more important things to think about than the War. The War was back then, and the oats is right now."

Evelyn Weaver didn't seem to know how to reply. She simply looked at him with a puzzled air of concentration. Suddenly she jumped up and went hurrying into another room where Clyde had gone, crawling and drooling and making baby noises. She fetched him back and deposited him in the middle of the floor. She admonished the other boys to look after him, but they all forgot the baby almost immediately, and the whole Weaver family (except for Clyde) sat or stood around the table looking impressively thoughtful.

Brian brought his meal to a brilliant conclusion with a couple of fried eggs. He pushed his chair back from the table, finished the coffee in his cup with a smacking gulp, banged the cup down on the table, folded his arms over his belly, and delivered himself of a resounding belch.

"Mister Ledbetter, you ain't got the manners of a hog," Evelyn Weaver said. He only chuckled. She looked critically down at the wooden peg thrust out before his large body. "Can you do much work in your condition, Mister Ledbetter? You ain't handicapped with that wood leg?"

"Mrs. Weaver, they ain't a man in the county that can work me down, don't matter how many legs he's got or what kind."

"Your place looks all right. You got clean fences. Dothan always said you could tell a farmer by his fences and his barn."

"You been by my place lately?" Brian asked. Curious surprise spread over his face.

"We rode by last week," Virgil said laconically.

"I was out riding with the children," Evelyn Weaver said. She was embarrassed, and her neck got red.

"Well, you ought to of stopped and set for a spell."

"Didn't look to me like your house was much to sit in," she said.

"It's a respectable place," Brian assured her.

"Well, it ain't respectable for a woman just to stop and call on a single man."

"Your barn ain't been whitewashed like ours has," Virgil said.

"My cows ain't proud," Brian said. He was in an amiable mood. He turned his great head and looked idly out the window. "You know, I just figured something out, Mrs. Weaver. This is the first time in weeks and weeks that I ain't smelled dust. Right now I can't smell nothing but the flowers. I just naturally hate to get back out there in the dust. I'd like to sit right here till it rains."

"That might be a long set, Mister Ledbetter."

"I don't think I'd mind, Mrs. Weaver."

"It's going to be bad tomorrow," Sam said.

Brian's amiability and his comfort slowly dissolved in his gloomy thoughts about the dust. "I ain't seen it so dry since Cold Harbor," he said. "*Lord,* that was dusty. We was all gray, the Rebs and us. I don't see how we stood it. But I guess that wasn't as bad as the Wilderness." He looked around at the little boys and particularly at Virgil. "Some of these days I'll have to tell you boys about the Wilderness. I'll tell you about the wounded that got burned up when the bushes caught on fire. I'll have to tell you how they screamed when the fire got to them, the ones that was wounded and couldn't move. I seen men blow up like firecrackers when the cartridges they was carrying got touched off by the fire."

"Hush, Mister Ledbetter!" Evelyn Weaver spoke softly. "These boys is too young. Way too young." Her face was stern and sad.

Brian looked at her to protest. "I guess you got a point there," he muttered. Then, after a moment, he said tiredly, "I guess we was too young ourselves. I guess we could of lived to be a thousand years old and still been too young to see what we seen in that war. Ever since the Wilderness, when it gets dry, the hackles on the back of my neck knot up when I ride through a woods. They done it this morning when we come over here. It smelled just like the Wilderness. And the dust. The dust was like the Wilderness and Cold Harbor. Same bad smell. It made it seem like it'd all happened yesterday. I swear the leg I ain't even got started to hurt me again, right in the foot where I was shot." His voice dropped off. Then with sudden, dismayed force he said, "Where do you reckon time goes?"

No one had any answer to that. Instead the sadness spread over them like glue and stifled the conversation. Even the smaller boys felt the mood change and turned solemn and expectantly quiet, looking from face to face and awaiting something they did not understand. The window drew the eyes of the adults through itself and onto the earth beyond, where the molten sunlight lay spilled on the ground. Across the splendid lawn they could see the distance where a world of desolate fields was rimmed by the heavy forest. Above all the quiet exhaustion of the land hung the merciless sky, ominous in its mighty silence and brooding without a touch of cloud.

Finally Sam said: "At night, if the wind stirs, I can hear the leaves scrape together. It makes me think they're rubbing themselves raw. It's a silly thing." He made an unsuccessful attempt at laughter.

"It ain't silly," Evelyn Weaver said gently.

Brian heard the cow bawling off by the barn. "Mrs. Weaver, if the corn don't get some rain pretty soon, we're all going to have to kill stock we can't feed through the winter. We might not be doing you a favor this morning."

Evelyn Weaver sighed and lifted her hands in helpless resignation. "We can't think about that, Mister Ledbetter. It's her time for the bull. We have to do things in their time."

Suddenly she bolted to her feet. "I almost forgot the apples," she said. "The fresh ones. Right from our own trees. They ain't so big this year, but they're sweet." She went to the pantry and opened it and took a large wooden bowl out of the cool shadows. It was piled high with apples, and they gleamed deliciously in their greenish-yellow skins.

Brian looked them over critically, took one, examined it even more critically, and bit into it. He chewed at the bite with careful precision and inspected the cavity he had made in the apple for worms. When he saw none, and when he had tasted the sweet-sour apple juice on his tongue, he made an approving gesture with his head. "Right good apple," he said. "Course I've always been a cherry man myself, Mrs. Weaver. They ain't nothing to satisfy the appetite like a good, juicy cherry. I like the wild ones myself."

Evelyn Weaver looked at him in calm disdain. "Cherries is all right in season, Mister Ledbetter. But this ain't the season. You got to take what's offered at my house. Anyway, old as you are a cherry'd probably make you sick. An old man has to watch hisself."

Brian took another large bite out of the apple without removing his eyes from hers. He was elaborately serious. "That's a real true fact when you think about it," he said. "This apple's pretty good, Mrs. Weaver. I reckon all the fruit in this house is tasty."

"How many acres did you say you have, Mister Ledbetter?"

"I didn't say, but all told I guess I've got two hundred more or less."

"How much of it is worth something?"

"Oh, I just got about half of it planted now. But it's all pretty good land. I get a crop off of it."

"Half of it planted! You could do a lot better than that."

"Well, up to now I ain't *needed* to do no better than that, Mrs. Weaver. But I reckon if the need was to come up, I could do better."

"You got good water, I hear."

"You heard right. My spring ain't never been dry."

"I wouldn't brag about it, Mister Ledbetter. The Good Lord might think you're proud."

"Mrs. Weaver, if I recollect, you just said *your* spring'd never been dry."

"I said it in a humble voice," Evelyn Weaver said.

"I'm proud to hear it," Brian said.

"You ain't sick much, I guess?"

"No ma'am, I ain't never sick. Not with nothing more than a bellyache once in a while."

"And you got good stock. I know you've got a good bull."

"Boston's the best around," Brian said. "I'm real attached to him."

"Why do you call him Boston?" Evelyn Weaver asked suspiciously. "That's a Yankee name, ain't it?"

"It's a city," Virgil said, enthusiastic at knowing something. "Boston, New York."

"Boston, Massachusetts," Brian said.

Evelyn Weaver sniffed. "That looks to me like you're just trying to insult the South. You hang a Yankee name right in front of us. That ain't gentlemanly, Mister Ledbetter."

"I guess I could of named him Robert E. Lee, but Boston don't look the part. Boston wouldn't look good riding a horse."

"Why'd you name a animal Boston anyway?"

"I don't believe you'd want to hear it, Mrs. Weaver."

"It must be something you're ashamed of," Evelyn Weaver said scornfully. "I shouldn't of asked."

"No ma'am, I ain't one bit ashamed of it. Boston was what we called a man that was real friendly to me in the War. He was Irish, and I don't recollect what his last name was, or even his first. We just called him Boston because he was from there. Like folks called me Tennessee."

"I don't believe I'd want to name a bull after any friend of mine," Evelyn Weaver said.

Brian leaned over the table and spoke in a confidential tone that was half a whisper. "Well I tell you, Mrs. Weaver, that Boston—the one that was my friend in the War—he had one of the biggest organs I ever seen on a white man. It must of been a foot long. It was the kind of thing a man ought to keep in a sling." He sat back and looked at her importantly.

There was a moment of strained silence, and then Evelyn Weaver said drily: "So that's why you named your bull Boston."

"So help me God," Brian said. "And that organ was something old Boston sure loved to use! The rest of us said he had a right. You might of said he had an obligation. The Good Lord give him the gift. He had to use it. It'd of been a sin not to."

"I think we've talked enough about it," Evelyn Weaver said. "I think we might go another hundred years without bringing the subject up again."

"Well you asked, and I didn't think you'd like it. I don't know whatever happened to the *real* Boston. It was the least I could do for a comrade."

"I'm sure he'd be proud," Evelyn Weaver said. "You've got the kind of friends that'd be just naturally proud of something like that."

Brian turned from her to the distant bawling of the cow. "That cow sure sounds pitiful," he said. He got up in his clumsy fashion, stretched, and laid the gnawed apple core down in his plate. "Pretty good meal," he said.

Sam got up as he did, and so did Virgil, and Evelyn Weaver got up too. Brian watched the smooth, purposeful motion of her body, and he admired what he saw. He wondered if the rest of her were as ripe and rich as the flesh exposed to his view. All in an instant overpowering fantasies filled his head. He longed to run his rough hands over her from her toes to her chin. He could imagine the joy of the surrender of a woman with the character of Evelyn Weaver. *She sure ain't no whore.* The silent observation was not an irrelevant thought, not to a man of his considerable experience in such matters. You never really could possess a whore. But Evelyn Weaver . . . Well, she *could* be possessed just because she was the kind of woman she was. Brian got himself all mixed up in his thoughts, and the only thing that straightened him out was a calculation: *She must be pretty healthy to have all these kids and still look so good.* Musing over this and entertaining fantasies of cool nights and clean sheets, the smells of spring through open windows, and the sounds of breakfast in the morning, he turned abruptly and went out into the yard.

They walked to the barn. They made a little procession under the high, hot sun. Almost at once they passed from the watered grass into the dry land that lay beyond, and they smelled not the flowers but the smells of the barn. Pleasant smells. Hay, straw, manure. And in the way of barn smells there was something peaceful to it. Something languid and unhurried. And something purposeful, too. That was the way the Weaver barnyard was, and Brian saw that it was good.

The cow was tied in the shadows in the entryway to the barn. She looked miserable. In the way of cows she stretched her neck low, thrusting her head forward, and she bawled in a torment of desire.

The barn itself was remarkable, and not just because it had been whitewashed a few years ago. It was stout and heavy, and when you looked at it you had an impression of something fatherlike huddling over the things inside, protecting them. Brian was very much impressed with everything he saw. So much impressed that he blurted out his sentiments. "You've sure got a nice barn! A *real* nice barn!"

Evelyn Weaver nodded proudly. "Dothan spent a lot of time out here. Him and his daddy built this barn. They sawed ever beam and plank and hammered ever nail. We keep it clean for him. It's sort of his monument." She looked around nervously, and all of a sudden in spite of herself, big tears welled up in her eyes, flashed for a moment in the blazing sun, and then rolled slowly down her cheeks. She did not sob. They were all respectfully quiet until she regained control over herself. At last she said in a calm, heavy voice: "He was a good man, my Dothan."

Virgil went over and affectionately placed his tanned arm about his mother. He looked very manly. But since he was so young he could only reach her thighs, and that is what he hugged. He did not cry. He was silently disconsolate. The other little boys drew near and huddled around them, mystified by the presence of sorrow, and they looked up at Brian and Sam in a puzzled, wordless chorus of grief. All except Clyde, who had been carried out and deposited by one of the others. He sat oblivious to everything sad and happily rubbed his hands through the dust and watched the red cloud flare up around him.

"I'll never forget our courtship," Evelyn Weaver said. "He was older than me. He'd been in the War, you know, and he never had got hisself a wife, and there I was without a husband in the summer of 'seventy-three, and he come over and asked my mamma for my hand. There wasn't much romance about it, I guess. He needed him a wife, and I was going on sixteen and old enough to be *somebody's* wife."

"That's a real true fact," Brian said with a grave nod.

"So he just picked me out. But my, my, my! It sure did give my mamma a turn. She didn't know what on earth to do. She told Dothan she'd have to think it over, and we sat around all afternoon and way into the night, and we talked about it and argued it up one side and down the other. Mamma cried over it and called me her little girl and her darling, and she said she didn't see how she could give me up. But then she knowed I had to get married *sometime!* I couldn't sit around the house and be an old *maid!*"

"It'd be an awful waste," Brian said.

"And she knowed I could do a lot worse than Dothan. My mamma thought a right smart of Dothan. Fact is, I always did think Mamma might of married him herself if he'd asked her. He didn't cuss. He didn't drink liquor. He minded his manners. And he took a bath every Saturday night."

"Them is real fine things," Brian said.

"Anyway, I got tired and went off to bed and left my poor old mamma sitting down in the kitchen with a lamp and the Bible."

"Your poor old mamma would of been about thirty-six, thirty-seven years old in those days if I recollect," Brian said. His eyes suddenly lighted with a thought. "You got any claim now to your daddy's place, Mrs. Weaver?"

Mrs. Weaver turned grim. "No, Mister Ledbetter, I ain't. My mamma got married right after I did, you know. Her second husband got her to sign over our place to him. I knowed when my mamma married a Sartin that no good'd come of it. I think Mamma went crazy over that man's curly hair. That's all she could talk about."

"Them Sartins sure is a trashy bunch," Brian said, shaking his head in great disappointment. "I don't guess I knowed how trashy they was until just this minute."

"That man didn't want nothing but my mamma's land," Evelyn Weaver said, her face clouded with wrath.

"A man that wouldn't marry a woman for nothing but her land ain't no better than a dog," Brian said.

"I'm glad to hear you *say* that, Mister Ledbetter."

"It's a real true fact, Mrs. Weaver. You was telling me about good old Dothan."

"I was. Well, I'd not no more than got to sleep that night when Mamma come and woken me up, and she was so happy she was almost singing. She'd been reading the Bible, she said. She'd opened it up to the book of Genesis. It's a real powerful book, Genesis."

"It's one of my real true favorites," Brian said.

"Well, what do you think she read?"

She looked at the two men in a rapture of enthusiasm. They looked blankly back at her, and Brian crooked his mind and tried to think of something he knew was in the Bible. Anything at all. But all he could think of was "Jesus loves the little children." So he said that, pretty sure at the time it was wrong.

But Evelyn Weaver impatiently waved his answer aside. "No, Mister Ledbetter, you got to do better than that."

At which moment Virgil, unable to contain himself any longer, shouted out the verse: "I heard them say, let us go to Dothan!"

"That's right!" Evelyn Weaver fairly shouted as if he had never said it before. "That's *exactly* what it said. Let us go to Dothan! Genesis thirty-seven seventeen!"

Brian started to say, "Well I'll be damned," but he managed to block the words. Instead he didn't say anything, though he tried to look wise and agreeable.

"Don't you see what it was?" Evelyn Weaver went on. "It was a revelation. God *told* my mamma what I ought to do. She said to me, 'You must go to Dothan.' "

"Did you get up right then?" Brian asked.

"Of course not, Mister Ledbetter. We waited till next morning. It would of been unseemly to go in the middle of the night."

"You done the right thing, Mrs. Weaver."

"You see, Dothan's a city in the Bible," Evelyn Weaver said. She wasn't really sure that Brian understood how miraculous it all was.

"My middle name's Elisha," Brian said hopefully. "Ain't there something in the Bible about Elisha?"

"He was bald-headed and fed a bunch of little boys to the bears when they laughed at him," Virgil said. He looked apprehensively at Brian's balding head.

"I might of knowed," Brian sighed. He cleared his throat and got back to business. "I think we ought to comfort this cow," he said gruffly. "This here's a right nice piece of cowflesh. Boston ought to be right happy. Christmas in June." He looked down at the children. "How about it, boys. If I get this cow back here before dark, you reckon they'll be something to eat?" They grinned shyly back at him.

"We always eat dinner at this house," Evelyn Weaver said. "If you can eat it, you're welcome to it, Mister Ledbetter."

"I reckon I can manage, Mrs. Weaver."

"I don't guess I'll come back," Sam said. "I'll stop off at home when we get done."

"Well, you give my best to your mamma, you hear? You want to be thankful for that woman, Samuel. She's got *stuff* to her, that's what. And Samuel . . ." She looked at him with a smile of good-natured remorse. "Don't pay no mind to some of the things I said. I don't mean no harm."

Sam smiled at her. "It's all right," he said.

"We better water the horses before we set out," Brian said.

Sam cast an apprehensive glance toword the sun. "Yes, we'd better," he said.

17

THEY RODE LETHARGICALLY along the dirt road. Brian felt a growing consternation about the sky. It was as if something were crouching up there, as if the vitreous blue dome that yawned overhead were really a filmy web hiding something so monstrous that Brian could not imagine what it was. Something silently taking its greedy measure of things and waiting and falling quietly back on its taut haunches, ready to spring.

In the midst of his sinister thoughts he felt foolish. Nothing crouched beyond the sky. But then, he reasoned ominously, there were lots of strange things in the world. And who could say that because something had never happened before that it could never happen at all. After all, *he* was alive, and he had never lived before. So in the same blunt way that he accepted the mystery of his own existence, Brian Ledbetter accepted the possibility that unheard-of things might happen. Another mystery might lurk up there, something perhaps on the verge of cracking open the sky and descending to earth with a devouring cry of hunger. "Good God Almighty!" he said aloud to himself.

His voice stirred the other two to look at him, and then he did feel foolish. So he said: "Goddammit, Virgil, you could of brought this here cow yourself and be coming back by now. She ain't no trouble."

"Mamma told me to fetch you," Virgil said. "Anyway, you got a breakfast out of it."

Brian barely nodded. His thoughts drifted to more earthly things than his foolish imaginings. "Your mamma's a pretty good cook for a woman. But I guess you don't eat biscuits like that *ever* morning."

"We do too." Virgil contradicted him sharply. "We *always* have biscuits."

"What else can she make? I mean besides breakfast?" Brian asked.

"She makes a mighty good rabbit pie," Virgil said. "We caught a rabbit in a box trap last week and had rabbit pie."

"I always did like rabbit pie," Brian said in dreamy languor.

"She's good at peach cobbler too," Virgil said.

"She's got a lot of good points to her, I guess." Brian said the last in a low, speculative voice, and for a while they rode along without speaking.

Then Virgil said: "One thing about it. Mamma says she ain't going to have no man around that'd be mean to us. Nobody's going to beat on us. You can bet your life on that." He spoke with an assumed confidence, trying to convey a certainty as factual as the multiplication table. But there was something obviously uncertain about his thoughts on the matter, and Brian caught a nervous waver in his voice.

Brian looked at Virgil now, and he started to chuckle, but when he saw the the fearful gravity in the boy's eyes he checked himself. Instead he said gruffly, "Well, I'm sure you won't never have to worry about nothing like that."

The cow bawled again, stupidly protesting her fate and the dust. They all took it as an excuse to smile.

"My daddy used to sing to all of us ever night, when we went to bed," Virgil said. He looked with shy importance at the others.

"I know lots of songs," Brian said. "Most of them's dirty."

"He'd sit us in the rocking chair on his lap. And he'd start with the youngest. That was Gilboa then because Clyde wasn't born yet. And he'd work up to me. He'd sing a different song to ever one of us. Gilboa had 'My Darlin' Clementine,' and Aaron had 'The Bonnie Blue Flag," and Joab had 'Dixieland,' and Caleb had 'Goober Peas.' " He stopped.

"What was yours?" Sam asked.

" 'Shennydoah,' " Virgil said slowly. "He sung it to me ever night in the world." The boy's voice had become very soft.

"I reckon your mamma does the singing now," Brian said. He was getting ready to add singing to the list of talents marked down in his mind under the name *Evelyn Weaver*.

But Virgil said, "No, she leaves it up to me. She said I had to take my daddy's place, and that's one of the things I do. The singing. I know all the songs. I even had to add one on. For Clyde."

"Well, what's that?" Brian asked.

"Right now it's 'Old Hundred.' But I don't like it very much. I want to get something else."

"Why don't you sing him 'Shenandoah'?" Sam suggested.

"Sure," Brian said. " 'Shennydoah' 's miles better than 'Old Hundred.' Hell, look how much longer it is!"

Virgil self-consciously dropped his eyes onto the slow swaying back of the mule. And all at once Brian understood why he didn't sing "Shennydoah" to Clyde. But Virgil explained it anyway, carefully, eyes steadfastly on the mule's back, speaking with a cautious, restrained sadness. "I sing that one to myself. When the others is in bed and asleep, I sit in the rocking chair by myself and sing 'Shennydoah.' Then I go to bed."

There was another long silence, broken only by the cushioned falling of hoofs in the heavy dust and the moaning of the cow. Brian wiped a sleeve desperately across his face.

"Well, you remember something about your daddy," Sam said at last to Virgil. "That's something. I don't remember much of anything about mine."

"Yours was good at singing, too," Brian said. "He knowed lots of songs I did. Lots and lots."

"Mamma says my daddy's in heaven—with your daddy and your Uncle Matthew and other folks she knowed," Virgil said.

Brian nodded and looked straight ahead. "Let's hope that's where we all end," he said with surprising gravity.

"He ain't, though," Virgil said stolidly. "I know where he is. He's in the graveyard. I seen them when they put him there. He ain't no place but in the graveyard."

The boy went implacably on. "When they taken us out of the graveyard, when the burying was all over, I ran off," he said. "Nobody seen me because they was all taking care of Mamma. I went back and hid in the bushes by the grave. Mamma said he was going to heaven, but I seen him in that box, and I knowed he hadn't left yet. I was going to wait till he *did* get out, and then I was going to get him to take me along with him. We'd of sung 'Shennydoah' all over the sky! But he didn't get out. They put the box in the ground and covered it up with dirt, and that's where he is today. I've been back to look, and it's just the way it was."

Virgil might have cried. Brian half expected that. But the boy was absolutely solemn, and his voice was firm with a conviction too strong for crying. It was a simple declaration of fact.

Brian frowned deeply, and the sunlight reflected over the crinkled skin in his face under his hat brim made exaggerated shadows there. "Virgil, look. You got to see this thing in the right way. There ain't much of anything any more complicated than this dying business. It *looks* like your daddy's in the ground. Only he *ain't!* That's just what you *see*. But there's lots of things you *don't* see." He shook his head in exasperation and turned on Sam. "Goddammit, *you* tell him how it is."

Sam shrugged and looked away indifferently. "I never preached a sermon in my life," he said.

"Well, I ain't neither, not by a damn sight," Brian said. "But I know when a man dies there's something left over. Else what do you do about ghosts?" He was on the point of launching an irrefutable defense of the immortality of the soul based on the observation of ghosts.

But at that precise instant the cow decided she was not going to go one step farther on a meaningless road. She came to a completely unexpected halt, went clumsily down onto her knees, and collapsed in a stubborn heap on the ground. As the dust gently subsided around her, slowly and methodically she began to chew her cud.

Sam jumped off his horse and went after the cow. "Come on! Come on! Get up from there. Get *up!*" He whirled the now loosened end of the rope and brought it down with a whipping lash along the cow's neck. She shuddered and stopped chewing her cud for a moment, but she resumed her bovine indifference as quickly as the sting of pain passed. Sam beat her again, but she was rooted to the spot. He stood over her with great gouts of sweat pouring off his face and panted for breath. "Goddamn," he said.

"Now we've had it good," Brian said with a thick sigh. He slid down off his horse and stumped over to the cow and kicked her in the side with his wooden leg, dragging it obliquely across her ribs for maximum effect. She shuddered slightly in her way, but quickly went back to her stolid chewing.

"What's wrong with her?" Virgil asked. His face was panic-stricken. "Is she sick? We ain't got but two cows, and if this one dies, we won't have but one."

"The boy can do figures," Brian said drily to Sam.

"She's all right," Sam said. "She just balked, that's all. A cow'll do that once in a while. Specially when she's in heat."

"What are you going to do?" Virgil wailed.

"That is a hard question," Brian said. This time he was deeply serious. His perspiring face was wrinkled up in thought. "A balked cow is about the hardest thing on earth outside of concrete to move," he grumbled.

Sam nodded. He had come to stand by Brian, and he folded his arms across his chest and looked darkly at the cow. She sat in unruffled state in the dust, regally chewing her cud as if that were the sole reason for her existence. Occasionally she switched her tail over her back to chase away the swarming flies. But apart from that she simply sat.

"Maybe we could bring the bull to her," Virgil said hopefully.

But Brian only laughed in scorn. "Bring Boston! *Here*? Hell, Virgil, if you turned Boston out of my lot, you'd have to fetch him back from Kansas!"

So there was nothing to do but experiment. Virgil rode back to his house and gave the news to his mother and sought her advice. On the strength of it he brought back a precious bucket of bran. The cow loved bran. That was what she was fed at night so she'd stand still at milking time. But now she only licked casually at the bran when the bucket was held under her nose. When it was pulled away she looked after it briefly and then turned her head obstinately away and ignored both them and it. Next they took Brian's horse and double-teamed it with Sam's and tried to haul the cow to her feet by main force. They nearly succeeded in choking her to death on the spot. Then Brian cut down some sassafras saplings and trimmed them smooth and laboriously beat her until the blood oozed out. She stopped chewing her cud under the beating. Her eyes grew wildly concerned, and her body humped with each stroke. But she did not rise. When Brian heaved to a stop, the sweat pouring off his body and the shirt on his back plastered to his skin, the cow went back to chewing her cud. At that Brian stood angrily over the animal and jerked his pants open and pissed directly in her face. This did upset her. She made a convulsive snorting and shook her head violently, and for just a moment it seemed she would surely jump up and run off. But Brian ran out of piss before she made up her mind. By the time Sam and Virgil stepped up in turn and did their duty, she was accustomed to it and only looked pained and embarrassed.

So at last the two men and the boy collapsed in frustration in the uncomfortable shade at the edge of the road, and they thought.

Finally Brian came up with an idea. "You know," he ruminated, "the best hand on earth with an animal is a nigger. A nigger is part animal hisself, and he can do things with a cow that we can't even think of doing." He looked proudly around at the others, but they did not return his glance, did not seem to know what he was talking about. "We can't get through to this damned cow because we're so much smarter than she is. But a nigger could do it. Yessir," he said with growing conviction, "a nigger could do it!" He felt that he had performed a considerable intellectual feat, and he sat trying to think of some modest rejoinder to the outpourings of admiration he expected.

But Virgil sat still on his haunches, contemplating the cow. His face was troubled. In his brown fingers he nervously twirled at a leafy twig. "Well, ole Jackson Bourbon—and Beckinridge—they don't live far down the road from here. I could go fetch one of them." He did not move and did not look as if he would.

"I don't know," Sam said skeptically. He lay back and stretched his legs. His face was so dusty that he looked like an unnatural Indian with blondish hair.

"You got any better ideas?" Brian grumbled.

Sam did not respond. Virgil said, "You want I should go fetch one of them?" He did not speak with much enthusiasm, and he still did not move to get up.

Brian was sitting near a large clump of honeysuckle which climbed a bank behind him. He sank heavily back into it and shut his eyes in comfort. "Hell yes! Go fetch us a nigger. And we'll take good care of your cow while you're gone." He sighed so deeply that it might have been a groan.

Virgil got uncertainly to his feet. All his motions had a doubtful cast to them, and he was plainly unconvinced about the whole enterprise. But then it was his cow, and he was willing to try anything. So he prepared to go, and he said: "You won't run off while I'm gone? You'll wait on me?"

"If we go anywhere, we'll go on to Mr. Ledbetter's," Sam said.

"*Brian,* damn it!" Brian said comfortably. His eyes were still shut. Even so he could sense Virgil's lingering glance and the last questioning hesitation. But at last he heard the boy depart—heard the *whump* as he threw himself over the sharp back of the mule, heard the animal move sluggishly off down the road, heard the great hot quiet of the day settle softly around them.

When he was alone with Sam, he opened his eyes and looked at the youth. He made some remark about Virgil and then about the heat. Sam only grunted in reply. So Brian shut his eyes again and let his thoughts stray where they would.

For a while he aimlessly pondered the oddity of the differences between a father he had known so well and a son he scarcely knew at all. Had he been sitting along a forest roadway with Samuel Beckwith, Sr., the air around them would have been blue with obscenity and raucous wit, and Brian's ribs would be cracking with mirth. Brian had worked several harvests with the son, but until today he and the young Sam Beckwith had hardly ever exchanged a meaningful word. The boy worked hard, kept his own counsel, and armed himself against the world with a faint smile which drew a shade over whatever it was he might be thinking.

Vaguely Brian recalled that the father could be serious, that there were rare occasions when Samuel Beckwith the elder could be struck down with silence, when he weighed something distant and beyond the ken of them all. People always remarked about it when it happened. It was like the unexpected passing of a cloud before the sun, throwing the earth beneath into mysterious shadow.

Mention of Virginia could do it. That was his home. When somebody unrolled some story out of the War and Virginia, Samuel Beckwith, Sr., was likely to fall into his serious mood, likely to mutter something about going back up there someday to settle some business. He talked about it, but he never went.

Brian chided him about it once. Did Samuel Beckwith, Sr., have any relatives up that way? Well, in a manner of speaking he did. Close family? Mother or father? Well no, no one that close. Did they know he was still alive? Of course they did. He had written, he said. Some day soon he was going back up there. Well, why in God's name did he put it off! Some winter, when work was slack, he could make it without a bit of trouble. Take his wife and boy with him. Brian had volunteered to look after the place while he was gone. It wasn't decent to leave family up there with never a sight of him. Fast as train travel was nowadays he could do it in a couple of weeks and have a fine trip out of it. Brian managed to work up a good heat about the un-Christian sloth of the elder Samuel Beckwith toward his kin.

Now, in looking back over the sleepy distance of time, Brian believed it was just then that Samuel Beckwith, Sr., broke off the conversation in a hail of mockery. Mockery that Brian Elisha Ledbetter, a reprobate's reprobate, would start talking about Christian duty. At the time Brian sensed something false in the laughter, a ring that was not humorous, and he never brought up the subject again. At times he thought about it—when he and the elder Samuel Beckwith were together in a good mood, when they jabbed at each other with laughter and sought remarks to prick the skin. But Brian always drew up silent before the deliberate mention of Virginia. It was something touchy with Samuel Beckwith, Sr. It was something better left undisturbed.

And there was also the letter. Like that last day he saw the elder Samuel Beckwith alive, the letter was a scrap of a child's puzzle left scattered in odd corners when the child died. The letter arrived not long before the death of Samuel Beckwith, Sr. It settled one morning onto the large, roll-top desk of Miss Kathleen Pedigo which, in those days, was the Post Office at Bourbonville. Written in a spidery, female hand, it was inscribed simply to "Samuel Beckwith, Bourbonville, Tennessee." An unusually thick letter, perhaps with something besides a letter folded inside. Miss Kathleen couldn't be sure of that. No return address. Only a postmark from some little town in Virginia. Someplace more obscure even than Cold Harbor, some exceptional place in Virginia not burned into public notice by cannon fire. Some remote place which slumbered through the War as if there had been no war at all and slumbered on to this day, a place as ordinary as sleep and death except that it was in some tenuous way connected to Samuel Beckwith, Sr., whom Brian Ledbetter recalled with such turbid uneasiness and affection.

Anyway, Miss Kathleen sent a boy to get Mr. Beckwith to come pick up his mail. Soon he appeared, nonchalantly received the missive without comment, scarcely looking at it. He stuffed the letter unopened into a hip pocket, and as if instantly forgetting it, he went back to his horse and rode away. Miss Kathleen was stricken with disappointment. She expected him at least to say: "Why, it's a letter from my mother!" Or "from my Aunt Bess" or "my Aunt Bert" or from *somebody.* Miss Kathleen thought it would have been only just if he had opened the letter right then and read it to her. Most of her customers did that. She vividly shared the lives of a lot of people she had never seen—people who dwelt in distant and magical places like Vonore or Mascot or Paw Paw Plains or Knoxville or even Chattanooga.

But nothing like that from Samuel Beckwith, Sr. Formal thanks. A flashing smile. Then he rode away with his mystery stuck noncommittally in his hip pocket. But perhaps the greatest surprise came later when with polite caution Miss Kathleen pressed the matter upon Sarah Beckwith. She hoped, said Miss Kathleen, that Mr. Beckwith hadn't received any bad news? No, Mrs. Beckwith didn't think so. *Didn't think so!* Didn't she *know*? Well, as a matter of fact she hadn't read the letter. Mr. Beckwith said it was something unimportant from up in Virginia. He said they'd have to take care of some things up there one of these days. No, it didn't seem to be bad news at all. And that was the end of it.

Miss Kathleen was staggered by the whole thing. She couldn't *imagine* (she said) that any man could get a letter from *Virginia* and his wife not know what was in it. In fact, the first thing Miss Kathleen asked Mrs. Beckwith about after the funeral concerned the letter. Well (she guessed aloud), now Mrs. Beckwith was going to have a lot of responsibility. Not just in raising that darling little boy. But wouldn't she have to go up to Virginia? To take care of that business Mr. Beckwith's letter had been about?

Alas, Miss Kathleen got another jolt. Mrs. Beckwith had forgotten all about the letter. She didn't know what on earth Miss Kathleen was talking about. And when Miss Kathleen went on trying to explain, Mrs. Beckwith dismissed the whole conversation so impatiently that Miss Kathleen was hurt. She even got the impression that Mrs. Beckwith thought she was a busybody. But *everybody* knew the only reason on earth she wanted to know about the letter was in case it was something bad and Miss Kathleen could do something to help.

Anyway, the letter was an event indissolubly attached to the memory of Samuel Beckwith, Sr. It was the only genuine *letter* he ever received. Miss Kathleen would have known if there had been others, and she frequently remarked about the fact that for a man who could read, Samuel Beckwith, Sr., got mighty little mail. The only person in the valley who got less mail than Samuel Beckwith, Sr., was Preacher Bazely. So the two men—opposite in most respects—were lumped together in the minds of some, and a feathery presence of mystery hung over them both. They were like trees rooted out of their original ground and transplanted, and in looking at them no one could help wondering what kind of forest had been their home.

So now Brian lay back and let his drowsy thoughts play as they would through his head. Deep in the toils of his musing he thought of questions he wanted to put to Sam Beckwith, Jr. After all these years he still wanted to inquire about the letter. He wanted, in a casual way, to ask Sam about his father's family, about things which, he knew, were really none of his business. So he could *not* ask about them. The invisible obstacle firmly presented itself. And just before his thoughts tumbled into filmy dreams, Brian Ledbetter felt the sharp, irritating presence of a hesitancy he had felt long years before, the same reserve he had sensed in talking to Sam Beckwith, Sr., about things any two friends ought to be able to talk about—home and family, childhood, youth, love, hate, longing and hope, the little things which indicate a sense of responsibility to the place where a man was raised. It was troubling to Brian—one of the several troubling things. He tried to form some sort of resolution about it there with the son beside him. But sleep was too much to fight.

He was awakened by the return of Virgil. Or rather by Sam's half-muttered statement, "There they are." Brian roused himself and looked out the road. There was Virgil, on the mule. Beckinridge Bourbon was sitting behind him. The Negro was balanced awkwardly with his thin legs dangling and his bare feet sticking out the ragged bottoms of his pants. His face was stolid. He looked ahead, over the boy's shoulder, beyond Brian, beyond Sam, and all that showed in his eyes was a studied vacancy. It crossed Brian's mind that something dangerous and impudent lurked there, something a nigger ought not to have in his eyes, but as they drew near he decided it was only the puffy bruise under Beckinridge's eye from the blow he had taken the day before at the hanging.

Virgil was clearly excited about something. As they came up he called out: "Beckinridge's daddy is dead. I seen his grave."

Sam got up, futilely dusting at his pants with his hands. "Dead? Jackson? Well, well. I'm sorry to hear it." He looked up at the Negro with real sympathy.

Brian got up, still a little giddy with sleep. He stamped around to get himself awake so his mind could take things in. "Dead is he! I guess he was a pretty good nigger. Knowed his place. That's more than you can say for some niggers." He looked significantly up at Beckinridge, but the black did not even glance at him.

"How'd it happen?" Sam asked.

Beckinridge slipped cautiously down off the mule without answering. When his feet touched the ground he groaned. He caught himself and hung dangerously onto the side of the mule. Carefully he took a deep, consoling breath, and Sam, seeing he was in pain, asked, "Why, what's wrong?"

"Nothing," Beckinridge said sullenly. Only he caught his breath when he said it, and when he took his arms away from the mule he moved them so painfully that all three white could see he was badly hurt. But without looking at them, the black turned to the cow and looked her over. He darted his tongue over his lips. They were thick lips. In his thin black face they seemed grotesque, and Brian, who had never had many thoughts about him before, decided Beckinridge was even uglier than most nigger men. He was impatient with the black's insolent silence, and he said irritably: "Dammit, Beckinridge, you ain't answered Sam's question. What happened to your daddy?"

Beckinridge went on inspecting the cow. "I woke up this morning, and he ain't breathing. So I dug a hole and covered him up."

Abruptly Brian recalled the day before. His face lighted with grim understanding. "It was that goddam Quillen Bradshaw that done it. He didn't have no right to jump on you two like he done. Goddammit, it'd serve him right if Hub went out there and throwed him in jail." Beckinridge seemed uninterested in that prospect. Brian spoke with real indignation but with an exaggeration all of them recognized. "Did you bury him like a *dog*? You didn't take him to the graveyard?"

"We don't have no wagon. Anyway, I had me a preacher."

"A preacher!"

"Preacher Bazely stopped by on his way somewheres. He was in a powerful hurry, but when he seen my daddy was dead he stopped long enough to preach a little sermon."

The black still contemplated the cow, and there was an ironic note in his thick voice which Brian could not fathom. All he understood was that Beckinridge irritated him. In some indefinable way he felt that he or somebody else was being mocked. But he could only scratch at this strange news. "Preacher Bazely! Preacher Bazely *preaching a nigger's funeral!*"

"He done it," Beckinridge said flatly.

"He must of gone off his head," Brian said. "The heat got him."

"He didn't look too good for a fact," Beckinridge said.

"It doesn't make any difference. The man's dead. Bazely's crazy enough to do anything." Sam spoke caustically.

"Well, he lives back there in the hills," Brian said. "He's got to pass Beckinridge's place to get out. And he *is* a strange one."

Beckinridge half shrugged, caught himself in an extremity of pain, but quickly mastered it. He turned all his attention to the recumbent cow. He looked her over with great care, but his face remained blank. Except for the habitual running of his tongue over his dark mouth, his face might have been dead.

"How we going to move this cow?" Brian asked peevishly. By now he had passed the word of Jackson Bourbon's death through his mind and accepted it. He had meditated briefly on the ephemeral nature of life, the erosions of time, and the gaping enormity of death. All with a twinge of inner embarrassment. A nigger's death wasn't anything to moon over. Even a nigger like Jackson Bourbon had to die sometime. Of course Jackson Bourbon was a sort of pillar in Brian's life. The old nigger had been around as long as Brian could remember. It was a little surprising to think that the old man would never be seen again by anybody except maybe by God. And nowadays whenever Brian heard that anybody he knew had died, he felt just a little as if a part of his own body had died. It inspired in him that same sadness that the loss of his leg had given him years ago when he faced the fact that his body would never be whole again. The loss of people he knew laid that sadness bare for a moment. Yet when this morbid sentimentality welled up in his throat over a nigger, he could only feel foolish. So he wrested his thoughts back onto the cow. "We got to get this animal to my bull, and we got to do it before dinnertime," he said curtly.

Beckinridge paid no attention. He bent and cooed softly at the cow, and with his slim fingers he scratched her ears and under her muzzle along her neck. She stretched her head out in pleasure and made her skin taut, and her eyes took on a comatose peacefulness. The black cajoled her like a lover. Then, very gently, he took up the end of the rope, and while he made clucking noises with his tongue, he got laboriously to his feet and invited the cow to rise as if asking her, delicately, to share his bed.

But she would not budge.

He put gentle pressure on the rope, bent and scratched her behind the ears again, and called at her in a louder voice, though still coaxing and gentle. She paid no attention except to shift her legs slightly so that she was more comfortable and more fixed than she had been before. He coaxed her a little while longer. His eyes were strained in his blank face, and his breathing was a succession of painful gasps, but he kept at it. He kept crooning to the cow, enticing her with a litany of affection.

It didn't work.

Finally he stopped and let the rope drop. His face remained so expressionless that Brian felt uneasy. Beckinridge muttered something.

"What's that?" Brian asked.

"Salt," the black said, still not loudly. He looked around at the others. It was the first time he had put his eyes to theirs, and his glance was fierce. "You get back," he commanded. They did, edging away. For a moment Beckinridge contemplated his hands with his blank, black face. They were rough and broken and ugly. Suddenly, like a cat striking down on a frozen animal, Beckinridge fell on the cow. He sank his fingernails into the tender flesh of her nostrils. In spite of his own evident pain, he whipped her head violently, plunging his fingernails ever more deeply into the cow's nose. Almost at once she began to bleed around his fingers—first a small trickle of blood running darkly over his black hand and then a flood bubbling through his fingers and rolling off his hands and wrists. It made a splattering of dark little puddles in the fine dust of the road. Sam's face twisted with revulsion at the sight. Virgil let his mouth drop open in consternation, but he was too frightened to speak. Brian grunted, startled like the others. The cow thrashed around in the road and moaned and heaved and fought to throw off this clinging horsefly of a man.

At last Beckinridge stopped.

The red blood came pouring out of the deep wounds in the cow's nose. She licked once at it. When she did she was wracked with a herbivorous loathing for the taste of raw blood, and she made a noise like vomit. She looked frightened and miserable, and her ears lay pitifully back against her head.

Beckinridge was gasping so hard that Brian thought he might die on the spot. But he did not hesitate. He went from his haunches to his knees. He put a hand down into a pocket and drew out a quantity of dirty salt. He looked hard at the cow, and his eyes slicked over with a sort of emotionless hatred. Brian recoiled a step. Beckinridge did not notice. The black was alone in the world with the cow. He made one swift, hard stab with his body and flung the salt into the cow's wounded nose and grabbed her muzzle with both hands to grind in the screaming hurt.

The cow's body shook with a wild convulsion of pain. She let out a terrible groan. It was a torment to hear her. She wrenched her head so violently that Beckinridge momentarily lost control of it and was flung panting onto his hands. But he did not give up. Not yet. He reached for more salt. This time the salt turned instantly crimson in his clenched fist. Brian dimly thought it was astonishing to see how red the blood was in the salt, how dark on the ground. His stomach heaved, and he tasted everything he had eaten that morning clogged at the top of his throat and sour with bile.

But Beckinridge went on with his ruthless work. The poor animal was choking and roaring with pain, and with it all she was coughing because she had sucked salt back into her lungs. Again and again she tore herself away. Again and again Beckinridge stuck himeslf back onto her, an enormous, stinging, unbearable, horsefly.

But the cow would not rise.

So at last he collapsed. He was worn out by his exertions and his pain. He went down onto his hands and knees and put his head down with his forehead in the dirt and sobbed for breath, trying to keep his mind from turning as black as his skin.

Brian realized all at once that Virgil was hollering. The boy had been shouting for several minutes when Brian first really heard him. One shrieking word over and over—"Stop! Stop! Stop! Stop! Stop!" The boy was crying for his pitiful cow. The tears were running down his tanned face, cleaning wet streaks through the caked dust.

"All right! All right!" To his surprise Brian found he was saying those words himself. They meant "Stop," "Enough," "Please God," or something else, but they were just "All right! All right!" stupidly repeated and repeated.

Sam was saying, "We can wait. We've got time. It's enough. Lord, we've got all day!"

When Beckinridge had caught his breath, he looked up. He was still on his hands and knees. When he lifted his head he looked like a defiant animal. The swollen bruise on his face warped his features. "We gonter get her outer here," he said. There was a deadly resolution in his voice. With that same resolution the black got to his feet, staggering. He held his right hand over his chest. A blood crust of salt gleamed dully in his fingers so that he seemed to be bleeding himself. His face was contorted with something. The hurt the others did not understand? The frustration? Brian wasn't completely sure. But he could tell that the black's eyes were implacable. Beckinridge looked at the cow with a gaze so unmercifully fierce that the white men fell silent before it. Brian saw the hatred burning in the black's eyes. No doubt about it. Beckinridge hated the cow. *That* was the awful thing. The cow hadn't done anything to Beckinridge. She was nothing but a poor dumb animal that wanted a bull so badly she didn't know what she was doing. She thought her long walk was completely unrelated to what she desired, which was the bull's healing service. She was so consumed with her passion she couldn't put any energy into walking, and so she sat down. Brian could figure that out well enough. And he had the foolish desire to tell Beckinridge—to beg Beckinridge—to explain it to the cow. He supposed that idea had been in the back of his mind when he sent Virgil in search of a nigger. A nigger could whisper something in the cow's ear, and she would cock her head and listen and slowly nod in agreement and get up and go, for she would understand somebody like herself. But here was Beckinridge hating the cow! Brian didn't want that. It was too much for him. Just too damn much!

Still, he had to get the cow moved. He just *had* to. So many things he hadn't even thought about before this morning depended on getting the cow to the bull and back. The calf, of course. The life the cow would create, and the lives that life would help sustain. That was important. And Brian's dinner. He had to get the cow back by dinnertime or else stand condemned to a meal of pinto beans and eggs and . . . It turned his insides out to think of his own wretched cooking. Evelyn Weaver seemed able to make meals spring out of the ends of her fingers. Evelyn Weaver . . .

Evelyn Weaver wanted a man with gumption to him. Brian wasn't really sure he wanted to be the man she wanted. But he knew he did want to qualify, and then he could make up his mind. But what kind of a man was it that couldn't even get a cow to a bull! Brian needed Beckinridge. Otherwise Brian wasn't going to shine in Evelyn Weaver's eyes. The more he thought about it, the more he wanted to shine like the moon itself. Only if he couldn't get the cow to the bull, he'd look like a simple fool. What if he had to send Virgil back to beg Evelyn Weaver to come tend to her cow herself. The prospect was so awful that Brian almost groaned aloud. So he had to depend on Beckinridge, and he began to hate the nigger for taking so long.

All the while Beckinridge was fingering his chest and standing there, looking at the cow. Then out of his hatred, he mumbled a single word. They did not really hear him, and they strained closer. He repeated it, a little louder: "Fire!"

The white men still did not understand. Brian repeated the

word soundlessly, moving his lips. Virgil looked up at them with his large, child's eyes, asking a frightened question he didn't dare speak.

Only when Beckinridge began shuffling about, gathering twigs and fragments of branches and making a little pile of them by the cow's back did they finally begin to understand.

"You want to burn her out!" Sam was incredulous.

"Burn her out!" Virgil's horrified words trailed off to a cry.

"Burn her out!" Brian was furious. *"Burn her out!* You goddam crazy nigger, you'll burn this whole woods down. I ain't dared light my pipe once this morning because I was afraid the woods'd blow up, *and you want to burn her out!* You goddam, crazy, good-for-nothing, ignorant nigger bastard!"

The outraged words collided with the obdurate will of the black. "We gonter have us a fire. We gonter move this cow." His eyes gave off sparks of hatred. The surprising thing was that for all the hatred, the words were so silken and soft.

Right then, if he'd had a gun, Brian would have killed Beckinridge. He had never feared a man so much. He would have killed him without a second thought, without hesitation, without a shadow of remorse. It would have been a nonsensical act, which people in the valley would still understand as they always understood when somebody discovered the thing Brian had seen and killed a black man. People would forget about it because they always forgot about it.

But without the gun Brian could do nothing but think. He wasn't up to clubbing Beckinridge to death with a stick. So the black went right on gathering his firewood and heaping it up against the unsuspecting cow, and Brian stood by speechless, eaten up by anger and by fear and abruptly startled by the dull hammering of memory.

Memories, rather, scattered around him like the dappled sunlight on the forest road. Memories of days embedded in another time, another world, memories floating vaporlike out of an age of singing. *As He died to make men holy, let us die to make men free . . .* On this day, in this moment, Brian was more troubled by the War than he had been at any time since that night he rode off to fight in it. He was bewildered by the mystifying way things had fallen out. Once, long ago, he had marched to a song. He had believed the song. That exalted thought—Freedom—cast hauntingly into the mellow dark by singing men . . . It was pure and noble because the men might well die on the morrow, and they all knew it. It made men cry. Brian had seen it. He had cried himself. It made strong men love one another. And afterward, rolled in their blankets and looking up to the shining heavens, for a few moments before sleep came, they were gladly willing to die. Freedom was worth a death.

Freedom for Beckinridge Bourbon! Freedom for this animal-like thing which walked erect to burn an animal which lay in the dust. Brian had a murky foreboding that he might now know what it was which crouched behind the lurid sky. He did not want to work the thought out. Why had he fought? Brian wanted to flee both the question and the scene. But he could not run. Fixed to the spot like a tree, he watched Beckinridge moving terribly about the business of making a fire, and he could not protest any more.

All three of the white men stood hypnotized by the sight. The black moving with insidious purpose. The unruffled irony of the cow, who sat with the makings of fire laid against her fleshy back and went peacefully on chewing her cud.

From his pocket Beckrinridge drew out a match. He struck it against a stone. The flame flew up, almost invisible, while he instinctively sheltered it from the nonexistent wind. Cautiously he applied the point of fire to the pile of tinder. It buried itself briefly in the dead pine needles, caught, and a blue flame spurted out, widened, turned yellow and then white, and the smell of burning rose beneath a plume of white smoke.

At first the cow paid no attention. She continued to chew her cud, to switch her tail languidly, to blink her ponderous eyelids. The blood on her muzzle was already drying. She had forgotten her pain. But in a moment the first tremor of the fire touched her. Her ears went back against her head. Her eyes opened wildly. She stopped chewing her cud. Her legs and then her whole body tensed, and now the pile of brush was burning fiercely and the cow could no longer doubt that something terrible was happening. She still hesitated. The fire licked at her back. The men could smell meat burning. Some dumb thing within the cow kept resisting. She shook her head in witless protest. The fire roared.

And the cow got up.

She got up staggering. Her back was smoking where the fire had scorched it, and there was a charred blot on her skin there. She bawled in pain, and before anyone was ready for her to move she began plodding on down the road in the direction she had been going when she stopped. The rope trailed behind her. It stirred up the dust in a long, serpentine line.

"Put out that fire," Brian yelled. He was back in charge of things. He had recovered from his mawkish feelings and now felt silly about them. Beckinridge was just another nigger. The War and Brian's part in it had nothing to do with him. "Put out that fire before you burn the whole damned world down."

Beckinridge and Virgil hurried to obey. They threw dirt on the flames. In a moment the fire was dead.

The black looked after the cow. His bruised face was set in indifference. She was moving swiftly. Sam had run after her and had snatched up the rope and was trotting behind her on foot. Brian was getting his horse, preparing to bring up Sam's. In a moment he had done so and was moving out, abreast of Sam, calling for the youth to mount. Beckinridge was left with Virgil, and Virgil looked in anguish after the men who were leaving him behind. "Can you make it home all right? By yourself? They're going to leave me if I don't go." He looked plaintively up at Beckinridge.

The black slowly nodded without looking at him and without a word. It was all Virgil needed. He snatched up the bran bucket, lunged astride his mule, and set out after the others with his heels kicking and his thin elbows flapping against his sides. He called after the men. A shrill cry in the still woods. They looked back, and Brian motioned him to hurry.

Beckinridge stood, bent slightly forward, holding his chest with both hands. He watched them disappear in the shadowy forest and heard their voices recede to silence. Then he set out, plodding with his bare feet in the dust, to go home.

18

SHE WAS IN THE KITCHEN idly wondering over dinner when she heard the voice calling her name from the yard. She knew at once that the voice was not natural, but she could not tell who it was.

"Sarah! Sarah! Sarah!"

It was so intense and so urgent that she went quickly through the house and out the door onto the porch to look. Lifting her eyes over the bright yard, she saw it was Mr. Bazely, sitting barefoot and without a saddle astride his worn horse at the edge of the road some distance away. He went on calling her even after she appeared. Something frantic and barely controlled in the calling.

Something in her froze to steel when she saw his dark form. "What do you want? What are you doing here?" Her tone was harsh and pitiless.

"I want to talk with you, Sarah. I have come for an accounting. After all these years I have come for an accounting."

"What do you mean?" Her voice was still imperious, but her heart kicked inside her chest.

"Come here, Sarah. I must talk to you here in the light. Come! Come! Into the sun where all is clear."

"My son is here," she lied. "He is coming in for dinner soon. I do not want him to see you here."

"I know all about your son. Do you think I do not know about your son? Come here, Sarah. We have things to discuss. We must talk, you and I!"

Slowly she went down the porch steps and out into the yard. She was afraid. "We have talked all we need to. We said everything there was to say years ago, and now I would appreciate it if you would leave."

"I kept my end of the bargain. I have kept it faithfully."

"And I have kept mine," she said rigidly.

"Ah, but Sarah, you said once that someday you might reconsider something. Do you remember what it was you said you might reconsider? Or have you forgotten? I believe you have forgotten, Sarah!"

"You know how I feel. I can't help that. I've never been able to change."

"Your dear husband would be touched."

"I loved him in spite of what he did."

"You loved him. And you love him still. And you cannot reconsider?"

"I can't. I've told you that."

"And yesterday your son wanted to strike me. He wanted to humiliate me before all those people in town. For doing God's will. He wanted to strike me because I was preaching the Word."

"My son has no part in our bargain. You know that."

Mr. Bazely laughed. It was darkly unpleasant laughter, and something in it quavered dangerously. Sarah Beckwith felt the fear prick up inside her. "I understood your son to be all the bargain," he said. "I thought we made the bargain just for him—and to give you a chance to *think*, of course." There was a note of bitter sarcasm in his strange voice.

"He was too young to be a part of what passed between you and me. Have you forgotten about the age of accountability, Mr. Bazely?" Despite her fear she could not repress her scorn.

"But yesterday he was with John Wesley Campbell. They combined against me before all the town. It made me think about our bargain, Sarah."

"If my son hates you, it is your fault and not mine. You did that thing to him."

"But because you wanted it! Please don't deny you wanted it. You were glad, Sarah." He laughed unpleasantly.

"I don't like you to call me Sarah. I never gave you permission."

"Your name is Sarah—like Abraham's wife! That Sarah thrust Ishmael and Hagar into the desert for the sake of her son. And you will exile anyone for your son. Anything for him. No matter what price others must pay, anything for your son."

"I have my duty," she said coldly, folding her arms.

"And I have helped you do your duty. You won't admit that, but it is true. I showed you the truth—twice! But you are not grateful, Sarah. Ingratitude is a grave fault in a woman."

"I did not ask you for anything."

"Then would you have preferred not to know?" He was mocking her. "I don't believe that, Sarah."

She was silent.

"You pled with me for mercy when I told you the truth years ago. Do you remember that, Sarah? You asked me to be like God, to be merciful. And when your husband died, you said you would consider marrying me. Not right away, you said. It wouldn't be proper. But in time. In time. You have taken all these years of time, and I have waited. But yesterday I decided I had made a mistake. It is not like God to be merciful. God is just, and justice is terrible. Do you agree, Sarah?"

Her face blanched. He could see it and was amused. She controlled her voice with an effort. "You have kept your word. I have done my best to keep mine. Please God, leave it at that!"

"At least you have not married anyone *else!*"

"I said it would be you if it were anybody. It wasn't anybody."

"All I wanted you to do was to try and love me."

"You cannot force love, Mr. Bazely." Her lips were pale and hard.

"Am I so unlovely, Sarah? Am I so hateful?" His question was a plea, but she looked up at him and said not a word. Her eyes spoke for her. He nearly whimpered before them. "I wanted you to love me more than I ever wanted anything else in my life. You never gave me a chance. Not a single chance."

"You are not my kind," she said wearily.

"I am not your kind? Perhaps that is so. But I loved you so much I could have made you happy. I *know* I could have made you happy. We did not have to be of the same kind."

"I think you had better go. We have nothing more to say to each other. Nothing ever." Her voice was like an iron file.

"You did not talk that way so long ago. You begged me to be patient. It took me a long time to learn that patience was forever. Then I felt that I had been deceived."

"There were other women," she said curtly. "You could have married one of them."

"I did not love any other woman. No one else could help me. Other women were not pure."

She looked scornfully at him. "You had strange ideas about purity."

"You are pure."

She broke into a harsh laugh. "You really must leave now. I cannot be responsible for what happens if Sam catches you here."

"Your son is not on the place," he said softly. "I saw where he has gone. To Brian Ledbetter's. I hid in the trees and watched them pass on the road. Brian Ledbetter, one of the Weaver children, and your son. He is nowhere near."

A sudden, new apprehension crossed her face. She took a step backward. "I cannot stay out here. I have work to do."

"I only want you to try to love me, Sarah." He moved the horse forward.

"Go away! Please go away!" She was frantic.

"You don't know how important it is. I can't even explain it to you. You would think me mad if I tried to explain."

"You *are* mad!" She was almost hysterical. She saw his eyes, and all at once she divined what was in them. "John Campbell was right. *You are mad!*"

"It is true. Just as I suspected. You have joined with Campbell against me. I knew as much."

"I haven't! I haven't. I swear I hate him the way you hate him! I haven't spoken to him in fifteen years. Not since the funeral. Anybody in the valley can tell you that. Not a word. Not a word."

"Please, try to love me. Just one time, try to love me. Out of all eternity you can spare one moment of love."

She turned and fled. But it was too late. Whipping his horse forward, he quickly overtook her. He threw himself from the horse onto her back and bore her down in the hard grass.

She fought against him with all her might. She felt his hard arms around her, his hot breath raging at her face, and she screamed. Her piercing cry rent the still air, but there was nothing in response. The thrumming summer day swallowed up the sound, and it was as if she were crying under water. She felt his hands tearing at her clothing, heard the fabric tear, glimpsed her own naked flesh appear like an eruption of white against the dead grass. She stopped screaming and used all her strength to resist him, and so their wild thrashing raged on in bizarre silence amid the greater silence of the terrible day. She would not yield to him; if he killed her she would not yield, and she struggled with him in the desperation of those who know they will lose and die but fight on from animal instinct to the very end. The grass stung her bare back, burned her bare legs, cut her bare hips.

And finally she was grappling with him to keep his body off of her own, and it was then that her frenzied hands found the gun. He had forgotten about it in his fury of desire, but it was still there at his belt, and she seized it, and jerking it free she swung it in a great arc and hammered it against his head, crushing his ear.

His whole body went limp from the sudden blow, and she had time to hit him again with smashing force, and he rolled off her like something dead. She jumped to her feet, out of breath, and he sat up gripping his head with both hands and looking at her with a blank face like someone waking out of sleep and not knowing where he was. She raised the gun, holding it in her two trembling hands, pointed it at him, and fired.

The pistol jumped madly in her fists, and the report of the exploding charge was a thunderclap. But she missed. The bullet tore into the grass at his side. He came to himself, and he had time to jump up and back away shouting "No!" before she fired again. But again she missed, and he turned and fled to his horse.

"Stop! Stop!" she cried at him, as if her command would arrest his flight and let her kill him for the sake of her son. But he lunged atop his horse, and when she fired yet again at his head the bullet went harmlessly by. She had time to think of shooting the animal, but her hands were shaking so violently and the sweat was pouring into her eyes and blinding her so that again her shot went wild. She shrieked with frustration as she saw the horse spurt into the lane and vanish. The preacher clung to the horse's neck and galloped away toward town.

Only then did Sarah Beckwith's strength begin to fail. She was exhausted in every muscle, and she lowered the pistol and stood in the torn remnants of her clothing and sobbed in helpless rage. "Don't tell! Please, don't tell! Don't tell!" She was crying still at the preacher, but her voice was scarcely a mutter, and the sultry heat blotted out her words.

But she could not let herself give up, even then. Moving in a stuporous daze, she went into the house and changed her clothes. She hid the torn dress, and she had the presence of mind to leave a terse note for her son. Then she made her way out to the barn and for the first time in an age called up a horse by herself, affixed a worn old sidesaddle, and rode off toward town, after the preacher.

The road descended from her house and entered a thick forest. As the shadows of the high trees passed over her, her mind sank into the elemental things of sense. She was hardly aware of where she was going, could not think how to do what must be done when she arrived. She only knew that she must go on.

The trees she passed were very old. They stood in solemn grandeur beside the road, motionless in the deathly still of the day. The green leaves hung from the lofty branches, and in their terrible calm the leaves appeared immovable to the end of the world. Against the infinite sky they stood sharp as mysterious carvings, and she looked at them, and her mind dwelt with an inarticulate fixity upon them, and in a vague, wordless way she pondered the dropping of acorns to the soft earth at a time when the world was young. It was an awesome thing to move through the great forest when nothing moved apart from herself, the horse, and the spumes of dust whirling up behind them. Not a murmur anywhere. Only the midday quiet. Occasionally the alarmed cry of a bird. And then the arching emptiness of the open day, open without protection against the enormity of sunlight and withering heat.

Out of the forest at last. Riding the dirt road between fields which spread away to the fringes of other woodland, and beyond that the mountains veiled in a mist of heat, and beyond them the ends of the earth. No shade now except for the insignificant shadow of an occasional tree, and the horse went quickly through that. The blackness swept briefly over her, and she was in the dazzling sunlight again, and the heat waves throbbing heavily upward from the red ground made the earth an inconstant wasteland. It baked in a waterless cauldron.

Her thoughts were tangled hopelessly in her head. That, really, was the clearest thing she knew. And she wondered, desperately, as if standing at the borders of herself and looking queerly in, if she would ever get them untangled again.

Yes! Yes! Yes! There were *some* clear things! Or rather one firmly unshakable thing, unshakable in spite of the waving illusions of the heat—the land itself. As long as she could cling to that! Here, without a hat, without even the shelter of the trees, she might die. But if she did die, she would fall onto the land, and in time the land would raise her up.

No, that was blasphemy. Wasn't it blasphemy? Her thoughts knotted up again. "Forgive me," she cried aloud. Or she thought she cried. There was no one to hear if she did. Her voice was barely a mutter, almost as breathless as the day. But her heart was contrite. God looks on the heart. And only God raised the dead. That was the supremely divine act. She would be raised *from* the land if she died upon it. "Dust thou art to flesh returneth." No, that wasn't in the Bible. Was it? Her confusion made the tears come up in her eyes. The sunlight caught in the teardrops as if in a prism and was reflected brilliantly into the depths of her brain, and all the fiery world around swam crazily in an incandescent sea.

Dust thou art . . . But if she were dust, she was dust of this land. That had to be. The irrefutable fact impressed itself on her mind with a mighty, purifying simplicity. It was like the breaking of clouds after a violent storm or else the first faint gleaming of day across the eastern sky at dawn. Her people had been here so long. They had absorbed the substance of the land, and in turn the land took them again unto itself when they died. It remained forever, a warm and tender mother, bringing forth from the womb, holding them all with its limitless favor. It had brought her forth. It had nourished her. If now it reclaimed her body, it would be no journey to the unknown, but only a return to a familiar and peaceful realm where she would rest from her labors. The land would greet her with the kiss of peace—like the father welcoming the prodigal son whom he saw from afar.

No, that was not right. Something was mixed up again! She knew fathers did not really embrace. She knew she was no prodigal! The prodigal had sinned. He had spoiled the fruits of the land. But she had guarded the land itself with all the compassion of her life. All she had done had been for the land! Had she not done her duty, the land would have languished, disintegrated, fallen fragmented into the stuporous decay of time. A part of God's creation would have been left without the dominion of the people God had set over it. All the universe would have been imperfect by that much. She had only served the purposes of God. Nothing more. Nothing less! No sin to her charge, but glory.

And she had seen the glory. When? She could not tell the first time. The glory was already there, she thought, pre-existent as the light which illumined the amorphous patches of her first memories, of her becoming. The glory of the imperishable land. And everything she had ever done—*everything*—was for the glory of the land and not for herself. She had done *nothing* for herself. She would defy God to accuse her of selfishness. God or the Devil! She had wrought righteousness. She looked defiantly upward.

Then recoiled. Her head ached from the heat. Whence this darkness rushing off the fields like an inverse falling of night? Whence this absurd tilting of the horizon? Whence this blank, vacuous pain?

"Dear God, forgive me!"

The cry, out of the depths, brought her back. Slowly the darkness receded from around her vision, and the trembling world grew still. She clung to the edge of the antiquated sidesaddle as if to life itself. When had that been used last? Suddenly it was a concrete, limited, and extraordinarily important problem. When *had* the sidesaddle last been used? Meticulously she went over the years and the memories, and as she was carefully piecing out the answer to this desperate question, the horse topped the last dun hill, and Bourbonville lay before her, straggling on its lowly ridges and edging the waters of the dark river.

19

MR. CAMPBELL took a short walk that morning to stroll along the board sidewalks and look at his town. The walk was even shorter than he intended. The sunlight crushed his spirit and hurt his eyes, and in a little while he gave up and came back to sit in the office.

By late morning the room was stifling. He allowed himself the concession of removing his coat. He had opened the door which went back to the kitchen and also the door which gave onto the back lot. Nothing did any good. The curtains, stiff with dust, hung dead by the open window, and he fixed his eyes on the window itself without looking for anything.

He was startled from his musing by the creaking of a wagon and the ringing of harness, the formally harsh cry of a man's voice shouting "Whoa" at his animals, a sheet of dust pumped up before his window as the wagon stopped. Mr. Campbell leaned over his desk and looked out.

He saw that Mr. and Mrs. Samuel Curry had arrived in front of his office, that Mr. Curry was clambering down from the wagon to secure his team, that Mrs. Curry, soundly protected against the sun by a great, white bonnet, was sitting poker-straight on the backless seat, and that both of them had obviously come to see him. Mr. Curry was in his Sunday best. That meant he was sticky with sweat and badly rumpled and perfectly miserable. But he maintained his dignity and his polite decorum, and he came sloshing around through the dust to his wife's side to help her descend. She carefully removed her bonnet and fixed at her iron-gray hair before taking his hand to step down. Her face registered uncompromising querulousness. Her black little eyes darted about, snapping at things in the street. Most particularly she scrutinized the house wherein reposed the office of John Wesley Campbell, Attorney at Law.

Mr. Campbell got up, took his coat down from the peg and put it on. He examined himself for the tenth time that day in the tall mirror which hung behind the door. He adjusted his collar and pulled at the bow on his string tie and went to the front hall just as Mr. Curry's slow, regular knocking officially announced their presence.

"Well, well! Samuel! Mrs. Curry! How do you do! Come in. Come in." The greeting was genuinely friendly, for Mr. Campbell liked the Currys. They were stanch farmers, and they had been Union people. Before the War they had been Quakers, but they hated slavery so much they became Methodists so they could in good conscience send their sons off to fight.

Mrs. Curry looked sharply at Mr. Campbell and picking up her skirts stepped by him into the hallway and turned into the office. She seemed to try to ignore his friendly smile and the gesture of welcome he made with his hands as if she had determined already that she would not be obligated to him for anything.

Mr. Curry very self-consciously came in and shook hands with Mr. Campbell. He removed his hat so swiftly that he might have been entering a church, and he held on to it as if hats were scarce. Mr. Campbell guided them into his office and made them sit down. He sat himself and looked expectantly at them across the desk.

But they said nothing.

So finally Mr. Campbell said: "Hot day, isn't it, Samuel? I don't think I've ever seen it so hot in June. Not in Tennessee, at least."

To which Mr. Curry responded with a nervous bobbing of his white head and a mumbled, choking agreement, followed by a great clearing of his throat and a more clearly pronounced agreement which was simply: "Yep! Yep, it sure is. Awful hot!"

"Guess you folks have all been well," Mr. Campbell said. "You both look fine."

At which Mr. Curry got hold of himself enough to say that the Lord had blessed them both and that they were thankful and hoped the Lord would see fit to keep it up.

To which Mr. Campbell replied that he was sure the Lord would do just that. The conversation lapsed again. Mrs. Curry had not yet said a word. For a moment Mr. Curry looked slightly more comfortable. But as the silence deepened, so did his jittery embarrassment. He looked so beseechingly across the desk that Mr. Campbell finally took pity on him. "Well, Samuel, I suppose you're here on some sort of business."

Mr. Curry cleared his throat. But all he said was, "We ain't able to work much nowadays. The drought."

"Yes, I know. The land looks skinned."

"Worst I ever seen," Mr. Curry said. "If it don't rain soon . . ." He let the words trail off to an unuttered thought looming darkly up before them. Tugging at his collar with a finger, Mr. Curry said: "It *sure* is hot."

Mr. Campbell immediately caught the insinuation and got to his feet. "Could I get you a drink of water?"

Mr. Curry nodded in great relief. "I'd like that right well. I mean if it ain't too much trouble. It's *awful* hot." Then, looking gingerly at his wife, he asked, "Would you like some water, Nellie?"

Mrs. Curry actually spoke! "I *am* thirsty," she said in a low voice, casting her eyes down.

Mr. Campbell apologized for not thinking about it earlier, and Mr. Curry said he hadn't really noticed how thirsty he *was* until just then. He was still apologizing and hoping he wasn't too much trouble while Mr. Campbell went back to his kitchen and pumped a stone pitcher full of fresh water. Then he took down a couple of glasses and carried them and the pitcher back into his office and poured a drink for each of the Currys.

Mr. Curry snatched up his glass as soon as Mr. Campbell set it down. Looking apologetically around, he gulped all the water in it down without taking a breath. Mr. Campbell refilled the glass, and Mr. Curry drank this one down, too, and he probably would have had another right then except that Mrs. Curry checked him with a firm: "Samuel!"

She had not finished her own glass. Mr. Campbell might have been surprised, but he remembered his own mother. She had always taught him it was bad manners to eat everything put on your plate. That might mean you wanted more, and your host might not have more to give. Mrs. Curry undoubtedly had a mother with an eye for manners. And Mrs. Curry was one of those women who would retain her own manners in hell.

So Mr. Campbell responded according to an ancient and accepted ritual. He fixed it so Mrs. Curry *had* to assuage her thirst. Holding out the stone pitcher he said, "Mrs. Curry, my wife and I dug this well. When people drink its water, it gives me a lot of pleasure. I think she'd be happy knowing somebody else liked what she liked. Please have some more."

If Mrs. Curry refused now, she would be insulting a dead

woman. Her sharp little face suddenly mellowed, and her black eyes shone with womanly sympathy. "I remember your wife," she said softly, and she did hold out her glass, and when Mr. Campbell had filled it, she drank it all down, though with reserve, and at the end she patted her thin lips with the very tips of her fingers. Mr. Curry was less fastidious. He took his third glass and heaved it down with a slurping gulp and thereupon expelled a mighty sigh of deliverance. He drew his sleeve across his mouth and wiped it dry and looked about with great satisfaction. "That's real good water," he thundered. Muting his voice a little he added, "Your wife was a pretty little thing. I remember when we seen her in here years ago. Let's see, what was her name?"

"Charlotte," Mr. Campbell said softly.

"Charlotte! I'd of said it was Rosemary," Mr. Curry said with a frown.

"No, it was Charlotte," Mr. Campbell said.

"Of course it was Charlotte!" Mrs. Curry said, snapping at her husband. "Charlotte Anne."

"Charlotte Jane," Mr. Campbell corrected gently.

"I'd of *swore* it was Rosemary," Mr. Curry said.

Mr. Campbell only smiled distantly, whereas Mrs. Curry looked so fiercely at her husband that she might have hit him in the mouth.

"Well, she had on a yeller dress first time I seen her," Mr. Curry said, undaunted.

"That's right." Mr. Campbell's eyes lighted with the memory. "She did have a yellow dress. And you were a young man, Samuel. We were all young."

"It's a fact," Mr. Curry said without any real conviction. His tone was that of a man hardly able to imagine what youth had been.

"I think you came in with your father," Mr. Campbell recalled. "He wanted to make a will."

"It's a fact," Mr. Curry said again. He cleared his throat and looked subdued and timid once more.

"Would that be your business, Samuel?"

Mr. Curry nodded stiffly and in deep melancholy. "Threshing's tomorrow," he said. "Life's uncertain. People get themselves killed in threshing time. You remember the Jamison boy last year?"

"Yes, I remember. They brought him into town to Doc Cogill. On a flatbed wagon! The fools! If the boy wasn't dead when they started, they killed him."

Mr. Curry nodded again. Indeed he had not really ceased his

grave nodding since admitting his business. Only with the recollection of a bloody death, the slight gesticulation of his head became more pronounced. He had a high, domed forehead with a sweaty strand of gray hair plastered over it by the pressure of his hat. When he nodded in his unsmiling way, he looked as sober as Father Time. "I've thought a lot about things since then. Mules and men, and that machine. The smoke and racket. It's a dangerous thing, and I've made up my mind. I want to make a will."

"Rubbish!" Mrs. Curry said. Mr. Campbell glanced at her, but she had spoken like a steel spring snapping, and her face sprang so quickly back into that stern frown of hers that she might not have spoken at all.

Mr. Curry looked at her apologetically. "Nellie don't think I'm doing the right thing," he said.

"We all need to make a will, Samuel," Mr. Campbell said in his official voice.

"I agree," Mr. Curry said.

"Rubbish!" Mrs. Curry said again.

Again the apologetic glance from Mr. Curry. "Nellie thinks if you talk about dying, why . . . You'll die. She thinks I'm tempting the Lord."

"Well, we're going to die whether we talk about it or not," Mr. Campbell said. He spoke the words to Mrs. Curry, but her eyes went stabbing off beyond him into space, and she seemed to ignore him.

"Not that there'd be any trouble if I was to die or anything," Mr. Curry said uneasily. "My boys is good boys. We've always got along. I leave things pretty much to them nowadays, and they work it out. But I've seen some bad things in my time. People wrangling over money. Children fighting over their daddy's coffin."

"Very true," Mr. Campbell said.

"Rubbish!" Mrs. Curry said. She was more emphatic than she had been, but her eyes were still fixed on space.

"And I tell you, this threshing's going to be bad. The worst ever," Mr. Curry said. He leaned forward, his face intent and venerable, awed at his own thoughts. "We start tomorrow at our place, and in this dust, this heat . . . ?" His voice ended in a question. "The animals don't like it, J.W.! The men don't neither. They don't like this weather, and we're all going to be skittish." He subsided into his chair. His tone became sad again. "Besides, I've had my warning."

"He had himself a dream," Mrs. Curry said with a hint of scorn.

"I dreamed I was out riding and passed a graveyard," Mr. Curry said. "That's a queer thing to dream, ain't it?" He uttered a forced laugh. "I ain't really scared, you understand. I'm ready to go. But I think there's a reason the Lord gives us dreams."

Mrs. Curry started to say "Rubbish" again, but she couldn't quite manage it. Mr. Campbell looked at her and saw that her eyes were filled with tears.

"She don't like to think about me dying," Mr. Curry said gently. He put out a hand and clumsily patted one of her wiry arms.

Mr. Campbell cleared his throat. "Well, Samuel, death's as normal as birth. We don't think much of the man who lets his wife come down to giving birth without preparing for it. Maybe if we had our wits about us we'd like to get ready for death the way we do birth. But we can't like it. The best we can do is to do what we should. And I think you ought to make a will."

Mr. Curry nodded solemnly, unable to speak.

"We've been doing so well," Mrs. Curry said in an accent of reproach.

Mr. Curry recovered his voice. "I've had a good life," he said. There was a hard undertone of pride in his words, and Mr. Campbell looked at him appreciatively. "We've had good health. We've worked hard. We've raised four fine boys, and they've got fine families, and we've all come through a lot. I've lived my three score and ten, and I can still work down most men in this valley, even them that's a lot younger than me. And I've . . ."

At that precise moment a confusion of noise erupted in the street outside. A shouting about something. A rush of pounding feet on the board sidewalk. And then a shot. Muffled, queer, but distinctly a pistol shot, followed by a howl of pain. Removed through the cry was, Mr. Campbell instantly recognized the voice of Hub Delaney in distress, and he was up and racing out the door before Mr. Curry could finish his lugubrious sentence.

Mr. Campbell arrived in the torrid street just in time to see the Reverend Thomas Bazely run out of the jailhouse barefoot with a pistol in his hand. Even across the street and in the glaring heat Mr. Campbell could recognize the long barrel of Hub Delaney's ancient revolver, and he could see an almost invisible line of black smoke trailing out the muzzle. Before the preacher the crowd which had come rushing up went bursting asunder, exploding in panic. Some went diving into the bushes growing along the fringes of the courthouse lawn, and others remembering old reflexes threw themselves to the ground, covering their heads, while still others simply rushed away in a straight, mad line in the frenzied, most instinctive reaction of men in danger of death. And in the midst of the turmoil he had created, reeled Mr. Bazely, clutching the pistol. He came lunging across the street like a man drunk on sunlight and fire. Mr. Campbell had just halted in the middle of the street when Thomas Bazely saw him.

And then the preacher laughed.

In the years that followed, that laugh attained a kind of immortality. Men remembered it when almost everything else about Mr. Bazely was forgotten. For many decades mothers told their children about it late at night when the dark crouched around the house. The laugh was a manifestation of the dark powers which inhabited the world. Men sat murmuring around in the places men gather in country towns, and they recounted it, and long, long after all the people who were alive in Bourbonville that morning had passed into the dust, the laugh was remembered. It became a roar, a demonic cry of vengeance shrieking through the collective memory of the little town, making the living shudder in vivid memory of the dead. Thomas Bazely laughed.

John Wesley Campbell realized with an almost serene working of his logical mind that Thomas Bazely was come to Bourbonville to kill him. And with that same tranquil logic he realized that his only weapon lay inside his office, in the drawer of his desk, buried under accumulated papers of months and years and probably not loaded. Instinctively he took one step backward, toward the door, and at that instant Thomas Bazely flung the pistol out at the end of a lanky arm and fired. The explosion in the open street was deafening, but the fact that he had heard it at all was proof to Mr. Campbell that the bullet had missed him.

Until that first shot all the reflexes stamped into him by two wars had been driving Mr. Campbell to do something, to run for his house or else to fling himself to the ground. But the blast of the pistol and its spout of fire behind the invisible bullet settled a huge calm down upon him. For years afterward people told how he seemed suddenly to compose himself, and some who were very near said he even folded his arms across his chest in a final, grand gesture of contempt. He had time to speak one imperative sentence to Mr. Bazley which the stricken onlookers never forgot.

"You go to hell, Bazely!"

The words struck Mr. Bazely like a slap in the face. In his lurching progress across the street to where he now stood, his eyes had been glazed and wild, and there had been a slack madness to his face, the accompaniment of his insane laughter. He was still laughing when he fired the first shot at Mr. Campbell, and when he stopped, still chortling, to take aim again, Mr. Campbell cursed him. He started to laugh again—a shrill, mad, animal howl—but the curse knocked the laughter out of him, and he fell into a staring silence. His mouth abruptly stiffened, and just when he raised the pistol to take careful aim at John Wesley Campbell's neck, Mr. Bazely seemed more sane than anybody in Bourbonville could ever remember.

Hub Delaney always swore that if only he hadn't been taking a nap on his cot in the jailhouse office, Mr. Bazely would never have been able to rush in and get his pistol away from him. He said he was still groggy with sleep when the preacher tore the pistol out of his holster and shot him in the chest, just above his left lung, tumbling him out of the cot in a shocked heap in a pool of his own blood.

And he thought it was a miracle, he said, that his own instincts from the War had survived. For they did survive. Otherwise he could not explain how something kept prodding his unwilling mind, demanding that he get up, though he wanted so badly to drift off to sleep again. But get up he did. He was sick at his stomach and giddy in the head, and his left arm dangled uselessly. He could not feel it, could not move it at all through the hot pain which burned the whole left side of his body. But he did not think about that except to note it in passing. He thought only of the 1866 Winchester rifle which had been an ornament for years on the wall behind his desk. And somehow he managed to get it down and to lever a cartridge into the chamber in a desperate rush of his failing strength. Then he stumbled out into the brilliant sunlight, and bracing himself against the side of the jailhouse and firing with his good right arm, he shot the preacher dead.

John Wesley Campbell heard the shot before he saw Hub Delaney. Instantaneously he saw the front of the preacher's chest blow out from the exploding impact of the soft lead bullet, and immediately the preacher himself pitched headlong on his face into the street. The dust roared up around him like flames, dense and furious. Still he held the pistol. With the last effort of his life he squeezed the trigger. The blast was terrific. The pistol leaped out of the swirling dust. But the bullet went wild, and Mr. Bazely lay quite still. The blood running out of his chest made a dark, widening puddle of mud in the dusty street beneath his body, and the dust he had raised in his violent fall drifted quietly back to earth and settled over him like a shroud.

Mr. Campbell had only to take about five steps to reach the body. He turned the preacher over, quickly and warily, and saw that the man was indeed dead. Mr. Bazely's eyes were still wide open, nasty with dust, and glaring angrily at the sky. Mr. Campbell gently closed them as the first astonished spectators came rushing up.

At once he was on his feet and running across the street to Hub Delaney. A crowd had clotted around him. The sheriff was sitting with his back to the wall and his legs straight out in front of him. His left arm sprawled on the ground. With his right hand he still held the rifle across his lap. When Mr. Campbell pushed through the ring of dumbfounded people and plunged down beside him, Hub looked at his friend with eyes slowly going blank and mumbled, "Damn it, J.W., I hurt." With that he passed out.

Mr. Campbell tore Hub's shirt off and exposed the wound. It was a gaping, bluish-red hole, and dark, venous blood was oozing out of it. Mr. Campbell quickly threw off his coat and in efficient haste ripped his own shirt off his body and made it into a pad. This he pushed down on the open wound. Holding it there with all his might he got others to bear Hub up in their arms and to carry him across the street to Mr. Campbell's house and to Mr. Campbell's bed. Doc Cogill arrived forty-five minutes later from delivering a baby in the country. He dug the bullet out with a pair of slim tongs, cauterized the wound with a red-hot iron in the best approved medical style, administered a stout shot of morphine, and announced that Hub would live. Surprisingly, he did.

Meanwhile a noisy committee established itself to get rid of the preacher's body before any more children saw the thing. They hauled the remains into the jailhouse office. Some of the men who carried the body noticed with a certain bewilderment how thin the preacher had been, how dirty he was, how tangled was his hair, and how sharply the bones of his face showed through his pale skin. He had always seemed larger than that, they thought. More imposing. It was a puzzling thing quickly forgotten.

Much later Mr. Campbell thought of the Currys. Doc Cogill was still sitting by the bed where Hub Delaney lay. The sheriff was in a profound, narcotic slumber. Men were stumping up and down the stairs to look in and to inquire after the patient and to go away and tell their news to each other. In the street a din of voices jangled incessantly in the indolent heat. It was getting on toward one o'clock. The torrid air compressed between the buildings by the heavy light made the street a furnace. But the cacophony of talk rolled through the air like waves. Mr. Campbell had washed Hub's blood off his hands, and he had put on a fresh shirt, and he had knotted a new black tie through his soft collar. He thought that now they ought to clean Hub up. And he was going down, coatless to the kitchen, to fetch up more water, when he remembered the Currys, looked into his office, and found them still waiting patiently before his desk.

He was surprised. He went in and began to apologize for forgetting them, and somewhat foolishly he apologized for being without his coat. But Mrs. Curry cut him off. "That man upstairs shot the preacher," she said. She was righteously aghast.

Mr. Campbell was holding an empty bucket in one hand. For the first time he felt exasperated with Mrs. Curry. "The preacher was trying to *kill* me," he said. He drew the bucket up and brought his other hand down with an impatient thwack along the side of it. The bucket was made of galvanized iron, and his flat hand made a booming noise against it, like a drum.

Mrs. Curry was just declaring that it was a bad sign when anybody shot a preacher when suddenly far, far in the distance there was another hollow booming sound as if in response to Mr. Campbell's hand. The second sound was faint. It quivered on the verge of audibility. But the noise of voices died in the street like a waterfall suddenly dammed.

Mr. Curry heard it and sat bolt upright and looked openmouthed around him, every muscle in his body tense and alert and listening. *"What was that!"*

Mr. Campbell walked to the window and stood, straining to hear. Outside in the street, the sound of voices again rolled upward, frenzied and confused. He hesitated a moment longer by the window and then walked back around his desk and sat down with a bemused, wondering expression on his face.

"I think it was thunder," he said.

20

IT WAS LATE IN THE MORNING when the cow was finally delivered to the bull. He seemed to smell their coming from afar. He came stamping into the rutting pen as soon as they led the cow—bawling from the fire, the dust, and her longing—into Brian Ledbetter's land. When they arrived at the fence the bull was pawing the earth and snorting in anticipation. Brian slipped through the barn and back of the pen and shut the gate on that side so the bull and the cow would not fly to the farthermost corner of the pasture. "One sure thing about a cow," Brian said philosophically. "She'll always get the best of you if she can."

He took a long, sharp pole and punched Boston away from the gate, and Virgil threw it open and jumped back, and Sam kicked the cow in the ass, and in she rushed with a bellow of delight. Sam leaped into the pen and pulled the gate to and seized one end of the cow's rope and knotted it around a post. After that the men retired to the shade of a chestnut tree and sat on the ground to watch and to wait until it was over.

Boston got right down to business, and the cow seemed pleased.

Brian drank in the scene with an expression of profound satisfaction. He shook his head in admiration and grunted and licked his lips. "If they'd let men and women bang off like that whenever they wanted, we'd all be a lot better off," he said. "A *hell* of a lot better off. I tell you what's a real true fact. It's a shame to think something as dumb as a cow has got it over the whole white race." He was about to go on ruminating aloud, but he cast a sidelong glance at Virgil and thought better of it. He fell silent. Rapt with pleasure, he watched the animals and grunted in approval whenever Boston got in an especially good lick.

Sam leaned back against the tree. "Oh, I don't know," he said at last in response to Brian. "How'd you like to be led in with a rope around your neck whenever you got the urge? And having people standing around to watch?"

"Well," Brian said with a sigh, "that's just about what happens at a wedding. Only afterward they ain't nobody around to lead you *away!*"

They laughed idly together. Sam felt the rough bark biting through his soggy shirt. Somehow it felt good. Virgil sat hugging his knees. He was silently absorbed in the furious scene. Except for the frenzy of the animals the whole world was sunken in drowsy indolence. In some blank way Sam could not fully put together in his mind there was a vexing oddity in the way the bucking intercourse of the animals could even take place against the hard, open stillness of the day. Not a breath of air stirred. Not a cloud stood in the pale blue sky. Yet in the midst of this seething calm, the animals kicked up the dust until they were nearly hidden by it and wallowed on each other with devouring lust.

Sam was thirsty. Very thirsty, in fact. But he did not get up to seek water. Water was nearby, and there was something delicious about contemplating a drink soon to be taken in the midst of dry thirst. So he sat and let his mind drift aimlessly like some wisp of spirit. These days, when he did not willfully restrain it, his mind settled Westward. The Great Plains he had never seen. To Emilie, riding erect and proud somewhere across their wide surface.

The sky would be blue there too. He drew from his imagination a vision of midday out there and saw the clouds coalescing from invisible moisture to stand like enchanted towers in the blue magnificence of the summer sky. He thought of places he had never seen. Places perhaps recessed in the memory of John Wesley Campbell, who had wandered there and returned to Bourbonville clad in his impenetrable mantle of strangeness.

Sam did not know Mr. Campbell very well. He wished that he did. In all his life he had had only one long conversation with the man who had been his father's closest friend. That had been recently. Emilie was just gone. Mrs. Simson was in her grave, and Mr. Simson awaited death. Mr. Campbell was taut and silent and preoccupied. In their mutual moods, when nothing was exactly natural, Sam encountered him one day in the street and blurted out the question: "Mr. Campbell, what's it like? Out West? What's it like out there?"

So they had talked. Mr. Campbell looked at him with worn gravity and struck fire to one of his inevitable cigars, and standing in the shade of the courthouse lawn, he told Samuel Beckwith the Younger what the West was like.

"Well, in the summer it's hot. Hotter than the brass dog that guards the gates of hell. You can't stand in the sun bareheaded. You have to protect yourself, and sometimes a hat doesn't do any real good. And in the winter, up on the plains, it snows so hard it sucks the breath out of your body. It can freeze you to death in fifteen minutes, but the bad thing is that it can drive you crazy.

"And there're people out there hoping to make it, and they haven't got a chance. Sometimes you'll be riding along on the plains, and you'll think you're completely alone. But then you'll stumble on some fool from back here, and he's living in a dugout, roofed with sod—living like a gopher—and he's thinking that tomorrow or next year or sometime he's going to be richer than Solomon because he's got land to farm. But you know he'll die in a blizzard come winter, or else he'll starve to death, or else he'll get a cough and spit his lungs out like tobacco.

"Oh, I can't say it's all bad. But *mostly!* Mostly it's awful, the West. The scum of the earth live out there. They're all running from something definite to something unknown. You don't have kinfolks out there. Or a past. Not in the West I know. Sometimes you don't even have a last name. You don't ask a man what his full name is. You may know a man one year, two years, and all the time you call him Kid or Boss or Tom or John or Ringo and that's all. If he likes you and gets to trusting you, maybe—just maybe—one day he'll screw up his face and drop his voice down to a whisper you can just barely hear, and he'll tell you where he's from and why he's run away and what his real name is. It's a weir of deceit, the West.

"But then . . . Well, I'll be honest about it. It's peculiar. But sometimes, if you're in a saloon somewhere, and you're all alone, and it's all dark outside except for the stars, and there's a Mexican woman playing a Spanish guitar and singing over it—low and throaty and sensuous—and the lamplight is yellow and soft, and it's cool outside the way the desert gets at night when the air's so dry, well, you don't care. I can't explain it, but you don't care about anything. You may think that tomorrow morning you're going to die, and maybe a week from now your carcass will be rotting where the buzzards can pick your bones. But it doesn't matter. You've got Now. That's the only thing that counts, and there's a freedom in that. If you've got four or five ounces of whiskey in your stomach and a silver dollar in your pocket, well then, so much the better. I never have forgotten that feeling. I suppose it takes a peculiar set of circumstances to make a person have it. But once you do have it, you never forget it.

"Oh, it's the asshole of America. I don't deny that. I affirm it. The drunks, the bawds, the poor, the insane, the people with the crazy dreams—they go West. People who can't make it here go West. And people who just have to wander.

"And yet . . . Well, sometimes I think all that human waste spread out there may make the flowers grow someday, somewhere. I'm being very serious. All those people out there, looking for some damned thing . . . You've got to ask yourself this question: Can they all be looking for something and not find it? Can *all* of them be *so* misled that the West is nothing but a big joke nature has played on America? It's an important question. A very important question.

"But for me the thing was the freedom. And I can't even tell you what it is. It's something you have to feel for yourself. I felt it when I was there, and that's all I can say about it. I think maybe it's because there's no past to the West. History doesn't smother you to death the way it does here. You think you can change things there. You can get a new start and begin something altogether different in the history of the world. That's the way the West makes you feel.

"You think it's ugly when you see it for the first time. Dirty towns strung out along treeless streets. Nothing is painted. Ignorant people grub for life any way they can get it. A kind of monotony, a boredom over everything. Land so flat in some places you can see for miles and miles and the curve of the horizon all around makes the world look like a green plate or a yellow disk. You're a speck in the middle of something huge. But a free speck. That's the great thing. You're so little and so forgotten that you really are free."

That was the West Mr. Campbell knew, and he knew also that it had changed from the time he had been there. Now there were cows, and he had read that people were afraid the buffalo might become extinct. There would be more towns now, and the squalid hamlets he had known would be teeming with denser life. But could things have changed *so* much? How could they fill up all that space! Thousands of square miles of space, dotted by those pitiful settlements crouching in the awful immensity, naked to the winds and the sun.

That is where Emilie and her father and mother had gone. They had vanished like a tiny cluster of stones dropped into a colossal lake. Gone. Quite gone. Sometimes Sam longed to stand in the room by his father's unsmiling picture and shout her name. Or else he wanted to rise in the middle of the night and split the silence by calling her name into the dark. A shout to ward off death.

All his life his mother had spoken in soft, melancholy languor of death. But only Emilie's departure made him realize what death was, and only when she had gone did he begin to start up sometimes at night in the terrible knowledge that he would die and that his bones would rot in the earth.

She was out there somewhere this very moment. She was in Texas or Kansas or on the way to California. Her father might drive West until the axle tree of his wagon washed in the ocean. Every straggling crossroad he passed made it more impossible that Sam should ever find her again. Even as he lay here, watching the bull and the cow, he had a sense of an infinite column of lost chances spiraling silently upward as four slow wheels turned patiently along somewhere, out there.

Women were scarce in the West. They were as rare as diamonds when Mr. Campbell was there and far more precious. They were still rare. Sometimes even yet the Knoxville papers carried a pitiful little box on an inside page, a few drops of lead type spilled into a sea of flamboyant advertisements for tonics and salves guaranteed to make the old young and the young immortal: "Lonely Tennessean with good holding in Texas would like to marry lady from Tennessee or anyplace. Will consider taking over children and will try to be a good father. Age eighteen to forty considered. Please write box . . ."

So Emilie would find her way in the West.

Mr. Campbell told him to forget her. That is what everybody said, but everybody else said it in either an imperial scorn of worldly wisdom or else in a jocular bantering accent of half-suppressed hilarity. Mr. Campbell said forget her with a deep, inflexible sadness in his eyes and with the sober calm of one announcing death at the end of a long night.

"Oh God!" Brian suddenly rumbled. "I'm dying for a drink! I'll fetch water down from the spring." He got stiffly up and stumped off through the sun, and Sam turned idly to see him go and saw how dark was the shadow the sun cast behind him as he went.

Mr. Campbell had said going West was a little like losing your virginity. Before it happened you thought you knew a lot, and while it was happening you didn't have time to think about anything, and then when it was over—well, things were never the same again. You carried something around with you, inside, invisible, and if you didn't do it again—like him, did not go West again—it grew in your mind and grew until your whole life moved in the shadow of that time, West. No matter what dull thing you might be doing in what bleak place, you knew that somewhere there were plains rolling away to the sky and air so clear you could see a column of smoke rising for miles across the empty land. Knowing there were things like that in the world made you different. And once you knew it, it was something you could never, never undo or forget.

"Nobody cares out there. People don't give a damn for you alive, and they don't care for you dead. The only reason they take the trouble to put you in the ground when you die is to keep you from stinking up their town. I've seen skeletons out there on the plains, picked clean by buzzards and worms, and people like you and me pass by without looking aside, without taking the trouble to put those poor bones in the ground. I've passed by myself.

"But do you know something? That's a part of the freedom! It's the price you pay. If nobody cares about you, you really are free. If you don't care about anybody, you're free. And that's the way the West is. It's stark, naked freedom. It's a powerful thing. A very powerful thing, and some men get drunk on it. Oh, you can't understand. You don't really know what I'm talking about."

But in a way Sam did understand. It was a terrible place, the West. A great, terrifying land. But a free land, a land where things were possible. For Mr. Campbell it was a land in which he had invested time. And that afternoon, when he talked about it in the cool shade, something came into his face. Sam saw it and pondered it. A look in his eyes dimly reflecting violet clouds standing in the immense sky of the past, memories fading imperceptibly into the immensity of time, memories of invincible sunshine, white stars, and the throaty twanging of a Spanish guitar from some place long ago.

"I will not go again," Mr. Campbell said with huge finality. "I am too old."

And I will not go at all, Sam thought now and shut his eyes and leaned his head against the trunk of the tree. He felt as old as the first Crittendon to come into the valley. His ancestors mounted guard on him in the night. From their graves they held him with invisible chains. He would live here and die here and be buried with them, and it would all be over.

Brian came back with the water. The tin dipper rattled deliciously in the full bucket. The front of his shirt and his overalls were dripping wet, and his head was slick with water. He had nearly thrown himself into the spring to assuage his thirst. Sam and Virgil drank deeply in turns. Sam made the boy go first, and then he drank, and they both drank again, and finally Brian said he was thirsty again and drank—then the bucket was almost empty at the end, and their bellies were uncomfortably full. They all belched and sighed with relief. Brian pitched the rest of the water out. Flying through the air it streaked in the sunlight like a glob of quicksilver and fell to earth with a hollow thump and pounded the dust up around the dark blot it made.

They all sat down again. They were unwilling to face the trip back right away. Boston and the cow still toyed with each other, but they were through. Their romance was dissolving before their eyes, though Boston still seemed to think something more might be got out of it.

"It looks like it's over with," Sam said in an unhurried tone. But still they sat for a while longer.

Finally Brian went through the barn and opened the gate which led from the rutting pen into the pasture beyond. Boston ambled serenely through it without concern. The cow ignored his going. The bull went on, and they saw him pass slowly down the hill and through a screen of scrub cedars. switching his stubby tail in triumphant indifference.

"We'd better hurry if we're going to eat lunch," Brian said. And so they set about to water the animals, and having done that they moved out. This time the cow followed them without complaint, and their passage was a steady plodding through the pressing heat and the nasty dust.

It was well after noon when Sam left the other two. They went on with the cow, bidding him a laconic goodbye. He turned up the back lane through the sweltering fields to his house. The sultry heat was so thick that he opened his mouth to breathe. He was uneasy. Once his mother would have been cross with him for being this late to lunch. She was prompt at meals, and she expected other people to be the same. Despondently he thought that she would not be irritated today. By silently accepting his late coming, she would show again how much he was loved, how impossible it was for *him* to inconvenience *her*.

So he was surprised when he came into the house and found that there was no meal waiting and that the stove was cold. He knew almost at once that the house was empty. It was troubling. He could not remember when he had come home and found his mother unexpectedly gone.

He went swiftly through the kitchen and the quiet rooms downstairs, and once he called out, "Mother?" But there was no answer. The picture of his father gazed at him. Sam paused before it, looked at the grave, staring eyes, and shook his head in a frown. He went up the steps and noticed that they creaked gently under his weight. He would have to look at the beams under them, he thought.

Very gingerly he went into his mother's room. It was as quiet as the rest of the house. As empty. He rarely entered it any more. Her bed—the big, double four-poster bed his father had died in—was neatly made, and the counterpane was stretched tight as a drumhead across it. Everything was in impeccable order.

A large, elaborately posed picture of her father hung against a wall. It was done in prosperous middle age. He was standing next to a shrouded column almost as high as his waist, one hand draped lightly over it, the other resting against his hip, thrusting his coat back. A large chain stretched across his stomach. His stance was imperial. The angle of his face with its hard eyes glaring off into space above the long-vanished camera made him look haughty and cruel. Decidedly cruel. Sam had not noticed that in his boyhood when he was more familiar with the picture, and now he reflected briefly upon it. Sometimes it seemed that the expressions of the pictures in the house were subtly changing with the years. There was no doubt that this was Matthew's father. No doubt also that this man was a different sort from the dark, gentle likeness of Samuel Beckwith, Sr., in the larger picture downstairs. Probably nothing more than the difference between a man who had made his fortune and was hell-bent to keep it and a man going to war and perhaps to death. But maybe something else in the difference. Some family trait in the Crittendons. Something fierce handed down in the past through a blood now running in his own veins. Where did he belong? Which likeness was his?

"Mother?" No answer.

His own room was empty too. He went slowly downstairs to the parlor. Only then did he see the single creased sheet of paper on the large dining table. He had overlooked it in his haste and surprise at finding his mother gone. It had his name written across the front. "Samuel." The bold handwriting of his mother, an unnatural tremor distorting her usually precise characters. The note on the inside fold was two sentences:

I have gone to see about the preacher. I love you with all my heart.

He could not understand the message. He read it over and over and turned it first one way and then another as if expecting some explanation to come to him. The enigmatic sentences baffled him.

He went aimlessly to the back door, still turning the stiff sheet of paper in his hand. He looked out into the torrid day, vaguely pondering, and it was while he was there, wondering what to do and what had happened, that he heard the first distant hollow crash of the thunder. His eyes shot up with a jerk of his head. The sky was still blue and cloudless. But something had changed. There was a prodigious, foreboding cast to the high canopy of light, and the air was more oppressive than it had been.

He realized then in a more profound and disconcerting way the emptiness of the house, the stacking of room on silent room behind him, and though he knew there must be some reasonable explanation for everything, the house became suddenly desolate in his mind, and its immobile vacancy was as ominous as death. For no reason that he could explain, he was afraid. He stepped out the door and went slowly and hesitantly into the yard. All the while he kept glancing warily at the oddly turned sky.

21

SHE ARRIVED almost unnoticed in the town. People were coursing about in all directions, almost beside themselves. Everybody was telling everybody else over and over what had happened. They were shaking heads in uncomprehending disbelief. And all mixed up with the preacher's death was the effusion of hope and skepticism over that lone blast of distant thunder. A buoyant and impossible longing for rain.

Most were already saying they had known for years that the preacher was crazy. In another week only a few stubborn souls would take up for him. But the others were already beginning the justification of their two decades of silence on the subject. They spoke out now in feverish haste, showing their profound and infallible judgment of human nature, piously demonstrating that Christian restraint and benevolence which kept them from saying what they had really thought before now. And they were calling up little details of the preacher's life and working them into the evidence. They spoke of the way he looked in the pulpit on the previous Sunday. Somebody suggested that he had actually foamed at the mouth in the midst of reading the Bible, and that he just barely got control of himself so he could go on. Soon all the others were saying they had seen it with their own eyes. Now everything he had ever said assumed vast significance. The people of Bourbonville were convincing themselves that they had possessed all the doubts any good judge of character should have had about the preacher. So they scarcely paid any attention at all to Sarah Crittendon Beckwith when she rode into town.

She came dazedly into their midst and heard the news as if in a trance. People parted for her horse and went on babbling at each other across the animal as it passed. Their voices were shrill and confused. She heard them all in bafflement.

So she passed on to the jailhouse door. She went there because that is where the crowd seemed thickest. She pulled up her horse almost atop the tangle of men lounging in the scant shadow of the building, and she said: "Where is the preacher?"

Her form was black against the brilliant sky, and men squinted to see her, and a curious silence halted their lively talk. She thought she had not been heard. So she asked again: "Where is the preacher?"

A murmuring bubbled across the surface of the crowd. They all recognized her by now. And portly, bald, bewhiskered Joseph Tilley stepped forward and removed his dirty old hat and said quietly: "He's dead, ma'am. Haven't you heard? He's dead."

There was a momentary silence as Sarah Beckwith looked from face to gaping face. Then she said: "Yes, I heard. Where is he? He came to my house this morning . . ." Her voice faltered in uncertainty. "I knew he was . . . I knew he was sick."

The murmur of voices surged with interest, and now other people were gathering around, and she looked down into a pool of curious faces, turned anxiously upward.

"He was at your *house*?" Joseph Tilley was alarmed. "Why, that man was crazy, ma'am! Are you all right?"

She tried hard to smile, but it was a weak attempt. More a twitching of the muscles of her mouth. "I am quite all right," she said.

"What did he want? What was he doing there? What did you do?" The questions flew at her from the crowd.

"He was talking . . . He said some most *peculiar* things. He rode into my yard and shouted something about . . ." She paused. The faces around her were more tightly pressed together.

"About what, ma'am?" Joseph Tilley shifted closer to her. His dome of a forehead loomed up at her, and his salt-and-pepper beard stood out from his chest. The beard was something her eyes could seize, something less formidable than the probing faces, the surgical glint of inquiry rising from a hundred eyes.

"It was foolish talk. It was about something he wanted to tell in town, something terrible he wanted everybody to know."

The murmuring rose up like steam from the encircling faces. There was a nodding, a great shaking of astonishment and inquisitorial excitement. And Mr. Tilley said, "Good Lord, ma'am! You might of been in danger! What did you do?"

Sarah Beckwith lifted her eyes from his shaggy beard and looked at him directly. She spoke now with a great, clear calm. "I told him to go away. I went into the house and locked the door on the inside and told him to go away. I was alone. I did not want him to know it."

"Well, ma'am, you sure done the right thing!" Joseph Tilley spoke with florid relief, as if he himself had been spared an awful calamity. And he explained to her what had happened.

Or rather he was the leader of a chorus of explanation which rose with his and fell away, disagreeing at some places, adding to other places, relating the facts which were momentarily in circumstantial dispute. The mad gallop of the preacher through the town on a horse frothing with sweat. The wild cry that he made, shrill and terrible, when he threw himself off his horse right here, at this very door. The lunge he made within, the scuffle with Hub Delaney, the first shot, Mr. Campbell coming on the run into the street, the encounter of the two men, the second shot, and finally Hub Delaney's already legendary feat with the rifle which sent the preacher sprawling dead on the ground. All this boiled up at Sarah Crittendon Beckwith from the faces which contorted all over again in excitement from the telling. Within the caldron of hot commotion she became more and more calm. And at the end, or rather when the uproar of voices fell to a mere clamor and became hopelessly confused, she got down off her horse.

"I want to see the body," she said.

Joseph Tilley was taken back. He argued with her briefly. It did no good of course. She started by him. In the press of sweaty men she could not have entered the jailhouse had anybody had a mind not to move. But they did move, Joseph Tilley first, and before her men stepped aside and hushed, and some with a habitual motion of respect took off their hats, and she passed through the open door.

The office was dark. After the painful sunlight she had to pause to let her eyes adjust. In the somber light she made out the cot and Mr. Bazely's thin body tossed carelessly upon it. She stood over him for what seemed a long time. She took in the minute details—the dirt under his long fingernails, the dust smearing his face and matted into his rough hair, the extraordinarily hollow cheeks under their high bones, the jutting chin with its frail cover of stubby hair. She could see how filthy his clothes were and see also the wide, dark splotch of clotted blood showing on the front of his shirt.

"The bullet went through him," she observed quietly.

"Yes ma'am," Joseph Tilley said with equal quiet. He had come in with her, and other men had pushed through the door; many others were standing in a thick half-moon outside.

"We cannot leave him like this," she reasoned half to herself. "He was a man of God." She turned on Mr. Tilley in sudden intensity. "He should be washed and cleaned up. Can you help me?"

Now Joseph Tilley was openly surprised. "Why, ma'am, you shouldn't trouble yourself about that! We'll get some men to bury him. It won't matter none whether he's cleaned up or not. I guess we was just waiting till it got a little cooler."

"Do I understand you to mean that you were going to put him in the ground like a dog? No matter what happened to him at the last, he was a man of God. He deserves a Christian burial."

Joseph Tilley started to interrupt again, but she cut him off. "It is not our duty to judge. But it *is* our duty to provide for his needs. Now will you help me, or do I have to get somebody else?"

Joseph Tilley had been in the Confederate Army at Vicksburg, and he had spent the last two years of the War in a Federal prison camp in Illinois. He came back from the War with few illusions left about anything, but this woman stirred something up in him he thought was dead. In her commanding presence some hard residue of the things he had fought and starved for still remained. And so with a reluctant, ponderous nod of his head, he acquiesced. Behind him a murmur of new surprise picked up in the street.

"Very well, we shall need some water," she said with crisp authority.

In a fussy, embarrassed way Joseph Tilley cleared the other men out of the room, speaking quickly to someone at the door and mentioning "water." Soon a bucket appeared. By the time it arrived, Sarah Beckwith already had Joseph Tilley removing the preacher's shirt. When the bucket was brought in she dismissed its bearer with a cold nod and shut the door in his face with a quiet bang.

The wound was almost directly in the center of the preacher's bone-ridged chest. It was livid and fearfully ugly and already hard around the edges. Without any compunction Sarah Crittendon bent, lifted the hem of her dress, and tore off a strip of white petticoat from underneath. Joseph Tilley flushed to see a portion of woman's underwear, particularly when it was being worn by a woman with the dignity of this one. He turned his head shyly and discreetly. She ignored him.

"This here's a bad wound, ma'am," he said. He spoke in a cautious, squeamish tone. "It might be too much . . . I mean, if you want me to . . ."

"I am quite all right, Mr. Tilley." And she was. She set efficiently to work. First she inspected the wound. She touched it tentatively with the tips of her fingers, pushed slightly at it, frowned, recognized its irrevocable fatality. Then she dipped the wad of her torn petticoat into the water and began to scrub Mr. Bazely's face. She swabbed out his hair, washed his neck, and then set grimly to scraping the incrustation of blood from the skin of his chest. Her wad of cloth turned scarlet in the process. She seemed unaware of it. Joseph Tilley stood circumspectly on the other side of the corpse and watched her and was reminded of a field hospital once, long ago in another world.

Once he did notice something. He exclaimed: "Why look ma'am, at his ear! Something's tore it most clean off. And look at his face! Something's gave him a bad lick right there." He pointed at a thick bruise.

She turned the dead man's head over slightly with her hand and inspected the mangled ear and the bruised face. "I guess he hit a tree when he went through a woods somewhere. The man was riding like crazy when he left my place," she said. She went back to her scrubbing with a look of professional indifference.

"True enough," Joseph Tilley muttered. "I guess he didn't even feel it. They say crazy people don't feel nothing."

She ignored him. Once she went to the door, carrying the bucket with its bloody water, and she commanded new to be brought. It was. She shut the door again. With the new water she set to work again. She got the wound thoroughly clean, and she even removed Mr. Bazely's cumbersome old shoes and washed his dirty feet. Looking about she spied a towel hanging over a crockery washbasin in a corner. She took the towel down from its peg, sniffed at it, and she was mildly astonished at how clean it was. With it she set to work again, carefully drying the corpse.

When she was done she combed the flaxen hair of the preacher straight back with her fingers. At the end he looked human again and in repose, though not even death could quite pacify his hard face.

Sarah Beckwith stepped back from her work and looked at Joseph Tilley. Little glistening beads of sweat were bulging out of her forehead. But there was a look of triumph in her face. She dried her hands methodically and gazed down at the body and pushed her long sleeves back into place. "It is up to you to wash the rest of him, Mr. Tilley," she said. He nodded again in deep respect. He was like an Old Testament prophet bending to the Word of God.

"He'll be clean all over," he said, repeating that slight but somehow profound inclination of his head.

"And you will get some decent clothes for him?" she said. "We can't bury him in those rags. He might have something better at his house. The clothes he preached in. Maybe we could find something here in town. After all he's done for these people you'd think somebody ought to have the clothes to bury him in."

"Yes ma'am," Joseph Tilley said.

"He must have a proper funeral. We'll need a preacher."

"I guess we can find one."

She fell into a reflective silence. "We must bury him by tomorrow," she said. "It's much too hot to wait longer than that."

"We could get him into the ground this afternoon." There was the slightest hint of rebellion in his voice.

"That would not be comely, Mr. Tilley. It'd be too soon."

"All right, Miss Sarah. Whatever you say. I'll do anything you want." His last resistance collapsed in a heap of affection.

Sarah Beckwith went on talking, measuring things out to herself. "But we need a preacher. Mr. Henck. He always spoke kindly of Mr. Bazely. I think he's at Kingston this week."

"I don't know, Miss Sarah."

"No matter. I'll see to it myself. Now . . ." She paused again, on the verge of a thought, and for a time neither of them said anything. In the close, hot silence of the room they heard the dull clangor of voices outside in the sun.

"Mr. Tilley, the body must lie in state," she said at last, almost in a whisper.

"What's that, ma'am?"

"People ought to come pay their respects. It's not fitting to bury him without that."

"I hadn't give it no thought," he said uneasily.

"He was a man of God. It's only right."

"You mean to watch over him all night? Well, there ain't no doubt about it, Miss Sarah. He's dead. You know the man's dead."

"It will be his last night above ground," she said in a preoccupied tone.

"That's true enough, Miss Sarah."

"If he had died in . . . in a normal way, we would have done as much for him."

"He sure didn't die in no normal way."

"He wasn't responsible, Mr. Tilley."

"I don't know nothing about things like that," Joseph Tilley said stubbornly.

"Well I do, Mr. Tilley. I know a great deal about things like that. We cannot disregard a man in death because in one moment he did an evil thing. We cannot judge a whole life because of one moment. The man had his reasons. We don't know what they were."

"Well, I guess we could stretch him out in here," Joseph Tilley said doubtfully. "I guess we could do that." The longer he thought about it, the more doubtful he became.

She looked around with distaste. The office was small, plain, and dismal. In some vague way its open yawn of bars made the room seem even more untidy and shabby. The whole place looked neglected and sad. Sarah Beckwith took it all in and shook her head. Then she made up her mind.

"You must bring him out to our place. That's all there is to it. He can lie in our parlor. I can do that much for him. He has meant so much for our family. It would be a farewell."

Joseph Tilley started again to protest. He even managed to get out a few period sentences in his clumsy, halfhearted fashion. He said there was no need. He said the man was plain crazy, that all this was too much trouble for somebody who had tried to kill two good men in cold blood. He said he thought Mrs. Beckwith was too *genteel* to get herself mixed up with anything like this. He said God and everybody else in the valley knew she was the best woman on earth, but this was really too much. It was just too much for her to bear.

But his efforts splintered against the granite of her mind. She kept coming back to her great conviction. The preacher was a man of God; he deserved a Christian burial. Joseph Tilley finally nodded in his uncomfortable resignation, and she left him and went back into the sunlight.

"Mr. Tilley will need some of you." She looked sternly around at the flock of curious men before the door. "Some of you go help him."

With that she went marching across the dusty street to the house of John Wesley Campbell, leaving in her wake a respectful drone of astonishment. Another loose tangle of men was on his steps and on his porch, and they took off hats and stood and nodded and mumbled reverential greetings to her as she swept up and through them. She did not give a sign of recognition in return. One of them rushed awkwardly forward and at the last minute pulled the door back for her. She strode through the opening, and lifting her skirts she went swiftly up the steps and was in the room where Mr. Campbell watched with his friend before he was aware of her presence.

Hub Delaney was still unconscious. She cast a brief look in his direction. Doc Cogill sat by the bed. Flies droned overhead, and from time to time Doc Cogill swept his hand over the recumbent form to clear them away. He looked up when she came in, and his eyebrows lifted in inquiry before he thought to rise himself. But he did rise, and the shuffle of motion roused John Wesley Campbell from his own deep contemplation of the river out the window to one side. He turned and found Sarah Beckwith facing him in a lordly, frigid calm.

But she spoke first to Doc Cogill.

"Doctor Cogill, I need to see Mr. Campbell alone."

Without a word the doctor looked first at one and then at the other and went out and shut the door behind him. She waited until she heard his steps descending on the stairs, his voice quietly ordering the seep of humanity up the stairs to descend with him. And then she turned to Mr. Campbell.

"And so we are the last ones left alive."

He nodded slightly. "Yes."

"I am grateful for what you did. Back then. I never had the chance to tell you."

"He was my friend."

Her voice was clear and cold, as if the words had been carved out of ice and tossed recklessly down into the melting day. His own was quite soft, and the edges of his words seemed worn down by memory as hard, as abrasive as impervious stone.

A profound and brooding cleft of silence opened between them for a moment. They gazed over it at one another, and something in her face relented. Her expression became one of sad relief. "I feel as though I had waked up from a long dream, a nightmare."

"I'm sure you do. Fifteen years. It's a long time to have a nightmare."

"They are bringing him to our house tonight, to lie for . . . for the viewing."

Mr. Campbell inclined slightly from the waist in something like acquiescence, and his eyes took on the glitter of a smile, though his lips were stern. "I suppose that is just. A fine mockery. Is it a mockery?"

She looked at him uncomfortably. "Perhaps it is. More a celebration, I think."

"Sam would have enjoyed that."

Her own face darkened. "Yes, he saw the comic side of things."

"He was a good man."

"I loved him," she said simply, and they were again silent.

Then she said, "I thought you might wish to come. I wanted to tell you that you would be welcome."

Mr. Campbell bowed again, very slightly, still with his eyes on hers, and still he did not say anything. She looked at him a moment longer. "I think we need a preacher for the funeral. I want . . . I want to end it in . . . in the right way."

"Whatever you wish."

"I think Mr. Henck is in Kingston this week. Could somebody go for him?"

"We could send a telegram through Knoxville. He'd get it sometime tonight."

"That would be very fine."

Once again she was silent, lost in her own thoughts. Then slowly and deliberately and with some embarrassment, she turned from him and fumbled in her dress. She undid a couple of buttons, retrieved something, did the buttons up again, and turned to face Mr. Campbell with a pistol in her hand. She held it out for him to take, and he did. "It was his," she said.

"The preacher's?"

"Yes. I . . . I took it away from him. He came to my house before he came here. He tried to do something terrible. I managed to get his gun and drive him away."

"I see."

"I told Mr. Tilley that I had locked him out. But that was not true." Her voice was quite strained.

"All right. You locked him outside."

"There are still two bullets in the gun." The strain became so intense that her voice almost broke.

Methodically Mr. Campbell broke the revolver down and checked the cylinder. He sniffed at it. "He shot at you?"

"No, I shot at him."

He said nothing, stood slightly weighing the old weapon in his hand, looking down at it.

"I saved the last two bullets. I wanted to be sure there were two left."

Still Mr. Campbell said nothing, but he looked inquiringly up at her.

"You will come tonight?" she asked.

"Probably. I'll have to think about it."

She turned as if to go.

"I am curious about one thing. Who were the two bullets for?"

She flung a majestic look of pride back at him. "One would have been for him. The other for myself."

"That would have been too much."

"I will do anything to save my son, Mr. Campbell." She spoke with unshakable force.

"Bazely was crazy, Sarah. It would have been a bad thing to give your life for him. A very bad thing."

"It doesn't matter now."

He looked soberly at her. "Two deaths just in the nick of time. You will forgive me for saying this, Sarah, but it strikes me that death has brought you luck."

Her eyes did not waver. "Perhaps there is a God, John." With that she did turn quickly away and pushed through the door. Holding her skirts above her shoes, she descended the stairs. Mr. Campbell stood pondering until he heard the small commotion she made as the crowd at the foot of the steps parted to let her go by. Then he went over to his front window and looked down, watched her stately progress to her horse through the motley conglomeration of the curious.

He heard Doc Cogill come wheezing upstairs. Very quietly he went to the chest of drawers in the corner and put the pistol away.

Overhead the steamy blue sky was darkening slowly to a coppery indigo. In the street below the crowd circulated aimlessly, and anxious faces inspected the changing light. The dull chatter of voices crunched on, but there was an indescribable hush over all that sound. In the midst of the tense throng a single word passed gingerly back and forth like something too delicate and precious to be spoken carelessly. The word—*Rain*.

22

IT WAS PAST TWO O'CLOCK when Brian Ledbetter left the Weavers and began his solitary ride back home. He had not stayed long. He was uncomfortable staying, and he was having a hard time making up his mind about what he wanted to do. All morning he had been playing idly around with a shining heap of dreams and speculations, and now it was speculation no longer. Something had to be done, and he wanted to get off to himself and decide what that should be.

Only he couldn't keep his mind straight. He was drowsy from all he had eaten. His large body rocked lethargically with the motion of the horse, and he could hardly keep his eyes open. The heat had grown more heavy with the ponderous accumulation of the day itself.

They had heard the first crack of thunder. He was just getting off his horse in the Weaver yard when it came pealing across the parching land like a giant broken bell flung down a stairway in the sky. It flattened everyone into silence, even the children. Evelyn Weaver, who had come out into the yard to reproach them for their tardiness, looked up in an anguish of longing. She forgot all the harsh words she had stored up for their arrival. "It's thunder!" she cried. "Rain! Hallelujah! Dear Jesus, help it to rain!"

Brian was pretty well shaken up by the thunder himself. For a moment he almost went jumping around the yard in his excitement. But he held on to his presence of mind and managed to shake his head as glumly as he could. One of the first articles of his faith was that everybody should be pessimistic about the weather. His pessimism was a sort of reverence, and he refused to violate it now though the thunder made his heart beat fast and set him to searching the sky. "Probably nothing but heat lightning," he said. "Lord knows it's hot enough for it. It probably don't mean a thing."

And he seemed to be right. The great glassy stillness of the day returned. They ate their meal in relative silence. They kept straining at the sounds outside, but they heard no more thunder. Finally, as he was grumpily thanking her for the dinner and saying it wasn't the worst one he had ever eaten, Evelyn Weaver addressed him formally: "Mister Ledbetter, I've got a crowd of boys to raise. I'm going to be needing me a man to help out with the raising. If you got anything you want to say to me you'd better say it in the next day or two."

Brian was embarrassed, and he felt that sharp, hard prick of reality plunge like a dagger through his candy thoughts. He dropped his eyes and felt his face grow hot and hoped she wouldn't see that in the shadow of his hatbrim. But he supposed Evelyn Weaver saw everything. He managed to mutter something about not rushing in where angels fear to tread, vaguely recalling something about the hostility of angels to matrimony. For some reason Evelyn Weaver took offense at that homely piece of wisdom. "Don't you go quoting books at me," she exclaimed. "This here's serious business!" And he rode off feeling that she was irritated with him.

So he went on his way with his poor mind all in a muddle and his body sleepy and so uncomfortable that he hated the motion he made in response to the swaying of his horse. His belly was heavy from drinking so much water, and he could hear water sloshing around inside him as the horse's steps jarred his stomach. In spite of all that he was thirsty again before he had gone a mile. He stank. The ripe stink of his body was foul and overpowering even to himself, and when things got *that* bad, my God they were bad! His skin was clammy and irritated under the scrape of his fetid clothes. He didn't think he could bear to go on living except that it was so much trouble to die. He glanced up at the sky, thought it might be changing, prayed that rain would come, and for a little while he even dared to hope. But with his mounting discomfort his hope died.

So he dozed miserably in the saddle, and his mind turned over and over like a wheel spinning in space, and memory flitted against the present, and he measured out the value of land and licked his lips over the muscular ripeness of the body of Evelyn Weaver. He was older than she was. That really did not matter much. He was strong, and he had a good lot of years left. (That thought seemed so monstrously presumptuous that it frightened him, and he said aloud, "The Good Lord willing." Said it in frightened haste.)

Maybe he drank a little too much. That could shorten a man's days. Maybe after all these years he had had enough of sitting with the stone jug on the platform of the railroad station with his friends. Maybe he had taken enough long trips home in the lonely night to fall into his solitary bed and to dream his absurdly melancholy dreams. Maybe he had had enough nigger whores, enough of their ritual passion, their bored yawning in the loveless dark. Maybe . . .

Oh God, how could he live in his heat! He could feel the itching sweat running around the place where his wooden peg was bound to his knee, and his tender skin smarted under the smooth leather straps which held it in place. When he bent to claw at it his fingernails only slipped under the sopping leather and he did himself no good at all. He pulled his hands away from any exposed patch of his skin and they were slimy with sweat and filth, and the only way to take the dust was to surrender to it and let it do its damnedest.

And perhaps he was thinking of surrender to the dust because surrender was on his mind. For, in a way, that is what it would be. It made no real sense to him, not in the whole run of his life. It made no sense at all to think that he had fought so hard in the War, had given up a part of himself, and now stood poised to marry a woman who thought what he had done was foolish and sinful. A woman who was willing to *forgive* him for the one thing in his life in which he took honest pride. Brian Ledbetter took a great many pains to assure everybody that the War was fought a long time ago, and that now people had to get on with the real business of life, which wasn't killing but living. He could always be counted on to nod in great piety whenever anyone mentioned forgetting the past.

But he could also be counted on to swell with unsuppressed glory whenever he heard a Fourth of July speaker tell men like himself what they had done when they saved the Union. Well, what *had* they done? Damned if he could tell sometimes. And what was he doing, thinking about marrying a woman who would never in his life admit that he had had a cause worth losing a leg for? And *was* the cause worth a leg? For the life of him Brian couldn't see much real difference in the way things had been before the War and the way they were now. There *must* be some sense to the way things had fallen out. If he could not see it, it was because he wasn't very bright, and he was resigned to his stupidity about things. The same way he was resigned to his wooden leg. But it did bother him. It bothered him one hell of a lot. If he married

Evelyn Weaver, he kept thinking, he would be just another man taking a woman to wife, and things like that happened every day. His past, her past, didn't really mean a damned thing in the long run of the world. It was like the oats. The War didn't matter. You could forget all about the War and harvest oats just fine, and marriage could be the same way. Except that the War did matter to Brian Ledbetter because he had been willing to give his life in the War, and he had ended by giving up a leg, and even after twenty years he missed the leg in the way that you might miss an old and dear friend.

My God! Could anybody on earth make sense out of it all? All so twisted and fearful and strange? He sniffed at the air, squinted against the dazzling waves of heat rolling upward off the land, and he thought. A sleepy, rambling thinking. The wheel turning lazily in space and shining with memory. The binding of sensations from out of the past with sensations now. Antietam, Gettysburg, the Wilderness.

He still thought of a dead squirrel he lay next to once in the Wilderness. There were lots of dead animals then, the garbage of battle. Birds littered the churned ground in feathery lumps of bright color. The fallen green branches of trees. And this single dead squirrel with the blood in his mouth, white belly upturned. Victim of the strange war, of men fighting in the Wilderness and burning the Wilderness over the wild things that lived there. And died there. What sense did the squirrel's death make? But men were different from squirrels. Wasn't the squirrel's death a different kind of death from the death of men who fell on the same ground that day? He was afraid of what the answer to that question might be.

He had been terribly afraid during the War. Fear was for him a hot wind rising violently in the fiery moments of those days. With the cooling years it had blown away until now it hung like a distant cloud, silent and gray, hardly bigger than a man's hand before the confused recollections of uncounted days at war. It was one of his more rational memories that he had been afraid. And at the time the fear made him hate the people who had brought all this bloodiness on the world, the people responsible for making him afraid. People like the kin of Evelyn Weaver.

It was strange how the fear settled on him at different times in different ways, the things it made him think. Oddly enough his most fearful time was not that morning at Cold Harbor, when he believed he was dying and his whole body was pain, when the great numb chill of shock came creeping upward from his mangled foot. It hurt too much to think. He could not even organize his thoughts enough to fear death. There was the rather bizarre rational conviction that this was the end. Behind that only the raw, red hurt.

At other times he was more afraid when he was more calm. At Gettysburg, for example. Then he lay for a long day and half behind a little rock wall and looked across the sunny fields to the gloomy line of trees where the enemy lay concealed. He lay in a nest of tranquility while he heard the battle crashing on the distant extremities of the Federal line, and he was so frightened of death that he could hardly talk.

He wondered then if anyone were copulating in the town nearby. It was not a particularly obscene thought. He just had a mind for incongruities. He was a man who thought about rolling craps across a church floor when the preacher was raising hell against gambling. Or else he thought of delivering himself of a long, windy fart in the midst of a formal wedding. And once in Washington City when he saw a beautiful girl lift her perfumed hand for her escort to kiss, Brian seriously thought of running over and biting it. So in his terrible fear he wondered if some frightened couple just might be copulating like mad in Gettysburg while all around people were getting killed.

He hoped that it was so, and he ruminated quietly and hoped in a sardonic way that fear drove many a solid prick into the warm receptacle prepared by a wise God who sure as hell knew what He was doing when He created woman. And at the same time Brian Ledbetter seethed in quiet hatred at all the people who had got him into this war and onto such frantic hopes. He lay there longing for peace and retribution.

At night at Gettysburg while he lay behind the wall, the stars were out by the thousands. They shone dully through the humid atmosphere, glittering nailheads of light hammered across the frame of the universe. It gave him a still feeling. He supposed that if he could ascend in an observation balloon, cut the heavy moorings and drift, he would rise to a cool and untroubled silence. Then the world below would fall away without a trace, and he would follow the winds and the clouds to some place where he would never be shot at again. But in those dreamy reveries he was startled by the thought that perhaps his mind had described death. Perhaps it was a premonition. Calling the peace "death" made him afraid. And it was with fear choking him like a thin wire that he fell off at last to sleep.

In the mornings when he awoke at Gettysburg, the mist shrouded the earth. The trees across the hostile fields were scarcely visible. The armies were not visible at all. Then it was as if the world were empty, and Brian felt that he might rise and go walking over the little hill by the cemetery and come down into the sleepy village and find his breakfast somewhere and go on, into the summery farmland, to find his peace.

He saw the mist on nearly every warm morning of the War. To most men, and even to himself most of the time, the mist was nothing more than a nuisance which gave him rheumatism. But on some days the mist seemed to be something else, and he could never quite fathom what it was. When he saw it, and the world rising out of it, it was like being near to God at the creation of heaven and earth. When the mist was heavy and impenetrable, everything was dimmed to likeness. Sounds were muted. The whole world was a soft, intangible thing in which all confusion was absorbed into one grand presence clothed with an infinite serenity. But as the mist rose, trees disengaged themselves from it. Shadowy forms assumed a vague, translucent reality, which with the streaming light turned hard and firm before his eyes and reassured him of his own life and the life of the world he thought he knew. Then the day passed. The night came down. The mist rose up from the ground and silently covered the earth, and it was all to do over again. A new day, hardly distinguishable from the one just past, lay in the womb of the mist and waited to be born. Gettysburg came and went. The War came and went. Brian Ledbetter came home, and things were just as they had been for him except that he was a little older, and he had lost a leg. A part of himself he knew as a child gone forever, he thought in that mawkishly sentimental way of his. Now he was a lot older, and the War—gigantic and terrible as it was—had fallen into the swamp of time and lay almost buried in a creeping muck of days, dull edges gleaming briefly and vanishing in the mists of years. Now Evelyn Weaver came sweeping over all that and made it more unreal, more indistinct.

It was all veiled in mist—his life, the life of the world, a confused tangle of things hidden under ignorance and somehow giving birth to something hard and solid—and fleeting. A mystery of white and silent awe, coming, going, coming again. Could he believe that out of Gettysburg, something *good* had come? Had his fight meant anything at all? And if so, what . . .

"There's something in it," he muttered firmly to himself and thought of Gettysburg and dead comrades and wondered how Evelyn Weaver looked naked in lamplight on a clean bed, and in his head he did idle sums of land and measured the growth of children and . . . and a certain *place* in the world. He squinted down the road and wiped the sweat out of his eyes with a hand. Was he disloyal . . . Was there such a thing as loyalty—or disloyalty—to dead men?

By God, there has to be something to it. Or did there? Gettysburg, the rushing, shouting men, and the thud of mortal resistance when a man leaps over a wall onto the exploding muzzle of a rifle and dies vomiting blood in your face! A purpose for a solitary leg, lost, buried, and rotted by now in some moldering heap of severed limbs, somewhere north? A purpose to this wide world of confusion and death? God . . . in the violence? Was this all the purpose there was?

He rode on through a place where the fields lay spread out under the sun and bordered by woods lying distantly on each side of the road. The road was a rusty streak, running through gold and green, oats, wheat, and standing corn—all muted with layers of dust—to the first trees, heavier green and silent. Much farther beyond lay the mountains, wreathed in their blue haze and blending almost with the sky, eternal and dreadfully still in the rich light of the afternoon sun.

Ahead the road climbed and curved over a crest of hillside. Here he stopped, and he could look south, down the valley. The sight instantly shattered his meditations, dissolved his memories, and brought him exulting to the present! For he could look across the still land to the horizon and see the heavy line of black cloud coming on and widening with each moment that he watched. He saw the jagged bursts of lightning spouting out of the storm. And here in this exposed place he heard the thunder distantly boom, reverberate, recede, grumble, and boom again.

Beneath the clouds he could see the shaking gray curtain of the rain.

He laughed aloud. He shouted his laughter. He kicked the horse violently with good leg and bad and howled with mirth, and the animal broke into a dusty gallop.

"By God!" he shouted. "By God, I'll *marry* her! Damned if I won't *marry* her!"

He kicked his horse again, and together they hurtled down the hillside in a tumult of dust and raucous joy, galloping full speed toward the coming rain.

23

THE RAIN SWEPT IN on the land like some huge enveloping thing, made of darkness. It came on from the south and was preceded by a blowing of wind. The wind, gusty and strong, pitched a hail of dust swirling into the air from the parched earth. In Bourbonville people scattered before the stinging dust in spasms of coughing, snatched at hats, often futilely, and turned their backs hunching against the wind and wanted to cry out with joy. Many chased hats which went spinning and rolling drunkenly down the wind and the dust, and they shouted obscenities and laughed and cursed in wild happiness as they ran.

Behind the first blast of wind came a thin, advance line of heavy raindrops. Falling into the streets and the fields they raised thousands of spumes of dust, and rolling across the dry rooftops they made a brittle crepitation like the passing of a ghostly troop of cavalry through the air. And then a perfect calm.

Calm, and the rich, sweet, pungent smell of nearby rain, soaking the atmosphere. Overhead, black and mysterious clouds raced to cover the last smears of blue sky, and down the storm the lightning split the darkness from top to bottom in dancing, angular lines of dazzling fire. Beneath the coming storm and the angry lightning, the tiny configurations of forest, dwelling, and field huddled on the waiting earth, shrunk to a terrible insignificance by the mighty clouds. And toward the heart of the storm the clouds came on so black that in looking at them some men lost the first mad joy they had felt and were possessed by a primitive and unspeakable awe. There were many in Bourbonville and in the valley at that moment who thought Mr. Simson had sent this storm blowing on them out of the pit of hell.

In the fields beyond town the first wind drove long waves rolling wildly across the crests of the oats and the wheat. But in its wake they snapped up again and became as still as stone. The corn, after a violent flailing of its slim leaves, stood likewise erect. The trees in the woods stood motionless against the lowering sky, and the green foliage was suffused with an eerie light.

Some children who looked out of windows into the strange vacuity of that moment never forgot it. Looking out their windows onto other storms, they would search for that fantastic green, expecting to die if they saw it again, or perhaps to reverse the processes of time. A wondrous, pregnant and shining green which meant something. They never knew what.

The calm passed quickly away. Then the storm burst in all its fury. The rain came rushing down in a torrent so dense that Mr. Campbell, looking out the window of his bedroom towards the jailhouse, saw that building slowly lose its definition and dissolve into a dull, watery reflection of itself which, with a blinking of his eyes, might vanish utterly away. The dust on the ground was drenched and pounded almost instantly to mud. At first an occasional straggler went splashing by. Dark, hurrying forms, indistinct in the gray rain. But soon the streets were deserted. The water carved channels for itself and raced torrentially along them, showing a dull gleaming to the raging sky. Men clustered on porches of houses and stores, wherever there was shelter, and thick knots of them hovered in the arched brick entryways to the courthouse and watched the rain roar down. Some stood with dripping clothes plastered to their skins and shook themselves with great energy and pushed soaked hair out of their faces, and some laughed and yelled at each other over the tumult of the storm, and some were so absorbed by the sight of the rain that they could only look at it in silence which was almost a spell.

The thunder crashed like doom rung down a thousand times. The blue lightning hurled its giddy bolts through the black clouds, and in its wildly quaking light solid things became lurid silhouettes, unreal projections of themselves. The lightning was so violent and the thunder so loud that people cringed before the blasts even as some hooted at each other for their cringing. But they all knew well enough that lightning could kill. And then it did strike a tree near the courthouse with a splintering crash so grand that the loudest of the hooters went silent. It was a blinding thing, and some who happened to be looking at that tree in that moment thought they had been struck themselves, and they mistook the darting blackness in their eyes for death. But when their vision cleared they could see the tree, a giant, full oak, still shivering under the deadly blast, showing a long white streak of fresh-broken wood open in its dark trunk all the way to the ground. The boards from the dismantled scaffold were stacked nearby, and there were some who saw great significance in the fact that the split in the struck tree seemed to point to the center of the earth.

Hub Delaney stirred drowsily to semiconsciousness at the noise of the thunder. He thought he was at war again. He thought the thunder was cannon fire and the storm was battle. Doc Cogill took him tenderly by the shoulders and soothed him like a child. "It's rain, Hub. Nothing but rain. Take it easy. Easy." And Hub lay back and tumbled off to sleep again. The doctor's eyes met Mr. Campbell's across the bed, and they smiled grimly at each other, and the storm went on beating at the windowpanes and picked up in its frenzy. Throughout the valley the wind blew with such furious power that the rain threatened to shatter the window glass, and mothers gathered frightened children to themselves and looked fearfully at their ceilings and wondered if their houses would hold. All creation was a shriek of unbearable sound.

The laughing and the yelling had everywhere stopped by now. Joseph Tilley sat with a couple of men in the dim light of the jailhouse office with the preacher's corpse. Mr. Bazely was cleaned and dressed to a string tie deftly threaded through the collar above his shirt. Mr. Campbell had unaccountably provided a suit for the preacher—a puzzling and wasteful gesture to the thrifty mind of Joseph Tilley. When the lightning burst outside, it seemed to make every still thing in the room leap up. Mr. Bazely's body appeared to start on its cot, his sharp face to twitch in the furor of electric shadows. The living had no doubt that he was dead. Rigor mortis had set in. Joseph Tilley and his helpers were at some pains to work the clothes onto the stiffening limbs. But the lightning gave a hideous life to that vindictive face, and the living kept their eyes averted from him. They said little to each other except to comment on some particularly violent clap of thunder. Through the dirty barred window of the jailhouse they glumly watched the storm and felt the stout building tremble in the raging wind.

In the countryside and down the valley the rain was hammering away. The oats could not resist the storm. The tall stalks bent beneath the unceasing downpour, bent and matted together, the hard wind blew inexorably at the brittle ears, and the rain threshed the grain from the mangled stalks and littered the ground with it. A sprinkling of golden drops over the turbulent mud. Farmers who had welcomed the storm now stood moodily at windows with hands thrust deeply into pockets and gave the oats up for lost. And the wheat. But at least the corn would be saved, and that was something. There would be pasture for the stock, hay for winter, and now the springs would live again, and so the rain was good. Too bad about the oats. The wheat. The farmers felt a formal grief for them, felt also something of the dull frustration farmers always feel in their eternal patient combat with weather. But this rain would not be a disaster unless the storm blew the houses down. And as the wind sucked and blew hysterically at the rooftops and jarred the window frames, the farmers wondered about that and made their deliberate calculations about what they would do if the gale did its worst.

In the woods the rising wind tore implacably at the trees, and in the forest there was a grinding and a tearing of wood as branches were ripped out of their sockets and sent crashing to the earth in a tumble of shivering leaves. And Samuel Beckwith, Jr., who had finally gone out in search of his mother before the storm found himself assailed by the suffocating wind and the unrelenting deluge of rain, and his horse was frightened almost beyond control by the flying debris from the forest. So he rode blindly for shelter, the first shelter he could find. And because he was on his way to the preacher's house, that first shelter was the shanty of Beckinridge Bourbon, to which he came, soaked through and all out of breath, and found not only refuge but the nigger slouched at the single table over a stone crock of whisky and glaring at him with yellow eyes from a face which, in the galloping bursts of lightning, Samuel Beckwith, Jr., recognized to be the face of death.

But farther down the valley Brian Elisha Ledbetter brought his horse gleefully into the barn and turned then himself and went tramping up through the gummy mud to his house and let the rain run down to his skin, and when the lightning exploded around him with its deafening thunder he yelled back at it and cried aloud with joy. Arrived before his door he took happy stock of his drenched clothing and his waterlogged shoe, and on a sudden plunging fit of inspiration he tore off the shoe and one by one stripped off the articles of his clothing and threw them down into the rain and stood at last clad only in the peg and its straps and put his face into the wind and laughed at it, howled drunkenly at it, and stretched his naked arms to the furious skies and thanked his God.

And in the great old house of the Crittendons, Sarah Crittendon Beckwith stood by the window near the picture of her husband and watched the unnatural darkness of the storm deepen over the land. She had arrived inside the house all wet and dripping. She saw at once that the windows had been shut, and from that she knew that Sam had been home. Her note was gone. But when she called there was no answer, and she was anxious for him. Yet she had been glad that for the moment she did not have to talk. And so she had changed her clothes for the second time that day, and on an impulse out of her secret longings she had dug down into an old cedar trunk and brought up not her customary black but a dress of her youth, faded lavender, smelling of mustiness, long and clinging—a party dress for parties of a bygone time. This she put on with a peculiar pleasure, perhaps that pleasure which arises from the sight of old ruins in an unexpected place, but something more than that. The air within the house was sultry and still, and as the rain cooled the outside, a thin glaze of condensed moisture formed over the window glass. The house shook in a subdued trembling under the repeated blows of the wind, and the wind itself cried around the corners and under the eaves of the roof and sobbed in the washing rain like the ghosts of the unredeemed dead. From her fund of history she recalled that Edward the Confessor had had himself buried under the guttering of his cathedral so that the rains might purge his bones of their sins. She stood quite alone with her thoughts. She felt cleansed and free.

And in the middle of her small parlor Evelyn Weaver sat on the floor with her little troop of boys huddled around her. She was singing them a lullaby. When the lightning blasted down nearby, her voice did not waver a single note. Clyde whimpered on her lap, frightened by the incomprehensible din outside. And with each sudden thunderclap all the children except Virgil pushed against her for safety. Virgil sat hugging his knees with his arms. When the lightning and the thunder and the wind banged the loudest, he only hugged his knees the harder and shut his eyes. All the while the serene, clear lullaby of Evelyn Weaver went on. She sang of angels and the Baby Jesus. She sang of children and paradise. She sang of the Lily of the Valley. And Clyde stopped his whimpering. Even as the storm went on building, he slept in her arms. The other children listened to the constant, invincible voice of their mother, and eventually, almost with reluctance, Virgil put his head against her and thought of his father's grave and wondered if

24

FOR A LONG TIME Sam sat in a hard chair before the fireplace and listened to the howling of the storm. There was no fire, and the hollow fireplace looked like the gaping mouth of something sick, something about to vomit, and it made the fetid room look more squalid and forlorn. An aroma of bitter decay saturated the air. A dank, unpleasant mustiness released by the pounding rain and stirred in drafts through the cabin by the shifting wind.

Outside the storm beat furiously in the trees and on the roof. Gradually the ancient shingles began to leak, and long, attenuated streaks of water fell glistening in the murky dusk. The leaking droplets fell with a soft, irregular pattering into the plank flooring. It was a distinct, gentle, and uncanny sound. Behind it and above it the shrill cry of the storm went on.

Beckinridge sat perfectly still. He had not moved since he let Sam in. He had not spoken a word, even as he opened the door. He simply looked blankly at the youth, heard his urgent plea for shelter, and made grudging way for him. Now he crouched over the stone crock and glared at his visitor. His yellow eyes snapped open and shut. The eyes were the only thing about him that seemed alive. All the rest of him appeared fixed in a skeletal frame of death.

Sam was uneasy. Each time he looked up the black's yellow eyes were clamped on him. He was irritated with himself for his qualms. He tried a couple of times to smile. He muttered something about being grateful to Beckinridge for getting the cow moving in the morning. He made some remarks about the storm. How violent it was. How it had nearly sucked the breath out of him. He was trying to be companionable, even friendly. But his words came out unnaturally harsh and nervous. Everything he said sank before the black's impassive scrutiny. Finally he stopped trying. He fell silent himself and resolved to wait the storm out and to go as soon as it was gone.

In the meantime he studied the cabin and its lone inhabitant. Beckinridge was dying. At first the youth thought he was merely drunk, and he was irritated at the slovenly habits which could make any man drunk in the middle of the afternoon, especially a nigger. As he went on thoughtfully gazing at the black, he concluded that Beckinridge was indeed drunk in a morose, silent sort of way, but there was something else. The working of alcohol had loosened the grasp on life in the black's face, letting it fall slack and revealing death lurking behind the membranous skin. Only the eyes held out. The thick bruise still showed on the otherwise emaciated face, the mark of the beating from the day before. The rest of Beckinridge looked incapable of supporting life. *He might die now, while I'm here!*

The thought was unsettling. To be here in this dingy light, with a corpse, in this storm, in this rotting shack. He tried to throw off the foolish uneasiness. But he could not. All the energy of the black's life seemed to be compressed in those blinking eyelids over the sick yellow eyes. All his vital force concentrated in making them flick open, shut, open, shut. If that minute strength failed, then the man would die. Sam found himself watching the eyes of the black with a terrible expectancy.

It slowly dawned on him that he was just a little afraid of Beckinridge. He had never been afraid of Negroes. He knew some people feared them. He thought his mother did. Of course she would never admit to being afraid of anything. But he had certainly not been afraid of blacks, especially not of Beckinridge Bourbon.

Long ago, after Sam's father died and before he could do the work himself, Beckinridge and Jackson Bourbon had hired themselves out to work the Crittendon place. They labored in the fields with old George. Toiled in staid lethargy with the slow rhythmic motions habitual to blacks. Three of them to do the work Sam did mostly by himself now. But they did keep the farm going until Sam got old enough to run things.

It was a sort of charity, his mother said in a self-satisfied way. She liked to say that without her a lot of blacks would have gone hungry after the War. Considering the way they had abandoned her when the Yankee Army came, the recollection of her own kindness to some of them gave her a lot of pleasure. It was like heaping coals of fire on their heads, said she, citing the Bible. She was fair with them. She gave them work and food, and at the end of the year when something of the crop was sold, they even got a little money. "They got one good drunk a year out of my purse," she said with rueful mirth.

Sam had to stop hiring Beckinridge. There were others blacks stronger and more willing to work. Beckinridge always looked as if he were slouching around trying to evade something. But the main thing was that he really wasn't healthy enough to do a hard day's work, and Sam considered things carefully and stopped hiring him.

Beckinridge didn't seem to mind. He merely shrugged and went shuffling off in the spring day without a word. That had been the last time Sam had spoken to him until this morning with the cow. It went to show that a black didn't really care anything about work, his mother said, for Beckinridge seemed indifferent to the whole business. And now it irritated Sam to think he was just a little afraid, here alone with a black he had so easily dismissed and scorned. The nearness of death added something to the man. Sam felt disagreeable and uncomfortable about it, and he was a little ashamed at that tiny sharp blade of fear which the black's blinking eyes worked around in his guts.

So finally he turned on Beckinridge and said, "We need a fire. I guess you're too drunk to build one."

The black said nothing.

"Well, goddam it, is there some wood? Can I build a fire myself?"

Nothing.

"Lord!" Sam said in exasperation. In the shelter of the dilapidated porch roof, he found some scrawny logs, some fragments of branches and a few sticks. Near the bed with its litter of filthy blankets there was a cheap tin lamp. When Sam picked it up and shook it he felt the heavy slosh of kerosene. He unscrewed the cap and poured what kerosene there was onto the wood. He struck fire to it, and the flame jumped up with a whoosh. In a moment the room was saturated with the strong smell of oily burning. Sam turned his back to the fire and felt the heat begin to work through his wet clothes to his chilled skin. Outside the rain went on in a flat, unwavering roar, and occasionally a vagrant draft swept down the chimney and blew the smoke out into the room so that his eyes smarted. But he was beginning to dry out, and he looked down at Beckinridge with more equanimity.

The black had shifted his eyes to follow him. Otherwise he had not moved. Sam spoke apologetically. "I'm sorry I spoke to you that way." He stopped. The apology died. He felt uncomfortable excusing himself to a black. It was a little like calling him "Sir" or letting him go first through a door. Besides, the apology kindled something in Beckinridge's raw eyes. Something that looked very much like the hatred he had flung at the cow in the morning. "I'll tell you why I was out in the rain. My mother left me a note. Something about the preacher. I'm sure she must have meant Preacher Bazely. She said she was coming to see about him. I'm wondering if you saw her go by here. She would have had to pass here to get to his house. Did you see her?"

At the direct question Beckinridge shook his head slowly. He still said nothing. All the time his yellow eyes did not leave Sam's face. All the while the thing kindled by the fumbling attempt at apology kept on burning there.

"You don't think you might have missed her?"

Beckinridge shook his head again. Sam looked at him doubtfully. "I guess everything's all right," he said in a tone of self-assurance.

Nothing.

But Sam was worried. Things were not adding up. All the combinations he put together in his head totaled perplextiy. He turned to expose his clothing more uniformly to the fire. He looked over at the bed again, wondered with revulsion how anybody could sleep in it, imagined the vermin swarming in the filthy blankets, thought abruptly that someone had died in it and only hours ago.

"I guess you feel bad about your father," Sam said in a sudden rush of sympathy. "He died right here, didn't he? Too bad. My father died in bed. But I guess you know that. I was too young to remember him very well. Still it was hard. I remember missing him for a long time."

"I liked your pappy. He brung us ground hog and squirrel onct in a while."

After the sullen quiet of the black the voice was unexpected. Sam turned jerkily around. The expression on Beckinridge's face had not changed. He still sat like a man gathering the last vestiges of his pitiful strength so that he might have the force to die.

"Oh, did he? I didn't know that. Nobody ever told me that." He shrugged his shoulders and felt vaguely that he was making too much of a trivial fact. "Not that anybody *should* have . . . I mean, well, I didn't know." He looked curiously at Beckinridge. But for the moment the black did not seem inclined to say anything more.

The fire blazed over the wood. It crackled in the fireplace and made a low and persistent noise against the steady drumming of the rain. By now the thunder and the lightning had begun to depart up the valley. But the wind kept its mouth at the chimney, and the fire rose and sank and flared again and sent liquid shadows spurting over the floor to splash soundlessly against the dark walls. The firelight, reaching out into the gloom, touched the black's face and made pools of dark reflection in his skin, and the flames showed in his eyes as if in tiny yellow mirrors.

"He brung us rabbit sometimes, too. And he come down here onct, and he eat some rabbit stew my pappy fixed up for him. He was sure big on rabbit stew, that man. He sure love to eat. And he was the onliest white man that ever eat in this house. He was the onliest one. My pappy think he the greatest man on this earth."

The voice was a level monotone, barely audible above the rain. Sam strained to catch the words. He was annoyed in the same vague way he had been afraid. There was so much he had not known, and in two days so much was dumped out on him that he could hardly take it all in. He had never connected his father and this place, never tied him in any remote way to this decaying shack with its slovenly inhabitants and the reek of filth and rot. Once again, as on the day before with other blacks, he looked dumbly at a place where his father had been and left a memory, and he saw it all with a strange wondering. The old forms became new and significant in a way that seemed just beyond his power to understand.

His eyes rose to the moldering roof beams sagging overhead in the damp gloom, and all the room made a vessel which, he thought, *must* preserve some fragile remnant of the moment of life it had embraced on a day long ago. His father at that table. Jackson Bourbon bending happily over him and wringing his black hands with pleasure. A pot bubbling in this fireplace. Laughter. And another form nearby. Beckinridge. Much younger. A child? Surely a little child. It struck Sam that he did not really know how old Beckinridge was. Younger than he looked, no doubt. And not old then. Looking on shyly, maybe suspiciously and even with fear, at the strange thing—the white man happily eating with niggers—which now he recalled in the same place and long afterward and over a vortex of change, a memory with the force to break the charm of silence over a dying man and make him speak into a storm.

Something within Sam wrestled with time. He struggled with the invisible river. But it rushed over him, and in its silent current he could sense a bubbling of mockery. His father was dead. His father was dead. The elder Samuel Beckwith would never laugh again. Never eat rabbit. Never ride. Never hunt. Never come to this miserable place again. Never smell its enwrapping odor of wet wood rotting, of oily fire, of bitter smoke. Never hear the tapping of water droplets against a floor of moldering wood. Never hear the rain, the crooning of wind against the chimney. Never. Never. Nothing was left here of the elder Samuel Beckwith. Nothing except the dull memory of a black who would soon die and bear even that remnant off into the dust where Sam's father had gone.

"I never knew he was here."

And Beckinridge with a languorous bubbling of words sticky with phlegm said: "He come here lots of time. Sometime with Mr. Campbell. Sometime by hisself."

Sam looked morosely around and said nothing.

"Everybody know your pappy. Everybody in the hereabout."

"I know. I mean it seems that way. He must have had a good nature."

"Your pappy was good to niggers. He never done nobody no harm. Nobody in this world."

There was something more in Beckinridge's voice than the words, and Sam looked at him curiously, still without speaking, still with his heavy, wordless thoughts.

"You pappy ain't like you mammy. He lots different than you mammy. All the niggers know how different you pappy is than you mammy."

There was the faintest of insinuations in the remark. Sam narrowed his eyes at him. But the black refused to cower and went on blinking in that quick, intense way out of his dead face, and Sam felt uncomfortable and did not know what to make of it.

"You member the snake?" Beckinridge asked in easy languor.

The youth nodded. "Yes, I remember." His voice was subdued.

"I never forget Mr. Snake."

"You shouldn't hold that against my mother."

Beckinridge laughed. The evil laughter surprised Sam and made him more afraid than anything else that had happened that day. It was an almost noiseless chortling, made mostly of hissing noises, and was as unpleasant as laughter could be. "Lawd, boy, I ain't going to hold no *snake* gainst you mammy! I wouldn't do nothing like *that,* white boy. Not no snake gainst a white woman!"

Again the mocking hint of an insinuation so slight that Sam

could not really reply to it with any dignity. "I meant you should not hold against her what . . . The thing she did. She was frightened. You startled her."

Beckinridge stopped his chortling, and his shriveled face took on an abrupt, malevolent gravity. "Oh, I knows that. She don't want no snake round her boy."

"I was the only thing she had then. It's like you and your daddy. You were all he had, and I was all my mother had."

"You was all you mammy have!" Beckinridge repeated the thought with a solicitude which was disagreeable.

"Yes, you see . . ." The youth started to explain in an apologetic way all the hopes his mother had vested in him, but the idea became silly even as he thought about it, and he fell silent.

Beckinridge nodded like a snake bobbing before a baby chicken. "I knows just what you means, white boy. You mammy break off a switch and thrash me for bringing Mr. Snake into the yard. My pappy tell her I don't mean no harm. But she thrash me anyhow, and she call me a nigger fool."

"I remember," Sam said. He wished Beckinridge would stop.

"I'm real proud of that snake. I pick him up under a tree, real fast, before he can move, and I think folks gonter say how big I is to pick him up. He just a blacksnake. But you mammy scream. Lawd, she *scream!* And she made my pappy kill him right quick with a hoe, and then she call me up. 'Boy! You, boy! You come here. You come here this minute!' " The black's imitation of his mother was excruciating.

"I remember how it was," Sam said. "You don't have to go on."

"And all that time she's pulling a switch offen one of them bushes and stripping the leaves to make it hurt more, and I'm scairt, and I say I'm sure sorry. And I'm crying. I'm crying something awful, but it don't do no good with your mammy. I say I'm *awful* sorry. But she whip me anyway. She whip me till she's tired, and my pappy stand there. He don't do nothing. I yell at my pappy for help when she's whipping me, but he don't do nothing. I don't know why he just stand there. I don't know then how it is with niggers. So she whip me till she's tired. And then my pappy take me home, and he try to make me stop crying, and he say a lot of things like you say to a little boy when he's crying. But it don't do me no good. She whip me till she's tired, and my pappy *can't* do nothing cause he's a nigger, and after she get through he take me home and he say a lot of sweet things, but that don't stop my skin from hurting. It hurt a long time. Sometime it still hurt from that whipping."

There was a great, gloomy silence. Outside the rain went on and on. Sam had lost track of time. It was growing dark.

In a little while Beckinridge picked up his slow monologue and went on, and now Sam was very much afraid of him and wanted to go and somehow couldn't quite get up to leave. The yellow blinking eyes of the black held on to him, and he could not move.

"I never knowed my mammy. She die before I can member. But I go home that night and cry for my mammy cause my pappy ain't doing me no good. I don't even know where my mammy's buried. Mr. Bourbon own her. He own all of us. Did till the Yankees come down here. Then nobody own us no more. Ain't nobody own us now. Nobody in this whole world own a nigger."

Sam jumped at a chance to change the subject.

"Yes, it's done. And I'm glad you're free. It isn't right to own slaves. I don't care what my mother's people thought. My conscience would hurt me if we owned slaves."

"It's my skin that hurts," Beckinridge said softly.

"I'm sorry."

The black dropped his eyes to contemplate the sliver of light reflected up the walls of the jug before him. "Is you you mammy's boy, or is you you pappy's boy?"

Sam sensed the import of the question, and he resented it. "I didn't know my father very well."

Beckinridge looked up at him again. "Then you belongs to you mammy?"

"I loved my father. I remember loving him. I just don't remember him very well."

Beckinridge nodded. Something weighty and menacing in the nodding. "You pappy and Mr. Campbell, they real good friends."

"I know."

"They was always hunting. Everybody know what good friends they was. Ride out sometimes in the morning, and sometimes they stay gone till dinnertime. Real hunters them two. They laugh a lot when they hunt."

"I know."

"Why sure you know, white boy. I guess you mammy tell you all about it."

The youth shrugged.

"You mammy don't like to cook wild stuff. She don't like rabbit.

And lots of times when they cotched something, you pappy bring it to me and my pappy. He never done nobody no harm, you pappy." The final note was wistful.

Silence except for the steady rain. The fire was burning down, the shadows settling into dark. No more wood inside. Sam's clothing was still stuck to him. He wanted to squat before the fireplace, to warm his back against the sinking flames. But he did not. He wanted to stand in the presence of the black. He wanted to look down. He was afraid not to look down.

"It's funny. I never remember seeing Mr. Campbell hunt," he said at last. "I've never seen him with a gun."

"Oh, he ain't since. I guess it take it out of him when you pappy die. My pappy say you pappy look like Mr. Campbell's boy. He say when you pappy die it's like Mr. Campbell's boy got kilt twict."

"Did he? Did Mr. Campbell's son look like . . . Did he look like my father?"

Beckinridge smiled that joyless, contrived smile and shook his head. "I don't know, white boy. I don't even member Mr. Campbell's boy. It's what my pappy say. That's all I knows."

Sam put a reflective hand to his face. In his mind something large and out of joint had just fallen neatly into place. He felt like someone who has just wakened in the middle of the night with the solution of a problem which had troubled him for years.

"They would have been about the same age, I guess. Maybe my father was a little older, yes, a little older. But not much. Just a year or two." He half muttered the words, thinking them out loud to himself.

Beckinridge said nothing. The sardonic smile was stitched across his face. The face which held the smile was dead, the eyes alone unnaturally alive. Like the malignant eyes of a snake peering out from a crevice in a dead tree.

And Sam looked about the room once more, his hand absentmindedly at his mouth and his mouth half open behind it, lips working at measuring the size of his thoughts. The thickening dark hovered under the ceiling. He wanted to leave and go off and think about this thing, maybe go see Mr. Campbell right then, tonight, and ask him about his son. But the rain went on without letup, and he began slowly to pace the floor, engrossed in his thoughts.

"I never thought of that," he muttered. He stopped and spoke sharply to Beckinridge. "Did anyone else say that? Did anyone else notice they looked alike, my father and Mr. Campbell's son?"

"Niggers all say so. I don't know what white folks think. Miss Idy, she say you pappy and Mr. Campbell's boy growed out of the same seed."

"Who is Miss Idy?"

"She's the nigger hag that reads hands." The black dropped his eyes to the table top. It was only a tiny gesture. But in his own sudden desire to know something, Sam caught the rebellion in it, the spurning, the flouting of the white man. And the youth could imagine the clots of feeling and memory, thought and hatred, which went spattering like excrement through the black's mind.

"You mammy sure love you pappy," Beckinridge said in a little while. He did not look up.

"Yes, I know. She still loves him."

"Us niggers know you mammy don't get married no more."

Sam stood almost directly over the black, just at his side, but still Beckinridge did not look up. He went on talking thickly at the whiskey jug.

"You mammy mighty pretty, and they's folks that say she gonter get herself another man. But us niggers knowed better."

Brooding silence. The rain still beating on the roof.

"Me and my pappy and George, we work that place. You got to thank me a little bit for getting that place of your'n along till you get old enough to work it youself. Ain't that right?"

"Yes, that's right. I appreciate it."

"You mammy done forget us all. She don't member nothing we done for her."

"She lost a lot. She's kind and good down deep. But she lost everything she had, and it makes her harsh sometimes."

Beckinridge nodded again. He still had not looked up. "Yessuh, she sure lose a lot. Lose all them slaves. They used to be lots and lots of niggers on that place. I members how my pappy talk. He say if you want a good piece of ass in the old days, you go up to the Crittendon place. They's bushels of ass lying round just waiting to be picked."

"I don't know about that," Sam said coldly.

"Too bad you Uncle Matthew don't live to tell, boy. I hear tell he could of told you lots and lots. He knowed, that man did! He *knowed!*"

Sam could feel his face burn in the gloom. "You don't want to go talking about my kin like that."

"Well, what's wrong with it?" Beckinridge said. He did look up now, affecting bewilderment. "Man see a lil' piece of ass, and he reach out, and he *take* it, that's all. Nothing wrong with *that.* And they was lots for the taking round here back in them days." He shook his head wistfully. "I gets my first piece of ass when I'm fourteen years old. The woman, she twenty-five, thirty. I don't know. I give her a nickel, and she give me a piece of ass. But you know something? She tell me I'se one of the bestest fuckers she ever have."

He halted, and a sly, malicious pride stole into his yellow eyes. His voice became an exaggerated, confidential whisper. "And you know something else? She'd had you Uncle Matthew, white boy. That girl'd fucked you Uncle Matthew." Beckinridge sat back, and his eyes shone with evil triumph.

"I think you've said enough," Sam said.

"I don't mean no harm!" Beckinridge spoke in an elaborately protesting tone. "Honest I don't. What's the difference, white boy? It's all gone, ain't it? They all dead, ain't they?"

Beckinridge folded his arms carefully across his thin chest and sat there hugging himself and rocking gently back and forth without moving the chair. He had looked away from Sam again. He smiled off into space in the confident way of men sharing an obscene joke. "And before you Uncle Matthew, they was you granddaddy. Oh, I knows all them things. They's lots and lots my pappy tell me. They say you granddaddy used to tell you Uncle Matthew which was the good'uns."

"Who said?"

"All the niggers said it, that's who. You don't spect to hear things like that from white folks, do you, boy? The niggers still talks bout them days. How you Uncle Matthew and you granddaddy love to fuck nigger women."

Sam knotted his hands tightly together behind his back. He said nothing. But he measured Beckinridge, calculated the distance around the table, the time it would take to lunge, the force of the blow it would take to kill him. Still he did not move. The black rambled on with the defiant courage of the weak.

"You ought to *know* bout such things like that, white boy. Don't you think you ought to know who you menfolks has fucked with?"

"I don't see that it makes much difference." The youth tried to speak carelessly, but his voice was husky with anger.

"But it do for you, white boy. It *do!* Now I been in you house. Long time ago I been in you house. And I seen all the pictures. All them pretty pictures of you folks. You ought to be real proud of you folks, white boy. *I'd* be proud to have pictures like them."

"I *am* proud," Sam said rudely.

"But that's what I'm talking about. You ain't got them *all*. Don't you see, white boy? You mammy leave some of you folks *out*."

Sam spun around and looked into the fire. He did not want to look at the black any more. Outside the rain went on pummeling the roof, and the sound of it was as steady as the grinding of timeless machinery against the axis of the universe.

"I'se done gone and hurt you feelings." There was a thick, hypocritical deceit in the voice, and a keen note of triumph, surprising in its boldness. Triumph at having drawn blood. The youth was startled to hear triumph like that in the mouth of a black. He had never heard it before, and yet suddenly something told him it had always been there, lurking just beneath the surface of the craven posing of Beckinridge Bourbon and the whole black race. They were looking on. They saw things. It really didn't matter what they saw, you thought. You did something in front of a nigger, and it was like doing it in front of a stump or a dog.

And then you woke up one day and saw that they'd been looking on all the time and taking everything in and seeing the white race with its guard down. Maybe that's why white men came to hate niggers so much.

"Which of the niggers around here are kin to me?" Sam pronounced the word *nigger* with rude, bitter force.

Beckinridge only smiled. "Round here? Oh, they ain't so many no more. Cleophas Blue, he call hisself. He live down Vonore way. He you Uncle Matthew's boy. You mammy know Cleophas Blue, only she ain't got his picture in you house I bet. She won't let him come on the place. And you got a real pretty cousin down toward Sweetwater. Name of Dewmawning. Dewmawning Crittendon. She one of you grandpaw's chillun, and last thing I hear she's got a pretty good whoring business. Got a nice yaller skin. Something bout that nice yaller skin gets a white man up. And you grandpaw give it to her. Without it, she'd not be nothing but a common nigger whore selling ass for a nickel apiece. Way it is, she's something special. Firstclass white man's whore. She don't have no truck with niggers. No fuck neither. I'se tried." He laughed again, softly, with tired languor and savored mockery.

"Is that all? Are there any more?"

"Not I know of round here, white boy. But Lawd! I don't member.

My pappy tell me a lot, but I don't member half what he say. Your Uncle Matthew had a boy name of Odell that cotched the measles and died just when the War's starting. He was old as me, my pappy says, but I don't member nothing bout it. They's lots of niggers that's gone up Knoxville way and ain't come back. White folks goes West; niggers goes to town. That's the way it is. I reckon if you was to go up Knoxville way and look, you'd find some of you folks."

"Did . . . Did my father have any children?"

"You pappy? No, boy. He come after the slave time. And he don't have no nigger children. Just you, boy. Just you."

There was a long, moody pause.

"Dewmorning. Is it one word?" Sam looked deeply into the fire. The flame was low. It burned with an ominous blue glare in the remnants of the wood.

"Hell, white boy! *Dewmawning!* That's what her name is. Dewmawning Crittendon. Just like you name." He chuckled again. "You moughten go see her sometime. I'se heard tell she was a right good fucker. She'd have you in a minute. Bet you life. And it'd be something! Like fucking you mammy's sister. Hell, it'd be like fucking you mammy!"

That was when Sam decided to hit him. It took some doing, and he was clumsy about it because he hadn't hit anybody since he was a child at school. But he was enraged, and the rage carried him swinging from the mantel and in a blind rush to the table. Reaching across it he struck Beckinridge full in the mouth with the flat of his hand. A streaking whiplash of a blow. The black tumbled over backward in the chair and hit the floor with a wallop that shook the house. Instantly Sam leaped around the table and leaned over him with his fist drawn back of his head like a hammer poised to kill.

But then Beckinridge laughed again. His eyes were closed. One hand was cast cast almost idly over his chest, the other thrown out on the floor palm up. A smear of blood widened around his mouth. Still he laughed—the tired, drunken, and mocking laughter of a man driven into a sea beyond disgrace and infamy. And Sam slowly lowered his arm before the awfulness of the laugh and unknotted his fist and stammered an apology. At which the black chuckled again, and his breath rattled like a piece of broken machinery while his eyes remained shut and the hand lay carelessly tossed over the thin chest.

"My pappy tell you pappy bout all the niggers that was kin to you mammy's folks, and you pappy laugh. He think it's the funniest thing he ever heard, and he laugh and slap his leg and get my pappy to tell him all about it. So now you tells me what I wants to know. You tells me you belongs to you mammy. You sure is you mammy's child."

"Get up. Here, let me help you get up." Sam felt his brain reel with what he had done. He bent down and reached for Beckinridge. "Here, get up."

But the black ignored him. "Listen to me, white boy. Leave me be, and you listen. I ain't done talking. Nawsuh! I ain't near done, and I ain't got much time left to talk." He lay with his eyes yet unopened, and he was grinning in that malignant way, and the blood oozing out of his mouth was dark in the darkening room. It made Sam think of the cow. He stood erect. Beckinridge panted for air, spoke intermittently and with a terrible deliberation.

"You see, white boy, I'se knowed something for a long time. A *long* time, and I reckon now I'se the onliest man in the world that does know it. You mammy don't know I know, and I almost yell it out the mawning you mammy whip me, but I'se too scairt. I'se scairt of what my pappy'd do to me and what you mammy'd do to me. He made me swear by all the devils of night and hope to die that I wouldn't never tell, and I done it. But it don't matter now. I'se gonter die anyway, if'n I tells or if'n I don't."

He halted and fought for breath. The rattle in his frail lungs was more pronounced. Sam gazed down at him and felt an indescribable horror creeping up his back. When the black resumed, his voice was a faint bubbling of words hardly audible above the sound of rain.

"I figures it this way, white boy. I figures I owes something to you pappy. Something for all that meat he brung us. I owes him vengeance, white boy. Vengeance." In spite of his weak voice the black managed to compress a terrifying force into that word, *Vengeance.*

Sam felt something alarming tighten about him as if the air in the cabin, gone to ice, had suddenly shrunk against his body so that he could scarcely breathe.

"What are you talking about?"

"Just hold on, white boy. I'll tell you. You just wait and let me breathe a little bit, and I tell you more than you want to know." The broken machine in the black's chest ground laboriously on. "You member the night you pappy die?"

"Yes, I remember a little."

"Well, old George member that night too. He wasn't nothing but a nigger. Nobody'd believe him if'n he tell, and he don't want to tell nobody anyhow. He love you mammy. Don't know why he love her, but he do, and he love you mammy's folks. He was foolish that way. He was the foolishest nigger I ever seen, and they's lots of foolish niggers."

"Get on with it. What are you trying to say?"

"Give me time, white boy. Give me time. I'se saying he love you mammy, and he's troubled, *mighty* troubled bout what he seen that night."

Sam shivered against the chill of the rain in his clothes. He looked down at the black lying at his feet, eyes closed, helpless, and near to death, and he thought that one swift, simple, and purifying kick would end all this forever. One quick jerk of his leg muscles. One impulse of his mind. Less force than the strength required to mount a horse or walk upstairs. Like kicking a snake to death. But he was entranced and could not move except to say: "What did he see? Tell me, quick!"

"They was a bright moon that night. Big and round and yaller. And old George was out in the woods like he was lots of nights when they was moon. He was hunting possum with his dog. Only the dog had run off somewheres, and old George was listening for him. He was sitting longside a stump and looking at the moon, real still and quiet. He was listening for the dog to tree. You understand? He was waiting for that dog of his'n to tree something so George'd know where he was."

"I understand."

"But old George hear something in the woods, and he know it ain't his dog. It's some*body* out there, close by in the dark. Somebody creeping up. One footstep after another, slow and quiet. He's scairt, he say, and he hunker down behind the stump of his'n, and he listen, and he don't hear nothing but the crickets and this *something* moving awful soft in the woods without a light. Then he pick it out in the moonlight, and he see who it is! It's you *mammy,* white boy, creeping through the woods and picking her way along. And old George's real worried first off cause he think something's wrong, and he wonder what you mammy's doing out there in the woods in the dead of night, and he almost speak to her. He *almost* speak. But he don't. Something tell him: No sir, George. Don't you say nothing. So he keep still like a mouse, and he watch. And he see you mammy's carrying something in her hand. Something that shine a little in the moonlight. It's a can of something, and she's got a pick, too. A little pick that she use to dig down in the garden with. I reckon you seen that pick?"

"Yes, I've seen it. Get on with it. Go on." Sam's voice was tight and husky. The menacing darkness swelled like something alive under the roof beams.

"Well, she's got that pick that night, and she taken it, and she dig a hole with it. A deep hole it was for a woman to be digging and at night like that in the woods. And while she's digging, that old dog of George's, he start to howl way off in the dark. Old George hold his breath. He don't know what you mammy's gonter do. He don't know what *he's* gonter do if'n she see him.

"But she don't. She look up and listen, and he see the moonlight on her face. It's white like he ain't never seen white on nothing alive in this world. And her long black hair's all down loose and floating round her white face. Old George say he wonder if he's really seeing you mammy there or if he's seeing a ghost. But pretty soon she start to dig again, and finally she satisfied, and she put the can in the hole, and she cover it up with dirt, and she spread dead leaves over the dirt—real careful. *Real* careful. And she go away. George say she slink off through the woods like some kind of cat. That's what he tell my pappy and me, and I member many's the time they sit up and talk bout it."

He opened his eyes then, large and lynxlike, and looked up at Sam with a grimace of contrived mirth. "Is you interested, white boy? Tell me true, is you interested?"

The youth barely managed to nod his head. The fire was a dull glow of embers sinking into the dark air of the room. The dusk outside was congealing into a thick night, and the rain kept falling in its interminable dreary beating. Sam was hypnotized by the dying face, its terrible grin, and by the prickly presentiment of horror rising in the room like a specter from the grave.

"So old George wait till she gone, and he don't hear no more footsteps in the leaves. That old dog of his'n, he still howling. George never *do* know what at. He always say he miss him a good coon that night. But he go out, quietlike hisself, and he dig up with his hands what you mammy bury in the ground, that can, and he taken it home with him. Only first he fill up the hole again and cover it over with the leaves.

"It's a long time after midnight when he get home, and the moon is low in the trees. Old George can't read none. But he can smell, and he strike a light, and he open the can, and he look good, and he smell. He smell *real* good. Then he know. Yassuh, then he know, white boy. He know the truth before that night is half done."

Beckinridge was droning on in a tired, languorous wisdom, and the syllables of his words were slurred together like something melting and losing its form in a cosmic heat. Only the cabin was ethereally cold. The room all around Sam went swaying in the pressing dusk, and his heart was pounding like the rain on the roof, and he thought he would die if he spoke. But speak he must. He had to work the question out through his rigid mouth: "What . . . What was it?"

"Why, can't you guess, white boy? Can't you tell by now? It was arsenic. Arsenic of lead. Poison, boy. *Poison!*"

And with that horrible word, Beckinridge began to chuckle again. His whole body shook. Like a snake caught on a rock in the naked sun and dying, his body quivered and shook. A soft trembling of diseased laughter. And Sam's legs nearly gave way beneath him. Around him the room's rolling sway picked up to a dizzy whirl, and he was sure he was going to fall. Then he thought he was going to be sick at his stomach, but there was nothing in his stomach to vomit. Beckinridge was wheezing with laughter and fighting off the pain and wheezing again, and all the while he was looking up through the faded light at the stricken youth with an expression of hilarious triumph.

"Then, long toward morning, you mammy begin screaming up at the Big House, and she say you pappy's dead. She yell for old George, and she say you pappy's died sudden in the night. His heart, she say. His heart give out." Beckinridge's laughter was a hysteria, exhausted, low like the fire, and almost lifeless, but a hysteria. "Poison do that to a man, white boy. Poison mighty bad on a man's heart. Poison, white boy. *Poison!*"

Sam veered around like a machine. Like someone in a deep trance, moving to a mechanical pull, an inaudible command. He went out the door looking straight ahead and down off the porch into the rain and untied his horse. He no longer cared about the rain, no longer noticed its falling, no longer was conscious whether it was light or dark. Behind him the black shuffled like a crawling animal and somehow picked himself up and came staggering out to the door, where he leaned upon the lintel with one long, black arm thrust upward, repeating his inhuman litany:

"Poison, white boy. *Poison!*"

Sam got onto his horse, and the rain poured down on him. He

was there in the open before the cabin, and there was nothing at all between him and the flooding sky. He did not care. He dimly wished for the rocks and the mountains to fall upon him, and he thought vaguely that they might come after the rain. He turned the horse back toward the trace of road slithering off into the gloomy woods.

"Boy! Hey, white boy! If'n you don't believe me, you do something, you hear? You go down there to old George's cabin, and find the can. It's still down there where he leave it when he died. Over his bed in the loft. It's a yaller can. You go find it. It's still got the poison in it."

He rode off into the rain, dumb and unthinking. The rain covered him up. Eventually the hard, slithering sound of it washed out the taunting of the voice behind him. In the opaque recesses of his being Samuel Beckwith the younger wished the rain would carry him off to nothing. He wished he could dissolve into it like powder, and be washed painlessly away into an eternal silence.

"Poison! Poison!"

It was the start of his longest ride.

25

AT FIRST HE FLED into the dark like a dumb spirit. His mind all frozen to ice. No words could break through the ice. Nothing deep inside his head but a furious pain which hammered down into his body with each stride of the horse. Burning ice tapped with a relentless hammer. Headache and nausea. Stomach wracked with the nausea. A heaving in his bowels. He shuddered violently. Every muscle in his long legs quivered, and his stomach heaved again. Muscles of his face contracted with the dull pain of the cold and the thing in his head. The rain fell streaming in the leaves, the grass, the sodden fields, and with a settled splashing onto the slithering road itself, and all the night was filled with the fierce roar of its tumultuous fall. A cataract of sound. Noise so loud that his ears screamed against it. Noise so penetrating that it made the cold iron thing in the middle of his head throb and ache.

He lashed the horse on. The agonized animal plunged and bucked in the slippery night. Several times they almost fell. Barely recovered, breathing with desperate labor, the horse plunged on to the mad cut of the bridle end. On they went, thrashing through the streaming night, and all he could think of was to go on and on until he and the horse fell dead together.

The countryside drifted by in the heavy night. Only the dimmest of forms were visible to him as his eyes set themselves to the dark. His own fields slipped behind him. Still he kept on until the horse pulled up with a gasp of fading strength onto the pike which plunged southward in the dark toward Chattanooga. Back north. Back toward Bourbonville he went. At last something asserted itself. A thought. A single word. A peaceful anodyne of death beating in the pummeling hoofbeats of the horse. *Emilie. Emilie. Emilie. Emilie.* And slowly the rhythm of the galloping hoofs communicated itself to him, and his brain went Emilie *never,* Emilie *never,* Emilie *never,* Emilie *never,* Emilie *never.*

Off the pike. An instinct of horse and man. The winded horse running like a wounded bird. Onto the particular road which toiled upward through the dense trees on the ridge overlooking the valley. The thin saplings slapped against rider and horse. The poor horse staggered to a walk, moved with hoofs of lead and heaved for air. A hot froth of sweat flooded out from the horse's body. The stark chill in the air around and the hot sweat oozing up under him. A small gust of wind. The trees creaked sorrowfully together. So lonely. So mournful their voices in the whisper of wind.

He had to get off the horse. He realized that at last. He pulled the animal to a laggard stop and dropped off. He took up the bridle and went plowing ahead on foot, the horse following, plodding. He stumbled forward and fell, flat in the muck. He lay there, sobbing for air. His face was in the mud. It was sticky and cold, and it pasted his clothes to his body and made them like plaster.

Then he got up and went on, lifting one iron foot and putting it down in front of the other. He could hear the distinct watery squishing his shoes made. He could hear the sucking of the mud when his horse stepped along, could hear also the stricken breathing of the defeated beast. Misery in himself, in the horse, the world filled with a misery like the rain which would never end. The pulse socking up through his bursting head made him almost faint, but he fought his way upward and at last came out into the clearing and sank down on his knees in exhaustion.

Below he could see the fluid gleaming of lights in Bourbonville. Nothing else visible down there. No river. No railroad. No green carpet of patched field mantled in sunny haze. No thin sound from the distance. No part of the scene fixed in his mind by Emilie's presence. Nothing but the dull cross of lights outstretched in the rainy dark far down below. A cross to crucify hope.

It was right here. The mocking thought jeered at him in the cascading rain. Soundless, scornful laughter rolled off the hill and shot out into the dark. Emilie so close in his mind, so removed in distance. *It was right here!* Emilie a sacrifice to his mother's vision of glory. He put his face up into the rain and shut his eyes. *Poison! Poison!*

He groaned aloud. It relieved him of something. He cried louder. A long screeching of pain flung against the sky. On and on he went.

A lonely, forsaken crying of hurt and unbelief, of need and bitter loss.

He stopped and felt his energy die. In an immensity of fatigue and apathy he looked out over the darkened valley. The rain was slackening. And there, above the eastern line of hills, a dull phosphorescence showed where the moon lay hidden in the cold calm of space. Thick clouds were roiling across the sky. They sped along, propelled by winds no human flesh could feel, and they showed heavy bellies of darkish white to the world below. All across the heavens he could see a buoyant shifting of motion, movement which in some strange way broke up the ice jam in his head and got thought circulating again. Dark and confused like the clouds overhead—but thought. He was still alive.

He could have killed the preacher right here that day. One short, sharp gesture of manliness, and he and Emilie could have dug a grave and put the evil man in the earth. Then they could have fled, gone West to be together with a murder to bind their marriage forever. No one would ever know what had happened to them, though some would surmise something of the truth. But no one would ever find the grave. The preacher would vanish in the same sudden mystery with which he had appeared in the valley long ago. And young lovers had vanished before. No one really had to explain that. Two little mysteries, unconnected, to be dumped in a corner among the many gathering the cobwebbed years in the valley. He and Emilie, guilty together of murder. But what was guilt when you could ride West and leave forever the narrow stage upon which something called murder had been done? Did guilt incurred in one drama really follow the actors who moved on to another scene?

Even without committing murder he could have gone away with Emilie. True, the murder done in partnership would have been a pure assertion of something. An effusion of blood to make something white as snow. Their love? But even without the blood, he and Emilie could have run away. Together they could have made a gesture as sharp and irrevocable in its own way as murder. He could have brought the knives down on his own past, done the daring thing. Done anything but what he had done—which was really nothing, nothing at all. For in his own weakness he had made a feeble surrender to a slow grinding of patient despair which carried him on from moment to moment and from day to day so that finally he was like a sodden and spiritless log borne on the sweep of a river. He could have *done* something. His mother had *done* something. Dear God! She had done something so dreadful he could not think about it! The people who *did* things ruled the earth. All the rest were their slaves.

The aching in his head was subsiding. His stomach had calmed, and he was conscious that he had not eaten since morning. He was still cold and weak, and he shivered, but the rocking world was settling down. The horse was also breathing easier. The rain was softening to a drizzle. The lights in Bourbonville were brighter. The rim of hills across the valley was distinctly visible, a darker dark against the brooding sky. His mind began to put one thought after another, though still dragging in a dreadful muck of hurt and wonder. His mind struggled to comprehend and went plunging into a jungle of memory so dense and dark that hardly a patch of light shone on the fallen things the jungle darkness hid.

Up the railroad to Knoxville, long ago. The train streamed along, and people in the fields along the rails raised their heads and shaded eyes with hands against the sun to watch the train as it hammered along. Children on porches and in yards sprang up sometimes from their play and waved joyously and yelled and ran barefoot after the train to be answered by a condescending hoot from the shrill whistle. The train swept grandly by them all. He felt superior to the children because he was on the train with his beautiful mother and they were not. Out of his superiority there arose an aching pity. He was having a great day, and they were having an ordinary day, and they might never ride a train because they were poor.

"Sam, you should write books!"

"Books!"

"Don't laugh. Don't act so *embarrassed!*"

"I never thought about it, that's all."

"But you tell such wonderful stories."

"*Everybody* in the valley knows the stories."

"But everybody can't *tell* them."

"I don't see why not."

"Samuel, you are being *modest.* You should not be *modest.*"

"Why are you laughing?"

"Because I *love* you, and you are so *modest.*"

"I would like to write books. Maybe I can write a book about us."

"You cannot write a book about us. You cannot write a book

about loves that continue. You can only write books about loves that die."

"I don't see why!"

"It is true. If you write a book about us, it will be because our love is dead."

"It will never die, Emilie."

"Then you will never write a book about it."

They went to one store in Knoxville. His mother was all silent and preoccupied with something, and she snapped at him to move along and not dawdle. She dragged him along by the arm out of the sooty railroad station where all the magic trains awaited the caressing gaze of a little boy's eyes. He remembered her sulky brooding, her impatience, because it was the ruination of his great trip. He expected her to be happy because she was always happy, but on this day she was not happy at all. They went into that single store, and she made her purchase quickly from a man in a blue apron. The man with the blue apron listened with his head cocked attentively forward and turned to a high shelf and lifted something down and put it into a paper bag and gave it to her and took her money and made change and said thank you, and they passed out into the street again. What was it? Something in a can. Something in a coppery-yellow can? The memory lay too deep in shadow. He wanted to know what was in the bag because he thought it might be candy or something else for him. She would not even let him carry it. When he nagged her for it, she got very angry with him and threatened to stop right there and spank him in front of all the people on the street. Passers-by turned around to look at them and to see the little boy about to be spanked. He was eaten up with shame. He had felt so *superior* on the train. Now his mother was ready to spank him out on the street where just everybody could see. Maybe the red humiliation of being reprimanded in public was the reason he remembered his mother bought something. They walked. They walked up the morning and down the afternoon, and his legs burned with fatigue. He whimpered. His mother was cross with him. They sat. Somewhere in the open, on a bench. His feet did not reach the ground, and his legs were numb. His whole body ached. He cried to sit in her lap. She would not allow it. Instead she scolded him. They walked some more. She spoke to no one, went into no more stores. She bought him no candy because she said he was a bad boy, and he did not know what he had done to be bad. Never in all the rest of his life was she to be as harsh and impatient with him as she was that day. Did she stop to buy lunch? He could not remember. All the remainder of that day rose from its sunny beginning to vanish in the frustrating haziness which was his memory. Vaguely he recalled the hard jouncing of the railway car against his sleeping head on the journey home. Noises from open space beyond the closed chamber of exhaustion where he slept. He knew he was missing the excitement of seeing the countryside pass by. He was sick with the thought that he was missing it. But he could only sleep, and that was all he remembered about that day. It ended in misery, and it was to be such a *fine* day.

"Sam, when I kissed you the first time, it was like something that never had happened to me before."

How many men have you kissed? Dear God, don't ever let me know!

"I knew it was going to happen. Did you know? I knew. I felt it coming on both of us. I suddenly wanted you to kiss me more than I wanted anything else on earth, and then I was afraid you might be too shy. Too *nice*."

Why can't I just ask you? Why can't I talk about how afraid I am?

"That first day, when I saw you on the street, I was just *interested* in you. All the other boys your age here, they don't have something in their eyes that you have. You are so full of life, Sam. It shows in your eyes."

It would be an insult to ask her if she ever loved anyone else. She would stop laughing and be hurt, and things might never be the same again. She would think I did not trust her. It doesn't matter anyway. Whatever she was in the past, she loves me now. Now is all we have.

"I didn't mean to fall in love. Not even when I came looking for you that day. I just wanted to *talk* with you some more. I was so lonely to talk with *somebody*, and you were the only *interesting* person I knew."

But if she had said all these things to someone else, then whatever it was didn't last. She's saying them to me now. Maybe tomorrow she will say them to someone else. What on earth can a girl like her see in me! It's a mindless infatuation. With all her experience, how can she really care for me?

"You can't talk to everybody. I've never really understood why you can't, but it's true. You can say words and hear words, but if you really *talk* you have to have somebody who is just enough like you to understand and just enough different to want to hear. And you have to have someone who is sensitive enough to listen the way you want to be heard. *Feinfühlig*, Samuel. *Du bist ein feinfühliger Mensch!*"

But what does it matter? Something could grow between us. What do I care if she had a thousand lovers in the past? What if she has a thousand more tomorrow! This is today. This is today.

"Oh Sam, you look at me so strangely sometimes. You understand me, and you *don't* understand me. Your face looks like a little curious rabbit's. You are funny, Samuel. My dear, lecherous, sinful Samuel!"

Why does she scratch herself under the chin like that? She looks so awkward. I know girls who are prettier than she is. Not as striking, but prettier. Why do I have to love her? What has possessed me? Why does she look so awkward when she is happy?

"Isn't it strange that we talk about the first things we did so much? I wonder if lovers always do that. Do you realize it, Samuel? Ever since the day you kissed me the first time, we have talked about it again and again. Isn't it wonderful how happy it makes us to talk about the way we *became* happy? I wonder what we will be when we don't talk about that any more."

His breathing was completely regular now, and the rain was hardly more than a fine mist. He was trying to see things in the right perspective. *It is all a nigger story.* The thought brought a great lightness to his mind. *That is the way of niggers. You can never trust the word of a nigger.* His mother said they would tell you anything that suited them. They thought it was true when they said it. That is why a nigger never would admit to lying. That was the difference between a white man and a nigger. A nigger didn't have any capacity to tell the difference between what was real and what wasn't, and a white man did. *But does* she *know the difference! Where is the line between her fantasies of the past and the hard, unbending edge of reality?*

"Oh Samuel, I feel like I'm sinking in the ocean. Don't let me go, Samuel. Please save me. *Please!*"

"Why of course, Sam, I remember that day so well! You were so young. It's a wonder *you* remember it, but I suppose it was the train ride that made it so vivid to you. I told your father I wanted to go to Knoxville just to see what had become of it since the War. We had had a hard time, and we had survived, and suddenly I wanted to shop in the big city again! Can you *imagine*? I wanted to get away from *here*. And that was just before your dear sweet father died! Oh Sam, you don't know the *times* I've regretted that day! What a poor, simple, silly little goose I was! I've only been to Knoxville one time since then. To get the picture made, the picture of your dear father. And I don't care if I never go again. Store? No, I don't remember that or the man with the apron. I suppose we went into several shops. No, we didn't walk far. I don't remember walking much at all, but you were just a little boy. It probably *seemed* a lot farther than it really was. Why, Sam! I'm *surprised* at you! I was not either cross! I have *never* been cross with you in my *life*. I *love* you, Sam. You know that. I *love* you." Was there a pallor around her dark eyes when she brushed his memories aside, or was it only a trick of his imagination played here in the cool, dark solitude of the lonely and troubled night?

"I want you, Emilie. Lord knows I want you more than I ever wanted anything else in my life."

He got on his horse again, and they went slowly back down the ridge to the valley floor. As the leather saddle moved to the plodding of the horse, he could hear the uncomfortable squeak of water. The mud sucked at the horse's hoofs, and he could hear that. He could hear the subdued tumbling of the drizzle in the leaves, a low, lazy pattering of fine droplets. The air was clean and unbelievably sweet, and an occasional fresh breeze made him realize anew how bad the dust had been.

He came back to the pike and turned north again. The horse went listlessly along. *Probably ruined,* the youth thought. He had no feeling left except a despondency so thick it nearly crushed his chest. All the frenzy had gone. He was still chilly from the water and the pasting of mud in his clothing, but he did not think about that. Something thick had settled inside him, and he was so tired that he could think the worst without panic or horror.

Who was it who summoned up the dead? The Witch of Endor. She called Samuel up, and Samuel pronounced doom. Poor Saul! There in the frightful dark with the witch cowering nearby and Samuel's ghost rising in supernatural steam from the underworld. The Philistine armies were in the plain. They had iron swords. Did the witch expect Samuel to come, or was the sudden apparition in response to her spell as frightful to her as it was to Saul? Was she a fraud, suddenly transformed without her knowledge into a seer by the stealthy hand of God? Or was it Samuel's hatred which drove him from the grave to curse his enemy? *I wonder if the nigger hags can call up the dead.* And if they could, what dark curse might his father speak?

He passed the fork of the road which curved across the front of his own land. Now other horsemen called out to him on the pike. He bowed his head and did not reply and passed on. He puzzled at their being abroad in such numbers at this hour, in this sodden night. But he kept on toward town, and he turned off down the little road which wound through the countryside to the Methodist graveyard.

The horse dipped tiredly into the creek, and from the way he labored and the way the water gurgled and sucked about his legs Sam could tell the creek was up. It grumbled heavily in the dark and went plunging off on its course to the river.

Away from the creek, into the depths of the countryside, the night quieted around him. No insects called. No night birds. Everything lay hushed under the soft rainfall. No sound except that slow pattering of the rain itself, and it was dying. The wind was down, and the horse's hoofs went plumping along, and the darkling land went stately by. The house of the nigger hags slipped off to the right. He was already beyond their pathetic lane when the door was abruptly thrown open. It showed a rectangle of pale orange in the wet gloom, and within the rectangle like something enclosed in an oblong bubble there stood a thin silhouette, bent forward, searching over the shrouded distance. He went on, and the door shut again without a sound. His mind went blank again.

Then the bulk of the church loomed up amid the larger bulk of the grove. Behind it stretched the graveyard with its weir of stones, and beyond that lay the thick woods—all dark and dripping. He slumped over the saddle, did not stop the horse at the hitching rail, but rode in defiance to all the good taste of the valley through the graves and knew the horse was leaving a muddy track which people would see later and reproach. The horse picked his way cautiously along and once or twice brushed against a stone. The youth might have been afraid on another night. Then he might have had so little on his mind that he would have feared ghosts.

He passed a plot of tall, thin stones slanting at crazy angles from the settling of the earth. He knew them. They were of rotting marble. Their inscriptions were hardly legible, and they stood off from the rest of the graveyard a little to themselves. The graves concealed the ancestors of a family named Hogan. The remnants of a sinister tale still circulated in Bourbon County about the early Hogans. Something about a massacre of redmen a long time ago, when the valley was mostly wilderness, when Bourbonville was a name given to an unhealthy clearing smoking in the vast forest and Indians still roamed the woods. An old yarn now all but forgotten even by those Hogans who lived on in the valley and noted in an uninterested way that their blood had passed on its way to them through these heaps of dust. Guilt or innocence; nothing mattered to the dead, and the crimes of the dead were atoned for by the earth in graves that did not speak.

He found the grave he was looking for. He sat the horse and looked down on the heavy monument. It was indistinct in the dense night, but in his mind he could spell off the sharp inscription carved into the granite. But there was a darkness beyond that which his mind could not penetrate. He pressed his fingertips against his eyes and rubbed at them and shook his head to clear his thoughts. *I must go home. I must get this straight.* But he could not communicate his resolution to his body, and the horse stood with lowered head like something drained of all its strength.

His father laughed a great deal. Sam remembered yet how still the house was when he was absent, how full of boisterous laughter it was when he was there. In his memory he saw a tall form standing in the kitchen at the same mirror which hung there now. The leaning form, occupied in shaving, was one of those little chips of memory like something broken out of the whole glass and tossed down in his mind to lie among the other unrelated bits of brightness he had carried off from his childhood. The form peered into the mirror and hummed some light air in a tone of laughter. Sam made it turn to greet him and recoiled in the dark from the monstrous image of a heavy gilt frame on the shoulders of a man, a frame which enclosed a dead picture, and the picture was solemn and staring and did not laugh or smile.

And what was it hidden behind that picture? Over what dark, dead things was the picture a stone which could not be rolled away. Who could tell him what might lie there? An opaque shadow rose in his mind, and a face emerged out of the pallid glow of the veiled moon, a face compounded of fantasy and memory and the diluted pallor of the night. Mr. Campbell. Of all the people in the valley only John Wesley Campbell might know and tell him the truth. If there were truth to tell.

Slowly his mind picked at the things he did know and tried to arrange them in some pattern which made room for the mystery he could not understand. His mother had built a glittering picture of the past streaming like a bright, full river over itself to rush into the vale of the present with life and grace, rapture and tragic beauty. Somehow his father had interrupted the harmony of her vision, perhaps threatened it with extinction. The bright river a sandy wasteland. So she had killed him. But what had he done? Mr. Campbell might know, but first the young Sam Beckwith must force himself to confirm what he could of Beckinridge's insane story. Something was left over from the past—a hard, small, insignificant relic molded by impersonal hands and set on a shelf with dozens of identical objects long ago. Now years and centuries weighed on that object—if indeed the object existed, if it were there where the black said it would be. And even then it might mean nothing at all.

The rain had stopped altogether. Slowly he rode back up through the graves and past the church and out the muddy road, past the house of the nigger hags where no doorway opened now, through the creek again, waters still rumbling with the heavy rain, making hollow sucking noises at its banks, breaking in efflorescent bubbles which caught the blur of moonglow and moiled it over the rocks. The sky was well on its way to breaking up. Sometimes the moon, on the slimmest edge of being full, would remain unconcealed for a couple of minutes at a time. Then it was a great, translucent yellow ball in the sky, a mocking parody of earth, and the woods beside the road turned silver in the treetops. But as quickly as it appeared it would pass again into the heavy clouds, and the world would be plunged into that nearly absolute darkness through which the youth passed in a lonely void. All around the owl-like silence lay brooding over the watery earth. The silence was a pensive spirit, free and undetermined and puzzling over what to make of creation, what to bring out of the great deep.

This was the South going by. His land. The dark trees with their silver profiles lined beneath the bitter moon. This was the South of dreams and languor and lost hope. And if there were ghosts, they surely maundered here, growling low at each other in the soft muttering of the night which they snatched up and used for voices. Ghosts of the raw men who settled this land, put strong hands out to grasp their dreams, drew hands away bloody, left the dreams themselves infected. And not just white spirits in this darkness. Nigger slaves sighing for rest like the wind seeking a bed under the leaves. Indians. The Cherokee nation, which had departed in the memory of some inhabitants of the valley. And if there were ghosts, the spirits of those Indians, like their white conquerors, filtered like dim light through the spreading woodland. The spirits also of their fathers who had died unvanquished. If there were spirits, they were watching on each side of the road as he passed by. Innumerable years of the past brooded against the infinitesimal present. This was the South going by in the dark. And like soldiers falling smartly out of ranks one by one to desert to the enemy, the ticking seconds of the present turned to take their places with the legions of the past, where memory blew a vain trumpet and all the battle flags were black.

The horse went plodding on. His head hung. His breath came hard. But he kept going, and the youth sat astride him with his own head down and his mind in a gummy stirring of thought. Was it possible that he could rescue anything out of this infinite throng of departed years stacked about him? Was it madness to think that it made any difference to separate fantasy from what had really been? Or was there simply a compulsion to know, which swept aside every rational weighing of the good or evil of the knowledge? He took the fork toward home when he came to it and then arrived at a place where the semblance of a path uncoiled itself through the woods. The path led back to the slave quarters, long abandoned. In the old days, his mother said, armed white men rode down that path regularly at night on patrol. Patrols kept the slaves from rebellion. But all that had been before the War.

Now the path was badly overgrown. He could tell its exit into the road by a tall chestnut, but only because he knew already it was there. When he came onto the path itself, he had to dismount and lead his horse. The moon shone for longer periods now, but its light falling unevenly through the thick foliage was spattered and uncertain. He had to keep feeling his way, confounded as much by the light as by the darkness. Once his feet slipped, and he fell again. But he got up quickly and yanked the horse impatiently on. And in a little while he came through the woods into the deserted and overgrown street of the quarters.

The cabins were all falling into ruin. The roofs of most had collapsed, and they lay like broken skeletons, hacked down by time and prostrate in decay. In one a pine tree went up from the middle of the house and stood tall and dark against the blueblack sky. He went slowly up the deserted street, leading the horse.

Old George had lived in the first cabin on the end as you came down the other way, from the house. He had rocked there in the evenings in warm weather and smoked his pipe. Recalling it now Sam remembered also sitting on the porch, listening to the regular crunching of the rocking chair on the planks, the languor of peaceful twilights falling into dreamy night. He remembered the way the fire in the fat clay bowl of the pipe rose and sank with the contented puffing of the old man's breath, remembered how when it was time to go that he had gone up the road and had turned and had seen that red fire coming and going like a friendly signal blinking in the dark.

Old George was like his mother in many ways. He talked with the persistent conviction that the best days were gone. It seemed that everything worthwhile had already happened. There was nothing left for a boy to do, nothing left to happen to him. The land as it had been ages ago spread out in the expanses of the boy's imagination. He peopled it with the men and women old George talked about—most all of them dead. Those dead memories moved together in a swaying dreaminess, like trees bowing in a gentle wind, and the boy looked on them from afar and with a terrible longing and wished he had lived with them. *Was he hiding something? Was every night that I sat here an exercise in concealment? Has my life been a masquerade where only I played no part, wore no mask?*

The questions made his skin creep in the moon-struck darkness. Was even the calm of this cabin in the long ago merely a thin net spread over horror?

He looked around. The moon was shining in a sky made of dark glass, sparkling with clean stars. The last of the clouds were sliding toward the north. Everything in the forest clearing lay as white as bone dust in the moonlight. He listened for the sound of a banjo. He listened also for the accents of a Yankee voice, for the excited jabbering of blacks, and for the slow settling of silence when the people had gone.

But he heard nothing. Nothing except the muffled, drowsy sounds of the wet night. He was more tired than he ever remembered being. If he could get dry clothes and sleep! If he could simply put this day out of his mind, dismiss all this year! If only he could fall back once more into the good ways and live undisturbed by knowledge! Was it sin or knowledge that drove Eve from the garden?

He thought of climbing back onto the horse, riding straight to the house, throwing his arms around his mother, and telling her how with all his heart he loved her. A confession of sorts. Her salvation, his own, the salvation of their land hanging on the thread of words. And tomorrow he could come down here and burn these ruins. There was a barrel of kerosene in the barn. It would make a good fire, and in a little while the woods would claim this place, and no one would care that there had ever been cabins here, with people who kept things dwelling in them.

Who told me the truth? Who in my life has told me the truth?

He stood in deep thought, seeing his own shadow cast softly before him. He made his decision by an act of hard will. He decided to step back to his horse. The muscles of his body shifted to obey the impulses of his mind, and he felt an overwhelming relief. But it did not last. Something broke down somewhere. There was something more powerful than his will, and with a heavy sigh of remorse he submitted to whatever it was. Carefully and deliberately he went forward and lifted himself onto the rotting porch. And a darkness descended on him again as he entered the door on a reaching carpet of moonlight.

26

IT WAS QUITE DARK when Brian Ledbetter came sloshing into town on his horse to find Mr. Campbell. But when he did arrive he forgot for the moment what had driven him out into the rain to find his friend. He came, full of wonder, his dripping clothes forgotten, upstairs in Mr. Campbell's house and saw Hub Delaney lying abed asleep under the spell of morphine. He had learned the story on the way in from dozens of travelers on their way to the Crittendon farm for the deathwatch. But he absorbed it all again as Mr. Campbell told it—the mad preacher, the shooting, the death, and the condition of Hub Delaney who had saved Mr. Campbell's life. It was enough to take his breath, and if he hadn't been so wet Brian would have sat down in astonishment.

"Goddammit," he said in exasperation, "I've spent this whole blessed day without knowing a thing was going on! You know, that makes me feel real funny, J.W. You and Hub nearly get yourselves killed, and I don't know a thing about it." He told Mr. Campbell something of how he had spent his day and then concluded: "I thought the thing I'd always remember about today was the rain."

"Maybe it was the most important thing," Mr. Campbell said with a tired smile.

"Oh, you don't understand, J.W. But it don't matter. It's just peculiar." He looked out the window where the soft rain was still pattering down. They could see the unreal images of themselves, raised by the lamplight, standing mystically thin and blurred in the glass, and behind the fragile reflections the rain whispered in the streets, and they could hear the low gurgle of water running in the misty dark. "I never seen a rain like this one," Brian said, full of reverent wonder. "It's cleaned the ground right down to the bone." He wanted to say something about Mr. Simson and the prophecy, but he could not frame the words or even form his thoughts.

"It's a little like Mexico," Mr. Campbell said in soft nostalgia. He laughed apologetically. "Funny how I've been thinking about Mexico today. I guess if you're close to death you think about things you did when you were young. And I was thinking about how dry it gets down there, drier than you've ever seen it here. And then the rain comes all of a sudden, and it falls like this rain did today. Like somebody blew up a dam in the sky."

"Mexico," Brian said in a sudden start of surprise. "God, J.W.! I don't even *remember* that war, and you fought in it."

"Yes, I fought in it," Mr. Campbell said flatly. "And sometimes it all comes back. Sometimes I feel I might wake up some morning and find myself out there again and have all my life to do over. Then I like to lie down at night and hope that that's the way it'll be in the morning. But it never is. It's a strange feeling." He stopped. His own tone was so concentrated and sad that Brian was looking at him strangely, and he felt he was talking too much without even the excuse of liquor. Out in the town, embraced by the dark, a few squares of yellow light marked the presence of other people —light quivering and washing and insubstantial in the faint rain as if the light had itself been water.

"I guess he always hated you because you made so much fun of him," Brian said.

"Yes, well he was insane, and sometimes the only way to protect yourself from lunacy is to laugh at it."

"You give him an awful hard time through the years," Brian said in mild reproach.

"I'd do it all over again. I'm not a doctor to take care of people like that. I'm a lawyer with a town to take care of."

"You don't have to defend yourself to me, J.W. You know I've always been on your side. Settle down." Mr. Campbell had become so heated all in a moment that Brian tried to soothe him. "Why don't you go to bed?"

"I don't need you to feel sorry for my gray hairs, Brian."

"J.W., a twenty-year-old would be all wore out after what you've been through today. And you ain't no twenty-year-old. Ain't you got a bed you can lie down on for a little while?"

"Oh yes. There's a bed in my son's room. I can sleep on it if I want."

"Well, you could," Brian said uneasily.

Mr. Campbell let a bitter laugh drop from his lips. "Of course I can sleep on it. Tonight or any night I want. He's long dead. He won't be home again."

There was a quick silence in the room. The night seemed to have sucked in its breath. The two men looked at each other, Mr. Campbell's face set in old granite and Brian's hurt and bewildered. The first time Mr. Campbell had ever uttered the words, and they were spoken with a toneless anger as if their speaker had some grudge against Brian Ledbetter. *He's long dead. He won't be home again.*

Brian lowered his head and looked glumly at the floor. The hurt deepened in his voice. "I don't mean no harm, J.W. I'm just trying to be your friend."

Mr. Campbell's face relented. He laughed, and the laughter was abruptly warm. "I'm sorry, old friend. It has been a long day. But I can't sleep now. I have to go out there."

"Out . . ." Brian was flabbergasted as the meaning penetrated his brain.

"Yes, to sit with the preacher. To do my duty to the dead."

"Oh, for Christ Almighty's sake, J.W.! You'll catch pneumonia in this rain, and then we'll be doing duty for *you*!"

"I think the rain is stopping."

"It's still not fitting for you to go out there, tired as you are!"

"I'll be all right. Besides, I've ridden in the rain before. Lots of times in the War I rode all night in the rain and fought in the morning."

"Oh I know that, J.W., but that was a long time ago, a *hell* of a long time ago, and there was reason."

"Twenty years. Twenty years and two months when I did it the last time."

"Well, you just can't do it tonight!"

"I not only can but I will, my friend."

"Oh Christ Almighty, go on then! See if anybody cares! Give her the satisfaction! I don't see how you can do it, myself. If I thought my dying would give anybody the satisfaction that your dying would give that woman, I wouldn't do it. I wouldn't *never* die. But you know best, J.W. You go right ahead and do it." Brian's last words were spoken in complete exasperation, and with a slapping one-two motion he brought his arms up over his chest and folded them and managed to look very much like a father wiping his hands of the pigheadedness of his children.

Mr. Campbell smiled again in his distant way. "I remember the day she was born," he said softly. "I remember it like yesterday. Her father came riding into town looking for help. You see, his wife had had her baby, but she was bleeding, and he couldn't get the blood stopped. He tried everything he knew. That meant he beat up the nigger woman who was helping, and of course *that* didn't do any good, and he yelled for a lot of the nigger women on his place to come up and help, but *they* couldn't do anything, so he came riding in to get my wife. I don't know what made him do that. He thought Charlotte could do something. I guess it was like praying to God when nothing else works because God is from so far away.

"My wife was pregnant herself, and I didn't want her to go. But she insisted, and of course I went with her. We went in his wagon. I thought he'd kill us, he drove so fast. Horses galloping over those roads, the way roads were back then. I remember Charlotte sat there beside me with her eyes closed and her teeth set, and I kept shouting at that crazy man to slow down, but he just whipped the horses on. And of course when we got there Charlotte couldn't do anything to help. She tried her best, poor girl, but the bleeding was way up inside that woman, and it kept on and on. Charlotte wasn't a doctor, and she didn't pretend to be one. I honestly don't know what Ben Crittendon expected. All Charlotte could do was hold his wife's hand while she died. The way I held Charlotte's hand when *she* died, later on.

"And there was this baby. You know, it was almost one of God's afterthoughts. But there was this *baby*, and that was Sarah Crittendon. All sweet and innocent. Not able to hate or love. Just a tiny body wrapped up in a blanket and spending most of her time asleep or crying for food. When I think about it, it's like I could walk out there right now and find that baby just like she was that day. Before Charlotte died. Before the Mexican War. Before I lost my boy. And I stand there in my mind and look at that sleeping little girl, and I can't believe how much of the destiny of so many people got itself tied up in that little child.

"Anyway, Charlotte said to Ben Crittendon, 'Well Mr. Crittendon at least you have a fine baby girl.' She was trying to cheer him up, you see. She didn't mean any harm. But Ben Crittendon thought the whole world had to stop and cry when something went wrong with his life. I don't think the man *cared* for his wife. No, I think he resented what she'd done to him by dying and leaving him to raise his children.

"And he thought Charlotte was mocking him. He never forgave her for trying to be cheerful when he was so downcast. He blamed her for it as long as she lived and me after she died. And do you want to know the truth? That was the thing that began the enmity between us. Oh, Ben Crittendon was suspicious before that. He was suspicious of anything he didn't control, and I was a young whippersnapper lawyer, and I wasn't from here, and he just naturally took a suspicion to me. But the *enmity* began that afternoon when his wife died and Charlotte tried to put a good face on and cheer him up. Afterward nothing was right between us. He yelled for a nigger to come and haul us back to town, and he said some bad things, and I lost my temper and threatened to kill him on the spot. Charlotte made me hush, and we went off, and Ben Crittendon and I never spoke a friendly word again. It shows you how absurd the world is, to think bad blood can run out of such a little cut of time and keep running for so long! I guess it's stopped now. Poor Charlotte! She didn't mean any harm. Poor girl. Poor dear girl."

He looked up slowly at Brian with a face that was haggard and full of sorrow. No sound in the room except the deep breathing of Hub Delaney on the bed and the soft drip of water beyond the windows. Brian stood there uncomfortable and puzzling. His arms were still thrown in a fold across his chest, but his look of commanding indifference was gone. In its place was an uneasy frown of compassion.

"Today everything has been very strange," Mr. Campbell said. "One minute I was in Mexico listening to the rain fall on the roof of a barroom, and the next I was here and seeing Ben Crittendon ride in with a face like a twisted rag. And I could go out there and make things *different.* I don't know how, but I could do something and make my *life* different. But it's all over and done, and there's no helping it now. No new start in life, is there Brian?"

Brian could only shake his head.

"When people are old," said Mr. Campbell gently, "they talk to themselves." He gazed at his friend in thoughtful silence for a few moments until suddenly his expression sharpened. "You didn't ride all the way into town to hear me talk. You never come in when it rains. And you didn't know what happened to Hub. What are you doing here anyway?"

Brian suddenly fell into a stuttering embarrassment, and he unclinched his folded arms and began to pace nervously about the room. "Well as a matter of fact, you got something there, J.W.," he said, clearing his throat and trying to sound hearty and confident. But he could not keep up the effort. He paced more rapidly and looked desperately out the window. "What I mean is that I was just thinking about how things has worked out, and I mean it's just like you said, J.W., we're all getting older ever day we live."

"Did I utter a truth as profound as that?" Mr. Campbell asked with perverse consternation.

"Well, I thought it sounded like something you'd said."

"Perhaps we should write it down to preserve it for posterity." Mr. Campbell made as if to search urgently for a pencil in the pocket of his coat, but Brian checked him with a tired sigh.

"This ain't the time to be making jokes, J.W. What I mean is that I'm not getting any younger."

"I see."

"And what I want is some legal advice. Now don't get me wrong, J.W. I'm willing to pay. *Willing and able*." He stopped and glared at his friend in the faint light and spoke these last words with a defiant pride. "Don't you go thinking I'm asking you for something free just because you're my friend."

"Brian will you shut up and get on with it! It's after hours. You don't have to pay me a damned thing."

"All right, I'm getting there. Now you recollect that once upon a time I had me a wife."

"Of course I do. I'm not senile *yet!*"

"I ain't saying you are, dammit. I just want to get it all laid out the way it ought to be."

"You just go ahead and lay it out all the way to Chattanooga. We got all summer, I reckon."

"Well, what I'm wanting to know in a nutshell is this: Am I *still* married?"

"It depends," Mr. Campbell said. "You have to tell me more than that."

"All right, now just suppose for the sake of supposing that I wanted to get married *again*. Oh for God's sake, J.W.! Don't look at me that way! I'm not saying I'm *going* to get married. Let's just suppose I'm *thinking* about getting married."

"I'll admit that supposition for the time being, but you must admit that it's a rather remarkable thought. I presume we're also supposing that the woman was born blind and that she's a full-blooded idiot!"

"No, we ain't necessarily supposing no such thing." Brian sounded tired and embarrassed rather than irritated.

"Go ahead, we're supposing you want to get married."

"Am I married to that . . . to my wife or not?"

"You mean to the woman that ran away with the fruit-tree salesman? You mean to the one that was called Josephine?"

Brian smiled in such absolute relief that he might just have delivered an enormous belch. "That's the very one!"

"Well, my friend, that wife is dead, and you're as free as a bird."

"Dead! My God, J.W., how'd you know that!"

"She's been gone seven years, hasn't she?"

"Seven! Hell, J.W., she's been gone seventeen! Longer than that. I lose track of things like that."

"All right, she's dead. The law holds that if you don't hear anything from a missing person in seven years, then he's legally dead."

"And that's the law for wives, too?"

"That is the law for everybody."

The already expansive relief on Brian's big face grew as large as the moon. "What about that!" he exclaimed. But his expression abruptly clouded over again. "Hmmmmm! Well, just suppose that I was to get married to somebody else and that dead wife of mine was to come humping up the road some bright morning. What would I do?"

"You'd just stick your head out the door and tell her she's dead. She may not know it yet. Then tell her to go away."

"With her *standing* there!"

"Standing, sitting, squatting, lying—what the hell! Hand her some flowers through the crack in the door and tell her you're sorry you didn't make the funeral."

"God Almighty!" Brian drank in the thought like white whiskey almost too strong for his stomach. "And what if she won't go?"

"Well, then I'd say the best thing you could do would be to kick her in the ass and tell her to get the hell off your land before you call the sheriff."

"It don't seem right to treat a corpse that way," Brian said.

"Oh hell, Brian. We're talking about the law. She's *legally* dead. It doesn't matter whether she's really dead or not."

Brian studied the proposition for a long time with an extremely puzzled look on his face. Then his wide smile came flooding back over his teeth. "God, J.W., the law's just as crazy as the rest of us."

Mr. Campbell laughed good-humoredly. "Yes, I guess it is," he said.

"But I'd still hate for her to come back," Brian said. "It'd sure mess things up."

"Oh she won't, Brian. Take my word for it. The woman probably went West. Where else does somebody like her go? She'll never come back. Hell, after all these years she probably *is* dead! If she went to some places I know she didn't last long. Women don't last long in the West anywhere."

"I guess that's a fact," Brian said thoughtfully. Then he pulled himself together with a shake of his wet body and made as if to go. "It was just something I wanted to know about," he said in a deprecating voice. "Now I'll know in case I ever need to."

"I understand," Mr. Campbell said in an equally offhanded way. "But like I said to Evelyn Weaver last week, you don't have a thing to worry about. You can get married any time you want, fair and square." He grinned slyly.

Brian cleared his throat uneasily and looked sideways at his friend. "Evelyn Weaver! She was in to see you, was she?"

"Oh yes. She came in one morning last week with all the kids, and we had a nice little chat. I guess I forgot to tell you about it."

"You don't say! Well yes, J.W., as a matter of fact you did."

"Of course I'm sure she told you she was coming."

"Told me," Brian repeated dully. "Last *week*? Well yes, yes. Sure, she told me all about it."

"I reckoned she did. She told me she was thinking about marrying you, and she knew it was complicated."

"You say that was last week? I mean it *was* last week."

"Yes, Wednesday I guess."

"What about that," Brian said, nodding with his mouth open.

"She was satisfied with what I told her. She said if it was good enough for the law, it was good enough for her."

"She's a law-abiding woman," Brian said. "That's a real true fact."

"Nice family too."

"Nice piece of land. Good water. Best damned barn in the county. J.W., did you know Dothan Weaver whitewashed his barn?"

"No, I don't guess I did."

"Damnedest thing I ever seen."

"Well, it looks like a pretty good deal to me."

"It is. I swear to God it is, J.W. And if you was thinking about such things, you'd have to say that my land tied on to her land would be a right smart of land."

"I guess I'd say that all right. Brian, I'll tell you what I think. I think that woman'd probably make you rich."

"I ain't never wanted to be rich, J. W. You know that. But now . . . Well, it's a thought."

Mr. Campbell laughed.

"Hell, J.W.! That's a good woman. I reckon I'm going to marry her."

"Well, I could have told you that last week. When's the day?"

"I guess we could do it tomorrow afternoon. Now that we ain't got no oats to harvest, I won't have nothing else to do."

It was Mr. Campbell's turn to gape. "Jesus Christ, Brian Ledbetter! You're not serious! *Tomorrow!*"

"It's as good a day as any once you decide to do it."

"Have you *asked* her? Have you even *asked* the woman?"

"*Asked* her! God Almighty, why should I *ask* her when she's practically *told* me?"

"You're just going out there and haul her off like a wagonload of green cabbage!"

"Well no, I ain't going to do that. But I thought I'd stop by tomorrow morning and pay my respects and tell her I've decided to marry her, and then we could get it done tomorrow afternoon."

"Lord God!"

"Well dammit, that's what I done with Josephine!"

"And Josephine ran off with a fruit-tree salesman who smelled like blackberry jelly!"

"That's a real true fact," Brian said in a worried frown. "But *she* ain't going to run off, J.W.!" He pointed vainly off in the dark in about the direction he thought Evelyn Weaver was located at the moment. "Hell, she *can't* run off. She's got six kids and a farm. She might haul the kids off, but you tell me how she's going to carry off one hundred and forty acres of land!"

Mr. Campbell shook his head wearily. "Maybe you're right, Brian. But it doesn't sound like any wedding to me. It sounds like you're buying a horse."

"Oh hell, J.W.! You're wanting me to make this thing up like some big love affair. Well, it ain't that way. Like she says, it's a business proposition, and if you ask me, it's a damn good one. Look what I get out of it!"

"And look what *she* gets," Mr. Campbell said.

"All right! I admit it! I ain't exactly no Prince Albert. But hellfire, she ain't no Queen Elizabeth!"

"No, she certainly isn't that," Mr. Campbell said with a wry smile.

They were silent again. In an air of abstracted thoughtfulness Mr. Campbell walked over and threw open the window giving onto the square. A cool draft was lightly wafted into the room from the dripping earth outside. The two friends stood together by the window and looked out, hearing the gentle murmuring of the wet night and the rhythmic breathing of Hub Delaney on the bed behind them.

Brian's mood deepened. When at last he spoke again he was solemn and thoughtful. "Anyway, I've been thinking about a lot of things, J.W. I mean here lately."

"Yes, it's been a thoughtful time."

"I've been thinking about me and coming in here ever night, year after year, and going home and not having nothing else. It's a long ride home in the dark, J.W. An awful long ride."

Mr. Campbell barely nodded his head in assent.

"I ain't thinking about what you're thinking," Brian said warily.

"You don't know what I'm thinking."

"Well, I ain't just thinking about the fucking around. I mean I ain't *not* thinking about it exactly, but it ain't the main thing."

Mr. Campbell smiled.

"It really ain't," Brian pleaded. "It's something more than that. It's . . . It's . . ." He wrestled futilely for words and could find none really able to express what he felt. So he only repeated with greater stress: "It's a long ride home in the dark, J.W. You don't know how long."

"I've been out in the dark myself, Brian."

Brian bit his lip. "I guess you have at that."

"Well, you'll have a nice family. All ready-made like a suit of clothes to jump into. I think you're probably a very lucky man."

Brian's face perked up. "And you know something else, J.W.? I ain't near as old as some folks think. I can still do my duty. I can do it any time I want."

"Old soldiers never die," Mr. Campbell said, laughing.

"So maybe I'll have some kids on my own. I can still do it. And hell, she can too!"

"You would need her co-operation," Mr. Campbell observed.

"You wait and see," Brian said.

"All right, I'll do that. I hope you have a son. Hell, you can name the little booger after me." Mr. Campbell tried to say the words in a bantering tone. But it didn't quite come off. Something deeply serious and sad forced its way into his voice. Both men were suddenly embarrassed.

"Well, we just might. You never can tell," Brian said with an artificial laugh.

"You're soaked through," Mr. Campbell said. Swiftly and deliberately he changed the subject. "If you catch your death you won't be able to do your duty or anything else. Why don't you go over to the station? You can sit with Clarence and dry yourself out. He'll have a fire going. He gets cold when it rains."

"I was fixing to stop by and see him." Brian drew closer to the window. He looked sadly out to the patch of clear light which marked the window of the railroad station across the square. "I need to look in on him. You know, he don't look good, J.W."

"He never has looked good."

"Yes, but this is different. He ain't long with us."

"I guess he should have gone back to Baltimore a long time ago."

Brian shook his head. "No, if he'd gone up there he wouldn't of had nothing. He don't have no folks in Baltimore. I asked him once. It's just the place he's from."

Mr. Campbell shrugged. "He doesn't have much of anybody here."

"He's got us. It's better than nothing."

"Is it?" Mr. Campbell raised his eyebrows. "Well, maybe it is at that." They hesitated by the window. Mr. Campbell took out his silver watch and looked at it. "I guess I need to go if I'm going." But he made no effort to move.

"I wish you wouldn't, J.W."

"I think Charlotte would want me to go." He laughed without mirth and stood holding the watch and looked at it with a distracted expression in his eyes. Then he hoisted the flap of his coat and put it back into his pocket. They were silent again. The sky was clear now, and the moon shone richly down through the moist air and bathed the town in a flood of tranquil light. Everything smelled clean and fresh.

"It was a hard storm," Mr. Campbell observed in a low voice.

"Hardest I ever seen," Brian agreed. He puckered his face in a puzzling frown. "I wonder how Simson knew."

Mr. Campbell did not even shrug. "Maybe he was a prophet after all."

Brian laughed. "Oh, I guess he was crazy and God thought He'd get Hisself a laugh out of it. My mamma always said God had a special love of idiots. You know, J.W., the world's so crazy there *must* be a God! It just couldn't of got this way all by itself."

They both chuckled. Mr. Campbell picked up his large black hat from the table. "Doc Cogill is coming back in a minute. He's gone home to supper. I guess Hub will be all right."

They looked at the prostrate form on the bed. "That was one hell of a shot," Brian said in admiration. "You know, I don't know if I could shoot with one hand or not."

"I guess Hub didn't know till today."

"By the way, J.W., you heard anything today about the general? Any news?"

Mr. Campbell shook his head. "Same as yesterday. He had a bad night. It won't be long."

"It's an awful way to go," Brian said softly.

Mr. Campbell did not respond. He went out of the room putting on his hat, and Brian followed him, and moving as quietly as they could, they went down the steps and out into the still moonlight. Brian departed for the station, slogging across the mud-caked square. Mr. Campbell went on down the street toward the livery stable to fetch his horse. He paused to bring a cigar out of the supply treasured in his coat pocket, and it was while he was lighting it and the sudden flame from the sulphur match was illuminating his face that he was accosted by a mud-splattered horseman from the dark. At the breathless hailing of his name, he looked up and with some difficulty recognized the slim form of the younger Samuel Beckwith glaring at him from the night. "Mr. Campbell, I've got to talk to you. It can't wait. I've got to talk to you right now." Holding the match aloft, Mr. Campbell could see that the youth's eyes were wild, and even in that indistinct light he could see that his face was dreadfully pale. Seeing, Mr. Campbell felt something thick and heavy shift behind a concealed door in his mind—the imponderable motion of something that should be dead—and he was suddenly afraid.

27

Mr. Campbell led the way back to his house along the moon-blanched street. The youth followed him on horseback and dismounted before the steps, secured his spent horse at the hitching rail, and went after the older man inside. The downstairs was dark and silent. Mr. Campbell's office was as black as a cave. But Mr. Campbell found his way unerringly to the desk and struck a match to the green-shaded lamp reposing there, and the light rose on the walls of the book-bound room. By its revealing glow he could see how smeared with mud the youth was, how exhausted were his eyes, and he could see more plainly the haggard pallor of his stricken face.

"Sam, are you sick?" Mr. Campbell looked at him in alarm.

"No, I'm not sick." The intonation was flat and lifeless.

"You're not well. Sit down."

"I'm too dirty to sit down."

"I hire a nigger woman to clean this place up twice a week," Mr. Campbell said impatiently. "For once in her life she can earn her pay. Now sit down before you collapse on the floor."

The youth obediently sat. But he perched gingerly on the edge of the chair as if afraid to let the full weight of his slim body rest upon the old leather. The two of them sat watching one another in a strained, anticipatory silence. The older man was stiffly composed. The younger was tense and weary and hardly able to speak.

Mr. Campbell carefully folded his hands at his chin and peered thoughtfully over them, the cigar smoldering listlessly in his grasp. "What's wrong with you, Sam?"

But instead of answering him the youth looked blankly around and made a vague gesture toward the outside. "Those people, tonight . . . All those people on the road . . . Where are they . . . *going?*"

Mr. Campbell looked at him through eyes narrowed in surprise, but he spoke with prodding gentleness. "You don't know what happened here today? You don't know about the preacher?"

"What preacher? Preacher Bazely?"

"Yes, he was killed out there in the street this afternoon."

"*Killed!* He's *dead*? That man is *dead*?" The youth gasped out the words and sat forward with a convulsive jerk. His eyes flared up wild and amazed—all signs Mr. Campbell absorbed with an observant and rigid self-control.

"Yes, he's dead. He was shot down in the act of trying to murder me with a pistol, as it turned out." And Mr. Campbell went slowly on to explain what had happened, told him the story in a carefully ramshackle narrative which ended with the appearance of Sarah Beckwith in town, though not with a true account of all she had said to him. No, Mr. Campbell told her share in the day's events as it would be narrated by Joseph Tilley, by people in the valley who heard it from him, and by those who would tell it long after everyone in town that day was dead. The crazed preacher had appeared at the Crittendon home. Sarah Crittendon Beckwith had perceived his madness and shut him out. As he departed in an insane rage, she realized he was coming to town to kill someone. She rushed off after him in a fearless dash to avert disaster but arrived after the preacher was already dead. And Mr. Campbell concluded with the restrained but admiring observation that she was a brave woman, a very brave woman.

His voice was low and mild, and his slow words were interspersed with an occasional grim chuckle. Beyond the open window the stillness of the town deepened as the night drew on. The narrative droned on in the tranquil room like a harmony of random chords, and the tense form of the young Samuel Beckwith relaxed and subsided into something more like calm. The youth heard the older man out without a word of his own, and as the story went on he sat back in his chair and surveyed Mr. Campbell with a long, searching, indefinable look of inquiry. Finally, when Mr. Campbell had done and a long, reflective silence had fallen over them, Sam said: "So my mother ran the danger of death to come to town to save your life." His tone was faintly ironic.

"She did not know he was going to try to kill *me*," Mr. Campbell said quietly.

The youth nodded slightly, his face set in a brooding mask. Finally with a great deal of effort he said: "Mr. Campbell, I came into town tonight to ask you some things. I've *got* to know some things, and you're the only person on earth I can ask. The only one."

"About what?"

"About my father."

Silence. A leap of invisible electricity in the book-quiet room. Mr. Campbell shifted ever so slightly in his chair, let his hands fall down into his lap, still holding the cigar, and with composed force he looked steadily back into the intense gaze of the youth before him.

"There's something I don't know about my father, Mr. Campbell."

"That's hardly surprising since the man died when you were a baby."

The youth sighed heavily. "I'm not here to play lawyer games, Mr. Campbell. I'm here to learn the truth. That's not too much to ask, is it? The truth? It's my *right,* isn't it? The truth about my father. The truth, Mr. Campbell. The truth. The truth." His voice dropped to the low, baffled repetition of a man not sure that someone else understands the meaning of an ordinary word.

"Would you like me to drag out a Bible and swear on that, so help me God?" Mr. Campbell reached mockingly for the old Bible on the edge of his desk, and a spark of scorn touched his words with fire.

The youth put a tired hand to his face and slowly rubbed his eyes. Taking the hand away he blinked hard and spoke with a great, tired patience: "Mr. Campbell, you can bully me if you want, but I'm still going to sit right here and ask you to tell me the truth about my father. I'll sit here until the moss grows down my back. I'll sit, and I'll sit, and I'll sit."

Mr. Campbell forced a malicious laugh, though his hands were still tensely set in his lap. "Well, you can sit right there till doomsday for all I care! Now, if you'll excuse me, I've got to be going. In fact, I've got to get out to your place to sit up with my old friend the preacher. We've got to be sure he's not breathing so we can plant him in the ground tomorrow in the blessed hope that he will be raised with an incorruptible body in the resurrection of the dead. Paradise, I am told, will be made up of one long sermon by Preacher Bazely, which is a pretty good argument for going to hell." Mr. Campbell spun the words off in a flurry of derision and at the end of them stood up to go.

But Samuel Beckwith jumped to his feet. "If you try to leave, I'll kill you with my bare hands." He stood lowering across the desk at Mr. Campbell with his fists clenched and half raised.

The older man mustered all the embittered disdain of his years and glared hatefully at the youth. "I hope you don't think a man of my age is really so afraid of dying that he'll take orders from the likes of *you!*" Placing a tone of acid scorn on the last word, he took a resolute step toward the door.

But the youth's face became so abruptly contorted that he might have been on the verge of tears. He unclenched his fists and put his open hands out in a gesture of entreaty. "Please, Mr. Campbell, don't treat me like a dog. In the name of my father's friendship, please hear me out. *Please!*"

The voice was so wretched and earnest that Mr. Campbell was arrested by it. Slowly he sat down again, his level eyes fixed on the wasted face of his visitor. Sam also sat. Mr. Campbell spoke to him with surprising tenderness. "What brought you here? What started all this?"

"Will you tell me what I want to know?"

"What *do* you want to know?"

The youth leaned nervously forward into the direct light of the lamp, and his pale face burned in the lamp's mellow gleaming. It was a haunted, twisted face, and in the full light Mr. Campbell sorted out features he knew so well from another face in another time. The young Sam Beckwith spoke in a thin, tight stream of anguished words. "I found something out tonight. A terrible thing. It's so terrible that I can't believe it, and yet I *do* believe it, and I've got to do something. But I don't know *what.* I just know I have to know something else before I can decide what to do."

"If you will permit an old lawyer to say so, you are not making your case very clear," Mr. Campbell said. His tone was not unkind.

"I'm not here to see you as a lawyer. I'm here to talk to you as a human being. *Please,* Mr. Campbell, for the love of *God* listen to me!" The youth was so vehement that the words flew out of his mouth like shards blown off an exploding bomb. For a moment Mr. Campbell thought he might be on the point of losing control of himself altogether.

"All right, Sam. You say your piece. Any way you want. Take all the time you want."

"Let's start with the things I know. Isn't that the best way? Yes. Well then. My father came here twenty years ago, just as the War was ending. Now, he met my mother by accident. Somebody happened to haul him out to our place so he could die in peace, and she nursed him back to health. They fell in love. He married her. I was born. My mother loved him with all her heart. Didn't she love him, Mr. Campbell? Don't I know that my mother loved my father?"

"Why Sam, she adored him. Everybody knows that."

"She adored him," the youth repeated blankly. "Yes, I guess I believe that. But still there was some way he didn't fit, Mr. Campbell. She had her world organized down to the last old picture hanging on the wall of the smallest room in our house, and in some way he just didn't fit. Five years after they were married, he did something wrong. Did my father love somebody else, Mr. Campbell? Was he unfaithful to my mother?"

Mr. Campbell replied in a steely calm. "Never in his whole life with her. I can swear to that."

"But there was *something!* Some way he didn't *fit!*"

"There was *nothing!*" Mr. Campbell spoke the denial with such tense force that it was like a shout in the still room.

The youth had raised his own voice, but now he resumed his tracking with an implacable quiet. "You are not telling me the truth, Mr. Campbell. Now listen, you were my father's friend. I am the son of someone who must have trusted you. Didn't he trust you, Mr. Campbell?"

"Yes, he trusted me." A confession, miserable and contrite.

"Then you owe me the truth because I inherited that trust. Did all the feeling you had for him die when he died? Are you the kind of man who forgets things like friendship? I am my father's son, Mr. Campbell, and you are not telling me something that I *have* to *know!*" The youth's eyes were like coals of fire burning far back in his head, and against the shadowed dimness of the wall behind him his intensity seemed spectral and almost frightful.

Mr. Campbell threw his hands up in a tired gesture of impatience, but above his hands his face bore a look of agony. "Sam, believe me, there is nothing else to tell. Your father and mother lived together for five years as happily as any two people could be. At the end he had a heart attack and died. That is the story of your father's life. It is all the story there is." Mr. Campbell accented the last sentence with an unspoken and desperate pleading to be believed and left alone. But Sam Beckwith was unflinching, and now it was in his eyes that there glittered an overwrought mockery—something faintly gleeful, ominous, and uncontained.

"And you believe he died of a heart attack?"

A far-off tocsin clanged in Mr. Campbell's brain. "Of course I believe it. It's what happened."

"But no *doctor* said so."

"There wasn't any need for a doctor. The man was dead."

"So what you mean is that my mother said he died of a heart attack, and everybody in the valley believed her."

"He had chest pains all the time."

"Did *you* ever hear him talk about those pains, Mr. Campbell?" The question was as deadly as a plunging knife, and the eyes behind the thrust were ablaze.

Mr. Campbell tried to evade it: "Your father wasn't one to complain about things in public."

"Did you *ever* hear him say one *word* about pains in his chest?"

Mr. Campbell lowered his head. "No, I never heard him complain." His voice was soft, resigned, old, and tired.

"I know he did not die of a heart attack."

"He's dead. It doesn't matter how he died. It's all gone."

"She killed him, Mr. Campbell. My mother killed him." The youth's voice had an almost hysterical lilt to it.

The older man raised his eyes in one last fiery counterattack. "You're insane."

"She killed him. I *know* she killed him. But I don't know why."

Mr. Campbell shook his head like a man rudely wakened from a drunken sleep. "No, you don't know a thing like that. Why it's insane, insane." The words were run together in an almost incoherent mutter, and he gazed blankly at the wild young face burning at him in the glare of light over the desk. The extinct cigar he held forgotten in his hand slipped out of his fingers and fell on the floor. He leaned dully forward onto the desk and gaped at his visitor. "Aren't you insane?"

The eyes of the younger man lost something of their leering brilliance, and he sank back against his chair, and his tired face was plunged once more into soft shadow. "It's true, Mr. Campbell. I'm telling *you* the truth."

"How do you know?" The question was a whisper of anguish.

So now the younger man uncoiled a narrative in the still room where the single lamp burned like a memorial to gods slain in battle. His homecoming to an empty house. The cryptic note. The plunge into the storm to find his mother. The refuge with the dying nigger. Their terrifying interview. And at last his discovery in the loft of the cabin where old George had lived—the insidious, dully gleaming thing buried under cobwebs and speckled with hardened rat dung, set on the decaying beam over the collapsed bed. The gently bitter smell of that finely crystalline powder—a smell like nothing else on earth. And at the end, the young Sam Beckwith said with huge conviction and calm, "So I believe it, Mr. Campbell. I believe she killed him."

The older man remonstrated. "Sam, Sam! You ought to forget all this! It doesn't do any good to ask questions like the ones you're asking. It's all over. It's finished. You can't call him back. You can't get all upset over a nigger story. My God, don't be a fool!"

But his words were faltering and unconvincing, and his thoughts got tangled up and crossed each other, and he was all at once unbelievably drawn and weary. Sam could see the age cracking out of his sagging face, saw the sorrowful lines eating across his temples from his gray eyes, saw the drooping mouth under the fierce moustache, saw also the dewlaps of tired skin hanging slack under his neck. Mr. Campbell had let his defenses fall, and age had overpowered him in an instant.

"I just want to know the truth, the truth you must know. I've got a right to know. He was my father." Again the implacable demand.

Mr. Campbell sighed miserably and got up and wandered in a torpor of fatigue to the window. He looked out on the dark town with forlorn grief. "I always wondered," he said in a slow, dazed muttering. "It seemed so *convenient* when he . . . died. The thought just naturally would enter my mind. I *am* a lawyer, you know. But I put it down the minute it came up because it just might have been true. And if it *were* true, I thought I couldn't live with it. Anyway, Preacher Bazely and I were the only people in the valley who had any reason to suspect, and I knew damn well *he* wasn't going to say anything. So I had to push it down and shrug it off, and I did my best to forget all about it. Just *forget!* And I did. I really did. I just said to myself so many times that he died of a heart attack—the way she said—that I believed it. I *made* myself believe it. You can make yourself do that, you know. Or maybe you don't know. You're so young. Maybe you don't know the tricks we can do with the past. It was like smoking opium, I guess. I took a deep breath and resolved to put the thing out of my mind, and I did it, and I felt a great peace over it. It was the best thing for everybody, I thought. And now suddenly here it is again, and I can't toss it off, and I think I may be too old now to bear it. Maybe it's harder for me to tell you what I know than it is for you to hear it. Strange the way these things are. Very strange. Very strange indeed. Yes, yes!" Mr. Campbell's normally strong voice seemed ready to degenerate into senseless babbling.

"Please tell me," Sam Beckwith said softly. "I have to know it all."

"Yes, yes of course. You're the son. You have to know, and it's your right. Of course it's your legal right." Mr. Campbell sought the youth with his dazed eyes and looked at him in perplexity as if trying to make out just who he was. He nodded again, gravely, and with an elaborate show of understanding.

Sam was alarmed at the changed appearance of the older man, and he asked anxiously: "Sir, are you all right? Shouldn't you sit down?"

"Sit down? No no, my boy. If I sit down right now, why I might never get up again. I'm all right. Quite all right." He turned back to the window and stood looking out as if trying to focus on a frame of moving shadows swirling in the street. When he resumed speaking his voice was more steady though it was still low and dazed and stricken with pain.

"Sam, you've got to understand that your father was one of the best men that ever lived. When you know everything about him—even the mistake he made—you still have to say he was one of the best men who ever lived. He was unselfish, and he was so full of life, so open, so *fresh.* Everybody loved him. Your mother wasn't the only one. *I* loved him. Do I shock you if I say that? I *loved* the man."

"Beckinridge said he looked like your son."

Mr. Campbell nodded so slightly that it might have been no gesture at all. "They were both . . . *tall,* and . . . *thin,* and there was something about your father's eyes and mouth when he laughed that reminded me of . . . yes, reminded me of my son. You could see your father standing with his back turned at a distance, and with his hair the way it was—long and fine and disheveled—and you'd just naturally think: Why that's *Tom!* But they didn't look *exactly* alike. Did Beckinridge say they looked alike? You wouldn't expect a nigger to notice things like that."

"He said all the niggers thought it."

"Well, well."

"You were talking about the mistake my father made," Sam said, prodding impatiently.

"Yes, yes. The mistake. But it's important about his looking like my son. I mean it's *symbolic* of everything that happened. You see, I failed my boy. It's a long story, and I was one of the chief actors in it, but even I can't tell you exactly what I did wrong or why I did it.

I just failed my son. I know *that.* And I guess I wanted to make up for what I'd done—or not done. I wanted a second chance to be a human being. This whole horrible business was pushed along by people who wanted a second chance in life. That's the real unpardonable sin, isn't it? To want a second chance in a life, where everybody gets only one real grab at fortune?"

"I don't know."

"Well, I'm older than you are, and *I* know. So that's a second point you ought to understand before you judge your father. Fact: Everybody makes a wreck out of life. We dream dreams and raise roof beams to nail the dreams on, and we always do *something* to knock the beam down and make all the dreams a wreck. Do you understand that? We all make blunders which tear our lives apart, and we do it at a very early age. A very tender and early age when we don't have the sense to know better. But the things we do then haunt us for as long as we live." He looked around at the youth with a wan inspiration, and Sam Beckwith nodded soberly and without a word.

"And most of the time there's nothing we can do even to make ourselves *think* we can undo the past. Our past hangs on to us like a death we carry around on our backs, and we can't get away from what we did then no matter what we do—*most of the time!*"

The old man lifted an instructive forefinger and shook it wisely at the youth. "*Most of the time!*" he repeated grimly. "But then, along comes a war! Now, war tears life out by the roots. Lord God! For most people who get themselves mixed up in a war, it's an unmitigated evil. War is hell. That's the truest sentence ever spoken. But every time a war comes along you get a flock of fools to shout and cheer the thing on, to yell themselves hoarse for the glory of it, and then to go charging off to give to the war whatever the hell it demands. And do you know why they're so delirious, so in love with war?"

"No."

"Because war means *change.* It's something terrible, but it's *different!* War kills a hell of a lot of people, but to some it gives a new birth. In all that death, some people experience a sort of resurrection. You can get out of the old life you had just as easily as you can pull off a glove or a boot, and you can slip yourself into a new one almost without thinking about it. And that was the way it was with your father."

Away out in the wet dark they heard the sad cry of the evening train, and for a moment they listened to its faint and gradual approach and imagined its swift pounding through the sleeping countryside up the line. Then Sam Beckwith said slowly: "So the War gave him—gave my father a new life."

Mr. Campbell nodded, still the slight, bleak gesture which was hardly a motion at all. His voice was still low, but it was stronger now. "Exactly, a new life. You see, he was from the backwoods in Virginia, and the fact is, your father had a poor background. You could tell that the minute he opened his mouth. That's one of the biggest differences between you and him. Your mother taught you the King's English."

"She's always been very strict about that. Sometimes I've wondered why."

"Well, she was embarrassed at the way your father talked. It was the only time I ever heard her irritated with him. He'd say something crude or ungrammatical, and she'd say, 'Sam, you sound so *common.*' But he would laugh and hug her, and he'd tell her he loved her in spite of her highfalutin language, and that would mollify her. You see, he *did* love her. But she was embarrassed about the way he talked, and you could tell his raisings had been poor."

"But when he married my mother, he got another chance." The call of the train was louder now, and in the distance they could hear the murmur of the engine and the extended gentle rumble of the trailing cars. The train was late.

"Yes, and in more ways than one. You see, he came here sick enough to die. He *would* have died if your mother hadn't nursed him back to health. No doubt about that. He owed his life to her. He always said he skidded through death's door on his ass, and your mother reached in and hauled him out again by the shirttail, and that's really about the way it was. Then one day he raised up out of his fever and looked around and saw he was resting in a pretty good place. And he must have seen something else that made him think twice about going back to Virginia. Your mother was in love with him. It was a deep and passionate thing, and your father knew it. He was always a little amazed at how much she cared for him. He never could understand it."

"She's always admitted she fell in love with him first. She even proposed, she says."

"I'm sure that's a fact," Mr. Campbell said wearily. "You see, your mother had a pretty lonely life, and not just in the War. Your grandfather neglected her pretty badly. He really *resented* her. I remember that very well. The fact is, Sam, your grandfather was having a pretty hard time making it before the War came along. Every year it got harder for him to meet his obligations, and I remember a constant rumor of talk that he might be about to lose the place altogether. Who'll ever know what kind of talk went on out there over that young girl's head! I think the confusion of the War saved your land. But before that your grandfather looked on your mother as something worthless that was going to cost him a dowry someday. So she was a lonely girl to begin with, and then she was left completely alone by the fortunes of war."

"She had old George," the youth said with a bitter smile. "An old nigger who loved her."

"Yes, she had that," Mr. Campbell said spiritlessly. "But then your father came along, and he was a handsome man, and he had this amazing ability to make people love him. Oh, I speak as if it were something *contrived,* a quality he *used* on people, and to tell the truth I think there *was* a little of that in your father. Let's just say that he knew how to make the best use of his gifts, and one of the greatest gifts he possessed was charm. He wanted people to like him, and he turned his personality into an art. He wasn't an educated man, but he was intelligent. Sharp as a fine tack, and he could appear instantly simple and unaffected and just naturally joyful. You'd meet him and listen to him talk about things, hear him joking, hear that spontaneous laughter of his, and you just couldn't help thinking that life had a bright, good side to it. *He* had a brooding side to himself, really a melancholy side, but people seldom saw that, or if they did glimpse it they didn't take it seriously because they didn't think it was real. No, what they noticed was the joy your father had at being alive, and something out of that joy always overflowed onto people and did something to them. You know, your mother was always a pretty woman. But your father made her beautiful! Before he came, she had a plain prettiness, but five years with him turned her into one of the most beautiful women I've ever known."

"Her face is breaking up now," the youth observed. "You can see it in little ways." He sat back in the shadows and watched Mr. Campbell's face, which was bent forward into the full glow of the light slanting under the shade.

The older man nodded slowly and sadly. "Yes, I know." They paused before the augmenting sound of the approaching train. The majestic entry of the night express was announced by its loud ringing bell and its prolonged whistle, rising and falling like a shrieking, bestial cry, and everything else in Bourbonville was reduced to a silence so profound that it might have been fear. Through the window they could see the fiery trail of sparks laid over the night by the great flared smokestack of the passing engine, and they could see the thick smoke roil black against the starry sky. The train halted in a screech of iron, and the boiler of the locomotive gave off a long hiss of power scarcely restrained, and an irregular clamor of voices rose around the station like a sudden, multifarious explosion. Then with another warning blast of its whistle and a grabbing of iron couplings and a measured clanking of prodigious driving wheels and heaving side rods, the train moved out of the station and, gathering speed, departed with an enormous sob of steam into the fresh summer night.

In the process, Doc Cogill came stamping up the front steps and into the house. He peered in and spoke to Mr. Campbell and with some surprise noted the presence of the young Sam Beckwith. But saying nothing beyond a grumpy hello, he turned and went toiling on up the stairs, trailing an aromatic whiff of pipe smoke behind him in the faded dark. Mr. Campbell went quietly to the office door and shut it and paced slowly back to the window and looked out and found his narrative again in the silken fabric of the moonlight.

"And there was something else about your father, and that was that he set out to *deserve* the fate that had given him a second chance. He told me many a time he didn't expect to live through the War. When it was over he was stranded down near Mobile, Alabama, and he had to walk all the way home. He was half starved from living on fatback and potatoes for four years, and it's no wonder he took sick. It was fate that brought him to your mother, and it was fate that gave him his life back. He always said he was lucky, and he wanted to make the best of it. I guess it was a religious feeling in a way—a gratitude to whatever gods there were for giving him another chance.

"In part that meant he worked like a dog. But there was more to it than that. He was good to people—good to everybody he met. Niggers, poor white trash, a country lawyer like me, your mother—good to everybody in this whole accursed valley. He had a streak of genuine kindness in him forty miles wide and forty feet deep. The kindness was a more real part of him than all the laughter and some of the other stuff he put on for public consumption. The man couldn't stand to inflict pain. I guess he had been so close to death that he thought he had perceived the real wisdom of life, and to him that wisdom was that everybody had enough hurt already without his adding to it."

Sam shifted restlessly in the chair which he had turned toward the window where Mr. Campbell stood looking out. "I know all that," he said with impatient energy. "I want to know what he did *wrong!*"

Mr. Campbell turned on him with a harsh scowl. "You'll have to let me tell it my way. I'm a lawyer, goddammit, and I'm making a case for a friend. You'll have to listen to the way I want to tell it, or else you can go to hell. Now is that good enough for you or not?"

The youth pressed both his hands to his face against this outburst, and he shook his head as if trying to rid his brain of a nightmare. He stared up at Mr. Campbell with a vexed and tormented frown. "It's so unreal, this *talk*—when we know what *happened,*" he blurted. "So *unreal.*"

Mr. Campbell chortled. "Do you expect a clap of thunder every time you get a backache? You'll find that men aren't that important, my boy."

The youth took a deep breath and lowered his eyes in submission. "Please go on. Please!"

"All right. I was saying that your father was just naturally a good man, and that's the first point I want to establish. But now there was a bad man who entered the picture. He was like your father in that he was from far away and that Bourbonville—this squalid little heap of human garbage—gave him a new chance for life after the War. His past was always a blank to us, though we've all heard some things. Now we'll never know the truth because the man is dead. He was killed out there in the street this afternoon."

"Preacher Bazely."

"Preacher Bazely. The man was a lunatic, and I argue that we can't judge lunatics after the ordinary standards of the law. But I think you can use all the excuses you want about madness, and after you scour away all the lunacy you still find something evil left in his bones.

"It makes you believe in mindless fatality when you think about it. Those two men came drifting into this town from different directions, and until they got here neither one of them knew the other one existed, and neither one of them intended to stay, and they both stayed because of your mother, and that got them eternally wrapped up together. They both fell in love with her. Preacher Bazely before your father. Don't look so black. You can't take vengeance on the dead, and it's all done now.

"I never did understand Bazely. But there was one thing perfectly clear, and that was that he took one look at your mother and wanted her to love him. Well, of course *she* was never going to have anything to do with the likes of *him!* He was scrawny and ugly, and he had a mind like the grate in a stove—made of cast iron—and all he could hold was bitterness and hatred and hellfire. Bazely preached hellfire all the time he was alive in this town, and I tell you the reason why. The man carried hellfire around inside him, and it burned in him day and night. I don't know what started it, but there it was, burning and burning.

"So they were very different men, your father and Bazely. A perpetual youth bubbled out of your father and made everybody around him young. But the preacher gave off hellfire like a volcano, and he devastated everything in sight. Your mother had the high good sense not to have anything to do with him, then or ever.

"I always heard that he went out there and spent the night in your barn on his way to wherever it was he was going. He took one look at your mother and lay awake all night thinking about her and proposed marriage in the morning. Your mother turned him down flat. She just laughed and put him off as if he hadn't even been serious, so I hear, and that should have been the end of it.

"But Bazely *wouldn't* give up. All at once he got an inspiration from God Almighty to stay here in the valley. So he wrestled up some money somewhere and bought that ratty little place of his back in the hills. I've always thought he probably got what money he had by looting poor devils in Kansas, but I don't know, and it doesn't matter now. Anyway he settled down, and pretty soon he let it be known that he was a preacher, and you know the rest.

"But I guess you don't know how he acted when he got word that your mother was about to get married to that invalid she'd been tending. He almost lost his mind. They say he rushed out to see her and begged her to reconsider. Your mother laughed in his face. I don't mean it was *mocking* laughter. She was much to happy to be unkind. But she laughed at *anyone* who suggested to her that she shouldn't marry her Prince Charming—your father. I know for a fact that she asked Bazely to perform the ceremony."

"Mrs. Weaver told me that this afternoon."

"Well it's true, and it's true that he refused. He never had a good spirit, but your mother's marriage ruined what might have been left of humanity in the man's soul. He became hateful. But you know what he was—silent and watchful, and so full of hate you couldn't get near him without feeling uneasy."

"I could tell you stories about that," the young man said in a low voice.

Mr. Campbell lifted a curious eyebrow, but he was enfolded in his own story, and he went on with it. "And naturally he hated your father more than he hated anybody else on earth. Your father just laughed it off, and I guess I was more preoccupied with Bazely than your father ever was. I realized the man was dangerous, and your father didn't. Even I didn't know *how* dangerous he could be.

"But that was when I started hooting at the man when he went by in the street. I used to beg him to throw me a little wad of his hellfire so I'd have something handy to light my cigars with. And I said a lot more than that. It was pretty mean, but you have to give me some credit for what I did to the man. Bazely was a marvel with words, and if I hadn't been here to mock him, well you don't know how far this poor foolish town would have followed him. But as long as I ridiculed him the way I did, the town just couldn't take him completely seriously, and maybe that saved it from madness.

"So that's the situation. You've got a good man, and you've got an evil man, and the good man doesn't want to harm anybody on earth, and the evil man is hungering and thirsting for some way—for *anything*—he can find to use to destroy the good man. And the poor good man—your father—just because he *was* good didn't have any way of protecting himself against what Bazely did."

"But what could he do? How could the preacher hurt my father?"

"I'm coming to that," Mr. Campbell said wearily. "Give me time. The first advantage Bazely had was that your father had a foolish, insensitive friend—me. In a way everything that happened was my fault because as old as I was—a lawyer and all the rest—I still couldn't look behind what a man *said* and figure out what it was that he *meant*. You see, one of the odd things about your father was that he never would tell you *exactly* where he was from. He was so frank about his reasons, and his heart seemed to be so open, that you just accepted what he said and dismissed it. He told everybody that his whole childhood had been a hard scrape against poverty and that he had a pretty miserable life before the War, and he didn't like to think about it, much less talk about it. Oh, if you mentioned Virginia, he was always saying that he was going to go back up there someday and settle some affairs, but he never said just *where*. It was something the man just wouldn't talk about.

"And you know how it is. You get acquainted with a man, and you know him for several years, and after a while you just forget that he came from someplace else, and that's what we all did with your father. We accepted him as part of life here in the valley, and he and I got to be good friends. We hunted a lot together. We both liked to be out in the morning, and to be honest, I was getting over the loss of my boy. Your father's company kept me from thinking about *that* all the time. I suppose I was trying to have the kind of friendship with him that I never did manage to have with my son. It was all part of that crazy business of looking for a second chance.

"Well, one day we were ambling along, and all of a sudden we saw this old dog slouching in the road, and your father pulled up with a look of the most intense pleasure on his face, and he whistled that dog up and got down and patted him like an old friend home from the War. Well, naturally I asked him what in hell he thought he was doing. And he said that dog was the very image of a fine old hunting dog he'd had at home in Virginia. And he just went on and on about how the two dogs looked so remarkably alike. And I said in passing, 'Sam, just what was the place you were from in Virginia? I might have fought through there.' I wasn't really very interested, and I could tell it wasn't something he wanted to tell me, but I was his friend, you see. I was your father's best friend, and he just couldn't evade the question, and the poor fool told me!"

Mr. Campbell's voice had been low and husky, and now it became so strained and tight that it almost broke. His wrung face was abject with sorrow and regret. "That was where he made his great mistake," he murmured with huge grief. "He told me where he was from. And I would have forgotten it right away except that it had a funny name for a town in Virginia. Union. The place was called Union, Virginia. I got a good belly laugh out of that, and I said it was a hell of a Union that produced Rebels like himself. But your father didn't laugh. He didn't even smile. I remember that distinctly because he was always laughing at everything, and he laughed hardest when the joke was on himself. But that day he didn't even smile, and I should have known that something was *wrong*. But it didn't seem important at the time, and I let it pass. And if that town hadn't been something I *remembered,* if it hadn't been called *Union,* that would have been the end of it, and your father might be alive to this day.

"But I *did* remember it, and one night there was a group of us loitering around at the depot. Your father wasn't there, and we got to talking about him and the way he could spin yarns and make people laugh. That was one of the reasons people loved your father. He could see the funny side of things and make people laugh. You'd get him and Brian Ledbetter in the same crowd, and I swear you'd go home with your ribs sore and wake up with your stomach stiff come next morning. So we were talking about that—talking about how funny he could be. And I said, 'But let me tell you what's the *real* joke on that goddammed Rebel refugee. He hails from a town called *Union.*' And I told them what your father had told me, and we all laughed about it, and the men repeated it in town, and it was something they remembered the way I remembered it without thinking it really mattered.

"And it wasn't more than a week or ten days after that that Preacher Bazely came down here one day and walked in on me. He stood right there. It was the only time the man was ever in this house. I can still see him and that evil curiosity on his ugly face. He said, 'Mr. Campbell, I heard somebody say that you said Samuel Beckwith was from a place called Union, Virginia. I wanted to see if it were true.' "

Mr. Campbell raised a frustrated fist and made a feeble beating motion against the air. "I *knew* then I'd done the wrong thing. I *knew* something bad was about to happen. All at once it came to me that Bazely had seen something that none of the rest of us had, and that was that your father had something to hide in Union, Virginia. Well, I tried to bluff it out. I told Bazely it wasn't any of his goddammed business, and I told him if he didn't clear out of here in a hurry I was going to break every spindly bone in his wormy body. But he'd found out what he wanted to know, and he just thanked me and left with a wise smile on his face. When Bazely smiled, you knew he was thinking bad thoughts.

"And next thing you knew, he had disappeared. It was the summer of eighteen seventy, and he got up in the pulpit one Sunday morning and announced he'd be gone for a month, and the next day he got on the train with a ticket to Knoxville and vanished. I must have been the only person in the valley who knew he was bound farther north than Knoxville, and I knew why. I didn't have the heart to tell your father. I was too sick to think about it.

"But Bazely stayed gone and stayed gone, and I got to thinking that maybe the man wouldn't come back. Maybe he had gone all the way up there and hadn't found a thing. Maybe everything was just the way your father represented it, and maybe we were all safe. If there *wasn't* anything, I was *sure* Bazely wouldn't come back. And as the days passed and the world kept on in its normal way, I felt a growing exhilaration. I was happier than I'd been in years because I thought we'd all escaped something terrible and that we were rid of Bazely to boot. I was even beginning to feel foolish just for thinking that somebody as open and honest as your father would have anything to hide.

"But then Bazely came back. I looked up from that desk one day when the afternoon local came in from Knoxville, and there he was, walking across the square with a carpetbag. It was like waking up and finding your nightmare crouching on the bedpost. He had a vile look on his face. I guess you'd call it a look of triumph—something like what Satan must have had when he made Adam fall. You could see it all the way in here, and right away I knew that things were bad. Very bad.

"In time I got to know the whole story. He did go to Union, Virginia—just as I knew he would. And he began asking questions about your father. It was a small town, and your father wasn't somebody people could forget right away, and Bazely got what he was after. He discovered what your father was hiding, and it was enough, entirely enough for what Bazely wanted."

The youth lowered his head, and his own voice was now abject. "I guess I know what it was."

Mr. Campbell nodded in lassitude, looking carefully out the window and avoiding the youth's face. "Yes, I guess you do," he said with a tired sigh. "Bazely found your father's legal wife."

There was a long, empty pause in their talk. The trees in the square throbbed and sang with teeming insect life, which against the vast sleepiness of the evening world seemed loud and melodious and infinitely calm.

"It all falls into place," the youth murmured at last. His voice was so low and worn that Mr. Campbell had to strain to hear it. "I knew it had to be something like that. But why did Bazely stay gone so long? I don't understand that."

"Well, the woman wasn't living in Union anymore. She'd moved over to Richmond after the War, and she was working in a mill there, and Bazely must have had one hell of a time tracking her down. But once he knew she was alive, he kept at it until he found her. He told her everything about your father. I met the woman later on. I'll tell you about that in a minute. I met her, and she was what you might expect of an ignorant country girl who'd moved to the city and was poor both places. I remember how bad her teeth were. Her hair was stringy and dull, and she was fat and undernourished at the same time. She wasn't even in the same class of human being as your mother, and knowing your father I couldn't believe that he'd been married to her. But by the time I saw her she was almost ten years older than she was when your father went off to war, and women like that age fast. I'm sure she'd changed a lot. They'd got married very young, she said. They tried to make it on a little dirt farm, and they couldn't even pay their bills. They were getting ready to pull stakes and move to Richmond when the War came along. Your father joined up, and that was the last she ever saw of him."

"Did they have any children?"

Mr. Campbell puffed his cheeks and expelled a thick breath of painful reluctance. "She had a child after your father left. A little boy. He died in the War because she couldn't feed him. They didn't have anything to eat for a while, and the child died."

"My happy, carefree father!"

"He didn't know anything about the child, Sam!" Mr. Campbell said in a quick tone of defense. "Not until just before he died himself. It hurt him. Believe me, it hurt him to know it."

Sam shook off the apology with an impatient gesture. "Go on. Let's get this over with."

"Well, she was grieved at what he'd done. It was hard for her to believe, she said. Once they had loved each other so much, and it was hard to think he'd do something like this to her. But she wasn't angry with him. That was his gift, you see. He could do so much wrong, and people loved him in spite of it. The man just unselfconsciously *used* people, and neither he nor they really knew what he was doing. I always have believed his first wife loved him just as much as your mother ever did."

"I'm sure we can say that *now!* " The youth spoke with dripping irony and tried to laugh, but what came out was very nearly a raw sob. Mr. Campbell hesitated an instant before taking up his story again, still studiously peering out the window as if talking to himself, meditating aloud over some antique puzzle which out of the enchantment of distance itself still obsessed his mind. Finally he did continue, speaking more slowly and deliberately than before and in a low, cautious voice which felt its way delicately along a difficult track.

"Well, the first thing your father knew of what had happened was when he got a letter from his wife up there. Bang! Like that, and the whole thing fell on him like the sky! The woman couldn't even write, and she had to get somebody else to do it for her, but it came, and it was enough to ruin your father's life. Bazely had put her up to getting a lawyer to collect some affidavits from witnesses who knew they were married, and she sent copies of them down to your father in the letter. Bazely told the lawyer how rich your mother's place was, and I guess the bastard expected to make his fortune on that case. At least it didn't work out *that* way." Mr. Campbell chuckled in grim satisfaction.

"Your father came to me right away and spread the whole dismal mess out here on my desk and asked me what in God's name he could do. She said that if he didn't come back to her, she was going to come down here and expose him. It was a pretty desperate situation.

"I guess I was pretty hard on him. You see, I felt so guilty at having spilled his secret so Bazely could pick it up. But then I was angry with your father for having given me something to feel guilty *about!* Lord knows I'd done enough bad to people on my own account without having to assume responsibility for wronging *him!* I gave him a pretty good tongue lashing, and he just hung his head and took it. Naturally I said the first thing he had to do was to make a clean breast of it to your mother. Then we'd work up a case, and we'd go back to Virginia or someplace and get a divorce or an annulment. Hell, I didn't know what we'd do, but we'd do *something* to straighten the mess out. After that he could marry your mother again all legal and . . . and fix things up for you."

The youth nodded sardonically. "I guess I *was* a problem," he said with a bitter laugh. "A bastard son doesn't quite fit in with my mother's glorious past. Not a bastard *white* son."

Mr. Campbell shook his head in dull sorrow. "It was a hard thing. A terrible thing for both of them."

"So what happened then?" Sam assumed a quick, false nonchalance and put his head back against the back of the chair and peered at Mr. Campbell through half-closed eyes.

"Your father did what I told him. It nearly killed your mother. It was like a blow on the head that left her almost bereft of her senses for a while. She didn't have any inkling that anything could ever be wrong between them until he broke the news, and then her whole life looked fit to fall apart in her hands. She hated me for having been so stupid as to drop your father's secret. And she was totally crushed by the fact that your father had deceived her the way he had.

"And then there was Bazely. Without him everything might have been different even if your mother had discovered the truth. But he knew the secret, and nobody could predict what he might do with it. Obviously he hoped your mother would rid herself of your father and marry *him*. And if she *didn't* do that, then he was likely to shout the thing from the pulpit itself. Bazely had been a standing joke to your mother and father all their married life, but suddenly what that lunatic thought of his chances of owning your mother became terribly important, and we all had to handle the man like a crate of eggs. I've always thought that must have been the most horrible thing for your father—lying there in bed with your mother at night where they had been so secure together and knowing that out there in the dark somewhere was a man they both despised who now had a pretty good chance of someday owning her body.

"Now, it seemed to me that there were two things they could do about Bazely, and I suggested both of them. Your father could have waylaid the man one night and picked him off with a rifle, and then we could have got ourselves up to Virginia to work something out in peace. But your father wasn't made that way. He felt wretched about what he had done, and he fell into an absolute apathy. It was really a stupor, and it was hard to get him to talk. He did whatever your mother or I told him—short of murder. That he flatly refused to consider. He didn't even seem very angry at Bazely, and he certainly wasn't going to kill him.

"So I said the other thing they could do was to tell Bazely to go to hell, try to work things out in quiet, and if he did spill the business, your mother and father could sell the place and pack up and go West. All of you could have got a new start someplace where nobody knew anything about you. Well, you can imagine how your mother reacted to that! She nearly died on the spot, and she said she would never, never leave that land until they hauled her off to the graveyard. So that's where we were.

"But then she seemed to relent, and on the afternoon of the last day he ever lived your father rode in here and told me that he and your mother had come to an agreement, and they wanted to start legal proceedings. He said they'd just have to hope Bazely was a human being under that hateful skin of his. But if he wasn't, well then your father and mother would sell off the place and take you West. So your father rode off, and next day I heard he'd had his heart attack and died. God knows he'd been through enough to have a heart attack. And that was that."

Mr. Campbell halted on a note of unbearable fatigue, and the two men faced each other in a prolonged, heavy quiet—the older man with his gaunt face staring bleakly out of the shadows, the younger with his half-closed eyes contemplating Mr. Campbell with a still expression now so emotionless that it might have been sleep. "I guess that's why my mother objected so much to Emilie," he said finally with languorous understanding.

"You can't blame her, after her experience."

"You went to see my father's *real* wife?"

"I went to see the woman in Virginia. Somebody had to go. Your mother didn't tell me to. I guess she had to hate me to placate Bazely, but I guess too she knew I'd go for your father's sake, and I did. I didn't want people in the valley to remember him as a bad man, and you know how people would have talked. So I went to Virginia and found the woman and told her what had happened. She was a good sort, really pitiful. *She* was sorry for causing *him* grief. She cried like a baby when I told her your father was dead. She said she knew there hadn't been much chance of getting him back again, but she had hoped and hoped that he might see her one more time and remember how he'd loved her when they were young, and just maybe he would come to himself and love her again. Maybe he would just take pity on her, and she said she would have been satisfied with that if he'd only come back to her. Here was this ugly, overgrown middle-aged woman crying over the only love affair she'd ever had, and I was looking on like a fool, and I was *angry* with your father! I was angry with him for making people love him so much. That charm of his . . . It was the gift of the devil."

"What ever happened to the woman?"

"I don't know. I never saw her again."

"And Mr. Bazely never told."

"No. I guess your mother played that with a cool hand. She must have promised Bazely she would marry him *only* if he never told about your father—and about you. I think he expected her to pass through a decent period of mourning, and then she'd give herself up to him, and he would own her down to the bone marrow. But your mother outfoxed him. She made a shrine out of your father's memory, and she's mourned after him for fifteen years! Bazely never could cut through it. The poor fool couldn't cope with a shade, and finally it just drove him insane."

Mr. Campbell plodded back around to his chair and sank down into it with an exhausted sigh. The feelings of both men were completely spent. They sat in the contemplative glow of the lamp and thought their separate thoughts in a dispassionate suspension of emotion. Finally Sam said in a dull monotone: "She really is a magnificent woman. Who else could have carried it off?"

"You've got to remember she did it for a purpose—for you."

"I wonder," the youth said in the same flat voice.

"There was no other reason."

"There are all the pictures in that old house. She could have done it for them."

They sat for much longer without speaking until they were roused from their lethargy by the somber crashing of the courthouse clock announcing midnight. Mr. Campbell stirred himself and sat up. "I guess we'd better be going out there," he said. "I'm sure your mother is anxious about you." He got slowly to his feet.

The youth stood up in a lanky collection of himself and waited for the older man to don his hat. Mr. Campbell adjusted the hatbrim low over his eyes and looked at his visitor. "What are you going to do, Sam?"

"I'm making up my mind," the youth said deliberately. "What are *you* going to do?"

Mr. Campbell had recovered his massive calm and self-possession. "I am going to do nothing. I am going to tell Doc Cogill that he did not see you here tonight, and I am going to pretend we never had this conversation, and I am going to do nothing." He pronounced the words with a firm hammering of syllables, and he looked at Sam with an expression so fixed it might have been either a threat or a command.

The youth only dropped his eyes. "Then I will not ride all the way in with you. Anyway, I have something to do before I get there."

"Remember, I don't want your mother even to know we talked."

"She will not learn it from me."

Slowly the two tired men walked out into the street and left the light gleaming alone on the desk before the silent books.

28

BY THE TIME MR. CAMPBELL arrived, alone, at the Crittendon place, it was nearly one o'clock in the morning. Knots of men sprawled over the darkened porch, and some stood smoking or chewing in little murmuring groups in the yard. The downstairs of the great house was brightly illuminated, and every window on that floor tossed a cheerful rectangle of lamplight into the wet and glistening yard. Above the lighted windows the upper story of the house rose in silent gloom before the sky, where the moon was already slanting down the west.

Mr. Campbell was greeted by a sudden stir of recognition, by loud exclamations of surprise, and by a flurry of questions. How was the sheriff? How was Mr. Campbell feeling? What had he thought when he faced the preacher? Why had the preacher tried to kill him? Because of the unpleasantness of the day before? And interspersed with the questions there was a general consent expressed again and again that Mr. Campbell had read the man's character plainer than most of them and that now he stood vindicated in the eyes of the valley for his judgment.

Mr. Campbell shrugged all these remarks off as best he could and went into the house. His entry provoked a chorus of welcome from the women, who had gathered in the kitchen. Sarah Beckwith stood up from the kitchen table and rushed forward to greet him, offering him a hand to take and momentarily to hold. "Why John! It's so good of you to come, especially considering all you've been through. So *very* kind. I'd given you up. Are you all right?" Her face beamed friendly concern, and when Mr. Campbell saw it, he managed a weary smile in spite of himself.

But almost at once she dropped her smile into a deep frown of anxiety. "Have you seen Sam?" she inquired urgently. "He's disappeared. I haven't seen him since the storm. I'm almost beside myself."

Mr. Campbell lied to her with a level gaze. "No," he said. "I haven't seen Sam since yesterday."

"Then *where* could he be? He might have been hurt in the storm."

"Sam can take care of himself, Sarah. He's all right."

"I'm worried sick," she said. Her voice was tight, and she wanted to say more.

But before she could go on men from the outside flocked into the house after Mr. Campbell, and suddenly he found himself the center of a warmly curious band of well-wishers. He had made his enemies in the valley, but now he was old. All at once people in Bourbonville took stock of his age and the narrow escape he had had. Suddenly they saw him as a distinguished landmark from a past which was romantic and bold, a character out of a saga removed by a generation from the ordinary lives of most of them. With that new respect, they also recognized the fragility of his life and, more dimly, the temporary nature of their own. And today in the hot street confronting violent death, he showed that he was a brave man, a very brave man, and even those who disliked him or envied him or simply mistrusted him all in an instant admired him. In his own flamboyant history and in his proud bearing before their eyes, they saw a part of themselves of which they were immensely proud.

All of them reflected on the thought that if Hub Delaney hadn't been the best shot in the world, Mr. Campbell might be lying in a box somewhere himself right now. But here? Under the heavily ornate frame enclosing the picture of the older Samuel Beckwith? That stiff portrait, itself a relic from a strangely bygone time! Would Mr. Campbell's body have rested here? Most assuredly not, they thought—uncertainly. For there was a faint bafflement at Mr. Campbell's presence. In the casual stream of talk, a quiet swell of inquiry rolled under the tranquil surface of the moment. There he stood, tall and gray and distinguished to the point of being picturesque, now sipping black coffee from a cup quickly placed in his hand—standing there in an offhand gallantry, and it was as if the long and bitter enmity between this house and his had never existed. People in the valley were accustomed to the enmity. It was part of their own lives, for it defined the world they knew. Seeing him here made them vaguely conscious of something that had shifted. Not something good or bad. Just something unexpectedly different and . . . baffling.

Slowly they did become accustomed to it. Other people kept

drifting in from the yard and pumping hands with Mr. Campbell. Some were self-conscious and uncomfortable, and others were openly exuberant. "Why, Mr. Campbell! You *are* here! Well, I declare! I do declare! How are you? How are you?" And passing once more in a ritual way to view the corpse, they made sage pronouncements about the wonders of fate and the slender happenstance which kept Mr. Campbell alive. It was a procession of handshaking like that which greets a new member in church, and it had its religious side. People kept saying over and over, "You really ought to be thankful." To which Mr. Campbell responded with his tired and distinguished smile and a murmur of assent.

And soon everyone was once again holding a coffee cup no matter how much coffee each might have consumed earlier in the evening. The powerful, bitter taste of the brew and its friendly warmth answered cravings, those that were conscious and immediately demanding and others which lay buried under a sediment of fear and obscurity, a yearning in the lonely inner silence of man for some way of affirming, "I am alive. I live. I am." All this in the near presence of death—a festivity because though death lay close by, life did go on, and for this supreme instant the people drinking the coffee possessed that life and were glad.

Mr. Bazely lay there before them. The coffin lid was off and discreetly laid behind the two wooden chairs on which the narrowed ends of the coffin itself reposed. In the mellowing lamplight the lines of the preacher's face were not so harsh. He seemed neither furious nor angry, neither strong nor weak, not quite asleep, not quite dead. Had he really lived among them twenty years? Had he a voice? Well, it was all over now, and the doors could be shut. All done, and he was dead.

So the men and women milled around Mr. Campbell and cast reflective glances at the preacher's corpse and filed by the coffin again and again and puckered their lips and clucked in simulated unbelief about the whole astonishing day. Unbelief simulated because everybody had begun to believe already that it *had* really happened. "I've been expecting him to go off," P. D. Lethgo said with a solemn shaking of his heavy chin, the superior gesture of a man who has known a secret he has not wished to reveal because he had a sense of decency and didn't like to gossip. "I ain't surprised. I ain't one bit surprised."

And others who heard him nodded wisely and affirmed that *they* had not been surprised, and the preacher's violent destiny was becoming something thought to be as inevitable as daylight and less startling than the mighty storm of the afternoon, the storm which was now departed with its lightning and its flooding rain.

The rain! The talk was full of it. People remembered exactly where they were and what they were doing when they heard the first blast of thunder. They recalled the first sight of the clouds which told them it was really a storm and not just a solemn deception played on them by the heat and their desire. They felt an irresistible compulsion to tell each other again and again. It was like Lincoln's death. Like Garfield's.

"I was down in the barn and thinking I'd have to kill animals this fall, and all of a sudden I heard that thunderclap! I didn't believe it. That's the way it hit me. I couldn't believe what I'd heard with my own two ears, and I run up to the house to ask the old woman if she'd heard it. But she met me out in the yard, running herself, and we was asking each other if we'd heard the thunder, and we was looking at the sky. We was scared. I can't explain it, but we was scared."

"What do you think, J. W.? Was Simson crazy? Or did he see something? What do you think? It's sure a spooky thing, ain't it? Do you reckon he seen a sign that the rest of us could of seen if we knowed what to look for? I ain't never going to forget it! Never!"

The women of Bourbon County flitted through the house like domestic birds. They fluttered into the kitchen and out again bearing their coffeepots aloft, and sometimes they alighted in the parlor with their men, and from time to time they perched at the edge of the coffin and looked down into the preacher's closed eyes and twittered with sadness. It was *such* a shame, they said.

They did not really mean it was a shame Mr. Campbell was alive and the preacher was dead. They were not speculative people except in matters of sexual sin. Mr. Campbell had not been killed. Mr. Bazely was dead. In the manner of country women from the foundation of the world, the women of Bourbon County were fatalists. Since Mr. Campbell was alive they reasoned that he hadn't even been in danger, and they could be free and expansive about their grief over the fallen preacher. So they were, and there was a little zone before the coffin where the women looked monumentally sad and spoke with hushed and sorrowful voices.

And even among the men the talk kept drifting back to Mr. Bazely. They talked about the storm, the way the rain had lashed their crops and the terrible lightning and the fear they had felt in spite of themselves. But they kept coming back to the preacher. They greeted Mr. Campbell and milled about, and they overflowed once more onto the porch and splattered into a dozen pools of talk there and on the moon-filled lawn. They wracked their memories. They called up M. G. Galyon's strange tale from the War. And they passionately wished to have the idiot blacksmith here now, erect, and in his right mind. They *knew* the preacher was crazy, had known all along. But there was something else. They wanted to know something else. Why? Why?

And that was the impossible mystery. Already they knew it would always be impossible. Never would they really understand it. Never. So they reduced the mystery they could not grasp to an excuse of sorts, which was the imbecility of M. G. Galyon. If only he could dredge some sense out of that warped and hopelessly idiotic brain! Sure, he was a liar. Everybody knew *that.* But he wouldn't let them down at a time like this. If *only* he were the way he used to be, they all might understand why the preacher had done what he did.

They spent a lot of time that night putting together the pieces of M. G. Galyon's story as best they could. With Mr. Campbell's arrival they kept asking him what *he* thought. But he would only grunt and shrug in his tired way and look as if he didn't very much care one way or another. And so in the end the insoluble mystery defied them as it defied their descendants for as long as anybody cared about it.

And while people were still jostling around Mr. Campbell and the night was awake with refreshed talk, Brian Ledbetter drove up in a flatbed wagon with Evelyn Weaver sitting proudly beside him and with the Weaver children mostly wrapped up and asleep in the back. Only Virgil sat with his feet dangling over the tail gate, and when the wagon creaked to a halt he slipped off and went away to himself to sit in a dark place on the porch. But Brian jumped down with his rough good will and handed Evelyn Weaver down, and the sight was so completely startling that for a while people could only gape and mutter over what they were seeing, explaining it to one another in a rattle of astonishment.

Brian and Mrs. Weaver came into the house, she holding the arm he gallantly crooked for her, and they paid their respects to the corpse and also sought out their surprised hostess and spoke to her. And then Brian, standing in front of the coffin, looking away from the sightless tallow face of Mr. Bazely, looking away also from the dark gazing picture of the elder Samuel Beckwith, announced to the wondering crowd that he and Evelyn Weaver were going to be married.

At which there was a startled eruption of happy exclamation which shot up and flowed racing through the house. And people were swarming around them with outstretched hands, and Rebels and Union men were patting the proud couple on their backs and wishing them well and telling each other it was all a damn good thing. And what was most surprising was the open pleasure the announcement gave to Sarah Crittendon Beckwith, who actually kissed Mrs. Weaver on her amazed cheek and took Brian's large hand with such glad fervor that she might have been ready to hug *him*.

"I got to thinking about it after we talked," Brian said to Mr. Campbell. "I thought *somebody* ought to go out there and tell Mrs. Weaver about what happened to that poor corpse alying there. I knowed *I* couldn't want to be sleeping when everbody knowed something I didn't, so I went out and woken her up and told her. And since she was up anyway, why I just decided to ask her to marry me."

"It was such a surprise," Mrs. Weaver said, "being proposed to in the middle of the night like that. I didn't never even expect to get married again. But then I have boys to raise, and a woman has to look out for her own."

Mr. Campbell gravely shook hands with both of them and stood back and smiled broadly for the first time this night and struck fire to a cigar. It seemed to some who stood nearby that he even winked at Mrs.-Weaver-soon-to-be-Mrs.-Ledbetter, but the light was uncertain in that crowd, and no one could be sure. The women of Bourbon County loved weddings even more than they loved funerals and watch nights for the dead, and here they had everything heart and soul could wish for in one night, and it was almost more than they could bear. They gasped and sighed their way around the happy couple and pushed in between them and the coffin and following the example of Sarah Beckwith they hugged and kissed Evelyn Weaver and praised her virtues and especially her sense of responsibility to her children, and a few even swelled up and cried.

And just when the excitement was subsiding a little bit, Preacher Henck rode in. He had come from Kingston. Clarence Jackson had sent a telegram up to Knoxville, and the agent there had relayed it out to Kingston on the Tennessee Central Line, and somebody had carried it to Mr. Henck, who was out trying to save the soul of a leather tanner named Hotchkiss.

Mr. Henck got on his horse right away, and he rode twenty miles and got hit by the full fury of the storm and came on undaunted and arrived at this dark hour of the night composed to perform his service for the dead. Some of the men immediately recognized the gait of the quarter horse Mr. Henck rode, and some recognized the ungainly skinny figure of the Methodist preacher himself, and before he had pulled to a halt some men were down in the yard reaching for the reins and others were reaching up to help the preacher down.

He hit the ground with a wiry, tireless bound, looked around, and demanded to know what had happened. He was told again and again by two dozen people at once, was told so many times and in such enthusiasm that he couldn't get it straight and had to ask some of the men to shut up so he could hear what the others had to say.

Once again, before the stove with a cup of coffee thrust into his hand, Mr. Henck heard the story, and this time he finally made sense out of it because Mr. Campbell told him. He stood quietly listening, drinking at his coffee and looking steadily at Mr. Campbell, asking a question or two, and at the end he went in to where the coffin lay and looked down at Mr. Bazely. He shook his head sadly but could find nothing to say. Somebody told him that Brian Ledbetter and Mrs. Weaver were going to get married. He broke out of his solemnity for a moment to smile in a distracted fashion at them and to shake their hands and to say how glad he was. Then he went back into the kitchen and sat down and muttered at no one in particular: "The poor man. The poor man." But he also looked up at Mr. Campbell and said, "I'm glad you weren't hurt, John. You should be thankful."

"I'm thankful to a friend who is a good shot," Mr. Campbell said with his slight, ironic smile.

"You should be thankful to the One who provided that your friend should be in the right place at the right time."

Mr. Campbell shrugged, still with the ironic smile, and sat down heavily in a chair somebody pushed up for him. "I guess he got away in the excitement. I didn't see him."

"John, John! I wonder if you'll ever change." But Preacher Henck liked Mr. Campbell. Or perhaps he just loved him. Preacher Henck delighted to recall that he had heard Mr. Campbell's father preach back in the old, old days when everybody was young, when some had not even been born, back in the good days when life was simple and even war was uncomplicated, when nobody in his wildest dreams would have thought that all which did come would come. "My heart was strangely warmed," he said in unflagging ardor to John Wesley Campbell. Mr. Campbell regularly dismissed the whole rapturous story with a short laugh and the comment that it was probably indigestion. At which Mr. Henck would raise his thin shoulders in a lost sigh and bite his lip and say no more until the next time he rode through town. But then he would always stop to chat a moment with the son of the man who had inspired him with the Divine Spirit which Mr. Henck felt that night in the forest, felt and remembered ever afterward like the recollection of roses on a wintry night or the sweet singing of a violin on a long road in the rain. Even more than Mr. Campbell, Mr. Henck was getting old. He had always been thin. Now he looked positively cadaverous. The skin on his high forehead sloped smoothly back into the fine tumbling of his unruly white hair, and his skimpy side whiskers were gray. He was given to preoccupied silences when he baptized children of late. When one day someone asked him why this was so, he said it was because he knew they would not remember him. He would be dead before they would be really old enough to know him. Sometimes when he stood in the pulpit he looked pinched and careworn, and not only the doting women but the stolid men of Bourbon County worried a little over him and suggested quietly to one another (though never to him) that he might be about ready to retire.

But still he rode his horse with an indefatigable vigor and an unquenchable purpose, and he had come twenty miles from Kingston this day through the wildest storm in the memory of man to do his duty. His horse was spent, too tired even to eat the oats which someone fetched out of the barn. ("Where *is* Sam? Where *could* the boy be?") And now Mr. Henck sat grieving in his chair near the stove. "I just wonder what was in the poor man's mind. If we'd only known what he was going through we might have done something. We might have helped him."

"We'll never know. Never, never! Not till we get to glory." It was Sarah Beckwith speaking. She stood over the conversation of the two men, stood almost directly before Mr. Campbell, and her bright face bore a look of feverish exaltation. "No one will ever know. No one but God."

Her voice was strangely charged and unnatural, and Mr. Campbell looked sharply up at her. "No, no one will ever know," he said. His own voice was quite soft, but it was as charged as hers had been, and his eyes flashed something which might have been a warning. He was about to say something else when a clamor burst out on the porch, another rise of voices, and one voice sharply heard above all the rest. "I'm all right. What's going on here? What are you all doing here?"

It was Sam.

And at the sound of his voice Sarah Beckwith went flying to the door. "Sam! Dear Sam, *where* have you been? Oh my darling boy! I've been so worried! I've been so afraid!" Her voice broke, and she threw herself into his arms and hugged him close and nearly cried. Probably Mr. Campbell of all the people there noticed that above the turbulence of her emotion the youth's face rose complacent and calm to the point of being immobile and that he looked around at the jostling crowd without a sign of surprise. Gently he put his mother aside and came in, and in the full light people could see his mud-plastered clothes.

"Sam, what happened to you? Where have you *been?*" His mother was almost beside herself with relief.

"Nothing, mother. Nothing's wrong," he said with a voice so deliberate it was almost languorous. "I did a foolish thing. I went out looking for you in the rain. You left word that you'd gone to see about the preacher, remember? I went to the preacher's house, but there was nobody home. On the way back the storm caught me, and I stopped at the cabin where the nigger Bourbons live, and well, I guess I went to sleep." He lowered his head at the last in a transparently affected gesture of embarrassment, but it was enough to deceive his mother and to deceive all the rest except Mr. Campbell. His mother laughed aloud and hugged him once more and held him tightly to herself. Once again he let her clasp him without making any physical response to her and with his complacent and settled face rising out of the storm of her emotion like a column of glacial ice.

"But the mud! How did you get so *filthy!*" She held him back from herself at arm's length and looked up and down at his plastered dirtiness, laughing on the faint edge of hysteria at the comic sight of his muddiness and his obvious safety.

And he with that same languorous deliberation said merely, "I slipped and fell in the road. It was nothing. Nothing at all. I wasn't even bruised."

"Oh Sam, dear Sam!" She was clutching him again, and his hands were at his sides, limp and unresponsive and tired. His eyes caught Mr. Campbell's for a second. Mr. Campbell's expression was mournful and astonished and old—woefully old—and both men looked quickly away from the searing touch of their mutual glance.

"What happened here? I don't understand what's going on?" He gestured with implacable self-control at the coffin, and it dawned on all of them at once that the youth would not know what all of them knew. He had been asleep. It had passed him by. And so they were swept up in the drunken compulsion to tell it, and they did. All in a vehement rush. They had all been there. They had all seen the preacher's last furious gallop. Years and years hence all the people in that room would be convinced that they had seen it. Wives, children, people who knew better would tell themselves so many times that they *had* been there that they would believe their own story.

And in a way they all *had* seen it. They knew Bourbonville. The place was fixed in their minds as indelibly as their lives. They knew the courthouse square, knew how thick the dust hung in the breathless heat of the drought, knew the preacher, his voice and his horse and the wolfish shining of his eyes, and they knew the way a horse sounded at the gallop in a dusty street. They knew Hub Delaney. They would see his stiff arm, and they would run their curious hands over the pistol the preacher had snatched away from him. They would convert the rifle Hub had used into a relic of sorts, and they would hear him tell his story times without number. They would talk to John Wesley Campbell, and from his laconic account breathed scornfully through cigar smoke, they would know what it was to stand there with death bearing down.

Mr. Campbell would die in time. He would be found lying rigid and cold in his nightshirt under the window in his bedroom, and most of the people in the house at this moment would be there to bear him to his grave. And while the red earth would be spaded thumping onto the coffin, they would tell each other all over again how it had been, recounting the most minute description about where they had been standing, the first glimpse they had had of the oncoming preacher, the first dim presentiment that something was wrong, and they would place Mr. Campbell there in the street beneath the naked sun and remember exactly how it had been when the preacher fired the first shot, the wild laughter and the empty calm, and Hub Delaney staggering out with the rifle and throwing it up one-handed to his shoulder and firing clean and true and killing the preacher with such velocity that the dead body was actually lifted off the ground before it went plowing into the dirt. They would remember. Wherever they had really been, a refraction of memory would shift across their minds with a motion as weightless and as mysterious as light, and they would put all the things they knew so well together in that hot point of action, and they would remember. In the annals of the valley they would all be there in the street at Bourbonville brought there by fatal coincidence in time to see the drama performed before their unforgetting eyes.

They told Sam with such jostling enthusiasm that they did not even notice the peculiar, steady-eyed tranquility which he maintained in their midst. He took another look at the preacher, turned away with hardly a fleck of interest, and looked at his mother.

"It is the first time we have had something like this since the death of my father. I have been thinking a lot about him today." His look at his mother was keen and penetrating. But she responded in something like ecstasy. "The boy *still* thinks of his father!" she cried. "You see, he still loves his dear father!" and she flung a pointing hand out toward the great picture looming over the coffin.

It was an outburst, something about it uncontrolled. Her face burned. Something like a fever raged across her cheeks and in her glittering eyes, something close to a delirium of relief and happiness.

Mr. Campbell said quietly, "Of course he does, Sarah. Of course he does."

She turned to him with beaming warmth. "Do you notice it, John? As Sam grows older he looks more and more like his father." She looked gaily around the room at the others. "John . . . Mr. Campbell here knew my husband. They were good friends. The best of friends." And to him she said again, "Don't you notice, John? Look at the picture, and look at Sam. Not that *you* need to look at the *picture!* You *remember* how my dear husband looked. But don't they look alike? Don't you agree they look alike?"

"Yes, Sarah. They are father and son."

She laughed. The giddy, nearly hysterical laughter. "Why John, I don't think you've been in this house since my husband died. I don't believe you've even *seen* his picture. You have neglected us, John." She admonished him with a girlish wagging of her finger.

"It's a good picture. It looks just like him."

Again the bright laughter with the burning core. "It's just as Sam says. That is the first time we have had a funeral in this house since my poor husband died. Think of that! Fifteen years since we had a funeral, and now it isn't even one of us! I guess this is the longest time this house has ever *gone* without a funeral. Isn't that *wonderful!* But I'm *so* sorry it had to be a man of God. Oh, that is just too bad! Just too, too *bad!*"

The crowd was emphatically silent now. All of them looked in bewildered anxiety at her flushed face and her bright, feverish eyes. Mr. Campbell stood up and rested a hand with unaccustomed familiarity and gentleness on her shoulder. "It's all right now, Sarah. Everything is all right." Her son kept on gazing silently at her in that mortal calm so that it was finally Mr. Henck who came to the rescue with a cracked sigh and a flood of sentiment. "I think something like this is a temptation of the devil. When a man of God does something like this, we're seeing something to test our faith. We'll just have to bear it, the way Job did."

Mr. Campbell looked darkly at the minister. "At least God spoke to Job out of the whirlwind at the last," he said quietly. "I have never heard the voice of God, Mr. Henck. Did you hear God in the whirlwind today? Did you hear God in that storm?"

Mr. Henck looked at Mr. Campbell in an abject and forlorn determination. "I hear the voice of God every day, Brother Campbell. When I ride my horse on the road, when I preach the Word. Yes, I heard the voice of God in the storm out there today."

"And what did it say, Mr. Henck? I should be most interested to know what the voice of God told you today."

"The voice of God tells me to wait, Brother Campbell. It tells me to be patient, and it tells me God is just."

"More coffee? More coffee anybody?" A woman pushed her way in among the tense and uncomfortable crowd. The curious tension which had been building up abruptly broke, and men looked around to retrieve their cups and to hold them out for more.

Mr. Campbell and Mr. Henck went on in their ancient theological disputation, but hardly anyone paid any attention. Sam heard their strained voices, and he followed their argument at a distance. But mostly it was all something detached and lost in a world beyond his, distant and unreal. He kept to his own world. Silently he saw his mother pass among the men in a state of dreamy serenity, bearing her coffeepot like a maid bearing a talisman of innocence in a harvest festival.

And he remembered Mr. Bazely, long ago, coming to visit, when his father had died. He recalled the way his mother sent him out to play, her voice dripping with false cheerfulness. He remembered the way they quietly but firmly shut the door after him, and the way also in which they broke off their low, earnest talk when he re-entered the room. He remembered all this through the translucent veil hung down between himself and fifteen years of time, remembered because he thought his mother wept on those occasions. He saw her afterward with her eyes swollen and red and her face wrenched with pain, and she went out with the preacher to his horse and talked beseechingly up at him as he sat there for a dark moment before riding away.

Or did he really remember anything at all? Again he was assaulted by the gentle, terrific mystery of time and the strange way memory could people this crowded room with the intangible forms of a dead age and dead men, the dead so superimposed on the living that the room was a confusion of shapes, all near, all as distant as Jerusalem. He clutched at the forms of the dead and found them to dissolve in his mind, leaving a soft impression of fading light and half-sentences, low, indistinct voices and an indescribable uneasiness hanging like a slight haze over the broad, slumberous calm of the twilit past. And beneath the cool shining of that calm, a profound blackness concealed a secret, an unutterable and unbearable secret.

Mr. Henck was just saying that on the other side of death we would see the full pattern of life, not just of our own but the life of the human race. He said there was a kind of weaver's loom in things, and that as life was being spun out, we could not see what it was becoming, but there would come a day when the pattern of things would be clear, and then we would see not only God but ourselves, and we should know even as we shall be known. Sam thought he saw something darken in his mother's face at the thought, though he could not be sure.

But in this life, a darkness. A comforting, concealing darkness. A darkness over all the earth. A darkness swelling lifelike from the familiar places, and out of it rose an overpowering fragrance of funeral flowers so that life in the valley and in this house was like being shut in a secret closet with a corpse. Sweet with an unbearable reek of rotting things in the stale air. He would have died choking in the sweetness, in the corruption of dead things, in the grinding embrace of half-forgotten men, in blood sacrifice to the dead.

Now he would not perish that way. And the dead should rest content with that. Surely they could demand no more service from him, now that he possessed his dreadful knowledge? That he should leave them with their profound sleep undisturbed by dreams of horror? Their line had not been tarnished. His mother had seen to that. It shone in the memory of Bourbon County. All the noble Crittendons strode manfully forward in the still death which was history—unblemished, untarnished, and unashamed. The dead possessed it so completely that they had no need for the living. The living were merely an inconvenience to the dead.

A sudden clamor on the porch! A frenzied scraping of chairs! A wild shouting. "Fire! By God in heaven, *Fire!*" People on the inside up and rushing out at the alarm. A hard, furious clatter of feet. A blister of voices. A storm of men and women bursting out into the yard to see. Children wakened and crying with fright at the noise. And there, out in the dark, a shaking finger of flame went reaching gigantically upward through the trees to place a burning touch on the sky and to point an oily smoke at the distant stars.

"The cabins! It's a fire in the slave cabins!"

Sarah Crittendon Beckwith knew her land, and she was the first to recognize the fire for what it was. She rushed instinctively toward the scene, drawing after her an agitated flood of humanity. They could all hear the roaring of the conflagration. They could see the huge sparks soaring and darting on the night air. And in spite of the drenching wet, they were terror-stricken at what the fire might do, and the fear cast by the fire drew them unto itself.

All but the younger Samuel Beckwith. He let the house drain of the living. Then he went loping up the stairs to his room.

Working swiftly, but with a worn, nerveless calm, he took down a heavy blanket from the closet and folded it into a long, narrow strip. On the blanket he made a pile of clothing. Finally he rolled the blanket around its contents, took some leather thongs and tied it carefully, and from a recess in the closet he took a heavy brown envelope and put it securely into his pocket. He took out his leather coat and threw it over one arm, and picking up the blanket roll he came quickly back downstairs.

The house was deserted of all the living but himself. He could hear the excitement receding toward the fire. A bright orange light was refracted through the windows and tainted the lampglow. He paused for a moment and looked up at the stern young picture of his father. Suddenly, acting on an impulse which came down to

My heart is sore pained within me:
And the terrors of death are fallen upon me.
Fearfulness and trembling are come upon me,
And horror hath overwhelmed me.
And I said, Oh that I had wings like a dove!
For then would I fly away, and be at rest.
Lo, then would I wander far off,
And remain in the wilderness.
I would hasten my escape from the windy storm
And tempest

—PSALM 55

EPILOGUE

MR. KAYRO LIVED ALONE with his dog in a neat little house on the riverbank and kept the ferry at Kingston. The sun was just up on the morning after the great rain when he went outside, scratching himself, and looked at the sky. Great heaps of snow-white cloud were floating lazily overhead in the soft blue of the fresh-washed morning. Beyond the river the houses of Kingston glistened against the early light, and the brass dome of the courthouse tower shone peacefully, throwing back a cheerful reflection of the sun. The air was cool.

At Mr. Kayro's feet lay the Clinch River. It came down from the north in a slow meandering of green to pour into the Tennessee just below Kingston. On this morning the water made a broad muddy track moving with sluggish, deliberate power through the land. The rain had brought it up and changed its color, and here and there along its moving surface tree limbs and other casual debris were swept along.

"It was a good rain," Mr. Kayro said in deep contentment to his dog. "Yessirree, Morton, that was a mighty good rain!" Mr. Kayro breathed in the soft air and smelled with delight the fragrance of life raised up by the rain, and he felt a contentment as deep as sleep. But he was not sleepy, and casting a glance to the other bank where the brown road ran down into the browner river, he climbed the rising ground to take a look at his flowers. They were roses, large and fragrant, a mingling of reds and whites dotted with yellows, and they were neatly woven through the trellis work he had constructed for them. Now each petal glistened with tiny droplets of dew. He thought they looked as if someone had stolen by in the night and sprinkled them with diamonds.

He was admiring them and smelling them and loving them when he heard the signal bell clanging across the river. When he looked in that direction he could see a slender young man standing by a horse and pulling at the bell rope. The pealing sound rang out over the water and made a throaty echo off the low hills on this side. Mr. Kayro liked the sound because it reminded him of a church bell and also because it was a summons to do his duty.

So he quickly bestirred himself and went down to the flatboat ferry and untied it from its mooring pier. Morton came down with him and with the long habit of custom jumped from the bank onto the boat and sank down panting on his haunches and looked toward the other side of the river.

The ferry was made of pine and rode high in the water. Mr. Kayro took up his long pole and laid his weight into it and made the ferry move. With his strong shoulders and experienced skill he thrust the boat upstream against the current until he was in the midst of the river. Then he let it drift down again, and expertly manipulating the boat and the river at once he brought the ferry to a crunching rest precisely at the place where the road on the Kingston side sank out of sight in the muddy water.

"Hey there!" Mr. Kayro called cheerily. "You're the first customer this morning. First since the rain in fact. Come aboard! Come aboard!"

The youth had his horse by the bridle, and he led the animal down to the boat. The horse was skittish, and once he jerked back, and his eyes turned up white and wild at the sight of the water. "It's all right. It's all right," Mr. Kayro spoke soothingly, and he laid a gentle hand on the horse, patted his muzzle, and then laid both hands over the horse's eyes with childlike care, and the youth was able to bring the horse up onto the boat without any trouble and to loop a rein over the guardrail to one side.

"Horses is always scared when the water's like this, and sometimes people too," Mr. Kayro explained in his loud, cracked voice. He took up his pole again. "But don't *you* worry none. I've not never lost nobody in the river. Man or beast. Not in forty years of ferrying, and you can ask anybody in Kingston. I've got over when it was a lot worse than this. A *lot* worse! Don't matter much about these summer rains. What's really something is the early spring, when the snow's melting up north. Then a little rain can make the water real mean. But it can't get mean enough for me. No *sir!*" And with the powerful emphasis on "sir" he threw the weight of his body into the pole, and it grabbed bottom somewhere out of sight below, the laden ferry moving slowly out into the slow river, pointed gently upstream.

The youth stood silently and looked at the muddy water flash white over the logs and planks of the boat. He appeared lost in thought. Mr. Kayro poled, paused to gauge his distance and looked at the youth, and poled again. The dog, after a brief, inquring sniff at the horse, had gone back to the center of the barge and now lay with his large muzzle in his paws and with slowly blinking eyes watched his master, moving only his eyes in time to the rhythm of Mr. Kayro's arms.

"I guess you'll be going West," Mr. Kayro said. "Oh, you needn't look so surprised. I can tell when a man's going West. Something in his face, not to mention his blanket roll."

The old man poled again with a droll grunt and looked across the river to the landing. "They's two kinds generally. They's the quiet ones like yourself, and they's the loud ones that comes onto the boat singing and offering me something to drink and shouting glory hallelujah. They're all going to the Promised Land, you see. But they's some that don't know what the promise is, and they's some that thinks it's all milk and honey and grapes so big it takes two men to carry a bunch. I don't know what it is myself. I just man the ferry. I've manned it forty years now, and I reckon that's longer than I *will* man it. But as long as I can stand, I'll be here, Lord willing. Everything's up to the Good Lord, you know. He tells you to go, and you go, and He tells me to stay, and I stay, and someday I reckon He'll tell me to come, and I'll leave."

He sighed and cast a longing glance at the sky. He looked back to the river, braced with the pole, and the ferry drifted downward again, making for the landing. "Don't know what folks like you'd do without me," he said. "Without me you'd have to stay here. Couldn't go West. And the way it looks now, everybody's going to go West someday or other. Don't look to me like nobody's going to stay here. And if the Lord takes me away—why, what'll folks *do!*"

There was a real perplexity in Mr. Kayro's voice. The youth said nothing. He might not have heard, for he continued to stand and to contemplate the water. Its low rustle over the bow of the flatboat was a whisper in the quiet morning. It was a peaceful sound, enough to take everything into itself.

"Well," Mr. Kayro said in something of a release, "I guess the Good Lord knows what He's doing. When He takes me, it'll be all right. Everything will be all right. And till He does, I'm going to be right here where He put me, and I'm going to ferry people over the river."

Mr. Kayro fell silent and tended to the boat. It slipped on through the water. The water reflected the clouds. The sunlight shone down with a heat as delicate as breath, and the day and the river seemed to flow in and out of each other, and then the ferry came sweeping out of them both and settled to rest against the gravel road which lifted itself out of the water.

"That'll be a dime," Mr. Kayro said. He threw a rope over a docking pile to secure the boat and turned to the youth with a large smile on his rubicund face. The youth paid him and led his horse off the ferry and onto the solid ground again. "See? I told you we'd make it," Mr. Kayro said heartily. "We're here."

They walked on up the steep bank together, and at the crest Mr. Kayro laid his hand on the youth's arm and said, "Wait a minute. I want to give you something." And stooping to his garden, he picked a rosebud, red and moist, and held it out. "It ain't much. Just a flower. But it means something to me, and it's all I have to give you. Take it along. Take it West."

The youth hesitated a minute and then put out his hand. Mr. Kayro laid the rosebud tenderly in the outstretched palm. The youth opened his mouth, moved his lips tentatively, and then murmured a soft, "Thank you."

"Not at all! Not at all! You take it and think of me." Mr. Kayro stepped back, and the youth swung up into the saddle and sat for a moment gazing down at the old man with a distracted and painful look of interrogation.

Again he wrestled to speak. "A month or so ago, a man and a woman—and a girl—a tall, blond girl with long hair—Germans—they passed by here. Do you remember? Her name—the girl's name—was Emilie."

Mr. Kayro squeezed his face up with the effort of recollecting and all at once broke into a sunny, affirmative smile. "They had a double-team wagon and a lot of stuff in it. The girl, she rode straddle—like a man!"

The boy almost laughed with his delight. "Yes, yes, that's the one! Did they say where they were going? I know they were going West, but did they say where?"

Mr. Kayro's own bright smile faded to a compassionate and sober frown, and he shook his head. "No, they didn't say. They didn't know, son. When they cross this river, they don't know where they're going. They're just going . . . West."

The youth's smile died in resignation, and he nodded slowly to himself as if speaking an austere thought to his own mind. "Thank you," he said again to Mr. Kayro. "Thank you." And with that he averted his face and gave an almost imperceptible nudge with his knees to the horse. Obediently the horse went off in an unhurried walk. Once the youth turned and threw up a hand in a gesture of farewell. It was the hand holding the rose, and for an instant the light caught in the shining flower, a small red flash in the tranquil day. After that the youth did not look back.

Mr. Kayro followed him with his eyes and shook his head. "That's a sad one, Morton. That's sure a sad one."

The Nashville Pike lay outstretched through a long, green valley flanked by the rising Cumberland Mountains. It passed as an irregular thin slash across the band of cultivated land in the valley floor. Above it, beyond the tattered fringes of the farmland, the timbered ridges brooded in the morning. Birds sang through the valley, and overhead the warm sun went soaring peacefully up the sky through the indolent clouds.

Mr. Kayro sat down on a bench in the midst of his garden. Musing, he watched the youth and the horse recede and diminish until the road carried them beyond the gate of the valley, and they vanished at last in the bright immensity which lay Westward.